THE HIGHLY
EFFECTIVE DETECTIVE DUO

THE HIGHLY EFFECTIVE DETECTIVE

THE HIGHLY EFFECTIVE DETECTIVE
GOES TO THE DOGS

by

RICHARD YANCEY

Mystery Guild
Garden City, New York

CONTENTS

THE HIGHLY EFFECTIVE DETECTIVE DUO

A Mystery Guild Lost Classics Omnibus

THE
HIGHLY
EFFECTIVE
DETECTIVE

ALSO BY RICHARD YANCEY

Confessions of a Tax Collector

A Burning in Homeland

The Extraordinary Adventures of Alfred Kropp

THE

HIGHLY

EFFECTIVE

DETECTIVE

A Teddy Ruzak Novel

RICHARD YANCEY

Thomas Dunne Books
St. Martin's Minotaur
New York

THOMAS DUNNE BOOKS.
An imprint of St. Martin's Press.

THE HIGHLY EFFECTIVE DETECTIVE. Copyright © 2006 by Richard Yancey. All rights reserved. Printed in the United States of America. No part of this book may be used or reproduced in any manner whatsoever without written permission except in the case of brief quotations embodied in critical articles or reviews. For information, address St. Martin's Press, 175 Fifth Avenue, New York, N.Y. 10010.

www.minotaurbooks.com

Library of Congress Cataloging-in-Publication Data

Yancey, Richard.
   The highly effective detective / Richard Yancey.—1st ed.
      p. cm
   ISBN-13: 978-0-312-34752-9
   ISBN-10: 0-312-34752-9
   1. Private investigators—Tennessee—Knoxville—Fiction. 2. Knoxville (Tenn.)—
Fiction. I. Title.

PS3625.A675H54 2006
813'.6—dc22

                                                                              2006042521

First Edition: July 2006

10 9 8 7 6 5 4 3 2 1

TO SANDY

Yet in these thoughts myself almost despising,
Haply I think on thee—and then my state,
Like to the lark at break of day arising
From sullen earth, sings hymns at heaven's gate
        —William Shakespeare, Sonnet XXIX

Take note, take note, O World.
To be direct and honest is not safe.
     —*William Shakespeare*, Othello

THE
HIGHLY
EFFECTIVE
DETECTIVE

CHAPTER ONE

I'D HAD THIS DOPEY IDEA TO BE A DETECTIVE EVER SINCE MY MOTHER gave me an illustrated Sherlock Holmes book for my tenth birthday. For months, I walked around the house with a bubble pipe and two baseball caps on my head, one turned backward so I would have that double-billed look. I outgrew the ball caps and the pipe, but never my dream of being a detective.

Then when I was twelve, somebody gave me one of those *Encyclopedia Brown* books, about a boy detective who was smarter than his own father, the chief of police no less, and solved all the crimes for him. The answer to each mystery was in the back of the book for those people like me who wanted to play detective but could never figure out what the solution was. I liked that kid detective so much, I started calling myself "Dictionary Ruzak," because "Encyclopedia" was already taken.

After high school, I went to the Police Academy, but they kicked me out. I couldn't run fast enough, and I never could pass the driving and the marksmanship tests. Then they put me in what they called "scenario training" and the bad guy always killed me. I must have died a hundred times, and would have died a hundred more, but the Academy concluded I wasn't cut out for police work.

After I flunked out of the Academy, I took a job as a guard with a company that provided security for a local bank. I wore a black uniform with a gold badge embroidered on the shoulder. I had the midnight shift, which I liked. It was quiet, I had a chance to read or listen to the radio, and nothing ever happened. I worked there for fourteen years. For ten of those years I lived with my parents, until Dad died of a heart attack and Mom told me if I didn't move out, I never would, because with him gone, the temptation would be too great to live with and take care of her as an excuse not to strike out on my own. She kept on me to go to college. I worked nights, so my days were free, but somehow, like a lot of things people plan for, I never got around to it. I also could never figure out how I was going to work a full-time job, go to college, and sleep.

So the day came when I was thirty-three years old and was still doing the same thing I'd been doing when I was nineteen. I was hunkered down. Flunking out of the Police Academy had taken something out of me, a pretty big chunk of my resolve or spirit or whatever you want to call it, and I was waiting for something. I couldn't put my finger on what I was waiting for. Maybe it was some kind of mystical call to action, but I was never the type who believed we all have a destiny to fulfill, like a cosmic apple hanging from a tree that we wait till it's ripe to pluck. My outlook on life tended toward the prosaic. I wasn't much of a dreamer or go-getter, since the two usually go hand in hand. But sometimes, usually midway through my shift, about 3:00 A.M., when things were their most quiet and I was tired of reading and all the late-night radio talk shows had signed off, I would feel an aching somewhere in the vicinity of my heart, not in the heart itself, but about two or three inches below it, which I interpreted as some soft groaning of my unfulfilled soul, only I didn't know what to do about it except wait for it to go away.

CHAPTER TWO

THEN ONE NIGHT IN THE WINTER OF MY THIRTY-THIRD YEAR, MY mother called me to tell me she was calling from her deathbed. So I drove to her house in Fountain City. It was the fourth house she had lived in since I'd been born. Dad was a salesman and moved around a lot. He wasn't a traveling salesman; he just wasn't a very good salesman and he moved to follow what he called the "consumer trends." I spent the first twelve years of my life in Brooklyn, where Dad sold furniture. Then we moved to St. Louis, where Dad sold cars. Then to Raleigh, where he sold life insurance. Finally, when I was sixteen, he moved us to Knoxville, where he sold more cars, more life insurance, and more furniture. The house in Fountain City was about fifty years old, renovated several times, big and drafty, with a pee smell in the hallways that Mom could never get out, so she burned a lot of candles, though Dad stomped around and said one day she was going to burn the whole place down.

Mom had cancer. When it was diagnosed, I told her she should find a smaller place. She said she felt closer to Dad there. She had had cancer for three years, and this was about the sixth call from her deathbed, so I didn't rush over. I even stopped first at the DQ drive-thru for a chocolate sundae. It was for her. Mom loved chocolate sundaes.

"Mom, I brought you a chocolate sundae," I said. She was lying propped up in the bed, with about a dozen pillows behind her back. She didn't look good, and I felt guilty for not going straight over there.

"I don't want a chocolate sundae. You eat it."

I sat on the edge of the bed and ate the sundae.

"Tell me how I look," she said.

"You look great, Mom."

"No, I don't. I look terrible. Don't lie to me, Theodore."

"I never lie to you, Mom."

"You lied about breaking my kitchen window."

"Mom, that was twenty years ago. I was a kid."

Her eyes narrowed at me. I looked away.

"How old are you now?"

"I'm thirty-three, Mom. Mom, you know how old I am."

"You've gained weight."

"I've always been big, Mom."

"Now you're bigger. You shouldn't have eaten that sundae."

"You told me to."

I set the empty plastic cup on her nightstand.

"Teddy," she said. "I'm dying."

"Mom, you say that every time I come over."

"This time, I am."

"Okay, Mom."

"I doubt I'll make it through the night."

"You want me to stay?"

"No, I'm sure you have to work tonight."

"They'll let me have the night off, if you're dying."

"Really? How kind of them." She coughed. She motioned to the box of Kleenex by her bed and I gave one to her. She pressed it against her mouth as she coughed, then examined it carefully for any sign of blood.

"Teddy," she said after she caught her breath. "I have a confession to make."

"Okay."

"When your father died, there was quite a bit of life insurance. I was working at the time, as you know, and we really didn't need the money, so I set it aside—the life-insurance money, I mean."

I didn't say anything. I was remembering all the times she'd complained about us not having any money.

"I knew if we started to spend it, it would just be gone. Woosh! Right out the window. So I invested it. There's quite a nest egg there, though the medical bills have taken their bite, and now that I'm dying and you're thirty-three years old, with half your life gone already, I thought it was time to give it to you."

I thought about it. It was a lot to think about.

"It's quite a bit of money, Teddy," she whispered. "And you shouldn't spend it. Invest it. Like I did. You make a good living. You don't really need it."

"How much is it, Mom?"

"One hundred and twenty-five thousand dollars, give or take a few pennies."

CHAPTER THREE

I FELT BAD WHEN SHE DIED THE NEXT WEEK. BAD FOR NOT BELIEVING she was really dying and bad for being angry with her for hoarding that money, which we really could have used. Most of all, though, I felt bad because she was my mother and she was dead. She was the only family I had.

I put the house up for sale and gave most of her things to charity. A couple of items, knickknacks she treasured or things I remembered from childhood, I kept, but I put them away in one of my closets.

They gave me the night off the day of her funeral, so I decided to eat out, though having a steak that night made me feel a little guilty. I drove to the Old City Diner on the corner of Western and Summit Hill. Felicia was working that night. That made me feel a little less bad. She was my favorite waitress. I liked her nose. It was a small nose and crinkled in the middle when she laughed.

"Teddy, how are ya?" she asked when she came to take my order.

"Okay," I said. "Except my mom died."

"Oh God! I'm sorry. Wasn't she real sick, though?"

"Cancer."

"My uncle died two years ago of throat cancer."

She took my order. I said, "She left me sixty-five thousand dollars."

"Get outta here!"

"No, she did. Plus a little insurance money to boot, and I've sold the old homestead. She told me not to spend any of it. Didn't make me promise, though."

"So what're you going to do with it?"

"Well, it's always been my dream to have my own detective agency."

She put her hands on her hips and laughed. Her nose crinkled. Felicia had goldish blond hair that she pulled up into a bun for work. I only saw her at work, so I didn't know how long her hair was or what it looked like when she took it down. She saw I was serious, and stopped laughing.

I pulled a piece of paper from my pocket as she slid into the seat across from me.

"See, I'm working on some names for it. So far, I've got Ruzak's Detective Agency, Detection by Teddy, AAA Detectives—you know, that way, you get the first listing in the Yellow Pages—Just Like Sherlock Detective Agency, and Dick Ruzak Agency. See, *dick* is another word for detective."

"I don't think you should call yourself 'dick,' Teddy," Felicia said.

"I'm not crazy about any of them."

"Well, I'm sure you'll think of something."

She left to put in my order. I studied my to-do list, things like renting an office and buying furniture and getting some phone and electrical service. Felicia came back with my steak.

"You know what I would do with sixty-five thousand dollars?"

"What would you do?"

"I don't know. But I'd quit this stinkin' job."

"I'm quitting mine tomorrow. It isn't the greatest job in the world, either, but it's the only job I've ever had, so it's been like contemplating the void, working myself up to quitting."

She didn't seem too interested in my contemplation of the void.

"How about the Ultimate Detective Agency?" she asked.

"Maybe something that's an acronym," I said. "You know, a title that spells something out, like CIA."

"CIA isn't an acronym, Ruzak. An acronym is a pronounceable word, like NATO. TUDA."

"TUDA?"

"For The Ultimate Detective Agency."

"That seems too close to *tuna*. If I'm going with an acronym, I should go with something that's related, not something that's going to make people think of fish."

"Related to what?"

"The thing itself."

"The thing itself?"

"Detection."

"How about Private Investigator & Gumshoe Ruzak?"

I thought about this. "Doesn't that spell out PIG Ruzak?"

Her nose was crinkling at me.

"Anyway," I said. "I'll think of something."

CHAPTER FOUR

The next week, I rented some space on Church Street, in the old Ely Building, about two blocks from the Tennessee Theater, where fading singing stars came for concerts and where old movies that hardly anybody came to see played on the weekends. My new office was one floor above the only dry cleaner's downtown. It was in a drafty old building, and you had to walk up this narrow stairwell to get to my door. The ventilation wasn't very good and I never could figure out a way to keep the stench from all those dry-cleaning chemicals from seeping up through the creaky boards. The other place I looked at was bigger, but it was above a Chinese take-out joint in Market Square and the rent was twice as much. I realized after a week that I should have taken the bigger place. I didn't take it because I didn't like Chinese food and the rent was higher, but smelling Chinese food all day would have been better than smelling chemicals.

I finally settled on a name and hired a man to stencil it on the door. I bought a desk, a filing cabinet, an electric fan for the top of the cabinet, an executive office chair, a typewriter, and a telephone. Everything was secondhand except the telephone. There was a little space near the door that could be a secretary's office, but I was trying to economize. I figured I would hire a secretary once I got my first client.

But I didn't get a client. I went to my office every day and sat by the phone, but the phone never rang. A couple of letters came addressed to "Current Occupant" and some bills, but no one called and no one came to the door.

I put an ad in the paper and printed some handbills. I hired this little Latino boy to walk around the block and hand them out, but I didn't monitor his work, so I don't know how many he handed out or if he handed out any at all. I drank too much coffee and ate too many Krispy Kreme doughnuts. I thought about my mother. I thought about my old job. I missed my mother. I missed my old job. I started leaving the office earlier and earlier. I'd go to the diner in the Old City and sit in my booth and Felicia would ask me how it was going and I would say fine and she would laugh and wrinkle her nose at me.

Then one day, there was a knock on my door. I thought it was another salesman, so I didn't answer it at first. About twice a week, the salesmen dropped by. I bought some stationery from one, and when it came in, it had my name spelled wrong at the top: Theodore Rusak. This really ticked me off, because people were always spelling my name wrong or saying it wrong. It was Ruzak with a z and pronounced "*Rue*-zack," not "Russ-ick" or "Ruh-zick." I called the salesman, but he refused to give me a refund or redo the job unless I paid him full price again.

The person kept knocking, so I got up and answered the door.

"Theodore Ruzak?"

"That's me."

"I saw your ad in the paper. May I come in? I know I don't have an appointment. . . ."

"That makes it tough," I said. "But I'll squeeze you in."

He was a small guy, maybe five four, no more than five five, balding, with little white wisps of the remaining hair dancing in the air like the tops of dandelion heads. Dandelions reminded me of summer and my father's irrational, visceral hatred of the weed, yanking me out of bed at six o'clock on Saturday mornings to pull them from the yard and flower beds, fussing at me for breaking them off at ground level, leaving the root intact to generate a new plant. Dandelions have very stubborn roots and are ingeniously designed to snap off at the top if you pull too hard. I've got one of those free association–type brains, where my thoughts bump around like pinballs, and I often come off stupid in conversations because I've bounced about ten thousand miles from the spot where I should be.

He was wearing Levi's, brown work boots, and a flannel shirt that was really too warm for the weather, like he was trying to come across as a farmer or a day laborer, but I wasn't buying it. He was too old for day labor, for one, and the shirt was pressed; I mean, what sort of farmer irons his flannel? I waved him to a chair. He was a spry little guy; he reminded me of Fred Astaire in that movie musical about the Irish leprechauns. He had the same thin, sharply chiseled features and the rather triangular-shaped head. I figured he was in his late sixties and kept himself fit, maybe with tennis or golf, despite the fact he wore flannel and people who wear flannel generally don't go in for the effete sports.

I sat down behind my desk, pulled out my legal pad and my mechanical pencil, and wrote the date across the top.

"My name is Parker Hudson," the old guy said. He didn't have an East Tennessee accent—definitely not a local, then—and his voice was strangely youthful, not cracked and quavering like you'd expect an old man to sound. He was no farmer all right. No self-respecting farm couple would name their son Parker. That was inviting trouble.

"All right, that's great," I said, and wrote his name beneath the date.

"Have you been a detective long, Mr. Ruzak?"

"Only about a month. But my background's in security."

"I tried going to the police," Parker Hudson said. "First they thought I was a crank; then they practically laughed me out the door."

I wrote beneath his name the words *crank* and *laughed.*

"What are you doing?"

"Making notes."

"I don't like the fact that you wrote 'crank' beneath my name."

"Sorry."

I erased the word. Now all I had was "laughed" beneath his name. I wondered how much sense that was going to make to me later, so I erased that word, too. *Police* made more sense. I wrote "police" while he watched me write "police."

"Do you have a license, Mr. Ruzak?"

"A driver's license?"

"A PI license."

"Do I need one?"

"You're the one billing yourself as a private investigator. Don't you know whether the state requires a license before you can privately investigate?"

"You know what, Mr. Hudson, I bet they do. I mean, you can't even fish in this state without a license, and PI work is at least as taxing."

I wrote "license (?)" beside the word *police.*

"So the answer to my question is, you don't have a license."

"Don't turn me in," I said. "I'll get one. Meanwhile, Mr. Hudson, maybe you oughta check out another agency. If I'm gonna make a go of this, I might as well do it legally. I know what right and wrong are. That's one of the reasons I became a detective, though maybe I shouldn't say that, because technically I'm not one till I get a license."

All of a sudden, he laughed. I wasn't sure why he laughed.

"Will you give me a discount?"

"Well," I said. I didn't really know what to say, since I hadn't thought out my rates. I tapped the eraser end of my mechanical pencil on the notepad and gave him what I hoped was a calculating look, like I was figuring what discount he might be entitled to, first for hiring an unlicensed detective and second for not turning me in for being an unlicensed detective.

"I'll pay you fifty dollars an hour, plus expenses, of course."

"Of course," I said. My mouth was dry. Fifty dollars an hour! My top pay at the security company had been twenty-two dollars an hour. Why had I waited this long to go into the detective business? That was the way my mind worked: On the heels of euphoria came depression, thinking about all the wasted years. "Expenses?"

"Gas and supplies and the like."

"Yes, and the like . . . that."

"Good."

"What is it you want me to do?"

"I want you to find a murderer."

I stared at him for a second.

"Did you say a murderer?"

"And once you find him, I want you to bring justice to his miserable soul."

CHAPTER FIVE

Parker Hudson paid me a retainer of two hundred dollars. I promised I'd be on the case the very next morning and we parted very up on each other. I honestly thought he thought he had found the right man for the job. I didn't have the heart and felt it didn't make good business sense to tell him I had no idea what to do next.

I drove to the diner in the Old City to celebrate. Felicia came over right away to take my order. She was wearing bright red lipstick and matching red nail polish. Her hair was up, as usual, and she wore the same white uniform with the name tag, and it occurred to me I had never seen her wearing anything but that white polyester waitress uniform.

"So, how's it taste?" she asked.

"How's what taste?" She had totally thrown me, since I hadn't even ordered yet.

"The canary. You look like the cat who swallowed it."

"I'm celebrating."

"You got a client."

"I got a client. How much do you make, Felicia?"

"What's that?"

"What's Freddy pay you to wait tables?"

"Two-fifty an hour, plus tips. Why?"

"I'll pay you twelve bucks an hour, with a two-week paid vacation every year."

"Huh?"

"I need a secretary," I said. "I'm getting clients now and I need somebody to answer the phone and do the mail and get the door . . . you know, a secretary."

Her nose crinkled. "You want to hire me to be your secretary?"

"Sure."

She thought about it.

"Okay," she said. She called over her shoulder, "Hey, Freddy! I quit!" She took off her apron and slid into the seat across from me.

"Okay, tell me about him."

"Who?"

"Your client, Ruzak."

"His name is Parker Hudson."

She took a sharp breath.

"You know him?" I asked.

"No. I just thought that I was supposed to do stuff like that. You know, like in the movies. Like, 'Oooh! Not *the* Parker Hudson!'"

"He dresses like a farmer, but he's a retired banker."

"He's loaded."

"I don't think he's hurting for cash."

"Ka-ching," she said. "But why would some big-shot retired banker with loads of cash hire someone like you?"

"The police won't help." It kind of bothered me, the way she said that, "hire someone like you," with the emphasis on the word *you.*

"Why won't the police help?"

"Well, technically I guess it's a crime, but it's not the sort of crime they take seriously."

"What is it, jaywalking?"

"Hit-and-run. Murder. Well, it was closer to manslaughter, but the 'man' part's misleading."

Her nose crinkled. "What is this, Teddy, some kind of joke? What really happened, his wife lose an earring?"

One of the other waitresses came over. Her name tag said LACEY. Lacey was an enormous woman with steel gray hair and very small hands for such a large woman. She told Felicia that Freddy was pissed that she had quit like that and doubly pissed because we weren't ordering anything. Only paying customers got booths. I started to order something, but Felicia stopped me.

"Let's get out of here, Teddy."

"It's my favorite place."

"We've been shut down three times by the Health Department."

"I'm hungry," I said.

"We'll pick something up. The food here sucks." She said this real loud. She wanted to make sure Freddy heard.

CHAPTER SIX

FELICIA KNEW THIS CHINESE PLACE CALLED #1 CHINA BUFFET DOWN on the Strip, the main drag through the campus of the university. A light rain was falling, the kind of rain that's between real rain and fog, kind of a foggy rain. It was never easy finding a parking place on the Strip; I had to park three blocks away, and we walked together in the rain. Felicia was wearing a green overcoat. I didn't have an overcoat or an umbrella.

"Since when do the cops not take murder seriously?" she asked.

"I guess it's got something to do with the victims."

"Victims? Like more than one?"

"Yeah, like that."

The rain made her face look softer somehow. Maybe it was all the moisture in the air.

We picked up our food and sat on bar stools at the long counter against the window and watched the people go by on the street, students mostly, since the Strip ran right down the middle of campus. She was having a bowl of noodles and I had some pork. The pork was soggy and the pieces seemed to take too long to chew. I didn't really care for Chinese food, which is how I ended up over a dry cleaner's in the first place, but Felicia had been pretty excited about the food here. I should have chosen the noodles, I guess. I wondered why only Chinese and American foods were done buffet-style. You never saw an Italian buffet or a Mexican buffet.

"So who were the victims?" she asked around a mouthful of noodles.

"Geese."

"Did you say *geese?*"

"Parker Hudson was taking a walk one morning a few weeks ago, and there's this nice big lake he walks around, and as he's walking, he sees these two geese with their babies, six of them, crossing the road."

"Okay, okay. I see where this is going."

"And while he's watching, all of sudden this big SUV comes roaring up behind him and—"

"Don't say it."

"Runs right over the baby geese. The goslings." That's what Parker Hudson had called them, *goslings*. I wasn't completely sure what that meant, so after he left my office, I looked it up. My name didn't used to be Dictionary Ruzak for nothing.

"Didn't slow down, didn't try to swerve. Parker's sure whoever was driving saw them. And if they didn't see them, they sure as heck *felt* them. So I asked him why they were crossing the road. . . ."

She laughed. "You didn't."

"Why not?"

"Never mind."

"Okay. Anyway, the two adults didn't get hit—Dad was leading and Mom was taking up the rear—and they went berserk, flapping their wings and honking to beat the band, refusing to leave their dead babies even when other cars came up, so Parker's running up and down the road trying to scare them back to the lake. . . ."

"Oh God. That's awful."

"Anyway, he didn't get the guy's tag number. Just says it's a big SUV with white-rimmed tires, something like a Ford Expedition or maybe a GMC. Might even be a Jeep. He's just not sure."

"So he wants you to find who killed the geese."

"Goslings."

"And when you find them?"

"First I have to find them."

"Okay, say you find them. Then what?"

I shrugged. "I guess Parker files charges, I don't know, reckless driving or something like that."

"He's a big animal lover, huh?"

I thought about it. "I don't know about that. I don't think it was the dead baby birds that got to him so much as the person who hit them, like life was nothing to him."

"It was probably just an accident."

"That's what I said," I said. "And he said, 'If it was an accident, why didn't he stop to see if the birds needed help? He must have known he hit them, so why did he keep going?' "

"He didn't care."

I nodded. "That's what got to him—Parker, I mean. That somebody killed something and just kept driving."

"The world's full of assholes, Ruzak."

"Yeah, but that doesn't mean you don't take them to account."

She pushed her empty bowl away. One of the dishes on the steam table had been Peking duck. There were Peking duck and General Tao chicken and sweet-and-sour pork and beef and vegetables. It wasn't disrespectful to eat the animals in those dishes, though. The whole reason they were on the earth was to be killed and eaten by people. The geese murdered that morning were wild geese that nested by Parker's lake every spring.

"Okay, detective, how're you going to solve this murder most foul? Sorry."

"I'm working on that."

"Witnesses?"

"Just Parker. It was pretty early in the morning."

"He lives around there?"

"House right on the lake. There're two or three subdivisions on the other side of the road, but he didn't see which one the car came out of. It might not have come out of any of them. The road connects to Kingston Pike."

"Busiest road in Knoxville."

"Right."

"Could be anyone."

"Right."

"Any one of about five hundred thousand people."

"Right."

"In a black SUV, the most popular kind and color of car in East Tennessee."

"Right."

"Or it might be someone from out of town, out of state, even."

"Right."

"Well, this should be easy."

"I'm not so sure."

"How much is Mr. Hudson paying you to hunt down this bird killer?"

"Fifty dollars an hour, plus expenses."

I was looking out the rain-streaked window, but I could feel her eyes on the side of my face.

"You're kidding, right?"

"He gave me a two-hundred-dollar retainer."

She whistled. "And I was making two-fifty, plus tips."

"Blood money," I said.

"Huh?"

"People like me. And cops. Even doctors, I guess. Somebody has to suffer so we can earn a living."

"Teddy, these are geese we're talking about."

"Tell that to the goslings."

"I never knew you had a sensitive side."

"Money never could motivate me that much, Felicia. Why else would I stay a security guard for fourteen years?"

CHAPTER SEVEN

I DROVE FELICIA BACK TO THE DINER TO PICK UP HER CAR. THE FOGGY rain had turned to just fog.

"I still don't understand why he decided to hire a detective," she said.

"He told me for three weeks he's been staking out that same spot and the car hasn't been back. He drove through all the neighborhoods around there, but he didn't see any car that looked familiar."

"So what does he think you can do that he can't?"

Again, she emphasized the word *you*.

"Well, he did say that when he wants his house painted, he doesn't do it himself. He calls in the experts. That reminds me. I gotta get a license."

"What kind of license?"

"A detective's license."

"Oh Ruzak. That bird killer's as good as in the cage."

"You're ribbing me. That's okay."

I pulled into the empty space beside her car. Before she got out, she asked, "Where's your office?"

"How come you want to know?"

"Don't I have to show up for work tomorrow?"

I waited until she was in her car and the doors were locked, so no crazed dope fiend or bum could get her. The Old City could be kind of rough. When she slid into the driver's seat, her white skirt pulled up and I saw a lot of thigh. Her stockings were the same shade of white as her uniform and she was wearing those thick-soled white shoes waitresses and hospital workers wear because they're on their feet all the time. A few strands of goldish blond hair had slipped from the back of her bun and hung down her neck, swaying as she got in the car. I watched her pull out and waved to her as she drove away, but she didn't wave back. Maybe she didn't see me.

Nothing can make you feel lonelier than hanging out with a pretty girl. All at once, I felt like crying. I knew I was luckier than most people. I had fulfilled my childhood dream. And so what if this wasn't the coolest or sexiest case any detective'd ever worked? At least now I was a detective and making more money than I ever had as a security guard. I guess if my mom hadn't died and left me that money, I'd still be a security guard making twenty-two dollars an hour, but at least my mother would be alive.

I drove back to my apartment, but I didn't feel like going inside. I decided to take a walk.

I walked up and down Gay Street, all the way to the Tennessee Bank Building and back. Not many people live in downtown Knoxville. Most of the people I knew by sight, though I didn't know their names. I passed three dedicated joggers damning the rain and some couples arm in arm, and the people walking past seemed more real to me than I did to myself. I'd always heard that the reality is never the same as your dreams when they finally come true. That it doesn't feel like you thought it would. Then I thought maybe it wasn't my dreams coming true that was making me feel so empty and ghostlike. Maybe it was something else.

By the time I got back to the apartment, I was hungry again, so I cooked some pasta, and right in the middle of washing my plate, I burst into tears and cried for about an hour. A lot of people say you feel better after a good cry, but I didn't feel better. I felt pretty crummy for the rest of the night. I took a shower and tried to watch some TV, but there was nothing good on. Maybe it's just me, but there's never anything good on TV unless you have something else you have to do and can't watch TV. I thought about walking to the video store and renting a good detective movie, but just thinking the word *detective* made me feel crummier. I told myself I was crying over my mom, but deep down I was wondering if I was crying because she died or because I felt bad I hadn't cried enough over her dying. Maybe it wasn't about her at all. Maybe I was crying because I didn't want to be a detective but had become one after a lot of hassle, just to find out that after all the dreaming about it, the reality sucked.

The next morning, I was still feeling lousy, so I stopped by the Krispy Kreme and picked up a dozen doughnuts and two large coffees. Felicia was waiting for me on the sidewalk outside the Ely Building. She followed me up the narrow stairs, pausing at the door.

"What the hell is this?" she asked.

"What? Oh, it's the name I picked for the company."

" 'The Highly Effective Detection & Investigation Company,' " she read.

"You like it?"

"What does that—Teddy, that spells out 'THE DIC.' "

"Yeah, that's another name for a PI. Only I couldn't think of a word that started with a *K*, so I left it off."

"What?"

"The word I couldn't think of that started with a *K*."

"So that's where I work now? I work at a place called 'THE DIC'?"

"I figured it'd be a catchy way for people to remember. Don't you think it's catchy? The copy in my ad says, 'Got a mystery? Come see THE DIC.' What's the matter? Too wordy?"

"No, it's just . . . well, it makes you wonder why it took you so long to get a client."

We stepped inside and she cried, "Dear God, what is that smell?"

"The dry cleaner's."

"We're gonna have to do something about that."

I showed her the fan and said it wasn't too bad with the fan on and the windows open.

Felicia ate two doughnuts and I ate the rest.

"You feelin' okay?" she asked.

"I feel pretty crummy."

"It's this place. It's a dump, Teddy."

I gave her the card of the furniture salesman and told her to go ahead and order a desk for herself and a chair and maybe a filing cabinet if she thought she needed one. Felicia was wearing a nice powder blue business-type suit and high heels. Her hair was down and reached just past her shoulders. It was the first time I ever saw her with her hair down and wearing heels, and I told her she looked nice.

"You want to go to the movies with me sometime?" I asked.

"I have a boyfriend."

"I didn't know you had a boyfriend."

"You never asked me."

"Some detective," I said. I went into the john and washed my hands. She was standing by my desk when I came out. She looked just like Lauren Bacall. I told her she looked just like Lauren Bacall and she asked who the hell Lauren Bacall was.

"Never mind."

The glaze from the doughnuts had given her red lips a luster, and for some reason I thought of a bowling alley, those lanes waxed and polished till they shone.

"What's your boyfriend's name?"

"Why do you want to know his name?" she asked.

"Just curious."

"His name is Bob."

"Bob?"

"Why, what's wrong with Bob?"

"Nothing."

"We've been dating for three years."

"That's a long time."

"He's a fireman."

"That's a very important job. I wanted to be a cop once."

"Why don't you have a girlfriend?" Felicia asked.

"I used to."

"What happened?"

"I had just flunked out of the Police Academy. She told me she wanted somebody with a future."

Her name was Tiffany, like the lamp, but everybody called her "Tiffy." We started dating my senior year. I made the football team that year, after four years of trying. I was big and hard to knock down, but I got confused in the huddle because studying the playbook gave me a headache, so I didn't play much. But if we got ahead in the game, the coach put me in at left guard and I would hunker down and just let them hammer me. "You've got a soft head and a softer body, Ruzak," he told me. "But we're leading fifty-two to ten, so go hit some people." Usually, the opposite happened. Tiffy played in the band, and one Friday night she noticed this guy standing out there like a big dumb post for two quarters, and something about this lummox standing in there play after play while he had the living crap beat out of him impressed her, so she asked the tuba player about me. The tuba player, who was actually bigger than I was, introduced us after the game and we dated the rest of my senior year. We were even talking about marriage once I graduated from the Academy, but of course I flunked out and she dumped me for a guy named Bill Hill, which is the kind of name you never forget, so I was stuck with always knowing the name of the guy my girl dumped me for.

I picked up the phone.

"What are you doing?" Felicia asked.

"I'm using the phone."

"How long are you going to be using it?"

"I don't know. Why?"

"I need it."

"What?"

"The phone, Teddy."

"Why do you need the phone?"

"I'm calling an interior decorator."

"Why are you calling an interior decorator?"

"For the office, Teddy."

"But I just gave you a furniture guy's card."

"This place doesn't need a furniture guy, Ruzak. It's gonna take a whole lot more than a couple secondhand chairs and tacky prints on the walls."

She disappeared around the corner. I wondered how much an interior decorator cost while I got the number for the Tennessee Private Investigation and Polygraph Commission.

"You can't be a PI unless you meet state requirements," the lady at the commission told me after I was on hold for twenty minutes. She had the same sharp, impatient tone as most people who staff telephone lines.

"What are the requirements?"

"They're on our Web site."

"I don't have a computer. That isn't one of the requirements, is it?"

"Are you saying you don't have access to the Web?"

"I'm saying I don't have a computer. That's what I said."

"But that isn't what I asked."

"But you can't have one without the other. That's like making a phone call without a phone."

"Do you want that address?"

"I might want it, if I had a computer, but I don't have a computer. Could you just tell me what the requirements are over the phone? I own a phone."

"Obviously you own a phone, sir."

"Well, what if I was calling from a pay phone?"

"Are you calling from a pay phone?"

"No."

"Then why did you say you were?"

"I didn't. I was posing a hypothetical. The bottom line is, I happen to own a phone but not a computer. Would it be possible—to save you some time and the state some money—to tell me what the requirements of becoming a PI are, right now, while we're talking?"

"Your local library should have Internet access. . . ."

"What, so I have to apply online?"

"Did I say you had to apply online? I said if you wanted to look up the requirements online, you could access the Web from your local library."

"Ma'am, in the time we've taken to exhaust the Internet-access option, you could have told me what the requirements are."

"That's an assumption on your part, sir."

"That may be, but you assumed I was talking from a pay phone, like I didn't have the wherewithal to own my own phone."

"Sir, you're the one who brought up the pay phone."

"I really don't want to quibble," I said. "I feel like we've started off on the wrong foot, and I'd like to step back onto the path and reach my goal of knowing what the requirements of being a PI are."

"Hold on," she said snippily, and music started to play in my ear. I was on hold for quite a while and began to wonder if she had cut me off or was taking a break, or if the list was so lengthy that it took this long just to assemble it.

Then she came back on and said, "Okay. There're eight."

"Now we're getting somewhere," I said. I waited with my mechanical pencil. "Now we're cooking."

"First, you have to be at least twenty-one years of age."

"I'm thirty-three." One down, seven to go.

"Then you can check that one off, I guess. Are you a citizen of the United States or a resident alien?"

"What's a resident alien?"

"I—I'm not sure. Do you think you might be an alien?"

"No, I'm a citizen. I was born in New York, though. Are you a resident alien if you were born in another state?"

"You can't be a citizen and an alien, sir, resident or nonresident."

"How can a nonresident be an alien in the United States? I mean, if you're not living here . . ."

"Sir, I have six other people on hold. . . ."

I told her I was sorry, but I reminded her we would be much further along if she hadn't bogged us down with the Internet option. I gripped my pencil hard to try to keep my thoughts from pinballing.

"Have you been declared mentally defective?"

"Not for years. But you know kids can be pretty cruel."

"By a court of competent jurisdiction, sir."

"Oh, no, nothing like that."

"Do you own your own company?"

"Yeah. It's my own company."

"Are you of good moral character?"

That one brought me up short. I'd always thought of myself as having good moral character, but who was I to say? What did the state want as proof? What did that mean, "good moral character"? I hadn't been to church since I was a teenager, so I'd be hard-pressed to find a preacher or other moral authority to vouch for me. It was one of those tricky questions where the answer flipped back and forth in your head. If I said yes, that I had good moral character, I might be lying, in which case, I didn't. But if I said no, that I didn't, that would be telling the truth when a lie would be better, and didn't that prove I did?

"Sure," I said. "You bet."

"Do you suffer from habitual drunkenness or narcotics addiction or dependence?"

"I have a beer every now and then."

Felicia appeared from around the corner and leaned against the jamb, crossing one ankle over the other and her arms over her chest.

"Beer? Who are you talking to?" she asked.

"Sir, you know that's not what I'm asking."

"The state of Tennessee," I said to Felicia.

"I beg your pardon, sir?"

"Nothing," I said to the phone lady. "No, no drunkenness or narcotic, um, ness."

"You also must submit your fingerprints for processing. All PIs must have a clean criminal background."

That sounded funny to me, "a clean criminal background." Did that mean I could have a criminal background, as long as it was clean?

"Okay."

Felicia rolled her eyes and disappeared again.

"And you have to pass the exam."

My heart gave a little roll. "There's an exam?"

"Tennessee also requires a minimum of six hours of continuing education per year, acceptable to the commission."

"What, like at a college or something? Do I need a college degree, by the way?"

"No, you do not."

"That's good, because I don't have one."

"Really? Is there anything else I can help you with today, sir?"

"Sure. How much does a license cost?"

"There's a two-hundred-and-fifty-dollar application fee."

I whistled. Her voice warmed because she was enjoying this part.

"And a one-hundred-and-twenty-five-dollar licensing fee, renewable every two years."

I didn't say anything, and she said, "Are you there?"

"Yeah."

"Would you like me to send you an application?"

"Sure. Yeah. That would be great. These fees, are they tax-deductible?"

"Sir, I'm not qualified to answer that question. Talk to your accountant."

"I don't have an accountant."

"Maybe you should get one, sir. Seeing that you're running a business."

"That's not a bad idea. Thanks."

I gave her my address so she could mail the application, then hung up. I was sweating hard and my fingers were shaking a little. Felicia came back into the room.

"Can I use the phone now?"

"Felicia, do you think I have good moral character?"

"I hardly know you, Ruzak. You're a good tipper."

She disappeared again. When Felicia was in the room, I felt bigger somehow. My mental weight expanded about twenty to twenty-five pounds. I wondered if I should call Parker Hudson and tell him it really wasn't moral for me to work as a private investigator on his bird case when I didn't even have a license, no matter that it didn't bother him. If I had good moral character, I wouldn't practice detecting without a license. But then I would give up the fifty bucks an hour, plus expenses, default on my lease, and fire Felicia. She would have to go back to waitressing, and she hated waitressing. I told myself not to worry so much about this PI exam. There must be study guides, and maybe it was even an open-book test. In general, people panic before they have all the facts.

I yelled into the vestibule to ask Felicia if she knew any good accountants, but she was already on the phone to some interior designer, setting up an appointment to "appraise the space." Maybe she would back off the interior designer thing if I hinted that only people with no taste hire interior designers. But then she might get sore at me. I'd have to balance the cost of her getting sore against the cost of hiring some fancy-pants interior designer. When I was younger, they were called interior decorators. *Designer* sounds more artsy, I guess, and somehow more technical, like an engineer, someone who designs rockets for NASA or something.

Felicia came back into the room and said, "They're coming this Thursday."

"To give an estimate, right?"

"What are you worried about?"

"I have to take an exam."

"You want me to help you study?"

"You'd help me study?"

"It's purely selfish, Teddy. You don't get that license and I go back to being a waitress."

"Why were you a waitress, Felicia?"

"What's that supposed to mean?"

"I mean, somebody as smart and pretty as you—"

She sat down across from me and said, "Maybe we should get something straight right from the beginning, Ruzak. My personal life is off-limits. Our relationship is going to be strictly professional. I won't stick my nose in your business and you won't stick your nose in mine."

"Don't get sore."

"I'm not. Look, I've got lots of single friends who'd love to—"

"Oh, I'm not looking for a girlfriend."

She narrowed her eyes at me. "How come?"

I shrugged and looked away.

"Are you still carrying a torch for her?" she asked, meaning Tiffy.

"She's married, Felicia. A guy named Bill Hill. Anyway, I thought you just said we weren't going to stick our noses in each other's business."

"Now you're sore," she said. "Don't get a crush on me, Ruzak."

I promised I wouldn't, though it probably wasn't worth the breath it took to say it. It goes back to moral character: You make a promise like that and there's no way you can know at the time if you can keep it.

CHAPTER EIGHT

A COUPLE OF WEEKS LATER, I WAS SITTING IN MY OFFICE, WHICH didn't even look like my office anymore. There were potted plants, some huge thing in the front that Felicia called a receptionist desk, a computer on that desk (with high-speed Internet access), colored prints on the walls, a throw rug, new towels and a fancy toilet paper holder in the john. My old second-hand desk was gone, replaced with a huge mahogany number and a leather executive chair. Two matching visitor's chairs were in front of the desk. There was a big globe of the world on a stand in one corner.

Felicia brought in the designer, and I guess they had a high old time. Felicia said I had to project a certain image or people wouldn't trust me to be their detective. "You have to look successful to be successful," she said. She was wearing a new designer outfit, though she said she'd gotten it on discount. She'd charged everything to the business account, even her outfit and the three others she had bought, also on discount. "It's like an advance. I'll pay you back, Teddy." The total for everything, including the shiny gold pens and stationery with the right name on it, was $26,546.74. This could have bought a nice car, even a convertible. I already had a car, but I'd always wanted a convertible.

Felicia had also bought me a tape recorder to make dictation on. All I had to do was tape my letters and reports and she would type them for me on the computer, to make everything very professional, she said. I was fooling with the taping machine when Felicia buzzed me on the new intercom system to tell me Parker Hudson was there to see me. She was sitting about ten feet away, so I heard her voice over the intercom and from across the room, as if there was an echo.

He was wearing a white sweater over a polo shirt, Docker slacks, and Birkinstock sandals. Except for the sandals, again he was dressed too warmly for the weather, which was eighty-three and sunny. Maybe he had poor circulation, like my mother, who had been dead now over two months, and still I hadn't been to her grave. That meant nobody had been to her grave, since I was the only somebody she had left. I clicked on my new tape recorder and said, "Flowers for her grave."

"Whose grave?" Parker Hudson asked. He sat down in one of the fat leather visiting chairs and looked appreciatively around the room.

"You've redecorated," he said.

"My mother."

"Your mother redecorated?"

"My mother's dead."

"I'm terribly sorry. I didn't know."

"I did."

"I'm sure you did."

"No, about the redecorating."

"Flowers would add a little color."

"No, the flowers are for her grave. I was just making a little reminder for myself, but I never remember to check the tape for reminders, so I'm wasting double the energy."

He nodded. He seemed confused. "I hope this isn't an inopportune time."

"No, pretty much any time is opportune." I pulled my pad in front of me and picked up my mechanical pencil, clicking out some fresh lead.

"I was in the neighborhood, visiting an old colleague at the bank, so I thought I'd drop by and check on the status of my case."

He stared at me and waited for me to say something.

"Is there a status on my case?"

"I'm working on some theories."

"Theories?"

"Scenarios. Hypotheticals. Possibilities."

"What are you talking about, Mr. Ruzak? It's been three weeks since you took my case and I haven't heard a word from you. Do you have any leads?"

"No, not really."

"Have you been to the lake?"

"I've been meaning to get out there. . . ."

"Canvassed the neighborhoods for any potential witnesses?"

"That's on my list."

He crossed his arms over his chest and said, "You haven't done a blessed thing, have you, Mr. Ruzak?"

"Legwork isn't all there is to detection, Mr. Hudson. Have you ever heard of Mycroft?"

"No."

"He was Sherlock Holmes's older brother. Smarter than Sherlock, if you can believe that, but he hated the legwork. He cracked cases completely in his head."

"And that's your strategy? To crack my case completely inside your head?"

"Like I said, I'm working on some theories. Without theories, you're just thrashing around in the dark and billing a lot of unnecessary expenses. I'm trying to save you some money here, Mr. Hudson."

"You're not charging me for all the time you spend concocting theories, then?"

"No, concoction is free."

"Because, after all, how could one call it work?"

"You couldn't in good conscience. Though most work these days is with your head, when you think about it. There're not many manual laborers left. . . ."

"Mr. Ruzak, I get the impression you're not taking my case very seriously."

"Oh, no, Mr. Hudson, I am taking your case very seriously. I think it's terrible what happened to those birds. It's a damned shame and whoever did it was damned shameless and you're to be commended for spending your money to track down who did it. And anyway, I'm grateful as hell for the work, but most of all for the confidence in hiring an unlicensed detective, though I'm in the process right now of getting one, a license, and letting him feel his way through his first case. To be honest with you, it's also my only case, so I've got a pretty strong interest in solving it. Maybe not as strong as you, but pretty strong."

He laughed suddenly, like he did the first time we met. One minute he was still and stoic as a Buddha, the next his face crinkled and cracked open and he was all teeth and tongue and guffaws.

"Well," he said after he got control of himself. "I suppose I can't complain too much. I haven't paid a penny and I've managed to find the equal of Mycroft Holmes."

"Oh, I never said I was his equal. Mycroft was very big in the smarts department. It's a matter of technique, not ability."

"That certainly seems true."

"But I'll get an answer for you, Mr. Hudson. I'll nab this bird killer. You've got my word on that."

He left after that and I was more than relieved. I was ready to throw his painting metaphor back at him, something like, When you hire somebody to paint your house, do you trail behind them, questioning every little stroke? Lucky for me, I didn't have to.

Felicia stuck her head in the little opening and said, "Two things."

"Yeah?"

"You wanna put a door here. I heard every word."

"I don't mind."

"Your clients might. One day, you'll get a case that requires delicacy, you know? Maybe something a little more serious than a dead bird."

"It was more than one."

"You know what I mean."

"I'll talk to the landlord. Have you ever heard of Mycroft Holmes?"

"Not till three minutes ago."

"Ever heard of Moriarty?"

"Sherlock Holmes's little brother?"

"No. His archnemesis. Maybe that's why I'm having trouble getting into this case. There's no, um, worthy adversary."

She just stared at me.

I sighed. "What was the second thing?"

"Paul Killibrew is holding for you."

"Oh. Who's Paul Killibrew?"

"He's a reporter for the *Sentinel.* He thinks this case will make a great human-interest story for the paper."

"Really?"

"Sure. It's got it all, Ruzak. Pathos, humor, a man chasing his dream. He said it might make the front page of the 'Lifestyle' section."

"That's terrific."

"And maybe the killer will read about it and come clean."

"That would solve the case," I said. I never considered myself a lucky person, but this was luck with a capital *L.*

"I wonder how he heard about it," I said, picking up the phone.

"I called him, Ruzak."

So it wasn't luck, unless you considered my hiring Felicia lucky. If it was, it was of the dumb variety. I thought I had hired her to answer phones and do the mail, not to be the brains of the operation.

CHAPTER NINE

PAUL KILLIBREW WAS A REAL NICE GUY AND SEEMED GENUINELY moved by the story of the dead goslings. He came by with a photographer after we talked and took a picture of me behind my desk, grimly gripping my mechanical pencil, the little point poised above the legal pad, as if he and the photographer had walked into the middle of some important detecting. The story ran on Sunday, a half-page spread with a big color picture of me behind the desk, holding the poised pencil. The first thing I thought when I saw it that morning was that I had no idea how fat I'd gotten. My weight had always been a problem and one of the big reasons I'd struggled so much at the Police Academy. The police take it very seriously, the ability to chase down criminals without suffering a coronary. The second thing I thought was how proud my mother would have been. I'd never been in the paper before, except when the *Sentinel* ran my senior picture, but they run everyone's senior picture, so that didn't really count. The third thing I thought when I saw it was that I still hadn't visited my mother's grave and what kind of son was I anyway?

So I cut out the article, threw on some sweats and my Nikes, and jogged down to the Central Baptist Cemetery on Central Avenue, where my mother was buried. The church's parking lot was packed when I got there; it was only a little after noon. After I caught my breath, I told her, "Ma, I didn't bring you any flowers, but I brought this." I laid the clipping at the foot of the headstone and weighed it down with a stick.

"I look pretty fat in that picture," I said. "So I'm starting an exercise regimen today. I ran all the way here—well, most of the way, anyway—and I'm going to run back. I'm taking up karate, and there's this new thing I saw an ad for in the paper today, this hand-to-hand battle technique perfected by the Israelis, called Krav Maga. It's kind of like street fighting, only more deadly, because it's their secret police who invented it, and those guys are some tough sons a bitches. Sorry, Ma. And I'm cutting back on the doughnuts and the Three Musketeers. And no more swinging by the DQ after work for those damned sundaes. Anyway, I wanted to show you that clipping because maybe you'll think I'll make something of myself one of these days. I'm getting some free publicity out of the deal, which is great for business, or at least that's what I hope. I guess I should tell you it wasn't my idea. It was Felicia's. I don't think you ever met Felicia, but she's this girl I know from the Old City Diner—you know, in the Old City—and she's really smart and nice, too, when her mood's okay. I think I've got this kind of crush on her, but she has this boyfriend named Bob, who's a firefighter. That's a pretty heroic profession, though being a successful PI is nothing to sneeze at in the courageous department."

I was still slightly out of breath from my run, and talking so much wasn't helping. I was tired of standing at the foot of her grave, so I sat down.

"So that's what I've been up to, setting up the office, hiring Felicia, working on this case. . . . That's why I haven't been by sooner."

I could hear voices behind me. I looked over my shoulder and saw people in the parking lot; church was letting out. I ducked my head. I had grown up going to this church, but I hadn't been back since I graduated from high school. My father had been a lapsed Catholic and never went, but Mom had been a dyed-in-the-wool churchgoer and dragged me in every Sunday when I was a kid. The old minister I knew back then had long since retired and the new guy was young and very energetic and kept getting Mom's name wrong at the service. Mom had been too sick to go to church much in her later years; this guy barely knew her. When Dad had his heart attack, he begged for a priest, until finally Mom relented, and then Dad got in an argument with the father during the Last Rites; the first priest he'd spoken to in thirty years and he gets in a fight with him, but that was Dad—very cocksure and querulous. I had trouble understanding why he'd summoned a priest to ready him for the afterlife, only to badger him about Church dogma. What especially set him off was the priest performing the sacrament in the vernacular. Dad wanted Latin, and when the priest said his Latin was rusty, Dad said, "What kind of goddamned priest are you?" I was worried he'd have a second heart attack, fighting with a priest, of all people, and that if there was anything to the Church's teachings, the priest would never get out of there, because Dad kept sinning up to and past receiving absolution.

I hunkered there until the last car left the lot, told Mom good-bye and that I'd be back soon, then started my run back to the apartment, thinking about a hot shower and maybe a package of those little white-powdered doughnuts ninety-nine cents for six at the Walgreens right on my way home. I told myself my problem was willpower, in that I didn't have any. I had just made a promise to Mom about sweets, and already I was planning to break it.

I stopped by the Walgreens on Gay Street, about five blocks from my apartment in the Sterchi Building, and bought three more newspapers for two dollars each, a bottled water, and a bag of unsalted peanuts. Peanuts are excellent protein and good for you, according to the Atkins book. I had never read the Atkins book, but I'd seen a lot of stories about it on television. I went through a phase in my twenties when I read every diet book on the market and bought exercise tapes and even joined a gym, which I never went to. I was into diet culture the way some homely guys get into porno. Maybe later I'd rent a movie (not porno) or call one of my old buddies from the security company, Glen or Farrell, to see if they wanted to come over and read the paper. Thinking of my old friends from work made me lonely all of a sudden, and I thought about getting a dog, even though it was prohibited in the lease. Then I thought how pitiful that was, so lonely that I was willing to pay for companionship. Growing up, I had just one dog, a collie named Lady, who died one summer while we were down in Florida for a family vacation. I begged for another dog, but my dad told me I wasn't going to get another dog until I learned how to handle my emotions better. I guess I never learned to handle them to his satisfaction, because we never got a replacement for Lady.

I jogged down the sidewalk, the green plastic Walgreens bag bumping against my thigh. You don't think a newspaper is heavy until you stuff three Sunday editions in a bag and jog with them. Traffic was very light on Gay Street. It was Sunday and the downtown pretty much died on the weekends, despite millions of dollars spent on revitalization and all the tax breaks and rent subsidies they handed out, trying to get people to move downtown. I barely glanced both ways before crossing at Jackson, and I was hopping onto the curb on the east side of Gay Street when it hit me—not the car itself, but the fact that it was a big vehicle and that it was black, and the fact that it was going very slowly, like it was following me.

CHAPTER TEN

Since I didn't know what to do at that point, I did what most people do when they don't know what to do: I just kept doing what I was doing. In this case, running. I slowed up, expecting the car to pass me. The speed limit downtown was twenty-five, but there was no way I was running faster than twenty-five miles per hour, so why was this guy driving so slowly if he wasn't following me? Maybe he had blown his chance to run me down like those poor damn goslings and he was waiting for another. I thought about stopping, just stopping and turning around to get a good look at him. It occurred to me I didn't have a gun and that, being in PI work, I might find a gun useful, but I hated guns—even when I was in the Police Academy I hated guns—and besides, I was a terrible shot—probably because I hated guns. I'd have to get a permit for one, and you have to pass a marksmanship class to do that, and I sucked at marksmanship. It had been my worst subject at the Academy.

I could see the Sterchi Building up ahead. Less than three blocks to go, and now I could hear the rumble of its big eight-cylinder engine and I tried to remember if the windows were tinted or not. It might not even be worth it to stop and look, if the windows were dark.

Then all choice was taken from me. The engine roared and the big SUV swept past, and I saw the windows *were* tinted. I also saw it was a black Ford Expedition with Tennessee plates. I was so overwhelmed with information at that point, I didn't catch all the numbers, but the first three letters were *HRT*.

I sprinted the last two blocks and up the three flights of stairs to my apartment, then collapsed against the wall beside my door, clutching my keys in my hand, saying over and over to myself, "HRT. HRT. HRT. History's really tough. Her rotten tomatoes. Harry rips tissue. . . ." I kept muttering things like that to help me remember.

When I had my breath back, I went inside, threw the dead bolt, dropped the Walgreens bag on the counter, and looked up Felicia's number in the phone book. A guy answered on the fifth ring. It sounded like I woke him up. I asked if Felicia was there. There was some mumbling, then a loud *clunk*, like somebody'd dropped the phone.

"Hello?"

"Felicia, this is Teddy. Did I wake you up?"

"No. No. It's my boss. . . ." She must have been talking to Bob. It made me feel funny, hearing her call me her boss.

"Did the article run today?" she asked.

"Yeah, but that's not why I'm calling. I think I spotted the killer."

"What killer? Oh. The geese. What do you mean, you spotted him?"

"He's stalking me." I told her what had happened.

"Teddy, the odds that—"

"The only thing I can't figure is how he knew where I lived. . . ." I looked down at the counter. "The phone book! I'm listed! He read the article this morning and looked me up!"

"Ruzak, think about it. Even if this was the person who hit the geese, why would he come looking for you?"

"I don't know . . . maybe because he's mad. I'm sorry. I shouldn't have called. I'm a little shaken up." My face was hot, and it wasn't from sprinting two blocks and three flights of stairs. "I visited my mother's grave this morning and I guess I'm a little spooked. I'm sorry I bothered you, Felicia."

I hung up. Bob must live with her, I thought, although last night was Saturday and it wouldn't be unusual for a guy to sleep over after a date.

Felicia was right: There were hundreds of black SUVs. It was crazy to think this was the one. Crazy, too, that the guy would be so incensed that he'd jump in his car on a Sunday morning to track me down and . . . and what? Stop me from fingering him for killing some baby birds? But if it wasn't him, why did he slow down like that, pacing me as I jogged? Or was he pacing me at all? Maybe he was talking on the cell phone, which people do, and they say that's as dangerous as driving while drunk. Maybe he was having a fight with his wife. One of the things you have to be careful about when you live alone is the tendency to put yourself too much in the center of the world, like everything that goes on around you is related to your existence, when in reality, your existence doesn't amount to a hill of beans. That's tough for a lot of people to swallow. For centuries, people believed the sun revolved around the Earth, because we thought we were so damned important. What's my life going to matter in a hundred years? Or fifty? Or even twenty? I wondered how long a goose's memory was, if that mamma and poppa goose still remembered their babies and mourned. Parker Hudson had told me they went berserk when that car flattened their children, honking and flapping their wings and refusing to move off the road. That tore him up almost as much as seeing those goslings murdered. That, and the way the SUV sped up right before impact, like he'd *meant* to hit them.

"It was him," I said aloud in my empty apartment, which seemed emptier than usual. I figured maybe I should get a more low-maintenance kind of pet, like a parrot, something you could not only talk to but that would also talk back. That way, I would have an excuse for talking to myself. But I had heard a parrot can live a hundred years, and that made me feel funny, having a pet that would outlive me. I went to the living room window, pulled up the blinds, and looked for his car parked on the street, but there was no black SUV.

I couldn't be sure it was him, of course, not like I was sure about the Earth moving around the sun. I couldn't *know,* but I *knew.* Black Ford Expedition with Tennessee tags beginning with the letters *HRT.*

It was a start.

CHAPTER ELEVEN

I took a shower, changed into some shorts and my NYPD T-shirt, made myself a roast beef sandwich on rye with some Lay's baked potato chips and a Clausen pickle, the spear-cut kind. Then I grabbed my keys and took the stairs into the garage below the building, thinking again about maybe investing in a gun. I could write it off my taxes, and being motivated might help me pass the marksmanship test, though in the Academy I'd been motivated—I'd really, really wanted to be a cop—but I couldn't get it down.

Checking my rearview mirror the whole time, I took Kingston Pike west into Farragut. After driving around for about forty minutes, I finally found the road Parker Hudson lived off of, with the lake sparkling beside it in the afternoon sun and the pontoon boats, waterjets, motorboats, and bass boats, and shrieking skiers and two little groups of fishermen angling off one of the neighborhood piers. A sidewalk followed the lazy curves on the opposite side of the road, broken here and there with entrances to subdivisions with names like Water Sound and Lakeview and Rocky Creek. Families were everywhere, kids on bikes and trikes and scooters and older ones on skateboards. It was a warm Sunday afternoon in late spring, the kind of day that makes your heart ache, although you're not sure what for.

I pulled into the lakeside park and shut off the engine. More families here, tossing a baseball or a Frisbee, and lots of dogs sniffing the bushes. I looked for Parker Hudson. Part of me wanted to see him and another part wanted him to see me. I'd tell him of my encounter with the evildoer on Gay Street and see if the make, model, and tag number jogged his memory. I checked out the cars in the parking lot, but although there were lots of SUVs and even some black ones, there weren't any with the tag HRT.

There was a paved walking trail that snaked through the park about fifty feet from the water, past picnic pavilions and under mature oaks and maples; then it wrapped around a softball and soccer field before looping back to the parking lot. I walked the trail, practicing my powers of observation, wishing I had worn a hat, because the sun was high and hot. Looking to my right as I neared the softball field, I saw them cruising the little inlet about a hundred yards away, two geese with dark heads and white bands around their necks, and I wondered if these were the parents of the babies who had been slaughtered. It occurred to me that, in a way, these geese were my real clients and Parker Hudson was just an agent acting on their behalf.

I left the trail and walked down to the water's edge and the geese checked me out in the way wild birds do when they're used to the occasional handout of stale bread. You would think after several centuries of humans giving them the bum's rush, wildlife would be more wary of us, but maybe there hasn't been enough time for the information to be encoded in their genetic memory. I was a little fuzzy on evolution; it taxed my imagination, getting from some slimy vertebrate dragging itself onto a primordial shore to Teddy Ruzak standing on another, man-made shore in an NYPD T-shirt and Nike running shoes.

A couple of shirtless boys, neither one older than ten, I guessed, appeared beside me and immediately found a couple of rocks and hurled them toward the geese. Before I even stopped and thought about it, I told them to cut it out. They gave me that shocked look of kids called down by a total stranger and took off toward the trail. "It isn't trivial!" I yelled after them. Life is not trivial, no matter whose life you're talking about, although some people might ask what mosquitoes or those tsetse flies in Africa contribute. That was Parker Hunter's whole point, why he got out his wallet, and the reason this case was important: You have to battle total disregard wherever you find it, in whatever form it takes.

The geese turned their backs on me and glided toward deeper water. To tell the truth, I have always been a little afraid of geese. They are the most aggressive of the freshwater North American fowl. I was charged by one more than once in my childhood, and I shrieked with terror and dashed behind my mother's legs.

It was a time for a silent pledge to the bereft parents, if these two really were them, but I didn't because I couldn't promise I'd find the killer, only that I'd try, and that would be more poignant than reassuring, and besides, to promise more would not reflect well on my moral character.

I walked slowly back to my car. A couple of lovers were reclining under the shade of a willow tree by the shore. He was reading something to her from a book and she was staring at the water with a bored expression, but it was like something out of a movie or a painting, and for a second I was pretty lonely and feeling self-conscious and sorry for myself because I was the only person in the crowded park who was alone.

I figured it was a good time to cruise the neighborhoods around the lake, since it was Sunday and the odds were better the SUV would be at the perp's house. If the perp lived in one of the neighborhoods around the lake, that is. If the perp had gone home after stalking me. If the car I saw even belonged to the perp. I drove slowly through Rocky Creek, Lakeview, and Water Sound, all newer developments with two-story brick or stucco houses, clean white driveways, and perfectly manicured lawns. I was thinking the whole time, This is it. This is the American dream, with bare-assed kids splashing in the plastic wading pools, big yellow fish painted on the sides, with the pretty teenage girls and shaggy-haired boys lounging on the patios beside blaring boom boxes, and the sometimes strained, disembodied laughter floating from unseen backyard cookouts, and the young trees, dogwoods and Bradford pears and oaks, their leaves still blushing the bright green of spring. Here there was no room for my sorrow over the goslings or my self-pity; here was bursting secondhand happiness and the riches of suburbia. No wonder people moved out here, a good twenty-five miles from the city. Twenty years ago, Farragut had been a sleepy little hamlet, a farming town named after the famous admiral who was born somewhere near here. The farms had been sold to developers, cut up into tracks, and the humans rushed in, pushing out the native deer and raccoon, rabbit and opossum. And the geese. I might have told Parker Hudson those babies were as much victims of urban sprawl as human viciousness and indifference, but we would both have known the truth.

I didn't see the Expedition, so I drove home.

CHAPTER TWELVE

I was late getting to the office the next morning. I hadn't been able to go to sleep Sunday night and kept getting up to stare out my window at the street outside until about 3:00 a.m., when it dawned on me that the goose killer was probably indifferent about my life, too. Then about three hours later, the sun itself dawned on me because I'd forgotten to close the blinds, so I crawled out of bed and closed them, then fell back asleep, not waking up until half past eight. For fourteen years, I was a night watchman, and that screws up your body's inner clock; it was still hard for me to stay awake during the day and go to sleep at night, though human beings are programmed to be diurnal.

Felicia was already at her desk when I came through the door at a little after ten o'clock. She was wearing a red short-sleeve sweater-type top and a short red skirt, but I thought it lacked something, maybe a red carnation behind her ear or a rose, although maybe that was too far on the flamenco dancer side. A stack of Sunday *Sentinel*s lay on the desk, along with a large frame with the backing removed. She was wielding a razor knife.

"I was about to call your apartment," she said.

"Sorry," I said, even as I wondered why I was apologizing to my secretary. "I overslept. You know, human beings are diurnal creatures and—"

She cut me off. I was disappointed. I wanted her to be impressed by the fact that I knew the word *diurnal*.

"Thought maybe you had a wild night."

"I was reconnoitering the scene of the crime yesterday." Again, a word worthy of any college professor, but she remained stubbornly unimpressed.

"Did you see it again?" she asked, meaning the SUV.

"No, but I saw the geese. At least I think it was them."

"Hard to tell. They all look alike."

"Unless you're a goose."

"Duck, duck."

"What?"

"Didn't you ever play that game when you were a kid? Duck Duck Goose?"

"Oh, sure."

"Well." The tip of her tongue came out of her mouth as she cut the newspaper with the razor knife. For some reason, this reminded me that I hadn't eaten breakfast, and I had a vivid image of a Krispy Kreme doughnut, then an even more vivid image of Felicia biting into one, the glaze glistening on her bottom lip, which was the same color as her sweater. Her tongue chewing also reminded me of my father, who'd had the same habit when he was concentrating on something. Thinking about my dad with one part of my brain and Felicia's lips with the other made me feel weird.

"What are you doing?" I asked, to change both subjects, the outward subject of childhood games and the inward subject of the odd pairing of my old man fixing a lawn mower with my longing to watch Felicia eat a doughnut.

"I'm framing your article. I'm gonna hang it on that wall right there so when people come in, they'll see it. They'll think you're a celebrity. People love celebrities, Ruzak."

"About the only thing I watch on TV is old movies, so most of the celebrities I love are dead."

"That's kind of morbid. Anyway, you are one now and you've got to make the most of it."

"Felicia, Ben Affleck is a celebrity. I'm an unlicensed detective with one case, which I can't even solve."

"That doesn't matter. What has someone like Sarah Ferguson ever really accomplished, except marry into a famous family and use that to sell diet plans? You put too much stock in personal achievement. Most of the time, it's just luck, being in the right place at the right time, or luck like Ben Affleck's looks."

"Well," I said. "I was never too lucky with that."

Though I kind of opened the door for her to argue with me, she didn't.

"We've had six calls already this morning."

"You're kidding."

"Three well-wishers, two potential clients, and a kid who wants you to find his lost hamster. He suspects his big brother's taken it, maybe killed it, even, and buried the evidence in the backyard. He's found a fresh hole."

"That's three potential clients."

"No pro bono work, Ruzak, until your bank balance is triple your IQ."

I was trying to figure out if she'd just insulted me as she went on. "Parker Hudson called, too; he wants you to call him back. I didn't tell him about your sighting or whatever it was yesterday. He's very excited, calling it a stroke of genius—the article, I mean."

"Did you tell him it wasn't my stroke?"

"Why would I tell him that? Anyway, nobody's called yet to fess up, so the jury's still out on whether it was marketing genius or detecting genius. Dear God, Ruzak, what are you wearing?"

I looked down at myself. My most comfortable pair of jeans, a white oxford that maybe was a little old and maybe one of the little collar buttons had popped off, but I thought I looked pretty good, in a casual kind of way.

"What's the matter with it?" I asked.

"Your shirt's so threadbare, I can see the moles on your stomach. Your jeans are about a half inch too short and your socks don't match."

"My jeans aren't too short."

"Then how else could I see your socks?" She proceeded to lecture me for about five minutes on the importance of image and how I had to project a certain kind. You're judged by the way you look, and people in the public eye especially are judged, and not kindly. Dress like a bum and be treated like one. Dress like a million bucks and one day you'll be worth it. The longer she lectured, the more maternal she became, and this didn't sit well with me, mostly because of the sweater and short skirt.

"It's like redecorating this dump. It's the same principle. People walk in expecting a professional's office to look a certain way. First impressions, Ruzak. Bad first impressions will kill you. Good ones will make you rich."

I told her I didn't have anything against getting rich, then went to my desk to call Parker Hudson.

"Hey, Teddy," he said. It was the first time he'd called me by my first name. "Terrific article."

I got right to business. I figured he'd appreciate it, because he was being billed for the call.

"Do the initials HRT mean anything to you?"

"HRT?"

"HRT." I told him about the black Ford Expedition and the slow, spooky "chase" down Gay Street.

"Well, the car I saw was definitely black and it might have been a Ford— those Expeditions are quite large, aren't they?"

"Huge."

"But HRT . . . I wish I could remember. I was focused on the geese. . . ."

"Sure. I saw them yesterday, by the way."

"You were at the lake?"

"Drove through those developments out there, too, but I didn't spot anything. Maybe I'm being overly optimistic, Mr. Hudson, but I'm thinking we might just have this thing cracked wide open by week's end. I've already gotten six calls."

"Tips?"

"Actually, no tips yet, but I'm thinking if our guy doesn't turn himself in outright, somebody else will. Might call or write a letter to the paper, or even to me. Meanwhile, I'm gonna figure some way to turn up the heat a little."

"How?"

"I'm working on that."

"Well, I thought the newspaper article was a stroke of genius."

Now was my opportunity to tell him it had been Felicia's stroke. I had assured the state of Tennessee I was of good moral character, and this was an issue of moral character if ever there was one. Felicia had acted like telling him the truth was counterproductive to earning a buck. And anyway, she didn't seem to mind giving me the credit, since she didn't tell him when she had the chance. I was quiet while I wrestled with these pros and cons.

"Teddy?"

"Yeah?"

"I thought we were disconnected."

"I am, usually. Mr. Hudson, you ought to know that article was my secretary's idea."

"It really doesn't matter to me whose idea it was. I should have thought of it, saved myself some money."

"Are you firing me?"

"Are you kidding, Teddy? You're doing a bang-up job. Keep me informed on your progress."

Felicia stepped into the room and said, "Why did you tell him?"

"Because the next one would be easier."

"The next what?"

"My mother always said that once you've told the first lie, the next one comes easier and the one after that even easier and so on."

She looked at me for a second. Her shoes, which I hadn't noticed till now, were the same color as her skirt, had three-inch heels, and were very glossy.

"You miss your mom, don't you?" she asked.

I nodded. "Is that a new outfit?"

"What's it matter?"

"The shoes are very shiny." I added quickly, "I've been practicing my powers of observation."

"Observe this," she said, and stuck her tongue out at me. She turned on her three-inch heel and disappeared behind the little wall.

"How about some Krispy Kremes?" I called after her.

CHAPTER THIRTEEN

A COUPLE MORE CALLS CAME IN BEFORE NOON. ONE WAS FROM AN old lady who wanted to tell me about all the skunks on the west side of town and how motorists kept smashing them in their haste to get to the mall or Wal-Mart or wherever their lives took them, then asked me if I thought anything could be done about it. The smell was awful, she said. I told her no, probably nothing could be done. The other call was from a potential witness.

"I know who hit those geese," the caller said.

I picked up my mechanical pencil and readied myself to crack the case wide open.

"What's your name?" I asked.

"I'd rather not give you my name."

"Sure, I understand. That's perfectly reasonable. It's a friend of yours?"

"A neighbor."

"Man or woman?"

"Woman. She's a nasty little woman, too, and I wouldn't put something like that past her. I see her all the time on that road in the mornings, and do you know what she's doing, Mr. Ruzak?"

"No. What?"

"Putting on her makeup! Can you believe it?"

"Once I was on Kingston Pike and I saw a woman strip off her work clothes and change into her aerobics gear."

"While she was driving?"

"No, it was at a stoplight."

"What in the world did you think?"

"I thought that life had gotten too hectic." I also felt guilt—guilt that I watched her and guilt that I had completely abandoned any pretense of keeping an exercise regimen.

"So you didn't actually see her hit the goslings," I said.

"Oh, no, nothing like that. But she drives a big black SUV all right."

"Ford?"

"No, it's a GMC, I think."

"You sure it's not a Ford?"

"No. I'm pretty sure it's a GMC."

"What's her tag number?"

"I have no idea."

"Could you get one and call me back?"

"I'm not walking over there and writing down her tag number, Mr. Ruzak."

"What's her name?"

"You want her name?"

"Isn't that why you called, to give me her name?"

"Why do you want her name?"

"Because the whole point of this case is finding out who killed those geese."

"If I give you her name, she'll know it was me."

"How could she know that?"

"Oh, she'll know. She'll know. You don't know her. She's a nasty, nasty person."

"Well, there's not much I can do about that. Not much of anything I can do, really, if you won't give me her name."

We went around and around like this for another five minutes. It was like playing Twenty Questions. "Does she live in Knoxville? Does she live on the west side? Does she live right off the road by the lake?" I continued asking questions, with her getting more and more cagey, until finally I gave up.

"Well, thanks for your call," I told her.

"No problem," she said. "People should stand up for what's right."

After I hung up, Felicia came into the room, holding her purse.

"I'm going to lunch."

"I didn't even have breakfast."

"I'm meeting Bob. Wanna join us?"

I thanked her but said I'd probably work through lunch. The thought of being their third wheel was mortifying. "How did you and Bob meet?"

"At his brother's wedding. His brother is married to my cousin."

"Doesn't that make you sort of related?"

"How do you figure?"

"I don't. Sorry. Is he nice to you?"

"You got a crush on me or something, Ruzak?"

"No, I just wanted to know if he's nice to you."

"He's very nice. Don't get a crush on me, Ruzak."

"Okay." I had never seen Bob, but I pictured him as tanned and buffed, like those models in the Calvin Klein fragrance ads, maybe mustachioed, possibly a black belt, and certainly possessing more than his fair share of machismo. In other words, the complete opposite of me.

"You ought to buy one of those little refrigerators and a microwave," she said on her way out the door. "That way, you wouldn't have to go out for lunch. Save yourself some money." Then she was gone, out to lunch. First, a complete makeover for her, then one for the office, and now a company break room. One of the reasons I'll never be rich is the financial concept of spending money to make or save money is something I've never been able to wrap my imagination around.

She hadn't been gone ten minutes when there was a knock on the door and an old lady stepped into the room. And I mean, as old ladies go, she was quintessential, from the shapeless flower-print dress to the blue-gray hair and the large purse clutched in both hands and pressed against her chest.

"Are you Theodore Ruzak?" she asked.

"That's me," I said. I went around the desk and led her to one of the visitor's chairs. She had those thick knee-high stockings old ladies wear and she smelled faintly of lavender talcum and cheap hair spray.

"Thank you," she said. "My name is Eunice Shriver."

I wrote down her name with my mechanical pencil on a fresh sheet of my yellow legal pad. When I finished, I stared at the name for a second.

"No, I am not *that* Eunice Shriver. No relation at all, though I've been asked all my life."

"Sure."

"My maiden name is Sparks, and in 1943, I married a young sailor on a three-week furlough. His name was Nathaniel Shriver—of the Kentucky Shrivers, no relation to the Yankee Shrivers."

"You bet," I said.

"I made quite certain of that."

"Who wouldn't?"

"His family owned several thoroughbred racehorses, though none ever raced in the Derby."

"Is that so? I'm not much into the ponies myself."

"The vice of vices!" she exclaimed. "It nearly destroyed my marriage, and it certainly destroyed my husband."

"He gambled?"

"Of course he gambled; he was from Kentucky and his family owned horses. When I say it destroyed him, I mean it literally: He died in a stable accident when a horse kicked him in the chest. Killed him instantly. I was thirty-four years of age, with four children, and he was gone. Not that he was a wonderful provider to begin with, God rest his soul."

"Insurance?"

"A little, but that's hardly any of your business, Mr. Ruzak."

"That's right. My business has to do with detective work."

"As I should well know! I saw the article in the paper yesterday and that is why I am here now talking to you, though you seem almost too interested in my private affairs."

"I'll back off."

"I never married again after the horse killed him, if you must know. I'd had my fill. Are you married, Mr. Ruzak?"

"Oh, no."

"Why not?"

"I guess I haven't found the right person."

"What hogwash! There is no such thing."

"Maybe you're right—you've lived a lot longer than I have and been around the track a few more times, if you'll forgive the pun, so I can't really argue with you except to say you gotta let the young be idealistic, because it's so darn hard when you get old."

"What's hard?"

"Idealism."

"You don't say!"

"Is there something I can help you with, Mrs. Shriver?" I had trouble understanding why she was sitting in my office giving me a hard time, as if I were the one who had arrived unannounced and without an appointment.

"I am here regarding the matter of those poor little goslings."

"Terrible thing, wasn't it?"

"You're to be commended, Mr. Ruzak. Most people could care less about the fate of six baby geese, particularly since the adults are such unpleasant and noisome creatures."

"Oh, I really couldn't agree with you there, Mrs. Shriver. I think a lot of people actually do care about it, or the *Sentinel* wouldn't have run the story in the first place. But now we're back to idealism."

"That's very insightful," she said. "Like several things quoted in the newspaper. You strike me as particularly sober and levelheaded for one so overweight, bless your heart. I mean to say, it's rare to find someone of your bulk so given to philosophizing."

"Really, you don't think so? Again I'll have to bow to your experience,

Mrs. Shriver, and the truth is, I can't think of a single fat philosopher. But my weight really is offset by my height; I'm nearly six six."

"Really! Did you play football in college?"

"I didn't go to college."

"I find that extraordinarily difficult to believe."

"Most people don't."

"And modest, too. I must say I find even more to admire in person, Mr. Ruzak. I believe I've made the right decision by coming here today."

"Gee, I hope so," I said. I looked at my watch, and she caught me looking at it and frowned.

"You won't think I'm wasting your time when I've spoken my piece, Mr. Ruzak."

"You're not wasting my time, Mrs. Shriver. Really, I'm what you might call a people person, and this is pure bread and butter to me."

She leaned forward and whispered, "I know who killed those goslings."

"I figured maybe you did."

"I was there. I saw it all. It was grotesque, terrifying, an absolute and utter tragedy, the likes of which I pray I never witness again. And I probably won't, because guess how old I am."

"You want me to guess your age?"

"Go ahead."

"Seventy-five."

"I'll be eighty-six years old next month."

"I'm not good with ages or names."

"And I still drive my own car."

"That's terrific. Now, you say you saw the car that hit these geese? What kind of car was it?" I was poised to write "black Ford Expedition" on my yellow legal pad.

"Why, it was my car."

"Your car?"

"Yes." She opened her purse and pulled out a white hankie and dabbed her eyes with it. "That's the worst of it. Now that's done. I had no idea how I would say it, but there, I've said it. The baby killer sits before you, Mr. Ruzak, in all her shame and sorrow."

"Oh, that's rough. I'm really sorry about the shame and sorrow, but . . . you hit those geese?"

"I just said so; must I repeat it?"

"What kind of car do you drive, Mrs. Shriver?"

"What does that have to do with anything?"

"Is it a black SUV?" It was hard for me to picture it.

"I don't even know what an SUV is. I drive a white Buick Monte Carlo."

"That's funny," I said. "Because my witness says it was a big black sport-utility vehicle."

"Well, your witness is mistaken."

"He seemed pretty sure of it."

"Then he is a liar."

"Why would he lie about that?"

"I have no idea why he would lie about that. Perhaps you should ask him, since you are the detective."

"Okay." I tapped the eraser end of my mechanical pencil on the pad. "Tell me what happened."

"Well," she said, scooching forward in her chair, bag clutched in her mottled grip and resting on her wide knees. "I was on my way to the market and running late, as usual, and I simply didn't see them until it was too late. Smack! Smack, smack, smack! Oh, it was horrible! Terrible!"

"Why didn't you stop?"

"I did stop! I am not a monster, Mr. Ruzak, no matter what that newspaper article implies."

"My witness says the driver didn't stop."

"Again, your witness must be lying."

"But if you'd stopped, he wouldn't be my client, there wouldn't be a newspaper story, and you wouldn't be sitting here." I laid my pencil on the desktop and said gently, "Mrs. Shriver, you didn't hit those geese."

"I beg your pardon, but I most certainly did!"

I thought about it. You have to pick your battles in life, and what was the point of arguing with the old lady? She wanted to confess; it made her feel better, for reasons I really didn't want to get into, so I dropped the whole thing, took a statement from her, which she signed with a dramatic flourish, and eased her out the door, promising I'd fax her confession over to the police ASAP. I warned her to be careful driving home, saying there were other animals and even pedestrians out there, though she'd probably already filled her quota. She got offended when I offered to help her down the stairs, and she huffed down to the street alone. I went to the window and watched her climb inside a sky blue Lincoln Town Car and pull with painful slowness into traffic.

I went back to my desk, tore the page off the legal pad, wadded it up, and threw it in the garbage.

About twenty minutes later, there was another knock on the door. Most businesses' doors you don't knock on first; what was it about PIs? I yelled that the door was open.

A Knox County sheriff's deputy walked into the room.

"Teddy Ruzak?"

"Hi, yes, that's me. How're you doing?"

We shook hands. He introduced himself as Gary Paul and pointed to the framed clipping now hanging on the wall directly behind Felicia's desk.

"Saw the article yesterday and thought I'd drop by."

"You're not the only one. I just took a confession."

His eyebrows went up. "Really?"

"From a professional. Not a professional goose killer. A professional confessor. Or maybe that would be confesstrix."

He laughed. "We get those types all the time."

"Have a seat." I waved him toward the chair Eunice Shriver, no relation to the Yankee Shrivers, had just vacated. "You want anything? The coffee's pretty old, but I could make a fresh pot." My heart was high up in my chest and I was slightly out of breath, a common reaction around cops, even back when I was at the Academy. That probably should have been a sign to me I wasn't cut out for police work. I was also thinking Felicia had a good point about the refrigerator. You want to make your clientele feel at home, and there wasn't so much as a bottled water in the place. I wondered how much those minifridges cost. Deputy Paul sat in one of the visitor's chairs and I plopped down in my big leather number behind my oversized desk and tried to look professional despite my threadbare oxford shirt that you could see my moles through and my too-short blue jeans. Deputy Paul's uniform was immaculate. He was probably around my age but about twenty pounds lighter and three or four inches shorter, with very small dark eyes and slightly oversized lips. His skin had this reddish tint to it, pocked and deeply scarred, most likely from severe acne in his adolescence. He was losing his hair but hid the fact by clipping it very short, like that guy on the *Today* show.

"What a creep," he said, referring to the gosling killer.

"Yeah. Either very cruel or very thoughtless."

"Either way, a creep."

"It's one of those things that can make you question the basic goodness of human beings. But again, all the calls this morning have had one thing in common, and that's a sense of outrage. Some people might say all that means is that people are basically silly and sentimental, but it gives me hope."

"Hope for what?"

"Oh, you know, for humanity. That everything's going to come out all right in the end. I'm basically an optimist; that's why I took the case in the first place, despite the fact there were no leads and no witnesses, besides my client." I didn't add the chief reason I'd taken the case—that I didn't have one and Felicia was draining the bank account for designer dresses.

"Well, that's kind of why I dropped by," Deputy Paul said. "I wanted to let you know not everybody on the force thinks it's funny what happened—couldn't believe it when I read that they laughed your client out the door—and also I wanted to help."

"Oh man, that's terrific, Deputy."

"Call me Gary."

"I couldn't appreciate it more, Gary. I'm kind of in a reactive mode, waiting for a tip or some kind of break, like the perp coming clean." This felt great to me, talking shop with law enforcement. It was almost like being part of the fraternity. Maybe your dreams do come true, but never in the way you imagine they will.

"Strictly on my own time," Gary said. "You know, informally. I've got resources you probably don't."

"That's true. You know, I went through the Academy a few years back."

"You were a cop?"

"No, I didn't finish. Another opportunity came up." This wasn't precisely a lie, but it wasn't precisely the truth, either. I never gave much thought to my moral character. Not many people do, I guess, because it's something most people take for granted, assuming theirs is pretty good for the most part. I didn't think most people sat down and considered whether their moral character was up to snuff. Maybe religious types do, like priests and certain fundamentalists. Although fundamentalists probably start with the assumption that everybody's moral character falls more than a little short of the mark: If everybody is so damned good, why do we need God in the first place?

"So tell me what you got," Deputy Paul said crisply. Down to business. He was probably on his lunch break, since he said he was going to help on his own time.

"Well, I've got a description of the vehicle from my client. . . ."

"What's his name?"

"Parker Hudson." I hadn't told the paper his name, but I didn't think Parker would mind if I told a cop. Gary wasn't taking notes. That meant either he had a good memory or I hadn't told him anything yet worth writing down. "Big black SUV with Tennessee plates. But I think I've got a little more on that." I told him what had happened on Gay Street with me jogging down the sidewalk with my Walgreens bag.

"What was that partial tag?" he asked.

"HRT."

"And it was a Ford Expedition?"

"That's right, fairly new, maybe a 2001 or an '02, with tinted windows. That's why I couldn't make the driver."

"Did you check with DMV?"

"Check with them how?"

"Motor Vehicles can run those letters through their database and match them up with registered vehicles throughout the state."

"Gee, I didn't know that."

"I'll have it run for you, if you want."

"That'd be terrific. That'd be great. This is an incredible stroke of luck," I told him. "I've been having this unbelievable run of luck lately, and to be honest, it makes me a little nervous. I forget who now, but somebody once said that luck is the residue of design, but I've always been a little deficient in the design department."

He laughed. He had needed some dental work as a kid and didn't get it. That and his pockmarked face got to me. Pity is the swiftest way to my heart. When I see a stray dog, I immediately look the other way, because if I didn't, I'd have half the strays in the county living in my little apartment.

He told me he'd give me a call in a couple of days with the list from the Department of Motor Vehicles, we shook hands, and he left. I was starving; it was nearly one o'clock and I hadn't eaten anything since Sunday night. I put up the sign Felicia had made on the new computer—GONE TO LUNCH. BACK IN ONE HOUR—and walked down to Market Square. I was feeling pretty ebullient. It was another warm, sunny day and the square was filled with the late-lunch crowd, and even though I didn't have a license, I was about to solve my first case. For the first time since Mom died, I didn't feel so crummy, and I had a salad for lunch with low-fat dressing and a glass of ice water.

CHAPTER FOURTEEN

FELICIA WAS STILL AT LUNCH WHEN I GOT BACK TO THE ELY BUILDING. On my walk back from Market Square, I got an idea to capitalize on my terror on Sunday. I was excited because, one, I actually had an idea and, two, it was a pretty good idea and, three, you should always find some way to exploit your fear, because otherwise it's just a destructive waste of time.

I called Paul Killibrew at the *Sentinel* and told him I might have a lead in the case and asked if he was interested in running a follow-up article based on my encounter with HRT. He sounded interested and said he'd run it by his editor.

About twenty minutes later, Felicia showed up, and there was something I'd call fuzzy about her: one side of her red skirt higher than the other, her blond hair windblown-looking, though there was no breeze, a fresh coat of lipstick. The Hilton was two blocks west of the office and she had been gone over two hours. She hadn't asked to take a long lunch, and I knew I had certain responsibilities as an employer, but would I be reprimanding her for the long lunch or the fact that she was fuzzy and the Hilton was only two blocks away?

"What's wrong?" she asked.

"Why do you think something's wrong?"

"You were smiling when I came in and now you're not smiling."

"I guess no smile lasts forever."

"Bob took me to the Bistro—you know, where all the bankers and lawyers and other big shots go—and the service is always slow there. And to top it all off, the waitress brought us the wrong check." Felicia, as a former waitress herself, could be righteously indignant when a fellow professional did substandard work.

"What'd you have?"

"The special."

"What was the special?"

"This some kind of test?"

"No, just curious."

"Why? Ruzak, did you skip lunch, too?"

"No, I ate at Market Square. A cop came to see me after you left."

I told her about Deputy Gary Paul and my idea to get another article in the paper about the latest development in "The Gosling Affair," as the *Sentinel* called my case.

"Only you don't know that Mr. HRT was our killer," Felicia said.

"Funny coincidence if he wasn't. Anyway, you've got to go where the leads take you."

"You know, one day after you're world-famous, I'm going to publish a book of your sayings. Like 'Go where the leads take you.'"

"Are you sore at me or something?"

"Why would I be sore at you?" she asked crossly. She went to her desk, out of sight, and now I was sure she hadn't lunched at the Bistro; she'd been at the Hilton, or maybe not the Hilton, but some other private place for a quickie (though technically, two hours couldn't be called a quickie), and her being sore had to do with guilt.

There were a few more calls in the afternoon. Felicia set up a couple of appointments for prospective clients and then around four o'clock, she said she had to take off early because she had a hair appointment. This made me wonder if she was a natural blonde. A lot of women in East Tennessee aren't but want you to think they are. My mother had called it "the Dolly Parton effect." After Felicia left, like some cosmic switch had been tripped, the phone stopped ringing. And I was out of ideas, since I'd used up my allotment for the day. I hung around till five o'clock, making notes, like "Check on minifridge" and "F/u on PI app." Then I cleaned off my desk and trooped around the office, watering all the plants Felicia and the decorator had placed around because they were convinced the oxygen produced by all the foliage would help cleanse the air of dry-cleaner fumes. By the time I finished, I was a little sore at Felicia. Watering plants was definitely a secretary's job, but then I realized the idea to call the newspaper with the story that might break the case was the detective's job.

There was a young woman standing on the sidewalk outside the Ely Building when I left. She was a good-looking girl of about twenty, with shoulder-length dark hair and very large brown eyes. She didn't have much shape, but she was tall and held herself well, like a girl who's had some breeding. She was holding a section of the newspaper—the "Lifestyle" section of the Sunday *Sentinel*. I could see the top of my shaggy brown head above the fold. What a sheepdog! I decided right then to get a haircut first thing in the morning.

"Guess what? I'm Teddy Ruzak," I told her.

"Oh, good," she said. "I didn't know if this was the right address. You saw me standing out here?"

"Actually, I was on my way home."

"I'm sorry. Mr. Ruzak, I need to talk to you. . . ."

"Okay. It's nice out. You want to walk?"

She hesitated, but only for a second, before nodding, and we set off east, toward Gay Street. The air had begun to cool and there was a springtime moistness to it that reminded me of flower gardens and the way wet grass feels beneath your bare feet. The gentle atmosphere played counterpoint to this girl's agitation. She was definitely distracted and nervous about something. HRT, I thought. She's going to tell me she's HRT, the goose killer. I cautioned myself not to get my hopes up. She might be a chronic confessor, like Eunice Shriver.

"Where are you parked?" I asked. "Because if you didn't feed the meter, they'll still ticket you after five. They're very aggressive about it downtown. It's a cash cow for the city." I thought I was being pretty clever. I wanted to see her car. If it was a black Ford Expedition with the partial tag HRT, I had her.

"I parked in the Hilton's garage," she said.

Well, there went that lever to pry the truth out of her. If she didn't confess, I could tail her back to the garage to check out the car.

"Did you want to see me about the article?" I asked.

"Yes." She dropped the newspaper into a trash can mounted on a light pole on the corner of Gay and Church. Her putting my picture in the garbage kind of hurt my feelings.

"My name is Susan Marks. I saw the article yesterday and . . . I don't know what good it's going to do, but . . . I wanted to ask you something, Mr. Ruzak."

"Go ahead. But call me Teddy."

"Okay," she said. "The article didn't mention the name of your client."

"I protect the identity of all my clients," I told Susan Marks. Of course, I had only one client, but she didn't know that. The trap of the human ego is the desire to impress other people, even total strangers. It's led to more misery than half the wars in history. I wondered if I should tell Felicia that one so she could put it in *The Wit and Wisdom of Theodore Ruzak, Master of Detection.*

"I understand that, Mr. Ruzak, but I hope that after you hear my story, you'll change your mind. You see, I'm a little desperate."

We turned left on Gay Street and walked north. A guy passed us walking a big German shepherd that was wearing one of those thick black leather collars with the rows of glittering silver spikes. German shepherds are very smart but too aggressive and big for my little apartment. I wouldn't want one of those little yippy-type dogs, though, the kind you dress in sweaters in winter, and the males especially annoy me, the way they daintily lift their hind leg to pee.

"Have you ever heard the name Lydia Marks?"

"No."

"Maybe you've seen her picture before."

She pulled a piece of paper from her purse, unfolded it, and handed it to me. It was a flyer with MISSING printed in bold black letters at the top. Beneath the word was a picture of a pretty woman with auburn hair, maybe around my age or a little older.

"They ran it in the newspaper a few days ago. She's my stepmother and she's been missing now for over four weeks."

"You want me to find your stepmom for you?"

"I want *anybody* to find her. The police sure haven't had much luck." Susan Marks had a small, slightly upturned, freckly nose and a full bottom lip that was out of proportion to her top one, which gave her a kind of puckish look. She went light on the makeup and could have passed for a boy if her hair had been shorter or maybe hidden in a ball cap. She had the fine features of a pixie.

"What's this have to do with my client, Susan?"

"When those baby geese were killed—that was around the time she disappeared. She always took a jog that time in the morning—always."

"She lived near the lake?"

Susan nodded. "We aren't sure she was abducted that morning. See, my dad travels a lot for business and my little brother and I live on campus. Dad flew to Brussels on Wednesday and didn't get back home till late Saturday night."

"You don't call or go see her on a regular basis?"

"We aren't that close. Don't get me wrong, Mr. Ruzak. I like Lydia, I really do, but she was Dad's thing, you know? He met her in Ireland about four years after my mom died. I was a senior in high school. She was a lot younger than he was, but they were in love. And it *was* love. She wasn't like some kind of gold digger or anything."

We had doubled back toward Market Square. She sat on a bench beneath an oak tree and I sat beside her. I was still holding the poster and I looked at her stepmother's picture as she talked.

"What have the cops found out?" I asked.

"Not a hell of a lot. There were no signs of a break-in. Nothing is missing in the house, the Mercedes is in the garage, and Lydia's purse is on the kitchen counter with her driver's license, all her cash and credit cards. The only thing we can't find are the house keys."

"And none of the neighbors saw anything suspicious?"

She shook her head. "Dad talked to her on Wednesday night. He tried calling again the next night, Thursday, but there was no answer. He wasn't too worried, because Lydia often goes to the movies at night when he's out of town."

"By herself?"

"She was—she's a very shy person. America was overwhelming to her. She hated America, I think, but Dad tried to help out the best he could. He even gave her a job managing some of his properties while he was away, Mr. Ruzak."

"Please, call me Teddy."

She nodded. "She didn't know anybody in America when Dad moved her here after the wedding and she didn't meet people easily. I don't think she has any close friends here."

"So what makes you think somebody abducted her? Maybe she hopped a cab and flew back to Ireland."

"That's the first thing the police thought, so they checked all the manifests. And anyway, you can't get on any plane these days without a driver's license."

"Maybe she ran away."

"She had nothing to run from."

"I mean with somebody else."

"Lydia's crazy about my dad. If you ever saw them together, you'd know that's impossible."

"Okay. No friends. No lovers. Enemies?"

She shook her head. "Not that I'm aware of."

"And your father was in Brussels."

She gave me a cold stare.

"The police must have brought that up, too," I added quickly. "Family members are the first people they look at in a case like this."

"My father loves Lydia. He adores her. I'm talking to you because he can't. Or won't. He's in some major denial right now. He can't bring himself to deal with this, so I have to. We're desperate, Mr. Ruzak. The police have no leads, no evidence, and no witnesses and I don't know where to turn. Maybe it's grasping at straws, but your client might have seen something. Even if he didn't see what happened to her, at least if he did see her jogging on that trail that day, we could narrow down when she disappeared."

I nodded. "Sure. That makes sense. I'll ask him."

She looked down at her hands. They were small and her fingers were very thin. I remembered a line from a poem I had read once, or maybe it was from a movie: "Nobody, not even the rain, has such small hands."

"Hey," I said. "Are you hungry, Susan? I didn't have breakfast this morning and all I had for lunch was a salad with low-fat dressing and a glass of ice water. You want to get something to eat?"

She looked up at me with a startled expression. The last thing she probably expected from me was a dinner invitation. I wasn't sure why I had extended one. It probably goes back to my weakness for the bereft of this world, those holding the short end of the stick, from stray dogs to poor people with bad teeth. She was obviously pretty broken up by her stepmom's disappearance and knew deep in her heart what all cops know: that the longer someone's missing, the greater the likelihood they'll never be found.

CHAPTER FIFTEEN

WE WERE A BLOCK FROM MARKET SQUARE AND THE TOMATO HEAD was still open, but I have this constitutional aversion to eating at the same place twice in one day. There're not a lot of restaurants or any kind of place that stays open past 7:00 P.M. in downtown Knoxville, because there're not a lot of people living downtown to patronize them. I thought about getting my car from the garage and driving somewhere, but we were about seven or eight blocks from my apartment and I was afraid if we walked all that way, it would give her too much time to change her mind. About the only other decent place was the Bistro on the corner of Jackson. It was attached to the Bijou Theater and frequented by the city's theater crowd at night, actors and other artsy types who constituted Knoxville's version of counterculture. The servers were all either actors or students studying to be actors and therefore could be counted on to be temperamental. I thought the place was overpriced for the quality, but it was kind of cool, with brick walls and wide-paneled wooden floors and a bar that ran the length of the room. A large painting of a naked fat lady hung over the bar; she was reclining on a bed with about fifty pillows and a small white dog, maybe a Pomeranian—I didn't know, as I wasn't up on the small breeds.

So we walked back to Gay Street and turned right onto Jackson. A breeze had picked up, the first real one in a couple of days, and some clouds were moving in. Susan Marks walked with her thin arms folded over her small chest. Maybe it's just my impression, but androgyny seems to be more prevalent in the upper classes. Look at all those royals and superstar celebrities, especially the singers, only they don't call them singers, but "recording artists." I guess you couldn't call people like Jack Kennedy or Paris Hilton androgynous, but those are the exceptions that prove the rule. It's like money breeds the sex right out of you, though you hear that money is the ultimate aphrodisiac—or maybe it's power, which in this world is the same thing. If I had a lot of money, I'd hook up with the most voluptuous woman I could find, just to safeguard against the asexual factor.

"Where do you go to school?" I asked. It was the first time I'd spoken since she said she'd have dinner with me. "The university?"

She nodded. She had this habit—probably born of self-consciousness, because her bottom lip was so much larger than her top—of sucking in her bottom lip and chewing on it with her teeth.

"What's your major?"

"I'm studying to be a vet."

"Hey, that's terrific. I love animals. I've been thinking about getting a dog, although technically it's not allowed. I haven't had a dog since I was a kid and my collie died."

"We always had a dog, usually two or three. And a cat. And a cockatiel, fish, turtles, a couple of hamsters—you name it."

"Since you're in the field, maybe you can tell me what the deal is with these ferrets that are so popular now and maybe what kind of dog I should get and your thoughts about somebody my age getting back into school. . . ."

She stopped walking all of sudden.

"What's the matter?" I asked. We were a block from the restaurant.

"This feels weird to me," she said. "Having dinner with you."

"Well," I said. "Why are you?"

She shrugged. "Why did you ask me?" She had folded those thin arms over her chest again and her dark eyebrows had moved close together. She wasn't exactly frowning at me, but she wasn't smiling, either. I guess she was wondering if this was some kind of seedy quid pro quo, like I wouldn't help her if she didn't have dinner with me. It wasn't that at all; she just seemed so lost and I felt bad for her. And, like a lot of guys, I equate eating with comfort—that's really what it was all about, comfort. But would she believe me if I told her that? I wondered. One of the saddest developments of the modern age is the cynicism of the youth. There was another quote for Felicia's book.

"I'm pretty hungry, to tell you the truth, and probably the last eighteen or nineteen meals I've eaten, I've eaten alone. It's pretty crappy to eat alone. There's nothing chic about it, and besides, it's dangerous to your health. I read somewhere you tend to eat more when you eat alone, but I might have that wrong, because sometimes you read things and you remember them wrong because you're justifying something—in my case, the fact that I need to lose about twenty pounds."

She laughed and her eyebrows sprang apart.

"It may have said that you eat faster," I said.

"You're funny," she said. "You're not what I expected at all."

We started walking again.

"What did you expect?" I asked.

"I don't know."

"Probably someone like Philip Marlowe or Columbo. You don't run into too many PIs in day-to-day life, so it's one of those professions where stereotypes flourish. I never liked Columbo, chiefly because there's something mean and snide about pretending to be stupid when you're not."

"Who's Columbo?"

It was a dark night for the theater, so we didn't have any trouble getting a table. Susan Marks folded her arms on the table and looked around the room; she had never been to the Bistro before, she told me. There was a tiny potted plastic flower arrangement on the table and an unlighted candle. I ordered a beer and Susan ordered a raspberry tea. I asked our waitress when her shift had begun and she told me four o'clock that afternoon, so she wouldn't have known if Felicia and Bob had actually eaten there. I wondered why I was trying to catch Felicia in a lie, then decided it was because detective work is a vocation, not a job; you can't leave it at the office at five o'clock.

I asked what she thought had happened to her stepmother.

"I think she was jogging and somebody took her. I don't think she ran off with the yardman or joined a commune or is playing some sick game on my father to get him to notice her or anything like that."

"But we're talking broad daylight on a well-traveled road with lots of moms around walking babies and retirees strolling the trail. Not exactly the ideal spot to be abducting someone."

"There's no other explanation."

The waitress came back with our drinks. I ordered the filet mignon and Susan ordered the North Atlantic scrod, which was one of the specials on the chalkboard at the front of the restaurant. I thought about telling her you should never order fish on a Monday because restaurants serve the leftovers from the Friday deliveries, but we weren't that intimate, and anyway, it was sort of a big brotherly or, worse, fatherly thing to say, so I kept my mouth shut.

"I guess the cops told you that's one of the hardest cases to solve."

She nodded. "Unless we can turn up a witness, there's not much hope."

Tears welled up in her eyes and I looked away. An older couple, maybe in their seventies, were eating at the next table, not saying anything to each other. You see that a lot when you eat out, old couples who've been married for a million years eating and not saying a word, but it never looks uncomfortable. After all that time together, they've probably said all that's worth saying. The best way to take someone's mind off their problems is to get them to talk about themselves, because most of us think our problems come from someone or something else, so I asked her about school—if she was going to specialize in any particular type of vet work, if she was going to work in the research field or be a practicing vet, if she was going to stay in the area when she graduated, and if vets had to do internships like people doctors. This kept the conversation going through the bread and salad and halfway into the entrée. When she relaxed, she had this habit of talking out of the right side of her mouth; she reminded me of those kids in that old movie *Bugsy Malone* trying to act like gangsters. She should let her hair grow some and wear more makeup, I thought, but vet work is kind of a butch science for a girl, a tomboy occupation. She had an athlete's body, inclined more toward swimming or basketball than softball or soccer. To test my theory, I asked if she played any sports, and she told me she was on the tennis team. Well, tennis would fit, too.

"I played football in high school," I told her. "Left guard. I wasn't very good, but I was big and could take a lot of hits. People just bounced off me like little moths off a naked lightbulb. I haven't been very active since then, but I'm gonna get into this Krav Maga deal. Don't know if you've ever heard of Krav Maga, but a lot of girls do it; it's a great workout, plus you learn self-defense. You really find out how to beat the living crap out of someone. I'm thinking I can write off the entire cost of the class, since knowing martial arts would come in handy in my line of work."

She asked how I got interested in my line of work, so I told her about reading Sherlock Holmes and the Dictionary Ruzak moniker. She laughed about me calling myself Dictionary Ruzak. She had very good teeth and didn't show too much of them when she laughed, like a lot of thin-faced girls, which reinforced my notion that she had some breeding, that here was a girl who had wanted for nothing in her life, that her stepmom disappearing was the first real trouble she had had.

The check came and she insisted we go dutch, but I told her I needed the write-off, because technically I was entertaining a client.

"But I'm not a client," she said.

"Well, it's sort of like you are, though one client removed, like a second cousin."

She laughed. "You say things that don't make sense and make sense at the same time."

I blushed, as if she had paid me a compliment. It was dark when we stepped outside, and I told her I was walking her to her car. Downtown Knoxville can be pretty rough at night, after the library closes and all the vagrants hit the streets. Knoxville is known as a good place to come if you're homeless: The cops don't hassle you too much and people are generous. The air was heavy with a storm coming in from the west. The leading winds of the front had died and there was that before-the-rain stillness in the air. We didn't say much on the ten-minute walk to the Hilton, and I was feeling a little like we were television reenactors on one of those true-crime programs, tracing Felicia and Bob's route from the Bistro to the Hilton, if they even went to either the Bistro or the Hilton.

Her car was parked on the third level, a brand-new cherry red Mitsubishi convertible. My car was a 1992 two-door Nissan Sentra. I stood a couple steps back while she opened the door. She thought of something, pulled a pen from her purse, and scribbled her number on an old bank receipt.

"Will you call me right away after you talk to your client?"

"You bet."

"An English sheepdog or maybe even a Great Pyrenees."

"Huh?"

"The kind of dog you should get."

"Oh. Okay. Thanks. I'll look into that."

A lopsided smile. A hand on my shoulder. A little bounce on the balls of her feet and a kiss on my right cheek. She got in her car and I waited until her top was up and she was pulling out to turn, then walked back to the stairs. The rain had started and I had left the umbrella at the office. I was going to get soaked to my Skivvies, and I'm not such a romantic that I like walking in the rain.

CHAPTER SIXTEEN

I CALLED PARKER HUDSON FIRST THING THE NEXT MORNING. A LADY answered the phone—his wife, I guessed—and told me he was playing golf. The rain that had moved in the night before was still hanging around, having turned misty overnight and now promising to stay all day. Sometimes the clouds swoop down upon us from the Cumberland Plateau and settle in the valley for days. I left a message for him to call. He must be a dedicated golfer to hit the links in this kind of weather, I thought, or else he is lying to his wife. Although Parker Hudson didn't strike me as the lying type.

It was Felicia's turn to show up late. She didn't get in till almost ten o'clock. She was wearing black knee-high boots, a suede skirt, and a white peasant-looking blouse that showed a lot of cleavage. As always, when she first walked in the room, I felt myself expanding like that fat kid in the Willy Wonka movie.

"Don't tell me I'm late," she said.

"How come?"

"Because I already know I'm late."

"Car trouble?"

"Yeah, something like that."

I wondered what could be like car trouble but not car trouble.

"You'll never guess what's happened."

"You've caught the killer."

"No, but the plot's thickened." I told her about meeting Susan Marks and about her missing stepmother. For some reason, I left out the fact that I'd had dinner with Susan.

"That's a weird coincidence," Felicia said.

"It would explain why the driver didn't slow down or stop."

"Because he was in the midst of an abduction?"

I nodded.

"On the other hand, maybe she's wrong and the stepmom took off on her old man."

"She's sure that didn't happen."

"Stepmom was a lot younger, right?"

"Uh-huh."

"Dad's out of the country a lot, right?"

"Uh-huh."

"Stepmom's a looker, right?"

"She's kind of pretty, yeah."

"A foreigner in a strange country, no friends, no family around except the stepkids off to college . . ."

"Maybe I should look into this deeper."

"Why?"

She was leaning in the entryway, one ankle crossed over the other, and as she talked, her thigh muscles clenched and unclenched.

"Is Susan Marks your client?"

"Not exactly."

"Is Susan Marks your client, Ruzak?"

"No. She's not."

"Is the Highly Effective—oh Christ, I can't remember how it goes—is the DIC a for-profit business?"

"Okay, Felicia. But I did promise I'd call Parker and ask if he saw anything that morning."

"Don't you think he would have told you already if he had?"

I shrugged. "Memory's funny."

"No pro bono work, Ruzak," she reminded me. The phone rang and I heard her say, "The Highly Effective Detection & Investigation Company. How may I direct your call?" even though there was only one place to direct it.

It was Deputy Paul.

"Teddy, I've got an answer on that partial tag for you."

"Hey, that's terrific," I said, digging in my desk drawer for my mechanical pencil.

"Well, it's probably not the answer you're looking for. You sure you got the letters right?"

"Hernando Radio Tango," I said, trying to sound very law enforcement.

"What?"

"HRT, that's what I saw," I said firmly.

"Well, there's no match, at least not to a Ford Expedition."

"Stolen tag?" I asked.

"I thought the same thing," he said, and I felt myself go warm with pleasure that I was thinking like a cop. Maybe I couldn't be one, but I could think like one. "But there's no record in the database. You sure it was a Tennessee tag?"

"One hundred percent."

"Okay. Huh. Well, sometimes not every number gets keyed in correctly. I could check the actual paper, but that takes time, Teddy."

"Look, I can't tell you how much this means to me . . . and to my client."

"Don't mention it, buddy."

I took a breath and said, "Does the name Lydia Marks mean anything to you?"

"No, should it?"

"She went missing around the same time the goslings were killed."

He didn't say anything for a second.

"Okay," he said. He was waiting for the punch line.

"Maybe it's connected."

"What?"

"Lydia Marks's disappearance and the killing of the geese."

"What was her name again?"

I spelled it for him. He said, "Who's the detective assigned to the case?"

"I don't know. I've been dealing with . . . an interested third party."

"A confidential informant?" There was a smile in his voice.

"Yeah, confidential informant, something like that."

"I'll ask around."

We expressed our mutual admiration and hung up. Felicia spun around the half wall as if on cue, as if this were a play and we had to keep the action moving.

"Three things," she said. "I hate our company greeting. It's too long and I refuse to say 'You've reached THE DIC.' We've got to change the name before it's too late. Also, Parker Hudson is holding for you, and what are you doing for lunch?"

"You're asking me to lunch?" I felt gut-punched.

"Relax, Ruzak, it's not a date. It's a working lunch."

"I didn't think it was a date," I said, but my tone probably gave me away. "What are we working on?"

"You," she said, and spun back around the wall. I was glad peasant blouses were making a comeback; I had always liked them.

I picked up the phone and asked Parker Hudson, "Have you ever been hypnotized?"

"I beg your pardon?"

"You know, where somebody puts you in this altered state. . . ."

"Teddy, I know what hypnosis is. And the answer is no, unless you include the spell placed on me by my beautiful wife thirty-five years ago." She must have been in the room with him; that's something you'd say if your wife was standing nearby.

I pulled the flyer about Lydia Marks out of my pocket. "She's thirty-seven, five six, a hundred and thirty pounds, auburn hair."

"Who is?"

"The woman you may have seen the morning the goslings died, maybe on the trail, maybe in the SUV itself. Her name is Lydia Marks and she's your neighbor, I guess."

"I've never heard of her. Or seen anyone like that. What's this got to do with hypnosis?"

"I figured you didn't have a memory of her or you would have mentioned it when you hired me. What I'm thinking is that they have that regression-type hypnosis therapy where you can reach suppressed memories. . . ."

"You want me hypnotized?"

"Totally voluntarily."

He laughed.

"You never know what might turn up," I went on. "Even if it isn't Lydia, maybe you'll remember the tag number, because my lead's not really panning out, or something else that'll crack the case."

"Why do you want me to remember Lydia Marks?"

I told him. He waited so long to say something, I had to ask if he was still there.

"I'd really like to help, Teddy. But I don't think I'd be comfortable undergoing hypnosis."

"What about your wife?"

"You want my wife to undergo hypnosis?"

"No, what if it was your wife who was missing? What would you think of a potential witness who refused to be hypnotized?"

"Now you're trying to manipulate me, Teddy."

"I'm just in the field, turning over stones."

He laughed. "Oh Teddy. You know what lives under stones. All sorts of nasty things."

He promised he'd think about it and we ended the call before I remembered to ask him about his golf game. I looked out the window behind the desk. My office was in the back of the Ely, so my view was totally blocked by the building behind me. It was 11:30, but it looked like dusk out there in the alley with the light rain falling straight down, making whispering sounds against the glass. I turned on my dictation machine and recorded a reminder to research hypnotherapists in the area in case Parker Hudson changed his mind. It had occurred to me during our conversation that maybe a shot of sodium Pentothal might open up his mind a little, but I doubted he'd go for it, since he was so hesitant about hypnosis, which was a lot less intrusive than an armful of truth serum, so I didn't bring it up. I also made a note to look into those psychic criminal investigators who the police bring in when they're desperate. I'd seen a special about them on A&E and, although I went in a skeptic, some of the stuff they came up with was pretty impressive. Thinking of psychics reminded me of another show I saw once, maybe on Animal Planet, about a pet psychic who could telepathically talk to animals, sort of a New Age Dr. Doolittle; maybe I could dig up one of those to mind-meld with the geese, because, apart from Parker Hudson, they were the only witnesses to the crime. I wondered if I was being creative or just getting desperate.

I called the number Susan Marks had given me and left a message for her to return my call. Her voice was very calm on the recording, very smooth, as if she recorded voice-mail introductions for a living.

Felicia came into the room and asked, "Did you drive to work this morning?"

"It was raining."

"So that means you did?"

"Yeah."

"Good, let's go."

"Where are we going?"

"Lunch, remember?"

I don't think I'd ever been as physically close to Felicia as when she slipped into the bucket seat beside me in the Sentra. I caught a whiff of peaches and thought of summertime. I took Cumberland Avenue west into Sequoia Hills, with the mansions lining either side of the road and the big Greek Orthodox church where every spring they have their fund-raising Greek Festival with all the food and dancing in the back parking lot, all the little Greek kids in their traditional Greek getups, their arms wrapped around one another's shoulders, and I wondered as we drove past the church if line dancing in country music had its origins in Greek dancing. I wasn't really hungry when we set out from downtown, but thinking of baklava got my appetite up.

"Is Bob a good cook?" I asked Felicia. "I hear firemen are great cooks because they're cooped up in the firehouse all the time."

"He's not cooped up all the time," she said, which really didn't answer my question, but I didn't press it. Something about Felicia tightened whenever I brought up Bob.

"Where are we going?" I asked. "And don't say 'lunch.'"

"American Clothiers."

"Oh, no."

"Think of it as an investment, Ruzak."

"PIs aren't known for their couture," I said. "Look at Columbo and Tom Selleck in those tacky Hawaiian shirts."

"What about Sonny Crocket?"

"Who's Sonny Crocket?"

"Don Johnson, *Miami Vice,* come on, Ruzak!"

"Felicia, I don't want to look like Don Johnson."

"I don't honestly think there's a danger of that, Ruzak."

"American Clothiers is very expensive."

"How would you know, Kmart Man?"

"I happen to know because I rented my graduation tuxedo from American Clothiers and even the underwear was seventeen dollars a pair, and that was fifteen years ago."

"You priced the underwear?"

"Anyway, detective work can be grungy, dirty business, Felicia. You sleep in your clothes sometimes and—"

"What times?"

"Like on a stakeout. And—"

"Why would you be sleeping on a stakeout? Doesn't that defeat the purpose?"

"I was just using that as an example."

"What kind of an example is it that makes no sense?"

"Sometimes what I say makes both," I said.

"Makes both what?"

"Sense and no sense."

She laughed. Some women have very unattractive knees, but Felicia's were top-notch. Her brown skirt with the cowgirl-like ruffles on the hem had ridden up to mid thigh.

"Do you ever line-dance?" I asked.

"Do I what?"

"You know, that kind of country-music dancing."

"Never. I hate country music."

"I don't like it, either."

"So why were you asking?"

"I don't know."

We were on Kingston Pike and the traffic was bumper-to-bumper. I looked at my watch. When I was a security guard, everything was very time-oriented: when your shift started and ended, when you made your rounds, even when you took your potty and other breaks. Now I was self-employed, it felt weird working without a strict schedule.

"That deputy with the sheriff's department called this morning," I said.

"I know. I answer the phone."

"Yeah. Anyway, he can't find that tag."

"Maybe you got it wrong."

"Maybe."

"Or they've disposed of the car."

"That could be."

"Or maybe he just missed it."

"Another possibility."

"I don't even know how you can see to drive, Ruzak," she said. "How long has it been since you changed the wiper blades?"

"Now I suppose I don't have the right kind of car."

"You're about to bring up Columbo again and that clunker he drove on the show, but you can't use Columbo, Ruzak. Columbo was a police detective, not a PI."

"So was Sonny Crocket."

We were close to West Town Mall and the traffic inched painfully along. Kingston Pike was always bad this time of day and the rain only made it worse.

I said, "You ever notice how when you get a new car, all of sudden you notice the same make and model all over the road, when before you hardly did? Ever since I met Parker Hudson, I've been seeing black SUVs. Look, there're three in the right lane up there and two in our lane . . . and another one behind us."

American Clothiers was on the west side of the mall, in a strip center with a Korean restaurant, a print shop, and a store called the Candy Factory, where every year I used to pick up some hand-dipped chocolate strawberries for Mom for Valentine's Day. American Clothiers reminded me of my mom, too; she'd taken me there to help pick out my tux.

"My only point is," I said as we walked toward the door. "My only point is PIs are eclectic when it comes to wardrobe. I don't want to walk out of this place looking like a banker."

"You're not fooling me. This isn't about clothes. Sometimes change isn't a bad thing, Teddy."

The store was ten degrees cooler than outside, and since it was only in the seventies outside, it was damn cold in that store. A salesman dressed like a banker swooped down on us immediately, like an ER triager who knew a critical case when he saw one. For the next hour and a half, I stripped, donned, paraded, and pirouetted for Felicia and the salesman, a guy named Simon, who handed me his card when it was all over, because now he was my man at American Clothiers, my wardrobe guy. I bought—or my company bought, since everything was paid off the business account—three suits, four sport coats, five pairs of slacks, six ties, seven pairs of socks, and two pairs of shoes. The total bill was $4,576.98. Everybody seemed very pleased with the outcome, with the exception of one key person. Simon called into the back room and a little Lithuanian guy emerged with a tape measure around his neck. I was just assuming he was Lithuanian because he was short, swarthy, and spoke with that harsh accent of Eastern Europeans, and Lithuania was the first country that popped into my head. Simon asked the Lithuanian when my clothes would be ready.

"Two weeks! Two weeks!" he shouted back unnecessarily, and disappeared.

When we were back in the car, I sat for a minute staring at the storefront, the smell of leather and wool still lingering in my nose.

"People have a comfort zone," I told Felicia. "You know, a boundary that if they cross over it, they start to panic."

"What, are you panicking?"

"Next you're gonna tell me I need a haircut and manicure and a full body waxing."

"Well, you do need a haircut."

"When I was on the football team in high school, the night before the biggest game of the year, all the guys got together and agreed to shave their heads."

"How come?"

I thought about it. "It's a guy thing. Anyway, I went home that night and shaved myself completely bald, and when I showed up at school the next morning, I was the only one. Nobody else shaved his head."

She laughed.

"I looked like Kojak, another detective not known for his fashion sense."

She laughed again.

"Seriously, what do you think about the body-waxing thing? I've got some back hair."

"I could have lived without knowing that, Ruzak."

I asked her where she wanted to eat, because now it was past one o'clock and I was starving. We stopped at Don Pablo's, a Mexican chain that featured a flagstone floor and round tables beside potted palm trees and round, wide hacienda-type umbrellas. That way, you could pretend you were dining outside in Mexico while you ate inside in Tennessee. Felicia ordered a strawberry margarita and I had a Corona.

"Speaking of comfort zones, our killer must have one," I said. "The thing is, how do you bring him out of it?"

She thought about it. "Pressure. You put the pressure on. Like with the newspaper article."

I mentioned that I had called Paul Killibrew with my idea for a follow-up story.

"Call him again."

"Why?"

"Tell him it might be connected to the disappearance of Lydia Marks."

"How's that help?"

"If all the person did was kill the geese, he might come forward, because he sure wouldn't want to be connected to abducting somebody."

"Susan said they wired the phones and staked out the mail, but nobody contacted them for ransom."

"Not a good sign."

"Not if it was a real kidnapping. I'm afraid Lydia Marks is dead."

"Probably."

CHAPTER SEVENTEEN

IT WAS ON MY MIND THE REST OF THAT DAY AND WAY INTO THE NIGHT, so the next morning I ran the numbers, and they did not look good. Felicia was late again. I paced the office until she got there around 10:30, and I almost didn't say anything because her mood was so bad. She slapped her lavender purse on her desk, kicked off her lavender heels, and flopped into the love seat ($3,125 plus tax from Drexel Heritage) across from her desk ($2,567 plus tax from Braden's), rubbing the soles of her feet and grimacing like she'd stepped on a sharp object. In fact, I asked her if she *had* stepped on a sharp object.

"I'm just not used to heels," she said, and I thought of those thick-soled white numbers she wore waitressing.

"Nice outfit," I told her. And it *was* nice, a three-piece ensemble—lavender skirt, white blouse, lavender half jacket, the kind with the sleeves that are cut short, like the jacket worn by the kid on the Cracker Jack box, whose name probably is Jack. "New?"

"Yes, it's new. Why?"

"I've been crunching some numbers and we're in trouble."

She rubbed her arches and said, "How much trouble?"

"Enough trouble that Parker Hudson's fifty bucks an hour plus expenses is not going to help."

"That's impossible. There's no way we could spend that much in two months."

"Look at this." I handed her my calculations. Her nose scrunched up and her tongue came out like when she was framing the newspaper article.

"Well," she said finally. "Looks like you're going to have to postpone that body waxing."

"We need a cash infusion."

"You're meeting with two new clients today and one tomorrow," she said. "Up your fee."

"I canceled them."

She stared up at me. She was still sitting and I was standing a couple feet back, and for a second I was afraid she was going to come out of that love seat and coldcock me. Her tongue disappeared and her lips thinned out.

"Why did you cancel them, Ruzak?"

"I don't have a license, Felicia. I haven't sent back the application. I haven't taken the test."

"That didn't stop you from taking Hudson's case."

"I'm only comfortable pushing the envelope so far."

"Oh, what horseshit! You're kidding me, right?"

"And I took his case before I knew I needed a license. One of the requirements, Felicia, is you've got to have a good moral character. And anyway, the more clients I get, the greater the risk the state's gonna catch me, and then I'll never get my license."

"I lost my driver's license for six months and I didn't stop driving."

"You lost your license? What did you do?"

"That isn't the point. Sometimes you gotta play the odds, Ruzak."

"I'm in the accountability business, Felicia."

"The what?"

"My job is holding people accountable for their actions. That's what a detective does. It wouldn't be right for me to make a buck out of that while I'm not."

"While you're not what?"

"Accountable."

"Are you firing me?"

"Huh?"

"Is this where this is going? You're gonna fire me?"

"Of course not."

"Because I can save you the trouble, Ruzak."

"Felicia, look—" We were like a married couple fighting about household finances. I knew what that was like; Mom and Dad used to fight about it all the time. The worst fights they had were over money, the main issue being that there wasn't enough. There was never enough. Even rich people will tell you that: There's never nearly enough.

"But you just need to keep in mind you wouldn't still have your one client if it weren't for me."

"I'm not going to fire you, Felicia. I was going to say we need to cut back a little on the, um, I don't know what to call them. The stuff like here, in the office. Is it too late to return any of it?"

"Of course it's too late, Teddy. It's used office furniture. It lost half its value the minute it came through the door."

I whistled. "That's like when you buy a new car and—"

"Oh please," she said. "Spare me the Ruzakian riff on depreciation or relative resale values or whatever the hell you're about to go off on. You're like the neighborhood bar know-it-all without the drunken charm. Are you always so goddamned *earnest?*" She heaved herself off the three-thousand-dollar love seat and began to pace around the little area in her stocking feet. I could see the red paint of her toenail polish through the nude mesh. After pacing awhile, she stopped and said, "You're going to have to take those clients, Ruzak."

"Felicia, I told you—"

"You're going to take them and charge them a hundred bucks an hour to be their 'investigative consultant.' You want to play Mycroft, now you can. You'll sit your wide ass in that chair in there and noodle their problems and give them possible avenues to explore, and every minute the tiniest thought crosses that complicated brain of yours—I don't care if you're sitting on the can—you're charging them for it."

I thought about it. "That seems dishonest."

"Oh Christ!"

She flopped back down on the love seat and proceeded to jam the lavender shoes back on her feet. Again I could see the pink tip of her tongue, and all of a sudden I wanted to cry.

"Don't leave, Felicia."

"I'm not leaving, you bonehead! I'm putting on my shoes!"

"Good," I said, meaning the "not leaving" part. She went to her desk. "What are you doing now?"

"I'm calling the people you canceled and I'm uncanceling them."

"But what about—"

"Do you want to be a detective or not?"

"Of course I do."

"Then leave it to me, Ruzak. Have I ever let you down?"

I went into my office and sat my wide ass down in my $850 leather chair. It groaned a bit. I mean the chair groaned, not my wide ass. *Wide ass. Bonehead.* Guys are willing to take a lot more from a pretty woman than they would from a homely one. A homely one would be on the street right now, looking for a new job. Thinking that and thinking about morphing in a nanosecond from detective to "investigative consultant" made me feel like I had betrayed something precious or violated some solemn vow I never knew I'd taken.

She spent the next hour on the phone, getting my ex-clients back and rescheduling their appointments. I listened to her explaining my fee—$150 for the initial consultation, $1,000 retainer, $100 per hour—and saying how if they checked around, they'd find my rates very reasonable. When I couldn't take it anymore, I motioned to her that I was going out for a walk. She had slipped off her shoes again and had both feet on the desk as she talked. I noticed a tiny hole in her stocking, on the pad of her right foot, and for some reason the sight of that hole broke my heart and I wasn't sore at her anymore.

When I got back, Felicia delivered the good and bad news that of the three prospective clients, two had balked at my rates, refusing to make an appointment. This was good news for the maintenance of my moral character and bad news for my business. The third wanted to think about it, so the end result was that for now, I still had only one client.

I called Susan Marks's number and got the voice mail again. I hung up without leaving a message. Twenty seconds later, I called the number again, and this time I left a message, giving her my home number and telling her to call anytime.

I pulled out the envelope containing the PI application from the state, which had been sitting in my top desk drawer for over a week. The thing that concerned me the most was the fact that it would take three to four months for the state to process my application—three to four months *after* I passed the exam, assuming that I passed it.

I had to make a grocery run after work. The nearest store to my apartment was down on Broadway, almost five miles. That's one of the problems with getting people to move into downtown Knoxville: There're no grocery stores or gas stations or anything very convenient except the bus station and the mission houses for the vagrants. I checked my messages when I got home, but nobody had called. Maybe if I joined a gym or took some Krav Maja classes, I thought, I'd make some friends and people would call me.

I was putting away the last can of Campbell's when the phone rang. I jumped a little, because I wasn't used to the phone ringing. She sounded even younger on the phone, a little breathy, and I could picture her biting that fat lower lip as she talked.

"Mr. Ruzak?"

"Hi, Susan."

"This is Susan Marks. I'm sorry I didn't call you sooner. . . ."

"That's okay. Don't worry about it."

"You said in your message you had some information for me."

"Yeah. That's right. Look, I talked to my client and he doesn't remember anything, um, specific about your stepmom . . . seeing her or anything."

"Oh."

"So I told him maybe we ought to consider some hypnotherapy. You know, sometimes that can bring out things."

"Do you really think so?"

I kind of really didn't, but I wasn't going to tell her that. Still, you want to be careful with giving someone hope. False hope is crueler than despair.

"You never know," I said. "He wasn't too hot on the idea. How're things going?"

"About the same. I'm real busy. It's exam week."

"Well . . ." I was trying to think of something else to say. "That must be tough, exams in the middle of all this."

"Yeah." It was barely louder than a sigh. I didn't know how to comfort her, though comforting her wasn't really my job, beyond the normal moral obligation to give comfort when pain comes your way. I had no point of reference besides sharing her humanity. My mother was never abducted, except in the poetic sense, and I had never taken a college exam. When I thought about it, I had practically no life experience at all—never been to college, never been married, never had a kid. I was over ten years older than she was, but I might as well have been ten years younger.

"And a bad answer is better than no answer at all," I said.

"It's like your life just freezes, you know? You can't grieve. You can't hope."

"Oh, you can always do that," I said. "Hope, I mean."

"Why?" She repeated the question, her voice cracking a little. She seemed intensely interested in the answer. *"Why?"*

"Because when you think about it, that's what makes us human, besides speech. I watch a lot of the Discovery Channel and Animal Planet, and let me tell you, there's not much that separates us from the animals." She was very quiet as I talked. I couldn't even hear her breathe. I was relieved. Maybe my topic was just right, since she was studying to be a vet. On the other hand, maybe she was smirking on the other end because here was high school graduate and Police Academy dropout Teddy Ruzak lecturing her on animals. "Take chimps. Now, biologically, they have ninety-nine-point-something percent of our DNA; we're practically identical. Chimps don't talk, but they communicate. They use tools like sticks to dig out termites from mounds. They play games like people, and there's even that old saying about a hundred monkeys hitting typewriter keys for a hundred years to produce the complete works of Shakespeare. . . ."

"Shakespeare?" she asked.

"Sure, William Shakespeare. All his plays. Maybe not the sonnets. I don't know. I had a high school English teacher who read all of *Macbeth* out loud to us, and she played all the parts; I still remember the ghost of Banquo and the witches: 'Fair is foul, and foul is fair!' "

Now I could hear her giggling a little. This only encouraged me. Sometimes "Ruzakian riffs" could serve a purpose.

"But anyway, they love and grieve and form tight social bonds and learn from their mistakes, but like those damn geese, they can't hope. If a baby chimp gets sick, they don't hope it gets better. If a drought hits, the chimps don't sit around hoping for rain. They just suffer. When those goslings got killed, their parents grieved for maybe a day, no more than two, I would think, and then it was forgotten. I guess my point is that hoping is human, and when you give up hope, you give up that one or two hundredth of a percent that makes you human."

"I guess so."

"It's all, um, you know, precious."

"What is?"

"Life. I mean, it's too important to be trivial. Even a virus like Ebola. It's kind of what you might call evil in that it really messes with you, but that's exactly why it's not trivial." I told her the story of the kids throwing rocks at the geese. "That's when it hit me that I was wrong to think of my case as silly or a waste of my time on earth. Life matters, and to give up hope for life is like— well, I'm not what you might call a religious person, but the only word for it is *sin.*"

She didn't say anything, and I wondered if I had trespassed by slapping down my soapbox smack in the middle of her heartache. Plus calling her a sinner, in effect, was probably not such a good idea.

"I'm sorry," I said. "I'm talking too much."

"No, I like to hear you talk. I've never known anybody who talks like you. I've never known anybody like you period."

"I'm nothing special," I said, which was one of those self-serving things people who think they're special say.

She didn't say anything, and so I went on. "Would you like to have a cup of coffee with me sometime? Not anytime soon—I know you're taking exams and stuff—but maybe in a couple of weeks I could call you?"

"Yes," she said. "I think I'd like that."

CHAPTER EIGHTEEN

FELICIA CALLED IN SICK THE NEXT DAY. I WAS SURPRISED BUT NOT shocked. There really wasn't that much to do. I decided she had a good idea when she suggested staking out the scene of the crime to see if the killer was a regular, so for the next couple of weeks, I got up at 5:00 A.M. and drove west into Farragut, parked my car in a spot closest to the road in the park's parking lot, drank too much coffee, and ate too many Krispy Kreme doughnuts, but I never saw a black SUV with HRT on the plates, which made me think maybe Gary Paul was right and I'd gotten the letters wrong. I wrote down the letters of the alphabet and tried to see which ones resembled *H, R,* and *T* the most. I came up with so many different possibilities and combinations that I gave up. I started to doubt the whole thing had happened at all.

One morning, Parker Hudson saw me sitting in my car and came over to say hello and tell me that he was glad I was still on the case. I asked him if he had given any more thought to the hypnosis thing, and he just laughed and shook his head.

I visited Mom a couple times, picked up my new clothes from American Clothiers after arguing with Simon, my wardrobe guy, that I should be able to return them for a full refund, except there was the problem that they had been altered to fit me and all purchases for altered apparel were final, and generally moped around, waiting for a break in the case or a break in the monotony of my life.

Another morning, I came into the office and saw Felicia sitting at her desk, going through the want ads. She stuffed the newspaper in her desk drawer when I came in. When I accused her of looking at the want ads, she denied it, and when I checked her desk after she left for the day, I found it locked tight.

Speaking of the paper, I checked it every morning for a follow-up story on the possible Lydia Marks/dead goslings connection, but no story appeared. I called Paul Killibrew at the paper and he told me that his editor had killed the story because he didn't think there was enough of a story there. I hung up thinking it was pretty wonderful human beings weren't stories, because most of us would be dead. Thinking that made me think of Susan Marks, but I got her voice mail when I called. Finals would be over now, and maybe she moved back home with her dad for the summer.

The weather turned hot and dry. By midmorning, the temperature was in the eighties. I sat in my little Sentra and sweated, watching the joggers and the walkers and the baby strollers on the trail, hardly paying attention to the cars as they went by. I was pushing the envelope on this case; I knew that. Nobody had come forward and I had no leads left. How long would Parker Hudson pay me to sit in my car every day and sweat?

Then one morning, a cop car pulled in directly behind me and flashed its lights at me. My heart fluttered and the adrenaline made my ears sing. I was busted. The licensing commission had found out I was conducting a stakeout without a license and had issued a warrant for my arrest.

A sheriff's deputy got out of the car and came up to my window. It was Deputy Gary Paul.

"Thought that was you," he said, and showed me his bad teeth. "How ya doin', Ruzak?"

"Can't complain," I replied, the phrase used by most people who can.

"You working or taking a break?"

"Both, I guess."

He laughed. "Me, too. Let's go have breakfast."

"I just ate six Krispy Kreme doughnuts."

"Then you're ready for a real breakfast. Follow me."

He went back to the car and I followed him out of the lot.

He took Concord Road to Kingston Pike, then turned north onto Lovell Road, where he pulled into an IHOP parking lot. He hitched his belt when he got out of the cruiser and slapped me hard on the shoulder on the way to the door. He ordered a Rooty-Tooty, Fresh & Fruity, and I ordered two eggs and sausage with a glass of orange juice, since I'd already had about thirty-two ounces of coffee that morning.

"I ran that partial through the system again," he told me.

"Don't tell me. Nothing."

He shook his head. "So I had a clerk pull the paper."

"No match there, either."

"Nope."

"You have much experience with regression therapy?"

"I don't even know what that is."

"I was recommending it to my client, but now I'm thinking I should do it. Maybe I'd remember the tag right. Also, you should never recommend someone do something if you're not willing to do it yourself."

"I also spoke with Harvey Listrom."

"That's terrific. Who's Harvey Listrom?"

"The lead detective on the Marks case. They haven't developed any suspect who drives an SUV. They haven't developed any suspects period."

"What's his theory?"

"Random crime. Husband's been cleared. No evidence the marriage was unhappy. Stepkids have airtight alibis. Bank account overflowing. Health good. No sign of forced entry. Nothing missing from the house. Looks like she was taking her morning jog and somebody snatched her. She was just in the wrong place at the wrong time."

"And now she's probably dead."

"They usually are after this long."

Our food came, but my appetite had left.

"That sucks," I said. "I met her daughter. I mean her stepdaughter. A really nice girl."

"Too nice to have to deal with something like this."

I nodded. "But it made sense to me, HRT being connected to both things. First, it came flying down the road ten, maybe twenty miles over the speed limit."

"On the other hand, I pull fifteen to twenty speeders off that road every month. Doesn't mean they kidnapped somebody."

"And call me naïve, but I honestly think most people would have stopped if they'd done something like that—hit a gaggle of baby geese."

"You're naïve."

"I've got that habit," I admitted, "of thinking people are going to react to something the same way I would. Still, if it was the kidnapper, that would explain why he didn't stop."

"So would being an asshole."

"But what about HRT? Why would somebody who hit some geese come looking for me, unless they were the kidnapper, too, and thought I could connect them to Lydia Marks?"

"Maybe HRT wasn't stalking you. Maybe that SUV you saw had nothing to do with Lydia Marks or the geese."

"It just seems too much of a coincidence, the geese, the SUV, and Lydia Marks."

He shook his head. "Maybe it is all connected, Teddy, but you can't prove it. It's like a Rorschach test: You see in the blob of ink what you want to see."

"You know what the funny thing is? I've been out there every morning for the past two weeks, and even before the sun comes up, there're people walking and jogging that trail. I can't believe nobody saw what happened. And on the flip side, I can't believe Parker Hudson was the only one who saw the geese die."

"People don't like to get involved."

"Did Listrom talk to Parker Hudson?"

He shrugged. "I gave him the name."

I hadn't touched my food, but Gary Paul's plate was clean. He had wiped it clean with his last slice of toast and jammed the whole thing in his mouth. Most cops I knew were prodigious eaters and did their eating fast. At least I shared that with them.

"Could you get me a list of all black Ford Expeditions registered in the state?"

"Huh?"

I repeated the question.

He sipped his coffee. He took it with lots of cream and three of those little packets of sugar. I also noticed that he bit his fingernails to the quick. When you're a self-possessed, procedurally oriented kind of guy, like this Gary Paul obviously was, sometimes normal human anxiety leaks out in little self-destructive habits.

"Do you have any idea how many black Ford Expeditions there are in this state?" he asked.

"I'll pay for it."

"That's not what I meant, Ted. You'd be looking for a needle in a haystack."

"I don't know what else to do at this point. Does the department ever use psychics?"

"Ever use what?"

"Psychics—you know, people who get in touch with the spirit world to solve the case."

"Not that I know of." He was smiling. "Why?"

"Just wondering. Seriously, I can't think of anything else—I mean, getting that list is all I've got left."

"Sure. Give me a couple days."

He wouldn't let me pick up the check, reminding me that he had invited me. I followed his patrol car out of the lot. He turned right onto Lovell and I turned left and jumped on the interstate, heading back downtown. My stakeout of the jogging trail was over.

Felicia wasn't in when I got back to the office, but she had left a message that something had come up and she might have to miss work again the following day. For once, I didn't mind. I watered the plants and locked the place up, and I half-expected to see Susan Marks sitting on my stoop as I went out the door. Then I did a funny thing: I went to a movie. I'm not sure why I went to a movie, but it felt like I was on some kind of vigil; I was waiting for something, but I didn't know what I was waiting for. The atmosphere felt pregnant, like the air just before a summer storm or on the eve of a big battle, or that moment right before the batter leans back to unload on a big fat change-up and you *know* he's going to hit it out of the park. I ordered a large popcorn and a Coke, which together cost more than my ticket, and hardly paid attention to the movie, which I think was a comedy, only there seemed an awful lot of bloodletting and cursing for a comedy, but the movies have changed a lot even since when I was a little kid, which might explain why I watch the old ones on AMT or Turner Classics. After the movie, it was time for dinner, so I went through the drive-thru at Buddy's Bar-B-Q and had a pork dinner with corn on the cob and coleslaw. I drove home, checked my messages (I didn't have any), and then settled down to *Biography* on A&E.

When I got in the next morning, Felicia was waiting for me, standing by her desk in lime green shoes, slacks, and jacket over a satiny black blouse, holding a newspaper. I felt something contract in my chest when I saw the expression on her face, but it wasn't my heart; it wasn't something physical. It went deeper than that.

"What is it?" I asked.

"Have you seen this morning's paper?"

I took the paper to my desk and read the entire article, then picked up the phone and dialed the number. Her voice mail picked up. I hung up and Felicia set a cup of coffee by my elbow and then went to her desk. I could hear her typing something on her computer. I stared out the window into the alley, where two pigeons sat on the windowsill directly opposite mine. I watched the pigeons for a few minutes, then called over to Felicia to say I needed a phone book. She came in and placed a single sheet of paper with Susan Marks's address and directions there, which she had pulled from the Internet. She had also printed out the address for Kenneth Marks in Farragut.

I passed the dry cleaner's at the bottom of the stairs. They were already at work, and it flashed across my mind that for weeks on my way up to my office, particularly when things weren't going well, I would think at least I didn't run a dry cleaner's, with all those chemicals and the smell and customers complaining I had lost their clothes or lost one of their buttons, that at least I didn't have to work over those steaming machines pressing shirts all day. And thinking that always made me feel fortunate, until I thought about it too hard and realized my good fortune had depended on my mother dying.

She was sitting on the bottom step, the same step I first saw her on, wearing shorts and a sleeveless white shirt. Her brown hair was pulled back and held by a pink scrunchy, which made her face look even younger and more boyish—that and the fact that she wasn't wearing any makeup.

I sat on the step beside her and we didn't say anything at first. Then she turned toward me and put her head on my chest and I put my left arm around her. She cried until I could feel the wetness from her tears against the bare skin beneath my new oxford shirt and undershirt. She said something that I couldn't hear, but I didn't ask her to repeat it. I just kept my arm around her and rubbed her bare shoulder with the palm of my hand.

Then she said something else, and this time I understood.

"You told me to hope."

"I'm sorry," I said.

She cried some more—not your wailing kind of crying, the kind you see on the news practically every night when the story is from the Middle East, but a soft, quiet crying, pressing her face against my chest. Her shoulders and arms were covered in freckles.

"Help me," she whispered.

"I'll help you," I said.

CHAPTER NINETEEN

Two hikers from New Jersey found the skull of Lydia Marks high on a ridge in the heart of the Great Smoky Mountains. The rest of her bones had been scattered by the wild animals that had feasted on her. One of the hikers slipped the skull in his backpack and they descended nine hundred feet down the mountain to the nearest ranger station, bringing the skull with them because, they told the newspaper, they were afraid no one would believe them.

Within hours, the forensic pathologist with the Tennessee Bureau of Investigation determined the skull belonged to a female between the ages of thirty-five and forty and that the quarter-size hole in her cranium had probably resulted from a massive blow to the head with a blunt object. Dental records confirmed it was the skull of Susan Marks's stepmother.

The article said the TBI and the Sevier County and Knox County sheriff's departments had formed a joint task force to investigate the abduction and murder of Lydia Marks. They had set up a tip hotline and were asking the public for any information that might aid in the investigation. A spokesperson for the TBI told the reporter they had no suspects at this time.

I asked Susan if she wanted to go up to the office for a few minutes, but she told me she had to get back home; her father needed her. I walked her to her car and asked if she needed a ride; I thought maybe she shouldn't be driving. But she told me she was okay to drive, so I went back to the office. Felicia told me both Deputy Paul and Parker Hudson had called while I was outside with Susan. I called Deputy Paul first.

"This is a huge break," he said.

"How so?"

"It's not a missing person's case anymore. It's a homicide. Top priority.

And now there's physical evidence. Something to work from. It's terrible. It's shitty. But the odds were always that she was dead, and now that we have a body, we've got a better chance of finding the son of a bitch."

"I don't think the Marks family considers it a huge break."

I called Parker Hudson.

"I wish to God I had gotten a better look," he said. "But I was focused on the geese. I didn't even think to get the license number."

"We don't know it's connected," I said. "But you should call the task force."

He said he would. I said, "And I'll get hold of a hypnotherapist."

"Really, Teddy, I don't think that's necessary."

"It won't hurt to try."

"I won't do it."

"You will do it, Mr. Hudson."

"What did you say?"

"I said, 'You will do it.' When something like this happens, doing anything less puts you on the wrong side—the bad guy's side. You understand what I mean?"

When I hung up, Felicia was standing in the doorway. Her arms were folded over her lime green chest.

"I'm going to help her," I said.

"How much is she paying you?"

I didn't answer. She said, "Why are you going to help her?"

"Because I promised I would."

"Is there a reward?"

"A reward for what?"

"Finding the killer."

"Sometimes it isn't about money, Felicia."

"So you're willing to break the law for honor. It's just at money you draw the line."

"It's not a bad place to draw it."

"Aren't you noble."

"What's that supposed to mean?"

"Come on, Ruzak. You know the real reason you want to help this girl."

"She asked me to help her and I promised I would."

"And why did you promise that?"

"She asked."

Felicia laughed. "Okay, whatever. You want me to find a hypnotherapist for you?"

"That would be great."

I picked up the phone again and, after getting transferred a couple of times, spoke with the head of the joint task force, a detective with the TBI named Janet Watson, which was the same last name as Sherlock Holmes's sidekick. I told her about the black SUV that hit the geese around the time Lydia Marks disappeared and about the partial tag I spotted when a black SUV that might or might not have been the same one that hit the geese tailed me on Gay Street. Deputy Gary Paul of the Knox County sheriff's office had run the partial for me and hadn't found a match, but he was checking it again, I said. Then I asked her if she went into law enforcement because she had the same last name as Dr. Watson. That was a mistake, asking her that, because after she told me she didn't know what I was talking about, she treated me like you would a crank.

Felicia came back in after I got off the phone and handed me a piece of paper.

"Parker Hudson has a three o'clock appointment for next Tuesday. You want me to call him?"

"I'll call him."

"Address is on the paper," she said, and turned on her heel without saying another word.

There was something else I wanted to do, someone else I had made a mental note to call, but now I couldn't remember, so I got up and watered the plants and waited to remember. The best way to remember something is not to think about it, but to think about or do something else, and then it always comes to you. Try it next time you lose your car keys or can't remember somebody's name. I was misting the fern on the windowsill when I remembered, and I got on the phone right away to Paul Killibrew, the guy at the *Sentinel.* I told him his editor might be interested in running the follow-up now that Lydia Marks had been found murdered. He said he'd check again. Then I called Parker Hudson, told him about his appointment, and hung up before he could argue with me. Sometimes doing the right thing makes people uncomfortable, which is why the right things don't get done more often.

Felicia told me something had come up and she had to take the rest of the day off.

"What's come up?" I asked.

"It's personal."

"Is somebody sick?"

"Didn't I just say it was personal?"

"Technically, it's a business question, Felicia. I mean, I guess I kind of need a reason before I let you take off."

"Okay, *boss.* I'm not feeling very good, if you must know."

"That's all I need to know." She didn't look sick, but women have problems men don't see easily.

"Good, because that's all you're gonna know."

After she left, I took out my mechanical pencil and began a to-do list.

The door opened and a man's voice called out.

"Hello? Is anyone here?"

I went around my desk and saw a tall man standing by the love seat. He was easily halfway to thirteen feet tall, dressed in an expensive gray suit that might have been purchased from American Clothiers, and fairly sparkling with diamond jewelry: watch, two rings, and a stud in his left ear. His hair was fashionably long and swept back from his massive forehead, which jutted out like the brow of a warship over a very long, very straight nose and full, sensuous lips. It was the lips, particularly the lower one, which gave him away.

"I'm looking for a man named Theodore Ruzak," the man said.

"I'm Teddy Ruzak. And you're Kenneth Marks."

"How do you know my name?"

"I see the family resemblance. Come on in. Sit down. Can I get you anything? The coffee isn't fresh, and I keep meaning to get one of those watercoolers, but Felicia, my secretary, might have something stashed in the filing cabinet, not that she drinks on the job, but she did have a margarita once when we had lunch."

"No thank you," he said, slipping into one of my visitor's chairs. "I haven't much time."

"No, I didn't figure you would—not have a drink, I mean, but have much time. I gotta tell you how sorry I am about all this. . . ."

"No sorrier than I, Mr. Ruzak. We are preparing to leave for Ireland in two days."

"Ireland?"

"For my wife's funeral."

"You're burying her in Ireland?"

"As per her wishes, yes."

There went my surveillance of the funeral.

"I feel really bad about all this," I said. "Like I said before. I didn't know your wife, but I do know your daughter, which I guess you know I do, since she was here this morning and now you're here."

He didn't say anything for a second. Then he said, "My daughter tells me you have promised to help us find my wife's killer."

"Something like that."

"You're aware the authorities are also investigating her death?"

"Well," I said, "it certainly isn't a competition. They've got me outgunned in terms of manpower and experience and the ability to make an arrest."

"Then what do you suppose you can do?"

I shrugged. "Who knows?"

"Indeed."

He put his elbows on the armrests and laced his perfectly manicured fingers together. Now, this guy radiated charisma and power. I'd never asked Susan what her father did for a living, but whatever it was, he was very good at it and he knew it. He was not somebody to be messed with on a financial plane, not that I had any intention of messing with him on *any* plane. Still, the spouse is the first person you look at, so I looked at him and wondered if he'd had anything to do with his wife's murder. If this was a movie, I would have said Mr. Marks was suspect numero uno: rich, arrogant, smart. A guy you love to hate. He certainly wasn't playing the part of grieving widower very well, but these business-genius types are pretty cold fish, pretty ruthless, like those takeover guys who move in and fire half a company in order to save it. I really didn't have a head for finances. I was past my twenties and nearly midway through my thirties, and I still didn't know what I did have a head for. I certainly hadn't proved myself in the detective line. I couldn't even solve the murder of a gaggle of geese.

"Perhaps you would be interested to hear what I'd like you to do?" he suggested.

"That would be great. But I see my role as an adjunct to the police. Sort of an advisory position, because, see, technically, I don't have my license. I'll be taking the test next month, but as of right now I'm not a PI."

"If you're not a PI, what are you?"

"I'm an ex–security guard who lucked into some money and didn't have the brains or maturity to think things through before stenciling 'THE DIC' on my door."

He laughed. It was a bled-white kind of laugh, a social formality he observed, like shaking hands in the West or kissing cheeks in the East or bowing in the Far East.

"How did you luck into money?" he asked. I must have touched on his favorite topic.

"My mother died."

"You consider that luck?"

"I didn't say it was good luck."

"My daughter told me you are the most unusual man she has ever met. I begin to see what she meant."

He had such a formal way of talking, I wondered if he was a foreigner, too, like his second wife. Maybe he was naturalized, but he didn't have an accent, as far as I could tell. But I wasn't very good at accents.

"She brought your name up several weeks ago, after she read an article in the paper about your case of the dead geese. I told her at the time I didn't think talking to you would lead anywhere, but perhaps it has, or might, and that is why I'm here."

Now was the moment to pull out the ol' checkbook and write Teddy Ruzak a big number, one with lots and lots of zeros, but he didn't. He just studied me over his folded hands, his very light blue eyes taking everything in. Maybe German or Swiss. He was a big-bodied, stolid kind of guy, which fit the German theory; plus, the name could be an Americanized Marx, like the guy who started communism and made Ronald Reagan's second career possible. But he also was precise in the way he talked, clipping off the end of each word very neatly and organizing his thoughts, and even in the way he held himself erectly in the soft chair without so much as twitching an eyelash. There was a stoicism about him that might be Swiss, plus my belief, not based on anything really, that the Swiss were very good with money. Maybe it's all the talk about Swiss bank accounts, and you never read about Swiss poverty or them running to the World Bank for some debt relief. You never hear much about the Swiss period.

"I want the person who murdered my wife," he said.

"Sure."

"And toward that goal, I am offering half a million dollars for the arrest and conviction of her killer."

I gave an appreciative whistle. "Gee, thanks for letting me know. I've been cautioned against pro bono."

"That money is for anyone who comes forward with information that leads to an arrest and conviction."

"You bet, I understand. We see eye to eye on that."

"However, I am prepared to offer you twice that amount."

His proposal didn't make much sense, but I was sure the blame for that didn't rest with him. I wasn't getting it.

"There is another proviso to my offer to you, Mr. Ruzak, and that is if or when you discover his identity, you do not tell the police. You tell me."

He hadn't moved a muscle. I was moving a lot of them, mostly the internal ones.

"Mr. Marks," I said. "Wouldn't I have to tell the police to fulfill the arrest and conviction part of the deal?"

"Our deal does not end with arrest and conviction."

"You know," I said, "when my mother died, I was pretty torn up. She died of cancer, and my first reaction was, Somebody by God's going to pay for this. Like, Look how long cancer has been around, and we still can't lick it? I wanted to mow down the entire medical community and maybe the government, too, for dropping the ball on the whole cure issue. I mean, we can put a man on the moon and build bombs that can blow up half the planet, but we can't cure cancer? Anger is pretty natural—I think it has its roots in our genetic history, something to do with the fight-or-flight response, and sometimes it's pretty useful, but it's always been my opinion that revenge is anger misdirected in an unproductive way."

"Then you are declining my offer?"

"All I ever wanted to be was a detective," I told him. "If I take you up on this and somehow I succeed, that makes me an accessory to a serious crime, and I don't think the licensing bureau would look too kindly on my application. Of course, it would also stink morally, ethically, and, besides, could land us both in prison for a very long time."

"You don't believe I could protect you?"

"What could you do to protect me?"

"Safe passage to a country of your choosing. A new identity. Or, in the alternative, my word that if things do not turn out as planned, I will take full responsibility and never reveal how I came upon the information."

"How's that protect me from my own conscience, though? What about the moral and ethical part—you know, the evil?"

"Don't presume to lecture me about the nature of evil, Mr. Ruzak. I am intimately acquainted with it."

"Mr. Marks, I wouldn't presume to lecture a dog, much less somebody like you. I understand you're something of a world traveler and I can only imagine some of the things you've seen in your travels. There's an awful lot of bad out there, which is fortunate for my business but unfortunate for the species at large. I was only saying, all things being equal, I'd prefer to be on the side of light—you know, a bulwark against the darkness."

"One-point-five million."

"Gee, that shows a lot of confidence in me. It's flattering as hell, but I really don't—"

"Two million, then. My final offer."

"I'm glad of that, because this sort of reminds me of a parlor game me and my buddies used to play in high school. Well, I called it a parlor game, but it wasn't played in a parlor. We usually played in my parents' basement. You know, where you'd challenge each other to see how far you'd go for money, along the lines of the old saying that everybody has a price. Like, Would you eat a bowl of dog crap for five thousand dollars? I just grabbed that number out of the air, but usually the dog crap fetched a price closer to a million. I believe I said I'd do it for five hundred thousand. I was in high school, you understand, and when you're that age, you're pretty materialistic. I remember I was ready to give up a foot for two million. Some people never grow out of that stage; otherwise, we wouldn't have so much insurance fraud, like those people who stage car wrecks."

He blinked several times, like he had something in his eye, or it may have been just the sting of the dry-cleaning fumes.

"Mr. Ruzak, you are either the most facetious man I have ever met or the most facile."

"You mean you can't figure out if that was a yes or a no. One of my problems is that I've got a restless mind, probably a result of spending most of my adult life sitting by myself in the dead of night listening to too much late-night talk radio. They didn't allow televisions, so that was really the only media outlet available to me."

"I don't think your problem is too much talk radio," he said.

"Well, that's a relief. That would be something you can't undo."

"So your answer is no?"

"See, that's the thing."

"What is? What is *the thing*, Mr. Ruzak?" he fairly barked at me.

"Am I hesitating because I don't know who did this to your wife? In other words, is my moral character predicated on my lack of knowledge or on a truly righteous underpinning? See, it's like that game I told you about. It's all abstract because I don't possess the key to the treasure chest. That said, I made a certain promise to your daughter that I'm going to do everything I can to help find Lydia's killer, but I'd be happy to settle for the half million and forgo the jackpot."

His hands came apart and spread wide in a vaguely European gesture of surrender.

As I walked him to the door, I said, "You know, I probably don't have to tell you there're maybe a couple dozen guys in Knoxville alone who would jump at your offer."

"And what would you do, Mr. Ruzak, if some unfortunate accident befell this person who murdered my wife?"

He meant would I rat on him.

"I don't know. I'd feel pretty lousy for everyone involved, but we all have choices to make, Mr. Marks. I don't have to live with anybody but Theodore Ruzak. That's tough enough."

CHAPTER TWENTY

Felicia called in sick the next morning. I got off the phone with her, called the downtown fire station, and asked for Bob. When he came on the line, I hung up. Then I felt crummy for checking up on her like that. Most people are honest and all have problems. You can't get cynical. Cynical people aren't a happy lot and they have tight mouths.

I was so deep in thought, I didn't hear the door open and didn't notice I wasn't alone until my guest was halfway to my desk. We needed a bell over the door or one of those buzzers like they have in retail outlets. When I saw who it was, I went around the desk and held the chair for her.

"Hello, Mrs. Shriver," I said.

"Will you call me Eunice?"

"If you'll call me Teddy."

Her hair looked shorter and less blue, perhaps her summer do. She was wearing a pair of those orthopedic shoes with the thick heels over the knee-highs and was carrying the same big handbag. I sat behind my desk, smiled at her, and waited.

"I shall call you Teddy, but only on the condition that you call me Eunice."

I told her we had a rock-solid deal. She asked, "How old are you, Teddy, if I may ask?"

"Thirty-three."

"My youngest son is thirty-four."

"Well, we're practically contemporaries."

"Samuel is thirty-four, Rachel is thirty-seven, Kirk is thirty-nine, and Vernon, my eldest, is forty-two."

"Wow, you must have waited to have them."

"On the contrary, I couldn't wait to have them. I love children, though more abstractly when I was younger."

"That's probably pretty common."

"Do you have any brothers or sisters?"

"My parents decided one little Ruzak was plenty for them."

"Are you close to your parents, Mr. Ruzak?"

"They're both dead."

"Oh, goodness. Ruzak, what sort of name is that?"

"Polish. I'm Polish on my father's side, German, English, and maybe a little Dutch on my mother's."

"I am third-generation Knoxvillian," she said proudly. "My great-grandfather Martin Sparks founded the first full-service laundry facility very close to here, in the Old City."

"That's something," I said. "You know, I've got a dry cleaner's right below me."

"He was also a bootlegger, but the family doesn't talk about that."

"Every family has a few skeletons."

"Tell me, Teddy, do you speak to your parents often?"

"Not anymore. They're dead," I told her again. "But I do visit them and talk to Mom, or at her grave anyway, though sometimes I throw a word or two at Dad. I wasn't that close to him. He worked hard and I didn't see him much growing up."

"It's never too late to mend fences," she said.

"You think so? I guess I always assumed death put the kibosh on patching things up, but hearing that really helps, Eunice. It lifts my spirits. You know, my mom died recently, leaving me a little money, and now any success I have will owe a lot to the fact that she had to die for me to have it, and that's been weighing on me."

"Oh, I know all about that weight. The weight of death."

Here it came. She paused, tears welling in her eyes. She seemed to be waiting for something. I dug in my desk drawer for my mechanical pencil and found my yellow legal pad under a pile of papers.

"I suppose you know why I've come," she said.

"I think I have an idea."

"Must I say it, then?"

"I guess you need to, Eunice."

She nodded, running her palms along the straps of her purse. Both feet were planted firmly on the floor and her back was straight. She had pretty good posture for an old lady.

"I am a murderess, Teddy."

"I thought so," I said. "Did you kill Lydia Marks, Eunice?"

She burst into tears, but her back remained straight, her feet planted firmly on the floor.

"Eunice," I said. "How could you?"

"I wish I could say it was an accident, a horrible accident, but that isn't the truth. I killed her. I killed that poor woman and left her body in the mountains as carrion. Oh, Teddy, what shall become of me?"

"How did you kill her, Eunice?"

"Stabbed her with my sewing needle."

"Really? The coroner said she was bludgeoned to death."

"Oh, yes, yes." She gave a little wave with her mottled hand. "That, too."

"So you killed her and then dragged her up the mountain to leave her for the carrion?"

"Yes. Yes, oh God forgive me, yes."

"Well, I gotta say that's impressive. A woman of your age dragging a corpse nine hundred feet up a mountain."

"I didn't say I acted alone."

"No?"

"You remember I mentioned my son, my eldest, Vernon."

"Sure. Vernon."

"He helped."

"Why?"

"Because the last thing he wants to see is his eighty-six-year-old mother sitting in the electric chair!"

"That would be the last thing anyone would want to see," I said. "What did the police say?"

"They told me to go away. They told me they didn't want to see me anymore."

"You see them a lot, Eunice?"

She didn't answer. She was dabbing her eyes with her white handkerchief.

"If the police won't arrest you," I said, "what is it you want me to do?"

"Help me," she whispered.

"This Vernon, he lives in Knoxville?"

She nodded. "He came over last Sunday and found that woman's body in my basement, covered with an old blanket. He said, 'Mother, why do you have a body in your basement?' So I told him I had killed her and he said, 'Mother, we must not leave this body here. It's begun to stink.' So we put it in the trunk and drove into the park and Vernon carried it over his back up the mountain. I stayed in the car, as a lookout." She looked away. It was hard to tell, but she might have been pretty in her day. Not a stunner, but pretty, and despite her wackiness, there was a dignity about Eunice Shriver, like with a lot of very old people, the pride of having outlasted so much pain and heartache.

"That's a horrible story, Eunice," I said.

"I know it's a horrible story. And what makes it more horrible is nobody but Vernon believes me."

"I believe you, Eunice."

She swung her eyes back in my direction. The hope in them was palpable and heartbreaking.

"Do you? Do you, Teddy? That's all I want. You asked what I wanted, and that is precisely it. I want somebody to believe me."

"Why wouldn't I believe you?" I asked. "You haven't lied to me yet."

"Then you'll help me, Teddy?"

"Sure I'll help you, Eunice."

CHAPTER TWENTY-ONE

THROUGH SOME ACE DETECTIVE WORK, I DISCOVERED THE NAME OF Susan's brother: Matthew. Matthew Marks. It sounded like some kind of joke, a biblical play on words. I discovered his name by calling Susan and asking her for her brother's name and phone number. He agreed to meet me on the Strip for lunch, a Mexican fast-food place called Moe's. You ordered your food and then watched them create your meal in assembly-line fashion. Moe's was famous for its huge burritos, which were long, stuffed to overflowing, and extremely bland. I didn't like Moe's—the food reminded me of myself.

He was a big guy, like his dad, with roughly the same haircut, except the kid wore his combed forward instead of back, like a bloated version of an Abercrombie & Fitch model. His face was wide and pockmarked with acne scars and he had a sort of hooded look around the eyes that reminded me of a lizard, though I'm not sure lizards have eyelids.

"I'm only talking to you as a favor to my sister," he told me after we carried our trays to a table by the window. The sky was overcast and therefore the world was shadowless, which always made me feel a little disoriented.

"Sure," I said. "I appreciate it."

I asked him about school. It didn't seem right diving right into the gruesome circumstances of his stepmother's death as we stuffed our mouths with beans, rice, and chunks of greasy ground beef. I also wanted a chance to size him up before getting down to brass tacks. He had a chip on his shoulder, I could tell, like a lot of rich kids who never want for anything. But I figured that chip might come from Lydia being murdered and left as a meal for wild animals.

He said he was just a freshman and hadn't decided on a major.

"What about business?" I asked. "You're the only son, right? Maybe your dad would—"

"My dad," he sneered. "Don't start with my dad. I hardly know the guy. He was never home when I was growing up. I was raised by my mother."

"Yeah, your mother . . ."

"Not Lydia. Lydia was never my mother."

"You and Lydia didn't get along?"

He shrugged. The shrug is a gesture we lose as we get older, reaching its peak usage when we're around twenty-five. I'm not sure why that is. Maybe there's less to shrug about, which is ironic, because you think you know it all at twenty. I have a theory the shrug was born with the advent of organized sports, because, no matter the sport, players always do it after a penalty's called against them. The shoulders hunch, the arms come up, hands palm upward, like, What? *What?*

"I didn't know her very good," Matt said. "You wanna know how all that happened? One day, Dad comes walking in the door and says, 'Kids, here's your new mother.'"

"What happened to the old one?"

"She died, man. When I was fifteen."

"That's tough. My mother died just recently."

"Yeah, but you're what, forty? I was fifteen."

"Actually, I'm thirty-three, but a lot of people think I'm older."

"You don't have the baby face like a lot of fat guys."

I set down my burrito and sipped my diet Coke.

"How'd your mom die?"

"Car accident."

"Bummer."

"What did you say? Did you just say 'bummer'? What is this, Ruzak? You trying to relate to me or something?"

"No. I honestly thought it was a bummer. Bummer was my first reaction to the news your mother died in a car accident. I thought, Bummer. So that's what I said. What happened?"

"A truck ran her off the road. She hit a tree. She died."

"I'm tempted to say 'That sucks.'"

"What are you talking about? It does suck."

"How did your father and Lydia meet?"

"Why don't you ask him?"

"Was it in Ireland?"

"No, it was in fucking Afghanistan. Of course it was in Ireland. She was Irish, for Christ sakes!"

"So he travels a lot on business."

"I think I said that. You're not much of a detective, are you? Yeah, he travels all the damn time. England, Ireland, the Netherlands, Russia, Turkey, South Africa, you name it, wherever the almighty dollar leads him."

"How's he make it? The almighty dollar?"

"Didn't Suze tell you? He's a smuggler."

I laughed.

"I'm serious, man. He smuggles. You name it—drugs, weapons, even people. Human contraband, Ruzak. You know, slavery. My dad is a slaver." He laughed. I wondered if he was putting me on and decided he probably was. I was wasting my time, but I told myself I wasn't always going to be dealing with a cooperative witness.

"Why do you think Lydia's dead?"

"Because somebody killed her. What do you think?"

"I mean, do you think somebody she knew—"

"Man, Lydia didn't know anybody over here. She refused to make any friends. She spent about two thousand dollars a month in phone charges to the Emerald Isle to talk to her family over there. I always wondered why the hell she married my father and moved here if she loved it over there so damned much."

"Susan said she loved your father. Adored him."

He shrugged again. "I guess it's easy to love somebody who isn't there."

I said, "Why didn't she travel with him? What kept her in Knoxville while he jet-setted all over the world?"

"What did my sister say?"

"I haven't asked her."

"If anybody would know, it'd be Suze. Really, I never hung around Lydia much."

"Well, that's understandable. I mean, it's hard to accept a stepparent in the best of circumstances."

"Oh, it wasn't that. That woman gave me the creeps."

"Why did she give you the creeps?"

"She never talked much. Just stared at you all the time with this stupid smile on her face." He gave his best imitation of the smile, but I didn't think he was very good at imitating attractive Irish women. "You know? And when she did say something, it was always . . . oh, shit, I don't know, always so calm and almost whispery, almost like she was putting on an act or was doped up or something."

"When your dad was around—were they real affectionate with each other?"

"Man, why would I notice something like that? You think I'm some kind of pervert?"

He finished his burrito in one awe-inspiring face-stuffing orgy of sauce and dripping hamburger juice.

"So . . . ," I said, knowing this was a signal my interview was almost over,

"Lydia wasn't having an affair or anything of that nature . . . as far as you know?"

"Ruzak, that woman was about as sexy as a telephone pole. No personality at all, you know? Kind of pretty, though she didn't have any shape. I never got what my father saw in her, but to each his own. I never saw the mailman hanging around, if that's what you're asking. But like I said, I wasn't around much. Maybe she was screwing the whole neighborhood."

He stood up. I kept sitting.

"One more question," I said. "Who do you think killed Lydia?"

He leaned over the table, bringing his face so close that I could smell the spices on his breath.

"The British secret service. She was IRA, Ruzak. Dad's a sympathizer and the marriage was a sham to get her out of the country. But the Brits found out where she was hiding and took her out."

"You think so?"

He just laughed and shrugged. "I gotta go back home and pack."

"Thanks for talking to me, Matt."

"Thanks for the burrito, dick. That's what they call detectives, right? Dicks?"

He sauntered out the door while I sat there watching his shoulders give a little roll—the same way his father walked. I didn't feel as if I'd learned anything, and now I had a very bad case of indigestion. What bothered me about where Lydia Marks was found was that it would take a pretty big guy to haul a dead body up a mountain through dense woods. Matt was big enough. But then she might have been marched up that mountain at gunpoint, and practically anybody can point a gun, even me. I just can't shoot one with any accuracy.

CHAPTER TWENTY-TWO

THE WHOLE MARKS FAMILY LEFT THE NEXT DAY TO BURY THE REMAINS of Lydia in the family plot in Dublin. Now, the first Mrs. Marks was buried right in Knoxville, which raised the vexing question (at least to me) of where Kenneth would spend eternity—beside his first wife in Tennessee or his second across the pond?

"Say you were married," I told Felicia.

"Why say I was married?"

"I'm posing a hypothetical."

"I love it when you talk like a college professor. How're you able to do that, Ruzak, seeing you never went to college?"

"I read the dictionary."

"Really? How often?"

"Every day. Usually while I'm in the john."

"Did anybody ever point out to you the dictionary's not the kind of book you *read*."

"It goes back to my Dictionary Ruzak days. When I was a kid living in St. Louis, this group of neighborhood boys invited me to join their club, which met over one of the kids' garage, and I went to one meeting where they swapped these mysterious hand signals and spoke in code words that meant nothing to me but a great deal to them, and they laughed the whole time at inside jokes that nobody bothered to explain to me. They told me I had to pick a handle only the club members would know—it was sort of a benign gang—and I told them to call me 'Dictionary,' because I was going through my *Encyclopedia Brown* phase. That cracked them up. For the rest of the meeting, they asked me to spell words like *xylophone* and *oxymoron*. It was the first and last meeting I went to."

"You know what, Ruzak? You're the kind of guy who gets asked what time it is and then tells the person how to build a watch."

"Can I finish my hypothetical?"

"Sure, I can't do anything anyway until my nails finish drying." The polish was bloodred, to match her dress. She might have been sick the past few days, but she had managed to drag herself out of her sickbed to visit the salon. Her hair wasn't quite so blond anymore and I detected a hint of auburn. Women in general are restless when it comes to their appearance. There may be a Darwinian component to this, but I never really took the time to think it through.

"So you get married and something happens to your husband."

"He dies."

"Or runs off on you or—no, let's just say he dies and at the time he dies, you love him."

"Okay. Husband. Dead. Love him. Go on."

"A few years go by and although you can't imagine ever falling in love again, you do, and you get married a second time."

"For what?"

"For a second time."

"No, I mean for what reason am I marrying a second time? Love? Money? Blackmail?"

"Love. Deep, deep love."

"Okay. I could see that happening."

"So then he dies."

"He dies, too?"

"Or you die—that really doesn't matter."

"We both die?"

"Not at the same time. Well, it could be at the same time for the purpose of the hypothetical."

"All this is going somewhere, right?"

"Right. So here's the hypothetical . . ."

"You love saying that word, don't you? You should see your lips when you say it, especially the 'po' part." She pursed her lips at me. "Hypothetical."

"Can I finish?" I was just acting sore. Inside, I was glad she was in a better mood. "So, which one would you want to be buried next to—your first love or your second?"

"This is important?"

"It's been vexing me."

"I don't know, Ruzak. It sounds like one of those questions the Pharisees threw at Jesus. Probably the first husband."

"Why?"

"He had dibs."

"So it's a question of first come, first served? What if you loved the second guy more?"

"You didn't say that in your hypo. You just said I loved him, too, which implies I loved him equally. Of course I'd want to be next to the one I loved the most."

"What do you think the odds are, one wife getting killed in a freak auto accident and the other murdered by some psychopath?"

"Pretty damn long."

"That's what I thought."

"You think that's what the cops are thinking?"

"But Marks was out of the country."

"People like him don't get their hands dirty, Ruzak. He hired somebody to do it, the same way Parker Hudson hired you to find the goose killer."

I thought about telling her of his offer to give up the killer for two million dollars, then decided not to. One hypothetical was enough for one morning.

"What's his motive, though?" I asked. "Susan said he was nuts about her and her him, and besides, even though I'm sure there was life insurance, the guy's already richer than God."

"Really? What did you say his phone number was?"

"Money really does overcome everything," I said. "This guy might have killed two wives and you're jumping in line to be number three."

"Maybe he didn't kill her to get money, but to save it."

"She was threatening divorce? But Susan said—"

"Okay, then. Money and jealously aren't the only motives for murder, Ruzak."

I thought about it. "Blackmail?"

"Maybe the kid was right in a way. Maybe the marriage was a sham, like she made him marry her and get her to America because she had something on him, and the only way to remove the threat was by removing her."

"But what could that be?"

She stuck her tongue out at me. "You're the investigative consultant."

I went to my desk and called Deputy Paul's number. The dispatcher told me he was on patrol and couldn't be reached. I left my number. Then I called Parker Hudson to remind him of our appointment with the hypnotherapist.

"You're really going to make me go through with this," he said.

"Well, I guess the only thing that could make you is your conscience," I replied.

"You know what I like about you, Teddy? On the outside, you're just a cuddly big ol' bear, but on the inside, you're a scrappy little bulldog."

"Makes for a lethal combination," I said.

I told Felicia I was going out for some legwork and she said it looked like I needed it. I walked out the door with downcast eyes, like a puppy scolded by its mistress. Verity comes at you that way: Parker Hudson described it; then Felicia encapsulated it.

I walked one block west to the Lawson McGee Library and took the stairs two flights up to the periodicals room. Matthew Marks was a freshman in college and his mother died when he was fifteen, which meant the accident happened no more than four years ago. I told the lady at the desk what I needed and she disappeared down an aisle that was marked EMPLOYEES ONLY. She came back after a minute with four microfiche cartridges, sat me down in one of the little booths against the wall, and showed me how to use the reading machine. Not to propagate stereotypes, but she was in her mid-fifties, wore no makeup, and smelled of old paper.

She left me alone. My eyes were pretty worn-out by the end of it, but I finally found the story two hours later in the September 17, 2000, issue of the *Sentinel*. I located the obituary that ran three days later and asked the periodicals lady to make copies. I paid her for the copies, fifteen cents per page, and made the remark that at fifteen cents per page, you wondered where all your tax money was going. She curtly asked if there was anything else she could help me with, and from that, I gathered she was trying to show that my tax money paid her salary. I told her yes, there was something else, and asked for a receipt.

I walked back to the office. Deputy Gary Paul was standing at Felicia's desk and they were both laughing, but they abruptly stopped laughing when I walked in. It was clear to me by that point that Felicia had a thing for guys in uniform—firemen and cops and probably military types—but drew the line at security guards.

"Teddy!" Deputy Paul said, and we shook hands. He followed me into my office and sank into one of the visitor's chairs. Like Barbara Eden sans the bare midriff, Felicia appeared at his elbow with a fresh cup of coffee. She left without offering me any.

"So what's up with the goose killer?"

"Parker Hudson is getting hypnotized tomorrow. We're gonna regress him to the day of the killing. It's a long shot, but—" I shrugged. I had noticed I was shrugging more after my meeting with Matthew Marks. I am very impressionable where tics and mannerisms are concerned.

"Kenneth Marks's first wife was run off I-Forty five years ago, going about eighty miles per hour," I told Deputy Paul. "Her car flew over an embankment and smashed head-on into a tree, killing her instantly. The other driver kept going and, as far as I can tell, was never caught."

"Okay."

"Witnesses described the other vehicle as a white delivery truck with no identifying markings."

"And?"

"And four years later, Kenneth Marks's second wife disappears into thin air."

"Yeah," he drawled. There were dark circles under his eyes. I wondered if he had been rotated to the night shift. Then I remembered the dispatcher telling me earlier that he was on patrol. "I'm sure the task force is looking very carefully into the affairs of Ken Marks."

"But if he's our perp, there's one thing I don't understand." I told him about Marks's offer to pay me two million dollars to find Lydia's killer and forgo telling the police. "Isn't that a crime?"

"Not the offer. It becomes one if you actually did it."

"But my point is, if Marks is our man, why would he make an offer like that?"

He shook his head. "No idea. If I had an idea, Teddy, I probably wouldn't be a patrol officer."

"Should I tell the task force?"

"That's up to you."

"Would you?"

"You bet I would."

"Where are they with all this? Do you know?"

"They believe Lydia was alive when she was taken into the Smokys. Killed where the hikers found her."

"How do they know that?"

"Logic, Ruzak. It would be next to impossible to hike twelve miles from the nearest road, up a mountain, and through dense woods carrying deadweight like that, unless you're Paul Bunyan."

That had been my theory, and I felt a flush of pride that I was thinking along the same lines as professional law enforcement.

"How was she killed?"

"Multiple blows to the head by a heavy object. Still working on what that object might be, but that and the kill zone pretty much rule out a professional job."

"How come?"

"Professionals don't operate that way—too much risk. A professional kills on first contact, quickly, and disengages ASAP from the kill zone. If Lydia Marks was a contract job, she would have been taken in her house in the dead of night, one shot through the head as she slept, or something like that. The way she was taken and killed—way too many opportunities for witnesses and mistakes."

"So they think it was somebody she knew."

"Or it still could be some psychopath, a stranger killing her."

"Which is another point for Kenneth. He was in Brussels when she died."

"Some people just have crappy luck, Ruzak."

"His luck isn't so crappy. At least he's still alive."

CHAPTER TWENTY-THREE

PARKER HUDSON MET FELICIA AND ME AT THE THERAPIST'S OFFICE ON Wiesgarber, between Kingston Pike and Papermill Drive, within walking distance of the Krispy Kreme place on the Pike. As we drove past, I pointed out to Felicia the HOT sign was lighted.

"We can't stop, Ruzak," she said. "We're late as it is."

"I like to sit at the counter and watch the conveyor belts in the oven room with all the rows and rows of fresh doughnuts going down the line."

"Maybe you should work a second job at the Krispy Kreme."

"But then I'd weigh about four hundred pounds."

Parker Hudson was not late. He was standing by his Mercedes in the parking lot, wearing a windbreaker over a polo shirt and tan slacks.

"What's that?" He pointed at the recorder I was carrying.

"A tape recorder. This has evidentiary potential."

" 'Evidentiary potential'?"

"Teddy reads the dictionary in the john," Felicia said.

"Old habit," I told him. "What do you read?"

"*Field & Stream* and *Golf Digest*. Sometimes *The Wall Street Journal.*"

"Seems too heavy."

"Depends on the bathroom I'm in."

Felicia laughed, for some reason. She was wearing a navy blue pantsuit with a white blouse and only moderately high heels. Parker Hudson eyed her backside appreciatively as we went through the door. It doesn't matter how old you get; the procreative drive stays with us to the grave. They say Picasso fathered children well into his old age. But being an artist, of course, he never really grew up, and responsibility wasn't high on his list. Not that he couldn't afford a stableful of progeny. I saw somewhere that his signature on a check for a million dollars would be worth more than the check for a million dollars.

It's probably hard to make a living solely practicing hypnotherapy, so Dr. Stephanie Fredericks also practiced your regular type of therapy. The diplomas on her walls said she had a Ph.D. and an M.D. from Michigan State. The receptionist gave Parker Hudson a stack of forms to fill out, including a medical release form stating he couldn't hold Dr. Fredericks liable if she regressed him to memories that drove him crazy. Under the question of who was financially responsible for the account, he wrote, "THE DIC." I guessed this was his way of registering his protest to the whole hypnosis angle.

"You should do it, too, Ruzak," Felicia said.

"How come?"

"Maybe you'll get the tag right, even a description of the driver."

"Yeah."

" 'Yeah,' you might if you did, or 'yeah,' you're gonna do it, too?"

"Our appointment is only for Parker. Maybe I'll come back."

"I don't see how I can be morally obligated and yet you have a choice," Parker Hudson said. He was clearly nervous.

"Memories usually get repressed only if they're involving some kind of catastrophic event," I said. "Like the dead baby geese."

"You've done some research into repressed memories?" he asked.

"I've looked into it."

"Oh, he talked to the shrink about five minutes," Felicia said. "Don't listen to him."

I gave her a look. Whose side was she on? My palms were sweating at the thought of being hypnotized. I'd never been what you might call a control freak, but the thought of entering some kind of altered state that included the danger of quacking like a duck unnerved me.

"Personally, I think it's all a bunch of hogwash," Parker Hudson said. "I don't think it works, and haven't there been studies that show a lot of repressed memories aren't really memories at all, but manufactured to fit someone's expectations?"

"No stone unturned," I said.

"Unless the stone is resting on your big fat behind," Felicia said.

"You know," I said, "I'm getting pretty tired of the remarks about my butt. I know I have a big butt. You don't have to point it out every five minutes." The receptionist was staring at me, but I didn't care. "I don't point out your pug nose to you."

"I beg your pardon? You don't point out my *what?*"

"Are you two married?" Parker Hudson asked.

"Good God, no," Felicia said, and that broke the tension—at least for her—and she laughed.

The inner door opened and Dr. Fredericks leaned out and smiled, waving us in. She was an attractive lady in her middle fifties, maybe, dressed in a conservative business suit with sensible heels. She led us to her office and I made the introductions. She explained how the procedure worked and what we could expect. Parker might remember more details, she said, or he might remember nothing new at all. She admitted she might not even be successful at putting Parker under; a lot depended on the patient. Parker sat directly across from her and rubbed the pads of his thumbs against his palms.

"Where do we do this?" he asked.

"Right here," Dr. Fredericks said. She had a very melodious voice, which probably came in handy in her line of work. "Just remember, hypnosis isn't magic and it has nothing to do with mind control. Our goal is to lower your normal inhibitions and let what bubbles to the surface bubble."

Her voice and manner seemed to calm Parker somewhat, and he followed her obediently to the sofa.

"How would you be most comfortable, Mr. Hudson? Lying down or sitting up?"

"I might fall asleep if I lie down." He sank into the sofa and closed his eyes, folding his hands over his stomach. Dr. Fredericks gave a little smile in our direction.

"What do you want us to do?" I asked.

"You can stay, if that's all right with Mr. Hudson. Just be quiet, please. If you have any questions you want answered, write them down on that pad right there and pass it to me. Once we begin, the only voice I want him to hear is mine."

She turned the lights down and pulled a chair close to the sofa. Soft music was playing through hidden speakers and I wondered when she had turned the sound on. I expected her to pull out a watch or hold up her pen, like on TV or in the movies, but she just started talking. Her spiel was very repetitive; she told Parker to relax and imagine himself completely at ease, in a place of his choosing, maybe on a little boat on a lake or, if he didn't like water, lying on the shore in the shade. She went on like this for maybe five or ten minutes, and Parker Hudson didn't move a muscle. For a second, I was afraid he had fallen asleep.

Then Dr. Fredericks said, "Parker."

"Yes."

"I'm going to take you back now. I want you to imagine there's a doorway in front of you. The door is closed right now. Can you see the door?"

"Yes."

"Parker, on the other side of that door is yesterday. I want you to go to the door and open it. It isn't locked."

"Open the door?"

"Yes. Go ahead and open it."

"Okay. I'm opening the door."

I realized at that point that I had forgotten to turn the tape recorder on. I hit the record button and it sounded very loud in the space. Dr. Fredericks gave me a look over her shoulder and Felicia jabbed me in the side with her elbow.

"What do you see?" Dr. Fredericks asked Parker Hudson.

"Yesterday . . ."

"Now you aren't just watching, Parker. You are really there, in yesterday. What are you doing?"

"Making a BLT."

"You're in the kitchen?"

"Yes. The lettuce is going bad. She should have picked up some fresh lettuce."

"Your wife?"

"Yes. Damn it. She always forgets something, though she walks out the door with her purse stuffed with coupons and a list half a mile long. Always something. Then she'll pick up a jar of pickles, when we have five jars sitting in the pantry. Or mustard. We'll be out of milk but have sixteen bags of M&M's lying around."

"How is your sandwich?"

"Good, except the lettuce is wilted."

Felicia looked at her watch. At this rate, we'd be on the lake with Parker by early fall.

"Parker, I want you to look up. Right in front of you is another door. Do you see it?"

"I'm not finished with my sandwich."

"Do you want to finish your sandwich?"

"No." He sighed. "I guess not."

"Do you see the door?"

"Yes."

"On the other side of that door is last week. I want you to go to it, open it, and tell me what you're doing."

"I'm playing golf. I'm losing. The rest of my foursome are drunk."

"You're not?"

"I never drink and play. But I'm losing, so maybe I should."

This went on for another twenty minutes or so. She led him through door after door, until they came to the last door. I glanced down at my tape. It was sixty minutes per side and we were already halfway through side A. I wondered if I'd wake him if I had to stop and flip the cassette.

"Do you see the door, Parker?" Dr. Fredericks asked.

"Yes, I see it," Parker said. His voice had been calm, but now there was an edge to it, the same edge as when he'd talked about the wilted lettuce.

"This is the last door, Parker. On the other side is the morning of April sixteenth. Does that date mean anything to you, Parker?"

"Yes. It's the day the goslings died."

"How do you feel? Would you like to go through this door?"

"Yes." He sighed. "Yes. I guess I do."

"Then open the door, Parker, and walk through."

She waited while he walked through.

"Where are you, Parker?" she asked.

"The trail."

"You are walking on the trail?"

"Yes."

"What do you see?"

"The park. The lake. The old fence. The field. Railroad tracks. The sun is just coming up. Mist on the water. I love that."

"You love what?"

"The way the mist rises over the water in the early morning. The lake is perfectly calm and mist rises on the surface. Beautiful . . ."

"Do you see anyone else?"

"No, I'm alone. It's very early. Dawn. Not a soul. I love this. My favorite time of day. Just me. Just me."

He was smiling, content as a Buddha.

"Can you take a picture for me?"

"I don't have my camera. . . ."

"No, but try freezing what you see."

" 'Freezing'?"

"Stop it. Like you're watching a movie at home. Pause the movie."

"Okay."

"Did you pause it?"

"Yes. The mist isn't moving now."

"Good. Start it again. Remember you can pause the movie whenever you want to. Whenever I tell you to stop the movie, will you stop it for me?"

"Yes."

"Good. Are you still walking?"

"Yes."

"Which direction are you walking, Parker?"

"East."

"And you're walking the trail on the north side of the road, so the road is on your right. And across the road?"

"The park and the lake. Oh, there're some geese."

I straightened in the chair and checked my tape. Felicia was leaning forward, her elbow on her knee, her chin on her fist.

"You see geese?"

"They nest here every year. I've seen these geese. I know these geese. Oh, it's a family! The babies have hatched!"

"Where are the geese, Parker?"

"Right on the trail, about a hundred yards in front of me. Two adults and—let's see—one, two, three, four, five goslings—no, six! I didn't see that little piker behind one of the adults."

"And still no people? Nobody on the trail?"

"No one. Oh, I wish I had my camera."

"What are the geese doing?"

"They're coming out of the field, crossing the trail. Going toward the road."

"They're leading the babies back to the water?"

"They must be . . . yes, there they go. The big male, he's leading, and there they go! How orderly they are, in a perfect line. He's leading the babies and she's in the rear."

"Now, Parker, I want you to stop the picture but keep the sound going. Can you do that?"

"Yes."

"What do you hear?"

"He's honking, just braying to beat the band. It's like he's saying, 'Watch out! Get out of our way! Geese crossing!'"

"What else do you hear?"

"Other birds. The sound of cars, very far off. My own breath. Oh, now there's something else."

He fell silent with a small sigh.

"What else do you hear, Parker?"

"A car. It's loud . . . getting louder . . ."

"Where? In front of you? Behind you?"

"Behind me . . . coming up behind me . . ."

"Okay, now I want you to start the movie again. You're walking on the trail toward the geese; the geese are crossing the road toward the lake. And now you hear a car coming up behind you. . . ."

"It's going very fast. . . ."

"You see the car?"

"No, but its engine . . . very loud . . . revving up."

"Do you turn toward the sound, Parker?"

"No . . . I'm watching the geese . . . middle of the road . . . stretched all the way across, like a cordon of geese. . . . Oh God! Oh no!"

"Freeze the picture!" Dr. Fredericks raised her voice slightly. Parker was breathing heavily now and I could see a sheen of sweat on his forehead.

"What do you see?"

"Black. Big. Middle of the road. Son of a bitch!"

"Describe it, Parker. What kind of car is it?"

"Oh God, it's going to hit the babies!"

"Focus on the car, Parker. Is it still frozen?"

"Yes."

"Then the babies are okay. Don't worry about the babies right now. Look at the car."

"It isn't a car. It's one of those gas-guzzling SUVs. It's big. Big tires. Black."

"Can you tell what make it is?"

He mumbled something and she repeated the question.

"I don't know cars very well . . . makes of cars. . . . It's big and black and it's very loud. . . . Don't they hear it? *Do* they hear it? Oh, they don't know. They don't know what's going to happen. Do they know?"

"Parker, you are in control. You can stop the movie anytime you want. Do you understand?"

"Yes. I am in control."

"Do you see the license tag? Can you see what state the car is from?"

"Oh, yes. Tennessee. It's a Tennessee tag."

"Are you certain?"

"It's very clear. . . ."

This was it. I knew what she was going to ask next. I held my breath.

"Can you see the numbers on the tag, Parker? Can you read them?"

"Oh dear God . . . dear God, those babies . . ."

"Parker, you're looking at the SUV now. The movie's stopped and you can study the car as long as you like. Are you looking at the tag?"

"Yes. Yes, I'm looking at it."

"What are the numbers?"

"It's letters . . . letters and numbers."

"Ah, come on," Felicia whispered. "I can't take it anymore."

"H . . ."

"The first letter is an *H?*"

"Yes. I see it very clearly now. HRT. Those are the letters."

I felt my heart thumping hard in my chest. I was going to solve this case. I was going to hand a terrific lead to the task force and maybe collect half a million dollars. Most importantly, I was going to keep my promise to Susan Marks.

"And the numbers? What are the numbers, Parker?"

"Seven . . . one . . . nine . . ."

"Seven one nine?"

"Yes. Yes. I see it very clearly. HRT seven one nine."

Dr. Fredericks looked over at us and gave a thumbs-up. Then she turned back to Parker.

"Now, the movie is still frozen. Can you see inside the car, Parker?"

"No. Black windows. Tinted. I can't see inside."

"Can you look around for me? Do you see anyone else? Is there another car on the road? Anyone walking on the trail?"

"There's no one . . . no one but me. . . . I'm going to start the movie."

"Parker, you don't need to—"

"No, I'm going to start it again. . . ."

"Parker, don't start the movie."

"It's moving. Oh my God! My God!" His body stiffened and his right hand gripped the couch's armrest. "He's going to hit them! Get out of the way! Clear out of there! He isn't going to stop! Oh, for the love of Jesus! Feathers! Feathers! Blood and feathers! And oh God, he didn't even slow down, the son of a bitch! He didn't even swerve! Oh God, they're flat as pancakes, but look—one's still alive! Half its body is smushed and it's crying! 'Mommy! Daddy!' And they're screaming. Mommy and Daddy are screaming and flapping their wings and their necks are stretched as far as they'll go, and oh, the rage! The rage and loss! Bloody road! Oh, the babies! The little itty-bitty baby birdies!"

I heard a sound beside me. Felicia had a hand over her mouth. Tears glistened in her eyes, but the sound I thought I heard coming from behind her hand was the sound of suppressed laughter.

CHAPTER TWENTY-FOUR

DR. FREDERICKS SLOWLY WOKE PARKER HUDSON FROM HIS MOVIE memories, and when she asked him how he felt, he said, "Very thirsty," and she left the room to fetch a glass of water. He was a little breathy and sweating pretty hard.

"Well, Teddy. I suppose you were right and I was wrong."

"You remember what just happened?"

"I remember everything now. HRT seven one nine. That was the tag."

"You're sure?"

He nodded. Dr. Fredericks came back with an Evian. She turned up the lights, went to her desk, and sat down.

"There's something we all need to remember," she said. "Hypnotic regression has not been shown to be one hundred percent reliable. I'm sure you've heard about cases that have gone to trial, particularly cases of past sexual abuse, where the victim has not actually accessed repressed memories, but invented them out of whole cloth, usually through the hypnotic suggestion of the therapist. I was very careful not to ask Parker any leading questions, but the danger remains that he is taking postevent information and inserting it into the event."

"Wow," I said. "What's that mean?"

"For example, after your encounter with a black SUV near your apartment, you told Parker you thought the letters on the tag were *HRT*. Obviously, since these letters were on the same type of car Parker saw, you assumed it was the same vehicle. You planted both the letters and the connection to the event in Parker's mind. Just now, as he was reliving it, it is possible he overlaid that information on the event matrix."

"So he could have seen different letters?"

"The likelihood, if that is what happened, is that he saw no letters at all, and his mind supplied the missing detail with information provided by you."

"But what about the numbers? I didn't see any numbers."

"He might have seen the numbers that day and they very well may have been seven one nine, just as he might have actually seen the letters *HRT*. But they could also represent any number of things—a date that's significant in his life, or numbers from a tag he casually glanced at in traffic two weeks ago. Or they may be completely random. The point is, you have to take any information gathered in hypnosis with a grain of salt."

"No," Parker said firmly. "I know what I saw. I saw them as clearly as I'm seeing you right now."

"This is terrific," I said, trying to stay upbeat. Dr. Fredericks had practically killed the party. "It gives us something to work from. It might be nothing, but it could be everything. Thanks a lot, Doc."

We said good-bye to Parker in the parking lot.

"That woman is wrong," he said. "I remember now. HRT seven one nine. That was the tag number."

"Well, there's still no proof it's connected to Lydia Marks, but if you're right, we've got your goose killer."

"And it's been worth every penny. I want that SOB prosecuted to the full extent of the law."

I told him I'd have an answer for him in a few days. I could get the name from Deputy Paul, but I wanted to talk to the driver first, to see if I could wrest a confession out of him. Parker Hudson agreed that probably was the best course of action. He didn't look good. He looked like somebody who had been laid up in bed with the flu for a couple of weeks.

I drove back to Kingston Pike and made a left toward downtown.

"You know," I said to Felicia, "we could grab half a dozen to celebrate."

"Are you always thinking about food?"

She started to laugh.

"What?" I asked.

" 'The babies! The itty-bitty baby birdies!' "

"Felicia."

"Well, I'm sorry. It's funny."

"It's grotesque."

"Your first case solved. How's it feel, Ruzak?"

"It isn't solved yet."

CHAPTER TWENTY-FIVE

I CALLED GARY PAUL'S NUMBER THE MINUTE I GOT BACK TO THE OFfice. The dispatcher told me he was off duty and refused to give me his home number, even after I told her it was a matter of the utmost urgency. I managed to wrest a promise from her that she would page him and give him my message. Felicia was staring at me as I hung up.

"Are you done? I have to make a phone call."

"I had a couple more calls, but go ahead."

She disappeared around the half wall and I leaned back in my big leather chair and congratulated my big bulldog self. My PI exam was coming up and I was sure I'd ace it with flying colors. Though there were lots of questions about Tennessee law. I had gotten hold of a sample exam from the administrating company, but I had no idea what some of the questions meant. I was brimming over with confidence, though. The newspaper article might have been Felicia's idea, but hypnosis had been mine, and it looked like hypnosis was going to be the hammer that cracked this case wide open.

"I'm changing my name to Teddy 'the Hammer' Ruzak!" I called out to Felicia.

"I'm on the phone!" she shouted back. Then she came into the room and said, "I have to go."

"Is something wrong?"

"No, nothing's wrong. I just have to go."

"Felicia, wait. . . ."

"What is it, Ruzak? I'm in a hurry."

"It's just that—well, you've been missing a lot of work lately. . . ."

"You're not going to try to fire me again, are you?"

"I didn't try the first time. I was going to ask if everything was all right. I mean, you've been pretty upset and distracted over the past few weeks. . . ."

"It's nothing. Okay? Everything's fine. I don't need anything from you, Ruzak, just a paycheck, which, by the way, has been sitting on your desk for two days and you still haven't signed it."

"Really? It has?" I dug through the papers on my desktop. "Jeez, I'm sorry. Here."

She snatched the check from my hand.

"We had a deal, Ruzak. Personal lives stay personal. Maybe if things ever got busier around here, my being gone would matter more."

"I get a feeling they will now."

"You and your feelings."

"Look, it isn't personal. I'm not trying to pry; I just want you to know if there's anything I can do."

"There's nothing anyone can do. I'll see you tomorrow."

I thought there was maybe a fifty-fifty chance of that, but I didn't say anything but good-bye. As usual, I felt smaller when Felicia wasn't around. The office got bigger and I got smaller. I went back to my desk and started to dial the number for the task force, then set down the receiver before I hit the last number. I really didn't have anything yet, and Detective Watson already thought I was a borderline kook. It would be better for the case and better for me if I waited till I had a name.

I set the tape recorder on my desk and played back the tape of Parker Hudson's hypnotic session. He whispered in some parts, but the part about the tag was very clear, because he was nearly shouting by that point. I turned it off before it reached the part about the itty-bitty babies. That was too tough to listen to. Parker Hudson had lived a long time, by statistical standards, and it was reassuring to know that not all of us go completely numb by the time our hair's white. The lives of six goslings still matter to some of us.

The phone rang. It was Deputy Paul.

"You've got the killer," he said.

"Hey," I said. "Sorry to bother you on your day off."

"I'm always happy to hear from my favorite detective."

"Thanks, but technically I'm not a detective yet. Still working on getting my license." I told him about Parker Hudson's revelation during the hypnosis session. I repeated the tag number twice for him.

"Looks like we might have him," he said. "Did you call the task force with this yet?"

"The therapist said it might be a blind alley—you know, a false memory or something like that. I couldn't exactly follow everything she said."

"Right. And we still don't have a connection between ol' HRT and Lydia Marks. Better to wait. I'll call my contact with the DMV and call you right back, okay?"

"That'd be great."

"Okay. And Ted? Good work on this, bud."

I hung up, my cheeks positively glowing. Maybe this detective thing wasn't such a dopey idea after all.

"HRT seven one nine, here I come," I said aloud in the empty room.

CHAPTER TWENTY-SIX

I SPENT THE REST OF THE AFTERNOON STUDYING FOR MY PI EXAM AND waiting for Gary Paul to call back with the identity of HRT 719. At 4:45, he still hadn't called, so I watered the plants, shut down Felicia's computer, and locked up for the night.

I went downstairs to the street. The lights were still on inside the dry cleaner's and I could hear the machines humming through the walls. When I first leased the place, I thought renting above a dry cleaner's was a savvy move on my part. Your businessmen and other professional types—who else would be dropping off dry cleaning downtown? Every time they came by, they'd see my sign on the side of the building, and who else except a professional could afford to hire a PI?

I didn't feel like driving home to my empty apartment. As I was waiting for Deputy Paul's second call, I was thinking I should celebrate solving my first case and figured I should eat at the Old City Diner, where I'd celebrated getting my first case. Technically, there was nothing to celebrate yet, but I was still hungry, the diner was close and, after studying for hours for an exam I had no prayer of passing, I didn't have the mental capacity to think of another place.

I ordered a steak, medium-well, a baked potato, and a house salad with Thousand Island dressing. Freddy, the owner of the diner, must have seen me sitting there, because he came around the counter in his white smock and thick-soled running shoes and walked to my table.

"Ruzak," he said. Freddy had bright red hair and a face full of freckles. "Haven't seen you in a while."

"I've been pretty busy with my new business."

"Oh, yeah. Detective, right?"

"Investigative consultant—at least until I get my detective license."

"Well, that's terrific. Good for you. How's Felicia doin'? She went to work for you, didn't she?"

"Yeah." I averted my eyes. He might be sore for me taking her away from him. He didn't act sore, though.

"She's a good little girl. Did you know she was about a semester shy of getting her nursing degree at UT before she dropped out?"

"I didn't know that. I just thought—well, I thought she was just a waitress."

"There's always more to folks than meets the eye, Ruzak. But you're an investigative consultant now; you know all that."

"We don't discuss personal issues in the office," I said. "Why did she drop out?"

"Never said."

"Can I ask you something, Freddy? Did Felicia miss a lot of work?"

"Called in sick a lot, but she always found somebody to cover for her."

"Was she? Is she? Sick, I mean."

"I don't see her anymore, Ruzak."

"Is something wrong with her, like some kind of disease she doesn't like to talk about?"

"There's a lot Felicia don't like to talk about."

"Like what?"

His small blue eyes narrowed at me.

"Maybe she wouldn't like me telling you things."

"I'm not being nosey."

"Sounds like you are."

"It's just—well, I don't know what I'm going to do. She's in only three days a week at most, and then those days she does come in, she usually ends up taking off early."

"Here's a radical suggestion: Fire her."

"She keeps daring me to."

"I know you got a kind of thing for her—"

"Freddy, I don't have a thing for Felicia. . . ."

"You always did. Got those puppy dog eyes for her. Everybody around here saw it. Hey, Lacey!"

She yelled back, "What?"

"Didn't Ruzak here have the hots for Felicia?"

"You bet he did. Everybody knew it."

"Everybody except Ruzak!" he yelled back, and that cracked everybody up, including strangers who were staring at me as they chewed.

He turned back to me triumphantly.

"It's business, Ruzak. You can't let your feelings get in the way. Fire her and tell her if she needs a job, I could always use a good waitress."

He walked back behind the counter, wiping his hands on his filthy apron before slapping a couple more burgers on the grill. My face was burning and I was sorry I had brought the whole thing up. He was hiding something, probably to protect her. Or maybe he was trying to get me to fire her so he could hire her back.

I ate my meal faster than I should have; you always eat faster when you eat alone. It sat like a brick on my gut as I drove home. I didn't really want to go home, but I had no idea where else to go. That's pretty lousy, home being the place you go when you have no place better to go.

You should feel good, Ruzak, I told myself. Why don't you feel good? You would think living alone would free me from all the normal burdens of responsibility that people complain or worry about, but all living alone does is increase your psychological weight, as if your soul were living on Jupiter. It tends to make you more important to yourself and exaggerate your problems to the point that they're insurmountable afflictions. This was probably what was behind my wanting a dog. It wasn't just about companionship; it was about responsibility, too. There wasn't a damn living thing that depended on me, except the plants in my office.

There was a message from Felicia the next morning, saying she wouldn't be in. She didn't offer an explanation. I dialed her number, thinking that when she picked up, I'd ask for one, but she didn't pick up and I hung up without leaving a message. Hiring her may have been premature, as rash as opening a detective agency without having a license or quitting a job without having the slightest idea how to run a business or actually solve crimes.

Parker Hudson called around ten and asked, "So, who is HRT seven one nine?"

"When I know, Mr. Hudson, you'll know."

"Why so testy, Teddy?"

He was a chipper old codger. Life will grind you down to a bitter nub if you let it, but Parker Hudson had come to terms with his. Of course, having lots of cash lying around in his old age didn't hurt. As that old saying goes and even some scientific studies have shown, money doesn't bring happiness, but the poor people I knew didn't seem any happier than your average millionaire. I'd take the cash and risk the misery.

"Do you have a dog?" I asked him.

"Yes, we do. A golden retriever named Prince."

"I've been thinking about getting a dog, but it's forbidden in my lease. When my mother died, I thought about subletting and moving back into the old homestead, but too many ghosts, you know? I don't mean my parents. I'm not too concerned with the paranormal, though that's been all the rage—I guess because we're living in such uncertain times. Like those TV psychics communing with dead relatives and bringing back messages from beyond. Everybody's looking for some reassurance, and to me, it all boils down to justice. You know, that life's so screwy and messed up, there better be a payoff when it's over."

"Oh," Parker Hudson said. "I firmly believe in justice, Teddy. Otherwise, I never would have hired you."

"What would you like to see happen to this goose killer, assuming HRT seven one nine is our man?"

"I've been thinking some sort of restitution, perhaps a generous donation to the World Wildlife Fund."

The door swung open and Gary Paul stepped into the room. He was dressed in his civvies—a pair of crisp, brand-new blue jeans and a plain white T-shirt that accentuated his pectorals.

"That's terrific," I told Parker Hudson. "I'll call you back. . . ." I gave Gary the eye as he slipped into a visitor's chair.

"Soon?" Parker asked. Gary nodded. "Soon," I told Parker Hudson. I hung up and Gary broke into a big smile that reminded me I hadn't been to the dentist in over two years. If there were no evident disparity between the rich and poor, we wouldn't have half the wars in our history. Maybe no wars at all, but that was old thinking. Theodore Ruzak, the Bolshevik detective.

"We got him," I said.

"We got him," he replied.

CHAPTER TWENTY-SEVEN

GARY PAUL OFFERED TO GO WITH ME TO CONFRONT OUR SUSPECT.

"Right now?" I asked.

"Why not?"

"Well," I said. "It's a question of thoroughness. I haven't been too thorough in my thinking up to this point—I mean in my life, not just with this case—and I don't want to go off half-cocked without a firm POA."

"POA?"

"Plan of attack."

"Detective lingo?"

"I wouldn't know. I just made it up."

"I thought we'd just drive over there and ask him," he said.

"That was my first instinct. It's direct and exploits the element of surprise, but that assumes this is unconnected to the murder of Lydia Marks."

He slowly shook his head. "I'm not following you, Ted. That's not unusual, but I'm thinking this is one of those times when I really should."

"If this guy's our goose killer, he might also be her killer, and I don't want to be mucking that up. I don't want to blow it for the task force. What if this guy takes off or destroys key evidence on the basis of our visit?"

"I don't think you go anywhere near that. Like I said, there may be no connection at all, but on the off chance there is, you don't bring it up. You stay on-message with the geese."

"Still, it might spook him."

"So it spooks him. I don't see how you can avoid it, if you want to solve this case. Besides, I'll be there."

In the end, that settled it for me. How badly could I screw up with a member of law enforcement at my elbow? Plus, in the back of my mind, I really did want to kill both birds with one stone. *All right, all right, you got me, Ruzak! I did them both, the goslings and the Irish dame! Take me away!*

The address was on the northwestern edge of the county, north of Farragut and just south of Oak Ridge, where they work on nuclear bombs or the technology for nuclear bombs—I was never quite sure which and didn't really want to be. Oak Ridge was sometimes called "the Secret City" because during World War II nobody knew about it, or if they did, they didn't know what they were doing up in those hills outside Knoxville. Gary offered to drive, but I told him it was my party, so he rode shotgun in my Sentra. Our perp, if he was our perp, lived in a newer subdivision, in one of those stucco two-story cookie cutter–type houses on a postage stamp–size lot with saplings still staked to the ground and straw still visible on the freshly seeded lawn. The house had a two-car garage, but the Ford SUV was parked in the driveway, and I saw the tag as we pulled in. At the sight of that tag, my heart rate picked up.

"Look familiar?" Gary asked.

"That's it," I said. "That's the car that tailed me."

I parked behind the SUV, blocking any possibility of a getaway, and Gary stopped me as I started up the walk to the front door.

"Hang on a sec," he said. I followed him to the front of the Ford. He squatted down and ran his hand under the front bumper, frowned, then lay flat on his back and reached underneath again, feeling along the edge of the front license plate holder. He pulled something free and held it up: a goose feather—or rather, a downy minifeather, a baby's feather.

"Bingo," he said.

He handed me the evidence and I slipped it into the money compartment of my wallet, between a five-dollar bill and an old gas receipt, which I was saving for tax purposes. On our way to the door, he said, "Maybe you should let me take the lead here, Teddy. The Marks thing does complicate matters, and I've got experience with dealing with these lowlifes."

"Sure," I said. "That's terrific. I really appreciate it, Gary."

He answered the bell right away, which made me wonder if he'd been standing on the other side of the door waiting for us. He was younger than I expected, maybe in his mid-twenties, and better-looking, though I really didn't know why I expected someone in his mid-forties, balding, and with a middle-age paunch. I guess my expectation was based on my assumption that whoever smashed those goslings was either a shallow housewife bent on getting to the mall before it opened or a midlevel executive late for his flight to New York to close that big deal. He was wearing Bermuda shorts and a Ron Jon Surf Shop T-shirt. His hair was wet, like he'd just stepped out of the shower.

"How ya doin'?" Gary said. "My name's Gary Paul and I'm with the Knox County sheriff's office. This is Teddy Ruzak. He's a private investigator."

"Investigative consultant," I said.

"We're looking for Michael Carroll," Gary said.

"I'm Mike Carroll," the guy said.

"You got a second, Mike?"

"Am I in some kind of trouble?"

"Well," Gary said, "let's just say we're not here to solicit donations for the Benevolence Fund."

"Ah, jeez. Okay. I'm kinda running late for something, but come on in." He asked us to slip off our shoes by the door because the hardwood was brand-new and cost sixty-five dollars a square foot installed, and we followed him into the living room. The house was sparsely furnished and had a Rooms-to-Go feel. There were some built-in bookcases against one wall with no books in them and a glass-topped coffee table with a lava lamp set in the middle, maybe as a conversation piece.

"Nice lamp," I told Mike Carroll as we sat down, in case it was. Gary and I took the sofa and Mike sat on a rocking chair without any padding on the rails, which made me wonder how much he really cared about the hardwood.

"Isn't it cool? Those got hip again a couple years back, but now they're waning again. I can't help it, though, I just love 'em."

"You probably have some memory attached to it," I said. "That's what usually happens."

He shook his head. "I've got nothing attached to it at all." He looked at Gary and wet his lips. He had the classical features of a Greek statue and very blue eyes. If his hair had been lighter, it might have been possible to mistake him for Brad Pitt or an Aryan god, like Thor, only I wasn't sure Thor was Aryan, being a Norse god. Weren't the Norsemen from Norway? And I was pretty sure Brad Pitt had brown eyes, and your classic Aryans were blond, all of which would mean Mike Carroll did not resemble Brad Pitt, or an Aryan, or a Norse god.

"Hey, Mike," Gary said. "We're gonna cut right to the chase here. For a couple weeks now, Teddy and I have been trying to hunt down the owner of that Ford in your driveway."

"Well," Mike Carroll answered. "I guess your hunt is over. That's my Expedition."

"Mike, we have reason to believe that vehicle was used in the commission of a crime." Then Gary added quickly, "Not a very serious crime as far as the statutes go, but in terms of human decency."

Mike slowly shook his head. "I have no idea what you're talking about, Gary."

Gary looked at me and nodded. I pulled out my wallet and drew out the gosling feather. Mike barely glanced at it.

"It's a feather," he said.

"We found it stuck under your front bumper, Mike."

"My client saw a black Ford SUV with your plates hit a gaggle of baby geese by Anchor Park in Farragut a couple months back," I said. "There was a big write-up in the paper about it. Maybe you saw it."

"Look," Gary said after the silence dragged out and no confession was forthcoming. "I'm gonna be straight with you, Mike. Nobody's here to arrest you or slap a fine on you and nobody will in the future, but we would like you to fess up so Teddy's client can have some peace of mind. He's kind of an old liberal tree-hugger type and he's been giving Ted here fits about this hit-and-run. All we want is some honesty and a willingness to stand up like a man and admit you made a mistake. We know you didn't intentionally kill those babies. It was an accident, right? You were in a hurry, didn't see them until it was too late, and who really gives a shit about six little baby geese?"

Mike nodded. He wet his lips again and ran his fingers through his damp hair, and in that moment I hated Michael Carroll like I'd never hated another being in my entire life. I wanted to grab that lava lamp and smack him over the head with it. He didn't have to open his mouth for me to know he was our perp. Gary had it nailed: Mike probably hadn't meant to hit the geese, but he didn't care that he had. And here it was midmorning and he had only now taken his shower, and he was dressed casually, so I guessed he didn't even have a job and lived off the largesse of his parents or maybe a girlfriend (he wasn't wearing a wedding ring). He drove a nice car and lived in a brand-new house, and this is what tore me up, the callousness born of privilege, like the rules didn't apply to him. And I knew, too, even without any proof, that he wasn't alone in that SUV that morning; that Lydia Marks was with him, maybe struggling, maybe not. Maybe I was sitting across from her boyfriend, who got mad when she wouldn't dump her sugar daddy for him, so he took a hammer to her head high on a ridge in the Smoky Mountains.

"Okay," he said softly. Then he laughed. "Okay, I guess I'm busted. Yeah, I saw the article," he said to me. "And I guess you know I went downtown that day looking for you. I'm not sure why I did that. I was kind of pissed, to tell you the truth. Like, Who does this fat ass think he is? Like, What's the big friggin' deal?" He spread his hands wide, then slapped his palms on his shorts and rubbed his thighs vigorously, like he had a circulation problem.

"You hit the geese," Gary said.

"Yeah, didn't I just say that?"

"Not in so many words."

"Well, what the hell do you want? A written confession? You said you weren't here to arrest me or ticket me. What the hell are you here for, then?"

"A check," I said.

"A . . . a what?"

"Made out to the World Wildlife Fund. I'm thinking maybe three hundred bucks."

"Three hundred bucks!"

"That's fifty per gosling."

Gary smiled. "Seems fair."

"You're kidding, right? Jesus, man, it was just a bunch of friggin' geese!"

"Gaggle," I said. "And tell that to the parents of those friggin' geese."

"No, why don't *you* tell them, Ruzak? You're out of your damned mind if you think—"

"Hey, Mike," Gary said. "Mike, Mike. There's no need to get all excited about it. I think Teddy's suggestion is terrific. Three hundred bucks isn't going to bring those geese back, but it tips the scales in the right direction."

"I don't give a crap about any scales," Mike said. "What the hell are you talking about with these scales? Look, I'm sorry I hit them, okay? And yeah, I should have stopped I guess and I definitely should have come forward when that story hit the papers, but it's not like it was a group of schoolkids crossing the road."

"You know, Mike," Gary said. "You say you're sorry, but your whole attitude lacks any kind of remorse whatsoever. It's troubling to me and I'm sure it's troubling to Teddy here and I have no doubt Parker would find it even more deeply troubling. So troubling he might decide to press charges against you."

"Charges? Like what charges? This is bullshit, man. Okay, okay, what do you want me to do? I sure as hell don't want to *trouble* anybody."

"Teddy's already told you. A three-hundred-dollar donation to the World Wildlife Fund."

"Tax-deductible donation," I added.

"You bet," Gary said. He was smiling broadly now at Mike, who was smiling back with perfectly even, perfectly white teeth, which were made even more perfect by the juxtaposition to Gary's.

"And an apology to my client," I said.

"Apology for what?"

"For hitting the geese."

"But that was an accident."

"I think he could have lived with that," I said. "Anybody can have an accident. It was the driving away part that got to him."

"I was in hurry. Didn't I say that? Jeez, am I the only one who sees the ridiculousness of this?"

"The only one in this room," Gary said.

"What if I don't have three hundred bucks to give to the World Wildlife Fund?"

Nobody said anything. Nobody needed to. Everything about Gary Paul's aura said, I don't give a flying flip about your excuses, pal.

Mike sighed, his smile faded, and he stood up. "Okay, I'll get my checkbook. It just blows my mind when I pick up the paper and see all the shit happening in this town and here's a guy who cares more about *geese*—I mean, these are fucking geese we're talking about, and here you two are banging on my door, kind of strong-arming me because I made a *mistake*. Why should I have to pay up if it was an accident?"

"Everything has a price, Mike," Gary said softly. "Even accidents. Especially accidents."

I had an idea as he started out of the room.

"You don't need to get your checkbook right now," I said. They both looked at me, a little surprised. "I'm sure my client would prefer the check and the apology straight from the horse's mouth."

He gave a little frustrated roll of his shoulders, as if the situation was slipping outside all bounds of normalcy. He looked at Gary as if to say, Save me from this freak.

"You have my personal guarantee I'll do everything in my power to keep him from popping you in the nose," I said.

"Oh, sure, that makes me feel a lot better," he said. "But that's not going to happen, Ruzak. First you come in here demanding three hundred bucks and now you tack on a personal apology. You guys keep upping the ante. What's next? Taking out a billboard?"

"I'm thinking more along the lines of a written apology." Gary said. "With a copy to the newspaper."

"I'm sure he'd prefer it in person," I insisted. "A letter to the newspaper isn't bad, either; I'll run that by him when I set up the meeting."

"I'm not meeting with him, Ruzak," Mike Carroll said, but he was looking at Gary. He had Gary pegged as the rational one, the good cop.

I said, "Is tomorrow, say four o'clock, good for you?"

"Didn't you hear me? I'm not meeting with him."

"Parker would prefer it."

"I don't give a shit what Parker would prefer. He gets a check and note, 'Dear Mr. Hudson, I'm sorry about killing those fucking baby geese.' If that's not good enough for you, then slap the cuffs on me now. I'm not a bad person; I'm a decent human being. And I really resent the hell out of you two showing up at my door like this, acting like I'm some kind of serial killer or something."

"I don't have my cuffs, Mike," Gary said. "But I'm afraid you're going to have to go along with this, or I'll come back with them."

"You're kidding me."

"No."

"Yes, you are."

"No, I'm not. You'll do this, or I promise you I will come back, and when I do, I'll be wearing my badge, Mike."

CHAPTER TWENTY-EIGHT

PELLISSIPPI PARKWAY WAS ONLY A MILE OR SO FROM MIKE CARROLL'S house, so I swung onto it, heading south toward the interstate.

"You in a hurry?" Gary asked, and I eased up on the gas, thinking maybe my speeding seven miles over the limit disturbed his cop sense.

"I guess not," I said.

"Let's have a beer, then."

"A beer?"

"To celebrate."

He directed me off the Kingston Pike exit, then west toward Farragut, then into a little strip center anchored by a Harley-Davidson shop called Biker's Rags. At the corner of the L-shaped center was a sports bar with a big screen on every wall, a pool table, a couple of dartboards, and a tired-looking waitress with dyed-blond hair and a tattoo on her shoulder that said BITCH. Gary ordered a Michelob lite and I had a Budweiser. We shared a bowl of stale pretzels, and the waitress ignored us after she asked if we wanted some wings or a slice of pizza and we said no.

Gary raised his frosty mug and said, "To Teddy Ruzak, ace detective, first case in the can."

I clinked mugs with him and said, "Investigative consultant."

"What's the difference?"

"One's legal and one isn't."

He shook his head. I wasn't sure what the shake of the head meant, but I didn't ask. Something was bugging me, and I couldn't put my finger on it. I should have been flush with pride, overjoyed at my perfect batting average, relishing my victory, but there was a shadow over me, or it was more like a thorn in my head, pricking my brain.

He laughed suddenly. "Did you see the look on his face when he realized we knew?"

"Hand in the cookie jar."

"This gives me incredible satisfaction, Ruzak. I just can't tell you. So many times I've sat there in court and watched these jerks walk and there was absolutely nothing I could do about it. It's a pretty frustrating job, being a cop. The pay is shit, the hours are lousy, and, five times out of ten, after all the shit work you get the pleasure of watching the perp walk. It can make you cynical, you know? Pretty down on everything. It's nice to see something come out the right way once in a while."

"Oh," I said. "You bet. But what's your gut tell you, Gary? Is he the one?"

"A black Ford Expedition with the same license plate that both you and Parker saw, a goose feather caught in the undercarriage, and a confession. Yeah, I'm pretty sure he's the one."

"I don't mean the geese."

"Ruzak, the only thing I know about Mike Carroll is that he's a very careless driver, a very casual dresser, and a very poor decorator. But you can bet the task force is gonna know his name."

"He never said," I said.

"He never said what?"

"Why he was there that morning. Why he was driving so fast. Why he didn't stop."

"Maybe he didn't because we didn't ask."

"I was nervous," I admitted. "Thanks for coming along, Gary."

"Oh, no, you did great, Teddy. My only criticism would be this setup with Parker. He was about to write you a check and you stopped him. What makes you think he's going to show?"

"I don't know."

"You're a trusting son of a bitch, you know that?" Then he laughed and finished his beer.

I dropped him off in front of the Ely Building. It was almost one o'clock and I hadn't eaten lunch. I doubted Gary Paul had, either, but for some reason I wanted to be alone. I thanked him again, we said good-bye at the steps, and I watched him walk down to Gay Street and disappear around the corner toward Jackson. Gary had that *High Noon* saunter affected by a lot of cops, like a toned-down version of the Mick Jagger strut, which I always thought had something to do with the gun slapping on the upper thigh—not Mick's, the cops'.

I ate a quick lunch at the Crescent Moon, a little bistro-type place half a block from the Ely Building. It was run by a couple of ladies I suspected were lesbians. My clues were the lack of makeup, the butch haircuts, and the brusque way in which I was always treated. They had terrific iced tea, though, and I drank about a gallon of it. Beer in the afternoon makes me extremely sleepy, and this didn't help the fog or shadow over my soul or the thorn in my brain, or whatever it was. When I got back to the office, the mail had come, and I carried it upstairs. I had closed the windows and shut down the fans before I left, and the place reeked of fumes. I rolled my big chair over by the window and went through the mail as I leaned on the sill, breathing through my mouth like a fish. I was trying to take my mind off the brain sliver, but reading the mail wasn't a mindless-enough exercise, so I tossed the pile on the desk and decided to water the plants. The ferns especially were looking a little droopy. I was thinking about a scientific study I had read about years ago, about how plants might actually feel pain, when the sliver in my brain slowly drew out and light burst through the fog. I picked up the phone and called Parker Hudson.

"Know anybody named Michael Carroll?"

"Never heard of him," he said.

"Well, he's heard of you."

"Who is he?"

"I'm not sure, but I'm going to find out."

"Don't tell me we finally have a suspect."

"I think maybe we do."

"I told you it wasn't a false memory," he said. "I can't tell you how grateful I am that you made me go through with that hypnosis, Teddy. I'm an old man and new things don't come easy for me, but you pushed and I'm glad you did, not only because now justice will be served but because I feel as if I've got a whole new lease on life. I am a bona fide believer, Ruzak."

"Everybody should be about something."

"In fact, I have an appointment with Dr. Fredericks next Tuesday."

"Next Tuesday? Why?"

"To do it again! That session was one of the most exciting, vivid experiences of my life. And let me tell you, Teddy, you don't get to be my age without having your fair share of exciting, vivid experiences. It felt more real than the real event, if that makes any sense."

"Sure."

"I highly recommend it. Tuesday, I'm going to ask to be taken back to 1974."

"Good year?"

"One of my best."

"Gee, that's terrific, Mr. Hudson."

"I figure I have fifteen, maybe twenty years left—plenty of time to relive practically my entire life, particularly since I'm skipping over the bad parts. By doing that, I'm actually living an extra forty years, by my calculations. Virtually speaking."

"Wow."

He must have noticed the lack of enthusiasm in my voice. "Are you feeling all right? You don't sound like yourself."

"No. No, thanks for asking, Mr. Hudson, but I'm myself. I'm myself."

He laughed. "That's good to hear. I would sorely regret your passing."

This struck me as creepily prophetic. "So would I," I said. "I'll call you back in a couple of days."

I hung up to the sound of him chuckling. My hand was shaking. Must be the tea, I thought.

I made three more calls: one to the Department of Motor Vehicles, one to the Knox County Tax Assessor's Office, and one to Harvey Listrom, detective with the Knox County sheriff's office.

Then I went home and took a nap. I was pretty tired.

CHAPTER TWENTY-NINE

FELICIA CALLED IN AROUND TEN THE NEXT MORNING.

"You're not coming in," I said.

"How badly do you need me to come in?"

"Are you sick? You don't sound sick."

"I'll be there tomorrow; I promise."

"Is there anything I can do?"

She started to cry. This took me aback. I had never heard her cry before.

"Sometimes," I said. "Sometimes it helps to talk."

"What are you, Ruzak, my mother?"

"Just trying to be your friend. I've pretty much demonstrated I suck at being your boss."

"What does that mean?"

"Even Freddy would have fired you by now."

"Do what you want, Ruzak. I didn't come to you, remember. You asked me to take the job."

I'm not sure how that applied to her questionable work ethic, but I let it go. It was probably Bob. In fact, I was sure it was Bob. In general, firemen are obnoxious, chauvinistic jerks, or at least that was my impression, based on nothing really, since I had never actually known any firemen. Stereotypes and prejudices flourish in the experiential vacuum of my own head. Although Felicia was probably not the easiest person to get along with—like a lot of strong-willed people—she was a seawall against which weaker wills crashed and collapsed. So maybe it was Bob and maybe it was Felicia; one thing I was certain of, it was the relationship that was the problem.

"I know who HRT is," I told her, to change the subject.

"Who is it?"

"Not at all the kind of person I expected."

"So the case is over?"

"Um. Don't know."

"How could you not know, Ruzak?"

"Like most things, there's an ambivalence there, a delicate shading. . . ."

"You're not going to tell me, are you?"

"Not yet. I'm pretty sure, but not completely. I've got this working theory though, finally, which is more than I had twenty-four hours ago."

"Maybe you're just drawing the whole thing out to bill Parker more hours."

"That would go back to my moral character," I told her. "Don't impugn my moral character."

" 'Impugn'?"

"What's wrong with *impugn*?"

"You have the vocabulary of a college professor without the intellectual and educational underpinning."

"Well," I said, "you just used the word *underpinning*."

"I'm hanging up now, Ruzak."

I hung up after apologizing for impugning her underpinning. It occurred to me I was too softhearted for this line of work. If somebody challenged me to name the chief characteristics of a successful private eye, being softhearted would not be at the top of my list. It certainly wasn't anywhere on the state of Tennessee's list. Additional cottony softness was located due north of my plushy heart, in the region between my ears. What if I was wrong? Sure, things as they had been presented to me didn't add up, but was that because I wasn't good with math? You read about genius and epiphanic moments, like the apple falling on Newton's head. I had the sort of head that would cry, Damn that apple! and then I'd go home to complain to my wife about my terrible luck, which only goes to show that geniuses are just like the rest of us, only more so.

In addition to being a very casual dresser and a very poor decorator, Michael Carroll was also very punctual: He arrived at four o'clock on the dot. He was wearing the same Bermuda shorts but had changed into a Tennessee Volunteers orange-and-white T-shirt. I offered to make a fresh pot of coffee, but he seemed in a hurry or upset by something, or maybe both. He sat on the edge of the visitor's chair, working his fingers through his damp-looking hair, and I decided I'd had it wrong the day before; his hair hadn't been wet, just gelled to saturation.

"I've got the check," he said. "Where's Parker Hudson?"

"Oh," I said. "Today's his foursome."

He blinked those gorgeous baby blues at me and said, "He's not coming?"

I shook my head no. If I had expected him to act relieved, I would have been disappointed. He slid the check onto the desk blotter and sat back. He had folded it in half and maybe was waiting for me to unfold it. I didn't unfold it. I didn't touch it. I watched his eyes as I asked, "Who is Lydia Marks?"

"Lydia who?"

He didn't blink; he didn't hesitate; he didn't fidget. He gave no indication he was lying, but I had no training in the area of lie detection—as I had none in any area of private detection. But it wasn't like I'd let that stop me.

"How do you know Gary Paul?"

"What's that mean? What are you talking about, Ruzak? Look, you've got what you wanted. There's your check, and now I'm gonna—"

He started to stand up. I told him to sit down. He stood anyway. I said, "That wasn't your car in the driveway. And that wasn't your driveway, either, because that wasn't your house." He sat down. He scrunched low in the chair because he was a young guy and that's what young guys do: They scrunch in their chairs or tip them back on their rear legs.

"The black Ford Expedition in your driveway yesterday, the one with the baby bird feather stuck to it, is registered to Deputy Gary Paul of the Knox County sheriff's department. And the house with your lava lamp on the coffee table is deeded to a man named Kenneth Marks, who happens to be the surviving spouse of Lydia Marks, who was murdered around the time that car hit those baby geese."

Mike Carroll wet his lips. Since that was a classic gesture of guilt or, at the very least, unease, I figured I had taken the right tack.

"So?" he asked.

"So, it's one thing to borrow a buddy's car and smush some waterfowl. It's something altogether different to smush a human being's head and dump her body in the mountains as fodder for the indigenous wildlife."

"Look, Ruzak. Look . . ." He gave a little laugh that tended toward a giggle. "I don't know anything about any murder, okay?"

"Then maybe you can help me out, Mike. Maybe you can help me and that way I can help you."

He wet his lips again and I fought an almost overwhelming urge to scream at him, And stop wetting your lips like that, pretty boy!

"Okay," he said.

"Yes or no, were you the one who hit the geese?"

He shook his head no.

"Gary hit them?" I asked.

"I have no idea who hit them," he said. "Look, okay, here it is. Gary and me go back aways. He . . . I . . . see, when I was a kid, I got into some trouble and Gary, he helped me out, okay? I don't know, he thought maybe there was some hope for me or something, but he arrested me when I was a junior in high school, marijuana possession, and I did my time, but not as much as I would have if Gary hadn't gone to bat for me. So I owed him one. A couple days ago, he calls me out of the blue and tells me he wants me to admit to this goose-killing bullshit because this pal of his—you—had this client who was all over his ass over this stupid thing and he wanted me to 'confess' to it to get him off your back. But you had to buy into it, too."

"Why?"

"He didn't say why, okay? He just offered me a thousand bucks, and what the hell was I going to say to a thousand bucks?"

"I guess you said yes."

"You're damn right I said yes."

"Awful lot of money just to boost my spirits," I said. "Especially on a deputy's salary."

"Man, I didn't ask him where the money came from."

"But why the meeting at a rental owned by Kenneth Marks?"

"How the hell should I know? He didn't say and I didn't ask. He said be at this place at this time and that's what I did."

"Where do you really live?"

" 'It's none of your damn business where I live, Ruzak."

"Probably nowhere near Farragut. He was being thorough—wanted to make sure everything fit—car, location. And it almost worked."

"Why didn't it?"

"You knew Parker's last name," I told him. "It kind of imbedded this splinter into my thinking, so I checked with DMV, which is something I guess I should have done a long time ago, but I'm too trusting and maybe a little lazy, to be perfectly honest."

He stared at me. "Whatever. So what happens now?"

"You don't tell Gary about this conversation."

"What's gonna stop me?"

I sighed. "How about a thousand bucks?"

"You got a thousand bucks?" he asked. I made a mental note to tell Felicia she was wrong: After I had poured thousands into this cramped, crappy space and thousands more in clothing for my rotundity, people still couldn't believe I was solvent.

I wrote him a check for a thousand dollars and told him the bank was right down the street and that he could go straight there after leaving and cash it. Then I took his check and slipped it into my top desk drawer.

"Hey," he said. "Give that back."

"Why?"

"I shouldn't have to pay it now. I didn't hit those goddamned geese."

"Well," I said. "I doubt there's going to be any other justice in that regard, so I'm keeping it."

"Then you should give me thirteen hundred to offset my loss."

"You already got a thousand from Gary," I pointed out, though I was sure the money had actually come from Kenneth Marks.

"I made him give me three hundred more to cover that check."

"Gee, you're a tough negotiator," I said. "You've got potential, and that heartens me. It reaffirms one of my core beliefs: that the book's never closed on us until the casket lid is."

"What the hell does that mean?"

"It means I'm not giving you three hundred dollars, since Gary already has."

"I'll stop payment on the check."

"That seems a pretty low gesture. Don't you care about nature?"

"You're an asshole," he said, getting up and staying up this time.

"And you might be an accessory to murder," I said. "So far, I have only a working theory, but there's room in it for you, Mike."

He slammed the door on his way out and, even though I saw that coming, I jerked in my chair. I've always been sensitive to loud noises. As a kid, I hated the Fourth of July. I pulled the tape recorder from its hiding place under the desk and checked the sound quality. My voice sounded much louder than Mike's, but you could still make out what he had said. I thought about following him to wherever he'd gone next, then thought better of it and decided to have a cup of fresh coffee, water the plants, and think instead. I doubted the plants were doing a damn thing to improve the air quality in the office, but they did seem to improve my thinking.

I had finished watering the plants and was shutting down Felicia's computer when the door opened and Eunice Shriver walked in.

I followed her into my office and offered her a cup of coffee.

"Do you have any Earl Gray tea?"

"Celestial Seasons. I think it's herbal."

She wrinkled her nose at the thought of herbal tea and settled for a bottle of Evian. I sat behind my desk and wished that, like every movie detective in history, I had a bottle of scotch stashed in my bottom drawer.

"So what'd you do this time?" I asked.

"What, murder isn't enough?"

"And conspiracy," I said. "You and Vernon."

"Are you mocking me, Theodore?"

"Mocking's not in my nature. Occasionally, I tease, but that's a whole different animal. Mrs. Shriver—sorry, Eunice—I know for a fact you didn't run over those geese and I also know for a fact you didn't kill Lydia Marks."

"And what is your proof?"

"I don't need to prove you didn't do it."

"Then who did?"

"I'm working on that. It's a process of elimination. I'd show you my list, upon the top of which your name has been crossed out, but I've lost it."

"Some detective," she sniffed. "I actually am not here about either killing."

"You've robbed a bank."

"That bordered on mockery."

"Sorry."

"Teddy, I would like to hire you for a job."

"A detective job?"

"Is that not your business?"

"Actually, I'm an investigative consultant."

"But the sign on your door . . ."

"Well, that's just a marketing tool. Like the way chiropractors call themselves doctors."

"Chiropractors aren't doctors?"

"You never see an M.D. after their name."

"I love my chiropractor."

"That's terrific. I've noticed your posture. It's very good for somebody of your years."

"I'll give you his name."

"Mine's a slouch," I said. "Nothing to do with spinal pain."

"I have money," she said. "To pay you, of course."

"That's good," I said. "But I don't want your money, Eunice. I'm pretty sure I don't want your case, either."

"But you haven't even heard what it is yet."

"I'll guess. Somebody's trying to kill you."

Her eyes widened. "How on earth did you know?"

"A lucky guess. See, a real detective wouldn't admit to guessing, but a consultant guesses all the time. Who's trying to kill you?"

"That's what I want you to find out. I have a list of suspects." She dug into her enormous purple purse and fished out four pages of typewritten single-spaced names, which she handed to me.

I whistled. "You've got quite a few enemies, Eunice."

"If I could narrow it down further, I wouldn't need to turn to you, Theodore."

It made me feel funny, old Mrs. Shriver calling me Theodore. Only my mother ever called me by my full name.

"Who are these people?"

"Neighbors, my children, of course, the ladies from my prayer circle, the postman, the mayor, among others."

"Why would the mayor . . ."

"Now, *that* is a long story."

I laid the paper on the desk, sighed, leaned back in my chair, and folded my hands behind my head.

"I'd love to hear it," I said.

CHAPTER THIRTY

It was close to seven o'clock when I left the office. I was hungry, but I drove home. The nesting instinct was strong upon me, and as I drove, I wondered if I faked some kind of illness, my landlord might let me keep a dog, like if I could provide a note from a competent physician or maybe somebody like Dr. Fredericks, who could vouch my lack of companionship was slowly driving me mad. Of course, I could simply bring a dog in and hope one of my neighbors didn't turn me in, but that reflected on the moral character issue I was trying to work on or work out.

I went straight to the refrigerator, but there was not so much as a slice of bologna, and all I had in the pantry was Campbell's cream of tomato soup and a can of sardines. I was checking out the fridge again, sniffing various containers, when the floorboards creaked behind me. I closed the door and without turning around, because I knew who it had to be, said, "Hey, Gary."

I turned around. He was sitting on the sofa in his full uniform, including the gun and the walkie-talkie strapped to his shoulder, and for some reason I thought of my old job. We'd had walkie-talkies, too, but working the night shift, there was nobody to communicate with, so I didn't even know how to use mine. *Walkie-talkie* is one of those archaic terms that's funny when you think about it.

"Hello, Ted."

"Guess I've blown a thousand bucks today."

"Probably not all you've blown, Ted."

"Maybe I'll sit down."

"Maybe you should. I'm waiting for a call and I thought it'd be best to wait for it here with you."

"Sure, Gary," I said. "You bet."

I sat on one of the bar stools by the counter.

"You want anything?" I asked. "I'm fresh out of just about everything, but there're a couple of Buds with good born-on dates."

"No thanks."

"Okay." I sat there for a second and thought, Maybe I should take up smoking so I would have something to do with my hands in situations like this. But there was a downside to smoking, of course, and I had enough vices for two people. Plus, odds were this was the last situation like this I'd ever have.

"I knew the second that dumb-ass said Parker's name that the thing was fucked," Gary said.

"You give me too much credit, Gary," I said. "I almost missed it, though the shadow of it was heavy upon me, like a splinter in my brain. It was like one of those *Encyclopedia Brown* moments—you know, like, 'Encyclopedia realized Mike couldn't have known Parker's last name, since Ruzak never mentioned it!'"

Gary Paul laughed. "You skipped to the back of the book."

"Is that where we are?"

He nodded. "Nearly."

"Are you going to kill me, Gary?"

His small eyes widened. "Why would I kill you, Teddy?"

"That's a good question. I don't have any proof, nothing that could get anybody in any kind of serious trouble. If I did, I would have called the task force. But there are a couple tapes. Hope I'm not being premature telling you that."

"Tapes?"

"Yeah. I've got a tape of Parker Hudson remembering your tag number under hypnosis and I've got a tape of Mike Carroll confessing to your setup at the Marks's rental. That might be a little difficult to explain to the task force."

"Oh," he said. "You mean *these* tapes." He then pulled them from his pants pocket and held them up.

"You broke into my office," I said.

"Right after you left tonight." He slipped them back into his pocket and adjusted the volume of his walkie-talkie. "You probably have a couple questions. Some loose ends. A couple extra splinters in your brain."

"That story in the paper—about the geese—that bothered Ken Marks?"

He hesitated, then nodded. "I guess it did."

"So he sent you to me, to find out what I knew and when I knew it. To throw me off or keep me close, or both, and when I got the tag number, you set up this deal with Mike to wrap my end up and keep me from nosing around and mucking things up worse than I already had. That's why you pretended to talk to Detectives Listrom and Watson. I don't know about Watson, but I know for sure you never talked to Harvey Listrom. Harvey doesn't even know who you are."

"Right on the money, Teddy."

"Only Mike blew it, and this puts you in an extremely awkward position."

"Bingo."

"It was you on the road that morning, wasn't it, Gary?"

"You really think I'm going to answer that question?"

"Oh, I only have one tape recorder, and that's at the office. But you know that already."

"I probably know just a little more right now than you do."

"I have a working theory. You want to hear it?"

"You bet. We've got a few more minutes."

I thought about asking him, A few more minutes till what? But I decided against it.

"Okay, here's my working theory. It still has some rough edges, and maybe since you're here, you can help me smooth them out. I think you're the goose killer. I think you grabbed Lydia that morning, probably just as she was starting out on her jog. She knew you, though, somehow, or maybe you were wearing your uniform; at any rate, there was some measure of trust there, but she realized at some point something was up, and I think there was a struggle going on when you hit those geese. You weren't watching the road and you couldn't stop, obviously: You had a job to do for Kenneth Marks. I think he paid you to kill Lydia like he paid you or somebody like you to kill his first wife."

He didn't nod or shake his head or make any expression at all while I talked. He just stared at me.

"I don't know why he wanted them dead," I went on. "I guess maybe it's the old money thing. As in it doesn't matter how much you have, because what you have is never enough. I don't know exactly what he does for a living, but my guess is that he lives pretty high on the hog and hiring someone to kill his wives was a way into some quick liquidity."

" 'Liquidity'?" he asked, smiling.

"Liquidity. And I don't know how he hooked up with a sheriff's deputy willing to go to the chair for a few dollars, but somehow he did—right? See, these are some of the rough edges in my theory, but not even Darwinism fits together completely, you know?"

"Gosh, that's one helluva theory, Ted. I don't suppose you've gone to the task force with it yet. They already think you're a nut—I've made sure of that—and what do you have? Without the tapes, what do you really have?"

I was about to say, I have Parker Hudson, but at that moment, like a cosmic turning of the wheel or clicking of the karmic gears, his walkie-talkie squawked to life and he pulled it to his right ear to listen. I couldn't make out what the dispatcher was saying, but it sounded pretty urgent. He stood up and said, "It's time, Ted. Let's go."

"Where are we going?"

"You know where we're going."

"No, Gary, I honestly don't."

"Okay, you don't know where, but you know what and why."

"You've been hanging around me too long," I told him, but because of that or in spite of it, I knew exactly what he meant.

CHAPTER THIRTY-ONE

I RODE SHOTGUN IN GARY PAUL'S CRUISER, AND IT OCCURRED TO ME that it was my first time in a police car since my Academy days, racing around the track in a mock pursuit, orange cones and life-size cutouts of pedestrians flying everywhere, the instructor, a little redheaded Irishman named O'Roark, screaming in my ear, "Accelerate through the curve, *through* the curve, you big dumb Pollack!"

Gary jumped on the interstate, heading west, and I knew the minute we mounted the entrance ramp where we were going. I didn't know precisely where, but I knew generally where. He turned on the siren and we roared west going ninety-five miles an hour till he reached the Lovell Road exit, which we took practically on two wheels.

"But here's the roughest edge," I said, raising my voice to be heard over the screaming siren. "Why would Ken Marks offer me a boatload of money to find out who was responsible if he was the one responsible?"

"Gee," Gary answered. "That *is* rough."

"Maybe it's like Jane Goodall and the chimps."

"What is?"

"You know, she hung with those monkeys for so many years, she started to act like them, think like them, even look a little like them as she got older."

"What you just said makes no sense to me, Ruzak. Sorry."

"He had to come see me, and why else would he come see me? He had to have a reason to come, a reason that would make sense to me. He wanted to know what I knew without tipping his hand, so his only choice was to play the part, the only part, I would expect him to play."

We pulled into the parking lot at Anchor Park. There were four other cruisers in the lot, which had been roped off with the yellow crime-scene tape, an ambulance, a fire truck, and a mobile crime-scene lab. Cars lined the other side of the street, parked illegally against the curb, and gawkers stood on the walking trail, moms in unflattering jogging shorts and baggy T-shirts and retirees in bright green shorts and sandals over white athletic socks. I followed Gary past the picnic tables and horseshoe court, down to the water's edge. The first thing that caught my eye was not the men in black wet suits wading toward the shape floating in the middle of the lake, but the two geese swimming nonchalantly near the shore. The water was sparkling in the last rays of the setting sun.

"Who is it?" I asked Gary.

"Who do you think it is, Ms. Goodall?" he asked.

"It's Parker Hudson," I said, and as if on cue, one of the geese gave a loud bray and ducked its head under the surface of the lake.

I turned away, leaned against a tree, and my empty stomach heaved. Gary put a hand on my shoulder in an obscene parody of sympathy and condolence.

"I think you're beginning to understand you're in way over your head on this one, Ted. Your reach has exceeded your grasp."

I nodded, head down, my arm wrapped around the tree, knees slightly bent. I wished I had eaten something; this dry retching really tore at your gut and burned your throat. This was the moment to pull free from Gary Paul's grip and run to the water's edge, shouting, "I've got him; I've got him right here! The killer's standing right over there by that tree!" But I didn't run anywhere or shout anything. Without the tapes and the only witness, what did I have? The guys in the black wet suits brought the body to the shore and laid it about fifty feet from us, and the people from the medical examiner's office hovered over it, taking pictures and gingerly touching, prodding, and poking Parker Hudson's body. He was dressed in shorts, sneakers, and a red polo shirt. I wondered what the hell was in that old man's head that he'd cared about what happened to six insignificant baby geese. Hadn't he realized the species would survive regardless? And why, if he'd cared so much, had he hired a hapless buffoon like Teddy Ruzak, who barely possessed the intellectual wherewithal to tie his own shoes?

"Let's go sit in the car, Ted."

He opened the back door for me and I slid into the seat behind the wire mesh. Gary got behind the wheel and slammed his door. His eyes were upon me in the rearview mirror.

"You agree, right? Way over your head?"

I nodded.

"Good," he said. "Now we've got to come to an understanding here, Teddy. I hope you appreciate the fact that I'm doing everything possible to keep you in one piece here. I'd like to hate your fat guts, but I can't, and believe me, I've tried. I took a big risk with that whole farce with Mike Carroll, and now I'm gonna have to ask you to think clearly for a second. What would be the easiest way to resolve this?"

"Kill me," I whispered.

"Kill you. You bet. What's the next easiest?"

"I don't know."

"Think, Ted. Come on. *Think*."

I tried to think. "Oh, crap, I don't know. Buy my silence?"

"That opens a can of worms, though, don't you think? Marks offered you a ton of cash and you turned it down. Maybe you can't be bought. Or I pay you off and down the road you change your mind or decide it wasn't quite enough. It's too open-ended. There's no closure."

I thought some more. I felt the answer floating in the ether but couldn't pin it down. Since there were no plants around to water to distract myself, I chose my usual method of distraction.

"That's something I've always been curious about, personally and professionally," I said. "Does it get easier? My mother always said lies were that way, and I've wondered if the same applies to your mortal sins—say cold-blooded murder. I mean, was it easier to kill Lydia than his first wife? Or maybe his first wife wasn't the first person you killed, I don't know, but even if she wasn't, was killing Parker Hudson easier than killing Lydia? Or is killing people one of those things that never gets easier, but something in which you find a comfort zone, like maybe flying an airplane, not easier or harder per se, just more relaxed?"

He smiled. "No, killing people isn't like flying an airplane."

"So you enjoy it?"

"Stop it, Ruzak. I know what you're trying to do."

"It is a little ridiculous," I admitted. "Trying to expand your understanding of the world while somebody's seriously considering putting a bullet in your head, unless you buy into the afterlife. How about that, Gary? I was never too religious myself, but you were born and raised in the buckle of the Bible Belt. Any qualms in that area?"

"You asking if I'm afraid I'll go to hell?"

"Well . . . yeah."

"I don't think about it."

I nodded. "I've got the opposite problem. I tend to think about everything, only I don't have the requisite wattage upstairs to accomplish it with any thoroughness or to bring anything to a conclusion. Like walking in circles: I get the exercise but never arrive anywhere. . . ."

He laughed, and as he was laughing, it hit me. In a way, the best alternative to killing me was worse than actually killing me. The answer was obvious, of course, and maybe it was slow coming to me because it was so obvious.

"Ah, come on, Gary, that's like . . . well, it really is beyond the pale."

"Then suggest a viable alternative."

I didn't say anything.

"There's really no way to protect her, you know," Gary said softly. "You try to hide her, I'll find her eventually. Do you really think I won't be able to find her? I'll know if you so much as breathe in the direction of the task force, Ted. You do anything, *anything,* and she dies. I know you're upset, and sometimes when people are upset, they miss subtle details, so my goal here is not to be subtle with you. I want the understanding between us to be crystal clear. Cross me and Felicia dies."

Neither of us said another word. He drove me home, pulling to a stop in front of the Sterchi. I stepped out of the car onto the curb and closed the door. He rolled down the passenger window and leaned over to call out, "You okay?"

I nodded, he gave a little wave, the window rolled back up, and he drove away. I watched him turn up Summit Hill; then I climbed the three flights to my apartment. It looked the same but not the same. I'd had a similar feeling right after Mom died, where everything familiar looked unfamiliar and strange. My insides felt hollow and my legs weak, and I realized I better eat something or I was going to have a major episode. Plus, I needed to think, and you should never try thinking, if it's of the serious variety, on an empty stomach. So I ordered a pizza, and while I was waiting for it, I went into the bathroom and washed my face and hands. My reflection in the mirror made my stomach give a slow roll and I bowed over the toilet in an attitude of abject prayer, but nothing came up. When the feeling subsided, I paced around the two rooms, moving aimlessly, and for some reason, I remembered the time I'd slipped in the shower, cracking my head against the tile as I went down. You hear those stories of people who die alone in their apartments and nobody finds them for days. There was nobody who would check on me if I went missing, and maybe in a week or two, Felicia might come by and find me bloated and stinking—you read about such things. When I left the security company, I lost my company benefits, including the life insurance. Now I had no life insurance, and if something happened, there'd be no money for the expenses and they'd throw me into a pauper's grave. But I had nobody to leave money to, so I wasn't too concerned about it.

At one point, I stopped dead still in the middle of my mindless circuit around the apartment and said out loud, "He's lying. He's just buying time till he can kill me without causing a ruckus. He can't afford the risk of me changing my mind or getting too big for my britches and running to the task force, thinking they'll protect me."

Then I thought, No, he really doesn't need or want to kill me. With each death, the risk escalated, and like he'd implied, I was a pussy. I didn't have the guts to do the moral thing, the thing that was right by Lydia, because doing the right thing conflicted with my self-interest. I had passed muster on every state qualification to get my license except that one, the one about moral character. It had thrown me for a loop because in thirty-three years, my moral character had never really been tested. It was a pretty scary thought, so I pushed it out of my head as quickly as I could. People in general spend a lot of their time worrying about wasting money or time, but the thing most squandered is thought. We waste a lot of it. The biggest successes in life are those people who are economical with their thinking. Losers like me are fooled into thinking that thought is cheap because it doesn't cost anything. But real thought, true thought, costs dearly.

My buzzer rang. The pizza. I punched the intercom button.

"Just bring it on up!"

"Mr. Ruzak?"

"Susan?"

"Hi. Can I come up?"

"Uh. Sure."

She came up wearing a black dress and dark hose with sensible low-heeled sandal-type black shoes, her dark hair pulled back in a severe-looking bun. I held the door for her and caught a hint of lilac as she passed.

"It's not too late, is it?"

The question was so ironical, I almost laughed.

"I didn't know you knew where I lived," I said, because I didn't.

"I looked it up in the phone book."

I threw the dead bolt on the door because she might have been followed or someone might be staking out my building, and what I was suffering from seemed to be exceedingly contagious: the pathogen of extreme violence. Parker Hudson had already succumbed to it.

She sat on the sofa. Her dress was sleeveless and terminated about two inches above her knees. Except for the shoes, she looked like she might be dressed for the theater. I offered her something to drink and she said Coke if I had it, which I did, and I poured her a glass with lots of ice in it, because I had heard in Europe they go easy on the ice—maybe two cubes at the most. You wonder why refrigeration is such an issue over there or if it's just a cultural thing, like not being able to get sweet tea above the Mason-Dixon Line.

"How was the funeral?" I asked. Bad topic for small talk, but it was really the only thing we had in common.

"Catholic and very, very Irish. The wake was incredible. I never laughed so hard—or cried so hard—in my whole life."

"I hear those Irish Catholics know how to throw a burial."

"It makes me wish I had known her better."

"Me, too. Not you, but me, I meant. How well did you know her, Susan? Did you meet before the wedding?"

"I didn't even go to the wedding. They were married in Ireland, honeymooned in Morocco, and flew to Knoxville six weeks later."

"You had no idea?"

"It was a total surprise."

"Matthew seemed to think there was some kind of fix involved."

She shook her head and again I got a whiff of lilac. "There was no fix," she said. "Matt's got a chip on his shoulder, that whole 'absent father' thing. Dad loved Lydia."

"He offered me a couple million dollars to hand him the killer so he could take care of things extrajudicially."

"Sounds like my father. Please don't report him or anything, Mr. Ruzak. He didn't really mean it. My father is the kind of man who always looks for the shortest distance between two points."

That was for sure. "I didn't report him," I said. "And I really wish you'd call me Teddy. Even the mailman, who I hardly know, calls me Teddy."

She nodded and sipped her Coke. "This is good. Thank you. I still have some jet lag, I think."

She slipped off her shoes and put her stocking feet on the coffee table, pulling the hem of her dress down demurely as she did.

"Speaking of Matt," I said. "He pretended he didn't even know what your dad did for a living."

"He's an investor. Real estate mostly. He started here in the States, of course; he's got half a dozen houses around town and some condos, but after a while, he got into the overseas market. He buys it, develops it, and sells it at a huge profit, I guess, because two million dollars is nothing to my father."

"I guess your dad's very economical in his thinking."

"What's that mean?"

"Nothing. I'm working on a theory of the economics of thought."

"Are you really?"

"No, not really. Sometimes things cross my mind that are beautiful but fleeting, like a shooting star—though more overwhelming. More like fireworks than a shooting star, I guess. So I get all excited and think I'm onto something profound, until I find out somebody else thought it or said it a few hundred years ago. It's hard to have a truly original thought anymore—I guess because we've been around for so long. Kind of like the monkeys typing Shakespeare."

She laughed. "Oh no. We're back to Shakespeare's monkeys."

"I'm not sure about that hypothesis, though. It's like that mathematician's theorem about the arrow never hitting the target."

Her eyebrows came together, creating a fine horizontal line that hovered over her nose.

"You know, anything that travels must cover half the distance before it can arrive at its destination. But before it can travel half the distance, it has to travel half of that half, and so on, and if you calculate that, always dividing by half, the arrow never gets anywhere."

"Sort of like our conversations."

"Sorry."

"No, I meant it as a compliment."

"You probably mean you never get any answers from me about your stepmom. I guess that's why you've come, but honestly, I don't have anything. Not a blessed thing." Even to my own ears, I sounded sincere as hell. I was a better liar than I thought I'd be, and I remembered Mom's saying each lie gets easier. "I thought I had something, but that fizzled out, so now your best bet is the task force. I guess you're in touch with them, too. You've got to remember that these people have access I don't. You know, forensics and databases and years of experience in this kind of deal."

She nodded. "I don't like that Detective Watson. She talks to me like I'm a moron or a little kid."

"Oh, I'm sure she's a crackerjack detective, though. You don't reach her level in a place like the TBI without having something on the ball. Did she tell you their theory?"

"Yes. That Lydia was jogging on the trail and a stranger pulled her or lured her into his car."

"So, um, they've ruled out somebody Lydia might know?"

"I guess that was pretty easy, since she didn't know many people."

"Why is that? Did she have some kind of psychological disorder or—"

"I think America was a little overwhelming to her. She wasn't an outgoing person at all, Mr. Ruzak. She told me once that when she was growing up, all she wanted to be was a nun. Why do you think she didn't marry until she was in her thirties? At the wake, her family said they used to tease her about being an old maid."

"So what was she up to when she met your dad? I mean, did she have a job?"

"Yes, but I don't know what it was."

"What's that story? How did they meet?"

"In a restaurant. She was at a table with some friends and Dad went over and introduced himself. He told her he had never seen a more beautiful woman in his life."

"Turned her head."

"He was good for her. He brought her out of her shell some—not a lot, but some. And she was good for him."

"How so?"

"She made him laugh. She was a very funny person, but her sense of humor was very subtle. Some people missed it, like Matt."

"Maybe he resented her. You know, that happens when a kid thinks his parent is trying to replace the original."

She lowered her dark eyes. "Maybe," she said softly.

"I looked into that a little," I said. "Your mother's death."

"I'm sure you did," she said. "I'm sure Detective Watson did, too."

I agreed she probably had.

"It sure is an odd coincidence."

"Exactly," Susan Marks said firmly. "And that's all it is."

My buzzer rang. She gave a little jump and I said, "I ordered a pizza."

Veggie lovers' supreme, heavy on the olives. I was being halfheartedly conscious of my weight. Susan said she wasn't hungry, but, like a lot of slight girls, she had the appetite of a horse. I fetched her another Coke and we ate sitting cross-legged on the floor, with the pizza on the coffee table between us. I was pushing the envelope even having her in my apartment. What if someone was staking me out? Was Gary already on his way to Felicia's? Susan picked the olives off and dropped them one by one onto my slice.

"The stranger theory doesn't work," I said.

"Why?"

"Location for one, if she really was snatched from the trail. A kidnapping like that is a crime of opportunity. She would have been taken from the house, which everybody agrees she probably wasn't."

She nodded. A piece of cheese clung to her plump lower lip and this produced a sensation in my gut that was pleasant and uncomfortable at the same time.

"They found remnants of her jogging shorts in the woods," she said.

"So she was either on the trail or in the neighborhood on the way to the trail, a little early for rush hour, but people might have been around anyway."

"Like the man who saw the geese."

The reference to Parker made my throat close up and completely killed my appetite. I set down my slice of pizza.

"Right. The second thing is, I don't know much about her, but from what you've said, Lydia wasn't the kind of person who would just jump into some stranger's car."

"No way."

"Would she have fought with him?"

"She was Irish."

"Okay. Let's try to imagine this. She's jogging along and this SUV pulls over and a stranger jumps out and grabs her. Does she holler? Kick? Punch?"

"Probably all those things."

"Or the car pulls over and the stranger asks her something, maybe tells her something, that would make her come over at least, close enough for the grab. Could that have happened?"

She shook her head. "She wasn't distrustful, but I can't imagine anything somebody could say that would have made her stop and go to the car. She thought America was a very violent place."

"That means a lot, coming from somebody from Ireland. So an organized killer like this one—and we know he's the organized type, based on how easily he got her in the car and how he killed her—just wouldn't have picked her randomly like that. Too much risk."

"But if it wasn't a stranger . . ."

"It could be somebody *she* knew, not necessarily somebody *you* knew she knew."

"Like a neighbor?"

"I'm sure the task force has covered all the neighbors. But it could have been somebody she met at a store or a restaurant, maybe even the bag boy at Fresh Market. I'm just using the bag boy as an example. She knew this person in passing at least; there must have been a germ of trust there, a note of familiarity. Or maybe even someone in law enforcement. Or, um, maybe even pretending to be in law enforcement, though not every cop is a saint—we're all human—but you know everybody trusts cops. I'm just using that as an example, too. I'm not saying it was a cop or somebody pretending to be a cop. Did she know any cops? Mention any cops to you? Maybe not, if it was a casual acquaintance, maybe even a mutual acquaintance—you know, of hers and your dad's. No? Well, you wouldn't necessarily know her casual acquaintances. I don't care how close you are to somebody, and it looks like Lydia wasn't close to hardly anybody, you don't know everybody they know."

I was spinning this and I knew it was all a bunch of hogwash, since, after all, I knew the truth, or most of it at least. And there was something terribly obscene about me hypothesizing about it, dropping hints and asking leading questions like some dime-store pettifogging shyster. But Susan Marks needed something to cling to. She was young; she wanted answers to life's horrors. There was also the seductive fact that she was one of the few people who seemed to hang on my every word. When somebody finds you interesting, you try to be even more interesting.

The cheese still hung to her bottom lip and it took everything in me not to reach out and pull it off.

"Maybe I don't know everybody she knew, but I know most of the places she went. I know where she shopped for clothes and groceries. I know where she had the car serviced, where she got her hair done. She managed Dad's rental properties here in town when he was away. Collected rents, dealt with tenant complaints, things like that. I could make a list for you and you could work from that."

She must have seen something change in my expression, because she said, "What?"

"Susan, I don't know how to tell you this, but . . . but I've got to let this go." I cleared my throat. "I don't want to let it go, but the truth is, I have what you might call an ethical dilemma."

"What's your ethical dilemma?"

"I don't have a license to practice detection."

"I don't understand."

"I rushed into hanging up my shingle before I even looked into the requirements. I'm taking the test in a couple of weeks, but as of now, I can't work on any cases."

"But I'm not paying you anything. Is that what you want, Mr. Ruzak? You want me to pay you? Okay, what do you charge? I didn't realize this was about money. . . ."

She had started to cry. I passed her a napkin and said, "If it was about money, I would have taken your father's when he offered it."

"You couldn't take it because you don't know who did it."

She had a good point. She had wrapped the napkin around her index finger and was dabbing the corner of her eyes with it. Prep school, horseback-riding and tennis lessons, and long afternoons at the country club sipping iced tea and gossiping with the girls. We might as well have been from different planets.

"Okay, maybe it's more accurate to say I don't have the experience to help you. It's more like someone asking you tomorrow to remove a cat's gallbladder. Only I'm not sure if cats even have gallbladders. My point is, my reach has exceeded my grasp on this one."

"Okay, Mr. Ruzak."

"Please call me Teddy. Why won't you call me Teddy?"

"I understand. I guess I'll have to find somebody else to help me. . . ."

"The task force—"

"You just said the task force had it all wrong!"

"I was speaking from the exuberance of inexperience."

"What?"

"Well, it's like when—"

"Oh, no, no, no. Don't tell me what it's like. Everything you say is like something else. When is something just what it is and not like something else?"

I tried to think of an example, but just thinking of an example proved her point. She stood up and her hem fell down. When she said, "No, no, no," she had shaken her head violently and a thick strand of her dark hair had pulled free from the bun and fallen against her cheek. Audrey Hepburn, that's who she looked like. Another simile; there really was no escape.

She jumped up and went to the door.

"Susan . . ."

"I just want somebody to help me," she said. "Why won't somebody help me?"

She pulled at the knob, not realizing I had thrown the dead bolt.

"Susan," I said. "There are some things I can't tell you. . . ."

This stopped her, giving me time to cross the room.

"What things?"

"I'll be frank," I said. "Frankly, I'm really torn up right now. I'm trying to figure out what's the right thing to do, and that isn't always clear."

"You don't think finding who killed Lydia is the right thing to do?"

"It's more complicated than that."

She slowly shook her head and another strand came loose.

"That's not complicated, Mr. Ruzak," she whispered. She had started to cry again. "You don't know what it's like . . . what it's like to lose some-body . . . to lose two mothers. . . ."

"No," I said. "I lost only one."

I don't remember who moved toward who first. The next thing I knew, she was in my arms and the smell of lilacs was all around me. Then I was kissing her. Our mouths came open and I could taste cheese.

CHAPTER THIRTY-TWO

SHE BROKE THE KISS FIRST. THIS WASN'T SOMETHING NEW IN MY EXPE-
rience, so my feelings weren't hurt.

"I don't know why I did that," she said.

"Why did you?"

"I just said I didn't know." She sounded cross. "I have to go. I think I really need to go." She looked at her watch.

"I'll walk you to your car," I said.

"Why? Am I in danger?"

"No. At least, I don't think so. You'd like to think there's a limit to evil—
you know, a line or a barrier that can't be crossed—but the ancient Greeks
didn't buy that and I'm not too sure I do, either. Let's just say the longer
you're here, the more somebody else is in danger."

"You?"

"No. Maybe. Probably, in the end."

The line deepened between her eyebrows. "You're trying very hard to tell
me something without telling me anything." She waited for me to say something. When I didn't, she said, "That's okay. I understand. Well, I don't understand, really, but that's par for the course with you, Mr. Ruzak."

"Stay here till I get back," I told her.

"Where are you going?"

"I'm going to walk around the block. I won't be long."

"There's something about Lydia you're not telling me. You know something."

I knew just about everything, but how could I tell her that? I trotted
down the stairs and into the night. I walked a block east toward the river and
back again, but I didn't see any suspicious persons hunkered in cars, or any

persons whatsoever, for that matter. I spotted her car parked across the street from my building. It was the only car parked on that side of the street.

Upstairs, she had to go to her tiptoes to kiss me good-bye.

"Thank you, Mr. Ruzak," she said softly.

"Wait," I said. "I'm walking you to your car."

I escorted her across the street, her small hand resting on my forearm as we walked.

"What's the matter?" she asked. "Why are you so jumpy?"

"It's a personality trait. Can you call me whenever you get where you're going?"

"Okay."

"Where are you going, exactly?"

"To my apartment. Why?"

"Matt staying at home with your dad?"

"Matt's staying in our condo at Riversound. Are you going to tell me what's going on?"

"Maybe later. I've got to . . . I've got some very keen thinking to do."

She laughed, threw her arms around my neck, and kissed me again. I stood on the sidewalk and waved as she made a left onto Summit Hill before disappearing from view. I stood there another couple of minutes, then went back upstairs, took a shower, sat on my unmade bed afterward for about thirty minutes, and cried.

CHAPTER THIRTY-THREE

I WOKE UP THE NEXT MORNING WITH THE SUN SHINING IN MY FACE. The last thing I remembered before falling asleep was the conviction I would never fall asleep. The phone was ringing.

It was Gary Paul.

"Hey, sleepyhead. It's rounding ten o'clock. Rough night?"

"It's been a rough twenty-four hours, Gary."

"No doubt. But, you know, I'm not entirely to blame for that, Ted. I just got off the phone with Felicia. What a nice gal. Is she married?"

I pressed the tips of my forefinger and thumb hard into the corners of my eyes. I had cotton mouth bad, but the phone wasn't cordless and I was trapped in the bed.

"She has a boyfriend, a firefighter boyfriend. Big guy, heavy into weight training and Krav Maja."

"What the hell is Krav Maja?"

"It's this hand-to-hand street fighting technique developed by the Israelis. Very deadly stuff."

"Seriously?"

"Oh, I kid you not."

"Sometimes I get the impression you're kind of putting me on."

"You wouldn't be the only one. Anyway, I've never met him, but I hear he's got a hair-trigger temper; you know, a real hothead."

"Hmmm. And he's a firefighter, you said?"

"Yeah. He's a fire-fighting hothead."

He laughed. "Look, Ted, the reason for my call. Two reasons, really. First, I was curious after our little conversation yesterday to know how you're gonna handle things from here."

"Well," I said. "I have no tapes, no witness, no client, and no money. Like you said, even if I went to the task force, they wouldn't believe me. I can't see any way to proceed except to shut my doors and try to get my old job back."

"Gee, that's really good to hear, Ted. I know you loved being a private eye, but sometimes things don't work out."

"Oh, I'm not sure how much I loved it. It certainly wasn't what I expected, but how many things can you say turn out to be the way you expected? You should never really trust your expectations. For example, there's about eighty percent of me that actually expects you to keep up your end of our bargain."

"Why wouldn't I?"

"Gary, you've lied to me from the day we met."

"Okay, but why would I make the offer if I planned to kill you? That's what you're concerned about, right? That I plan to kill you?"

"It's crossed my mind."

"Believe me, Teddy, if that was the plan, you'd be dead already."

"That's crossed my mind, too."

I washed up in the sink, brushed my teeth, and drove straight to the office without consuming so much as a slice of toast. It was a bright, sunny day with a forecasted high of eighty-seven degrees.

Felicia was there, standing by the sill behind my desk, staring at the brick wall of the building through the window.

She was wearing a clingy gray sleeveless dress with matching gray heels and no hosiery. Her legs were nicely tanned and I wondered if she used those tanning sprays or if that was what she'd been doing yesterday, maybe lying out by a pool.

She barely glanced at me. "Where have you been?"

"I overslept." I sank into one of the visitor's chairs. "Felicia, we have to talk."

She nodded and sank into my executive chair. She looked tired, the skin on her face not as tanned as her arms and legs. It had kind of a saggy, worn look to it, and there were dark circles under her eyes.

I got up, poured myself a cup of coffee, and sat back down.

"That cop friend of yours called," she said. "He said he was off duty last night and didn't know till he picked up the paper this morning."

"Okay," I said.

"Then he asked me for a date," she said, and laughed.

"What about Bob?"

"I didn't say yes, Ruzak. To tell you the truth, he kind of gives me the creeps."

"How come?"

"He's too . . ." She gave a little wave of her hand. She was wearing a charm bracelet and the charms tinkled against one another as she waved.

"Nice?"

"No. Yes. I don't know."

"He has bad teeth."

She laughed. "And Paul Killibrew called."

"Who's Paul Killibrew?"

"The reporter from the *Sentinel,* remember?"

"Oh, yeah."

"Jesus, Ruzak. Anyway, he wanted to talk to you about what happened yesterday."

"I don't know anything about what happened yesterday."

"You called him after the first story ran, remember? After you saw HRT. He's thinking of doing a story on it now."

"On what?"

She sighed loudly. "On HRT seven one nine, the geese, and Lydia Marks. Whether there's a connection."

"Boy, it would be a helluva coincidence if there wasn't."

"What's the matter with you? Why are you talking like this? Tell me what's going on, Ruzak. You know something."

"Did you tell Paul about HRT seven one nine? I mean, did you give him that number?"

"No—why would I do that?"

I sipped my coffee. Felicia made it too weak for my taste. I figure if you're going to drink coffee, you might as well go for the high octane. It's like those people who smoke low-tar cigarettes. It kind of defeats the purpose of indulging in the vice in the first place.

"The real question is," I said, "Where do we go from here? My only client is dead."

"What about the reward?"

"What reward?"

"The reward for finding Lydia's killer."

I almost laughed aloud.

"I'm dropping it, Felicia."

"You're dropping . . . what? What are you dropping?"

"Everything. This." I motioned to the room.

"You're not quitting, Ruzak."

"I don't have a choice, Felicia."

She folded her bare brown arms across her chest, leaned back in my executive chair, and asked, "Because?"

"Because? Because for one thing, I'm way over my head and, like a panicked swimmer, I just keep flailing around in the water, sinking deeper the harder I try to stay afloat. Let's face it, I'm all wrong for this kind of work. I'm disorganized, I'm sloppy, I don't have a logical mind, and I tend to get too personally involved with my clients." My cheeks were hot. I was close to telling her about Susan Marks and our impromptu pizza party. I sipped some coffee to steady myself, but coffee isn't known for its steadying influence. "Plus, most importantly of all, I've bottomed out. I've got no evidence, no witnesses, no leads, no case, no license, and no money. I've come up against it, Felicia. I've hit the wall pretty hard."

"What wall, Ruzak?"

"You know, reality."

"So," she said. Her lips had gone thin. "That's it. You're done."

"I think I'm done."

"You asshole. You come into my life . . . you make these wild promises . . . you drag me into this deal so you can act out your childhood fantasies, and now when things get tough, you throw up your hands and say, 'Oh, well, guess that didn't work out. Good luck to you, Felicia.' "

"Look, it's not that bad. . . ." I fumbled in my pocket for a handkerchief, then realized I didn't even own a handkerchief, so I went into the bathroom and pulled off half a dozen squares of toilet paper and tried to hand them to her. She pushed my hand away.

"I'm not dabbing my eyes with toilet paper!"

"Right," I said, and stuffed the wad into my pocket. "Anyway, it's not that bad. I talked to Freddy, and he said—"

"When did you talk to Freddy?"

"Couple days ago."

"*Why* did you talk to Freddy?"

"He came over to the table—"

"You have no business talking to Freddy about me."

"Why not?"

"Because you have no business in my business!"

"And you have no business in mine!" I bit my lower lip hard, what I usually do when I've mouthed off and there's no way to take it back, so I guess biting my lower lip is a form of self-punishment.

"Well"—she leaned over the desk and hissed at me—"you wanna know something funny, Ruzak? I absolutely agree with you: You're not cut out for this line of work. You're probably the worst-qualified PI on the face of planet Earth, but that's not the point anymore. Whether you like it or not, you're in this thing, and now you've dragged me and . . . and my life into it with you, and throwing up your hands and walking away is not going to get either of us out of it. Before, maybe doing things half-assed was an option, but that option doesn't exist anymore, Ruzak."

I nodded, but I didn't say anything.

"So which is it?" she asked softly. "What are you going to do?"

I dropped my head. "I'm scared," I said. I raised my head. "I'm afraid, Felicia."

She nodded. "And I'm unemployed. Thanks a lot, Ruzak."

CHAPTER THIRTY-FOUR

WE ARGUED FOR ANOTHER HALF HOUR WHILE I SLUGGED DOWN THREE more cups of the weak coffee and she clicked around the hardwood floor in her heels, but I held firm to my "I'm just a big fat pussy" defense, which came off convincingly because it dovetailed so well into everything she knew about me. What about justice? she asked. What about my promises? she wondered. Promises I'd made to Parker and to Susan and to her especially? The whole thing was leading into "What is your measure as a man?" territory and that was a place I'd be lost even with a map. Finally, when she realized I wasn't going to give in, she grabbed her matching snakeskin gray purse and pounded down the stairs to the street. I followed her outside, where I found her fumbling in her purse for a pair of sunglasses, which she jammed over her eyes with such force, I thought she must have bruised the bridge of her nose. I had drunk too much coffee, being fooled like those low-tar smokers who just smoke more, and, as usual when I drank too much coffee, I had the peculiar sensation of my legs being too long for my body; I seemed to lope.

"What are you doing?" she asked.

"I just wanted to say I'm sorry."

"Who cares about your 'sorry'?"

She shouldered her purse and set out toward the Hilton. She parked there for seventy-five dollars a month, but that was paid for out of the company account. She could never say after that and all the paid time off and the free designer wardrobe that she didn't have her share of perks.

"I'm sorry, Felicia. I really am," I said, loping after her. "I never thought taking on a wild-goose case would lead—"

"Oh, save it, Ruzak. It's over. Now you can crawl back to the security company and beg for your old job and I can go plant a big fat wet one on Freddy's pimply ass. And whoever killed Lydia Marks will get away with murder."

I followed her into the garage, thinking you shouldn't assume just because a guy is on the large side that his ass is pimply. She asked why the hell I was following her into the garage. I didn't answer. When she slid into the car seat, that clingy gray number pulled up on her thigh and I saw a lot of bare tanned leg.

"Get in the car, Ruzak."

Her tone brooked no argument, so I climbed into her Corolla without any argument. Too much had happened in the past twenty-four hours to absorb in its entirety. The danger of life in general is that you get so worn down, there's not enough left of you to fight. You see this especially among the poor, but nobody's immune, even nations and whole civilizations. Everybody's gotten so tired, they get to the point where they just don't give a damn anymore. I'm not a big believer in the spiritual side of things, but I suspected I had disturbed some balance in the cosmos by calling myself "the Hammer." It flipped some kind of karmic switch.

Felicia took the Henley Street Bridge over the river, and a couple of boats were out, with young women lounging on the bows in luminescent bikinis. We passed Baptist Hospital, where my mother died, on the opposite shore, then continued south, now on Chapman Highway, heading toward Seymour. She didn't say anything and I didn't say anything, even when we passed Baptist Hospital and I was overwhelmed with memories of chemotherapies and biopsies and radiation treatments, of long silk scarves wrapped around my mother's bald head and how she seemed to shrink inside her gown as the cancer ate her from the inside. Sometimes it's not enough for life to wear you down; sometimes life just eats you alive. It cleaves you in two. A lot of people spend the majority of their lives running from that fact, but in life, death has a way of bringing you up short, grabbing you by the nape of the neck, and slinging you around to face the Big Dark.

Felicia made a left onto a little side road off the highway. We drove for about half a mile before she turned into the driveway of a small frame house, once white behind a white picket fence, but now both house and fence were badly in need of a paint job. She pulled in behind an older model Toyota truck parked beneath the corrugated overhang attached to the house and cut off the engine. Someone had removed the first two and last two letters of the make, leaving the letters *YO* on the tailgate. Felicia took a big breath and told me to come on, and so I followed her up the overgrown walkway to the door, and we went inside.

The blinds were drawn. A television provided the only light in the small family room, so everything had that blue TV tint, making it hard for me to tell even what color the carpeting was. A large shape rose from the sofa, and instead of being Bob's, like I expected, the shape was that of Lacey from the diner.

She stood still for a second, absorbing my presence. Felicia said, "Lacey, you know Ruzak."

Felicia dropped her purse on a straight-backed chair set by the front door and asked, "Where is he?"

"In his room," Lacey said. "Why are you here?" she asked me, or more in the direction of me.

"She drove me," I said.

She gave me a look that said she didn't care for smart-asses. A door slammed somewhere in the back and a kid came barreling into the room wearing shorts and a yellow T-shirt with Spiderman's red face on the front, and he flew into Felicia's arms as she knelt to grab him. She picked him up and spun once around with him.

"How's my captain?" she asked. "How's my little knight?" And he was all giggling and slobbering, and I guessed he was maybe four or five, but there was something wrong with this kid. His head looked too big for his body, and he was pretty hefty for a five year old, with small eyes and very short, fat fingers. He noticed me and the giggles stopped like a switch had been flipped. Felicia set him down and said, "Honey, this is the man Mommy works for. Or used to work for. Can you say hi to Mr. Ruzak?"

He kind of lunged forward on those thick legs and grabbed my hand and pulled me so that I lost my balance and almost landed right on top of him. Then he wrapped his arms around my knees and twisted his body back and forth, wiping his mouth on the leg of my pants.

"Okay, no wrestling holds on Ruzak," Felicia scolded him, and behind me Lacey was laughing. I was looking straight down at the top of the kid's head, and his hair was very fine, like a baby's hair, and I could see the irregular shape of his skull.

"Ruzak, this is Thomas," Felicia said.

"My name is Thomas!" the boy said, tilting back his head and shouting up at me. "Thomas Kincaid! Who are you?"

"I told you, honey. Mr. Ruzak," Felicia said.

"Ruzak!" the boy shouted. "Ruzak! Ruzak! Ruzak!" He let go of my knees and did a little dervish sort of dance in the space between Felicia and me. He was giggling again and a thick line of spit ran out of his mouth and trailed down his chin.

"He likes your name," Lacey said.

"Ruzak! Ruzak! Ruzak!" Thomas Kincaid shouted.

"Now you know why I dropped out of nursing school," Felicia said.

CHAPTER THIRTY-FIVE

FELICIA TOOK THOMAS BACK TO HIS ROOM AND AFTER A LONG TIME, maybe an hour, came back with red eyes, like she'd been crying, and told Lacey she'd be back after she ran me back to the office. While she was with Tommy, Lacey and I sat on the sofa with the volume on the TV turned low, and it was a long hour, because Lacey was the kind of woman who didn't like men in general, or maybe just me in particular.

"He's not right, you know," she had said after Felicia left the room. "He's got 'developmental issues.' A preemie—four pounds, six ounces when he was born. Doctors think the cord got wrapped around his neck in the womb or something like that, cutting off the oxygen to his brain."

"Who's the father?" I asked.

"Somebody Felicia met at the diner while she was working through school. He took off."

"Does he know?"

"Know what?"

"Well, did he take off when she got pregnant or after the baby was born?"

"What's that matter?"

"I guess it doesn't."

"Freddy was real good about it," Lacey said, implying I was not. "Real understanding. Course, we were always willing to cover for her when something was going on with Tommy. She's all he's got, Ruzak."

No wonder she got so upset. Now either way things went, I had toppled the applecart. You never fully appreciate your effect on others. I was like a malevolent Jimmy Stewart in *It's a Wonderful Life*, screwing up the lives of everyone in my path.

When we got back in the car, I asked Felicia to forgive me.

"Forgive you for what?"

"Assuming you were, I don't know, a goof-off or something. Why didn't you tell me, Felicia?"

"What would that accomplish? I don't want pity, Ruzak, just a paycheck."

That made sense to me. Felicia was an awfully proud person, and awfully proud people never want special consideration. Unless they also happen to be rich—rich people usually want special consideration, based solely on the fact that they have more money than you. Like Kenneth Marks offering me the insider deal on finding his wife's killer. Money can make you arrogant, but it isn't the only thing that can. There's a certain kind of arrogance born of ignorance. Sometimes I felt like Rip Van Winkle: fifteen years on the night shift, awake when the world slept, sleeping while the world went on. I froze at the age of nineteen, when I took that job, and completely missed those life experiences that would have matured me. So in my arrogant ignorance, I had assumed Felicia was missing work because she was a goof-off or had some kind of nymphomaniacal dysfunction.

"It's Marks," she said.

"What is?"

"The killer."

"But he was in Brussels."

"He hired somebody, dummy."

"And that somebody followed me after reading the article, then killed Parker because he knew he was a witness?"

"Right. See, you're not such a bad detective, Ruzak."

"It fits the facts," I said. "But you don't need Marks in the picture for the facts to fit."

"What about the first wife?"

"That still could be a coincidence. And what about the fact of him offering me money to find the killer?"

"Done to throw you off. He knows you won't find the killer, so what's he got to lose?"

"How does he know I won't?"

"He thinks you can't. He thinks he's too clever."

"Maybe he is."

"Apparently for you."

She was trying to goad me. Appeal to my manhood. It wasn't going to work, but not for the reason she thought it wasn't. She dropped me by the front door of the Ely Building.

"Are you going back to the diner?" I asked.

"What do you care?"

"Well," I said, "I do."

"Maybe I'll take the exam and get my detective license. I don't know. Or maybe . . ." Her nose crinkled. "Maybe I'll marry Bob and he can support me."

"Has he asked?"

She rolled up her window and drove away. I thought about going upstairs to the office, but what was I going to do up in that office?

Instead, I drove to Wal-Mart and picked out a semiautomatic handgun. I filled out the application and was told I could pick up my gun after the waiting period. I told the clerk the clock was ticking but that on principle I believed in waiting lists and background checks and wondered if any exceptions were ever made based on dire circumstances. The clerk had never heard of any, and I didn't doubt that he was a highly trained professional, but still he was a Wal-Mart clerk, so I decided to look into the matter more thoroughly. You couldn't expect a Wal-Mart clerk to be an expert in all the ins and outs of federal law.

Then I drove north on Broadway until it turned into Maynardville Highway, about four miles into the Halls area, and Sharp's Ridge towered in the distance, its TV towers stretching like long fingers against the backdrop of the overcast sky. I hadn't been to Halls since the week after I buried Mom; her insurance agent was out there, Harry Conrack, a burly ex-marine with a crew cut. I explained what I was after, and Harry looked me up in his actuarial tables and told me if I lost twenty to twenty-five pounds and got out of my risky line of work, I could reduce my premium by forty-five dollars a month. Then he performed some calculations—burial expenses, plus outstanding debts, plus my last four years' income, plus the time remaining on my leases for the apartment and the office—and came up with a value on my life of $250,000. That struck me as strangely too much and not enough.

"Who do you want as the beneficiary?" He had been a drill sergeant in the marines and tended to bark his questions at you, looking down his nose over his little half glasses like you were a raw recruit just off the bus.

I gave him Felicia's name. He scribbled it on the form.

"Anybody else?"

I didn't answer at first.

"Listen! You can do it two ways, Ruzak," he shouted. "Cobeneficiary or contingent beneficiary, in case she's dead, too."

"Contingent," I said. "Thomas Kincaid."

He told me a nurse would be calling in the next couple days to arrange a physical. Then he sold me a rider that stated if I was ever hospitalized, I would receive a stipend of two thousand dollars a month. I thought that was a particularly sweet deal, since being healthy never brought in that much.

Then he asked if I had renter's insurance.

"No."

"You're buying some."

"I am?"

"Damn straight you are, Ruzak!" They say the best salesmen fit their pitch to their personalities. Harry had all sorts of awards on his walls and pictures of himself with celebrities and politicians and other important-looking people whom I didn't recognize. Harry's pitch was perfectly meshed with his military background.

So I left his office insured from the soles of my feet to the top of my head. He informed me I was an extremely lucky individual, since nothing horrible had happened since the hanging of my shingle, and gave me two coffee mugs, a calendar, some brochures on financing my next vehicle through him, and a prospectus on mutual funds. The burden of being a truly responsible adult felt new and strange to me, but at the same time I felt liberated from my childhood in a way my mother's death could not deliver.

I stopped for lunch on the way to the office, so it was after three o'clock when I finally walked through the door. The place was lonely without Felicia around. She had hardly ever been around even when she was around, but at least the potential for Felicia had been there. It was lonely and hot and smelled bad. I went through the mail, then checked my messages. There was just one, from Susan Marks.

"Hey," I said when she answered the phone. "I was going to call you. I probably should tell you I'm getting out of the detective business, too, but anyway, how are you?"

"Oh, I'm okay." She sighed into the phone, and for some reason, the cheese clinging to her bottom lip immediately leapt into my mind. "I'm starting my summer job, working for a vet full-time. Dad's planning another trip overseas and Matt's taking some summer classes because his grades were so horrible."

"You hear anything from the task force?"

"They don't talk to me. They talk to Dad."

"Does Dad talk to you?"

"What does that mean?"

"I mean about what's happening with the case."

"Oh. No. No, not much."

"When's he leaving?"

"In a couple days. Paris this time."

"Would you like to have a cup of coffee sometime?"

"That would be great," she said in a tone that told me it probably wouldn't be.

The call ended with both of us feeling a little relieved that no definite plans had been made. She was a nice girl, but our connection was based on death. It's always hard to forge something tender out of that.

CHAPTER THIRTY-SIX

THAT NIGHT I MADE THE MISTAKE OF FALLING ASLEEP TO THE DISCOV-
ery Health Channel, which late at night airs very graphic shows of operations.
I dreamed I was in Mom's hospital room when a Code Blue went off and the
doctor decided there was no time to get her into the OR, so they cut Mom
open right there and the doctor reached in and pulled out Lydia Marks's head
from Mom's stomach, and the head began to talk in a lilting Irish brogue,
only it was one of those dreams where you couldn't make out the words, but
it was clear enough from the head's attitude that I was a deep disappointment
as a detective and an even deeper one as a human being. I woke with the word
reword on my tongue. I stood in the shower a long time, wondering why I
woke thinking of *reword,* until it occurred to me that maybe what I should
have thought was *reward* and, to protect myself, my brain turned it into *reword.* Of course, in some private depths, I must have realized the day before
what I had to do. It was really the only option left to me, and why I'd decided
to buy a gun and life insurance at the same time I'd decided to quit. Timing
was a problem: Marks was leaving the country in two days and the waiting period on the gun was six. I guessed I could have borrowed a gun from somebody, but the only person I knew who owned a gun for sure was Gary Paul.
On the other hand, I wasn't sure what I would do with a gun. I'd failed
marksmanship in the Academy, but just the thought of having one made me
feel better, like keeping an emergency kit of batteries and fresh water and non-
perishable canned goods tucked in a closet in case of a terrorist or nuclear
attack.

I looked up the address in the phone book, then got in my car and, instead of heading west, took Broadway to Central, to the cemetery where my
mother lay.

"Well," I told her. "I guess I've solved my first case, but it looks like it also might be my last case, and the one thing I didn't plan for or tell anyone was where I want to be buried, which, of course, would be right here next to you and Dad, but both places are taken up by other families, so I don't know where they're gonna lay me. I guess Felicia will decide that. If I had any foresight, I would have told her or written a note, but my problem is that I can't think of everything. Of course, if I had any foresight, I wouldn't have taken up this whole cockamamy detective thing in the first place, but it's like you always said, Mom, you gotta play the cards that're dealt you, even in solitaire. I never told you this, but I don't much believe in heaven or an afterlife, but I like Whitman's idea that we become part of the grass and all the green growing things, even those dead goslings, though there're some schools of thought that hold animals have no soul. Then somebody close to you dies and you've got to justify your loss with the fact that you suspect it's permanent in the cosmic sense. There's also that whole question of suffering and why it happens if there's a big Someone absolutely great and good looking after us, so I suspect the whole reason I'm not more spiritual is my shorts in the brains department. You know when I was little how I loved those seek-and-find word puzzles? I think that deal was me trying to convince myself I was smart, as if finding *artichoke* out of a jumble of letters proved anything. I love you, Mom, and I miss you, but I probably won't be back."

The traffic was heavy and slow on the interstate heading west through the ubiquitous construction zones. For the past ten years, the interstate had been torn up at various places as Knoxville's population expanded, though I suspected it had more to do with politics and the lining of the big construction company's pockets as payback for campaign contributions. It was easy to believe, but most cynical things are. Cynicism is easy; optimism takes real effort.

The house was in a development about a half mile from the park where the geese lived and Parker Hudson died. It was easily the most impressive abode in the most impressive neighborhood in Farragut. Three stories, huge columns in front, built to resemble a European castle but on a small lot, like the houses around it, with a half-circle cobblestone driveway and a life-size statue of a naked lady holding a bowl out of which water trickled into a pool. Water lilies floated on the surface, and underneath you could see the white and orange spots of the large koi, which sold for two or three hundred dollars a pop. I rang the bell and could hear it echoing inside as I waited for a guy called Jeeves to answer the door in white tie and tails. When I was in my twenties, like a lot of guys in their twenties, I imagined myself as fabulously rich, and my chief fantasy entailed a manservant who would shave me every day, because that was the essence of true wealth in my mind: It meant never having to shave myself, because, like most men, I hated to shave. I waited, but no one named Jeeves came to the door. Maybe it would be a sweet curly-haired thing of French ancestry in one of those frilly-skirted maid numbers. I rang the bell again and after about thirty seconds I heard the lock turn. The door opened, and Kenneth Marks was standing there, wearing a business suit and holding a cup of coffee.

"Mr. Ruzak," he said.

"Mr. Marks," I replied. "I was going to say I was in the neighborhood and decided to drop by, but actually I drove straight here from my apartment. Well, I stopped by my mother's grave first."

"I see."

"I'm unarmed."

"I'm relieved."

"We need to talk."

"Urgently, I assume."

"Yeah. Pretty urgently."

He stepped back and I stepped forward and then he closed the door behind me. We were standing in a huge entryway that soared the entire three stories. The floor plan was more open than I'd expected; I'd thought the rooms would be small and I'd anticipated a lot of dark nooks and crannies, because when you think of evil, you picture a kind of spider's lair of labyrinthine complexity. That was probably a comic-book approach to evil, but I'm a product of my generation, where most movies are just comic books that move.

I followed him into the living room, or it might have been a very large formal sitting room, where one entire wall was comprised of two-story-length windows with a view of the lake and the high ridge on the opposite shore. There was a piano in one corner and a sixty-five- or seventy-inch big-screen television in the other. Above the sofa upon which I sat was a massive oil painting of the Marks family: Kenneth in the middle, with an auburn-haired woman seated beside him, and Susan and Matt standing behind their parents. Susan looked around fifteen or sixteen, so I assumed the woman I was looking at was not Lydia, but Kenneth Marks's first wife. I wondered how Lydia felt looking at the picture of the Marks family, seeing the first wife sitting by her husband and Lydia standing on the outside of the picture, as it were, and for the first time I began to understand how terribly lonely Lydia Marks must have been.

"Would you like anything, Mr. Ruzak?"

"No thanks."

He sat across from me in a leather recliner that faced the TV, crossed his legs, and waited.

"Nobody knows I'm here," I said.

"Is that important?"

"I thought it might be. I'm also not wearing a wire."

"A . . . wire?"

"You know, a listening or recording device. You can frisk me if you want."

"I have no desire to frisk you, Mr. Ruzak."

"That's good. That's terrific. You trust me. This isn't going to work unless you trust me."

"What isn't going to work, Mr. Ruzak?"

I took a deep breath and let it out slowly, but that didn't steady me, so I commenced to cracking my knuckles, and the sound of the popping seemed very loud.

"Mr. Ruzak," he said. "I can think of only one reason for you to come here, so may we proceed? I'm rather busy getting ready for a business trip."

"That's right, you're going to Europe. Paris, right?"

He nodded. "How did you know?"

I swallowed. "I know pretty much everything by this point, Mr. Marks."

"Really?" He crossed his legs and pulled the cloth on the upper knee with his hands.

"Well, some things I know with certainty and some things I know with just reasonable certainty, but others with less than certain, um, certainty. Maybe I will have something. Maybe a glass of water?"

He got up at once, disappeared around a half wall, and came back with a glass of water with no ice. If I had Ken Marks's money, I thought, I'd have a little silver bell to ring when I wanted a glass of water. I thanked him, took a sip, and put my glass on the glass-topped coffee table in front of me. There were no coasters, and I worried irrationally about leaving a ring.

"You know who killed Lydia?"

I nodded. "You know I do."

He stared at me from across the room. I took another sip and saw it on the coffee table, the damned ring of sweated water.

"Okay," I said. "Enough beating around the bush." I was talking to myself as much as to him. "Let's strip it down to the bone. It occurred to me as I was working through this problem that the only way to go was to the top. It's like when you can't get satisfaction from the clerk, you go to the store manager. Or like my phone bill. My phone bill is always messed up. Month after month, there's something wrong with it, and month after month I call the phone company on that toll-free number where they put you on hold for twenty minutes and at the end of it you're talking to some barely literate, poorly trained customer service representative who usually has some kind of foreign accent. Like the last time I called. The rep sounded Indian—not American Indian but Indian Indian. You know, from India. Which he probably was, because of all the outsourcing. And after another twenty or thirty minutes, you're transferred to someone higher up and have to go through the whole spiel again, until you finally reach somebody invested with some decision-making capabilities. My point is, if you want any kind of satisfaction, you've got to go to the string puller."

He nodded. "The string puller."

"The guy in charge. That's why I'm here. Because this whole deal has really put me in an untenable position, Mr. Marks. I've closed my doors as requested, but I can't spend the rest of my life looking over my shoulder, waiting for the other shoe to drop. Eventually, the logic's going to overwhelm you, and my ass—if you'll excuse my language—my ass is grass."

"Forgive me, Mr. Ruzak, but I'm having some trouble following what you're saying."

"See, that's been a problem of mine for some time. I think I told you I worked as a night-shift security guard for a lot of years, and night work tends to do things to your head. You don't get the normal distractions and interactions of the waking, working world. You know, coworkers and lunch dates, things of that nature. You lose the grip on your own thoughts and you develop a tendency to ramble. You become susceptible to all sorts of verbal and physical ticks, like cracking your knuckles, for example, or mumbling to yourself. Mumbling is a particular hazard. You start to do it without realizing it, and the next thing you know, people are staring at you in elevators and enlarging their personal space. I've had a hard time adjusting."

"I can see that."

"But I just can't see this situation continuing indefinitely. Sooner or later, the hammer's going to fall, unless you and I can reach some sort of understanding."

"I would like nothing better than to understand you." He looked at his watch. "What do you want, Mr. Ruzak?"

"The, um, reword. I mean, the *reward.* I believe—um, I think I have this right—I believe the offer was two million dollars."

He laced his fingers together and studied me over them with an inscrutable expression.

"You have proof?" he finally asked softly.

"I have enough," I replied.

"You are satisfied it would be sufficient for a court of law?"

"Sufficient enough to get the task force extremely interested. Enough for search warrants and subpoenas. Enough to make things uncomfortable for the parties involved."

He nodded. "And what is this proof?"

"I have tapes. He took the originals, but I made copies." I held my breath. If I were him, I thought I'd demand to hear the tapes. If he did, the jig was up.

"Tapes of what?"

"The witness to Lydia's abduction identifying the getaway vehicle. The patsy set up to take the fall for the goose killing."

"I see."

"These tapes are in a location known only to me and to one other person. Nothing will be done with them and no one will know about them unless something should happen to me or to someone else."

"To whom?"

"You know whom."

"The other person?"

"Exactly."

"And what if something should happen to both of you?"

"You're getting confused, Mr. Marks."

"I have been confused, practically since you walked in the door, Mr. Ruzak."

"This other person with knowledge of the tapes is not connected to the person to whom nothing must happen. Neither you nor the person who killed your wife knows who this third person is. But they have instructions from me to turn the tapes over to the authorities if something should happen to me or to the second person."

"The second person?"

"The person who was threatened by the first person."

"I thought the second person was the person with the tapes."

"No, that's the third person. I just mentioned them first."

"Would not that make them the first person?"

"Now I'm getting confused," I said.

"I thought you were the first person."

"No, the first person is the person who threatened the second person."

"If the first person is the person who threatened the second person and the third person is the person who has the instructions, who are you?"

"I guess I would be the fourth person. You'd be the fifth. It really doesn't matter how many persons there are, Mr. Marks."

"I'm relieved. You were saying you want to collect the reward—not the public reward, but the private one, the gentlemen's agreement between us?"

"There you go." Now I was relieved. "You've got it."

"I think it might be best if we backed up a bit," he said. "I'm not entirely clear on some points."

"Oh, I know you think you've got me over a barrel here, but even if I didn't have the tapes, I probably have enough. A reporter's been snooping around, and even if Gary disposes of the Ford, I've got Mike Carroll and the rental house and Gary paying him a thousand bucks to take the fall for the goslings. Plus, I know he was trying to drive home the point, but it was really a boneheaded move for Gary Paul to take me to the lake. The only way to keep a lid on this whole deal is my silence. Now, there are only two ways to ensure my silence. The ham-handed and dangerous approach of killing me— or killing the second person, or maybe she was the third person, I can't remember—or buying my silence. I figured you, being the savvy investor, would realize it's a much safer bet to give me the cash."

"Of course," he said. "The deputy. Gary Paul."

"Yeah, the deputy Gary Paul, the first person."

"You have proof he murdered my wife?"

"It's more like evidence, and it's circumstantial, like I said."

"And you won't take this proof or evidence to the task force?"

"You've got my word on that."

He studied me over those thick fingers for a long time. Then he smiled. "Will you take a check?"

"I'd prefer cash."

"It will take a few days to arrange."

"That's fine."

"And what about, as you put it, the evil?"

"Oh, you can't get away from it," I said. "Nobody will ever go to trial for the murder, though you can never tell. Maybe the task force will break the case on their own. I've got to live with that, but at least this way there's a chance I'll be alive to live with that. That's where self-interest trumps moral character, Mr. Marks. I don't want to die and I especially don't want somebody close to me and completely innocent to die."

He nodded. "The spilling of innocent blood calls for justice. That is the ultimate moral issue, Mr. Ruzak. I am at peace with that."

He rose and offered me his hand. I took it, and his grip was very hard and he looked unblinking into my eyes. A chill went down my spine, as if I had walked over somebody's grave.

CHAPTER THIRTY-SEVEN

I DROVE BACK TO THE OFFICE AND CALLED ROGER NEWSOME, MY landlord.

"Ruzak!" he shouted. "How's the redecorating going?"

"That's one of the things I wanted to talk to you about," I said. "I'm closing up shop."

"What?"

"I'm going out of business. Things didn't work out and I need out of the lease."

"Oh, Teddy, that's too bad. It's dog-eat-dog out there, ain't it?"

"In a week or so, I can pay you back, as well as the balance on my lease."

"That's damn good to hear, Ted, because if you don't, I'm gonna take you to court and sue your fat ass for breach of contract."

Next, I called Felicia's number, but there was no answer. I should have gone home or, better yet, booked a flight to Bermuda, because if Marks and Gary were going to make their move, it probably would be sooner rather than later. Instead, I stayed and cleaned out my desk. I called the paper and placed an ad for a going-out-of-business sale. I figured the computer and furniture were worth at least a couple grand, even at forced-sale prices. I calculated the cost of paying out both leases, for the office and for my apartment, and wondered where I should move and how much of the two million Felicia deserved for my bulling my way into her life and nearly getting her killed. At least half. Around three o'clock, I lugged all the potted plants down the stairs and loaded them into my car, because I didn't plan to be back until the date of the sale and because, like I've said, it's all precious; life matters because there never has been and may never be proof it exists anywhere else. I drove to my apartment, where I pretty much holed up for the rest of the week, except to go out once to shop for groceries.

I had trouble sleeping at night. I figured this had something to do with my circumstances, this waiting for the other shoe to drop, because Marks was a businessman who weighed risks every day, and what was the life of some mediocre amateur detective worth against the possibility of the death chamber? Probably falling asleep or trying to fall asleep with the television on contributed to my sleeplessness, but the silence in my apartment was deafening without its sound, and when I turned it off, I could feel the nothingness represented by that silence pressing in upon me, literally squeezing my head, and my heart would pound with such force that I was afraid a couple of times it would explode. I'd crawl out of bed and stand by the window and look down at the empty street below and think if I moved to some tropical locale with a million dollars, I could live like a king, especially if I chose one of those terribly poor islands like Jamaica. Not only would I be rich but also safe, even from a terrorist attack. What terrorist in his right mind would ever think about attacking Jamaica? When I thought about Jamaica, I thought of goats, for some reason, hundreds of goats wandering dusty streets, and brightly colored stucco buildings with raggedy-assed children wandering around begging you for money. That would be my downfall: I'd give all the money away by the second week and be just as poor as everybody else there. You have to have a hard heart to make money, real money, and a harder one to hang on to it. Bill Gates gives away millions every year, but he makes that much in about ten minutes.

So I was wide-awake when my phone rang at two o'clock in the morning, six days after my meeting with Kenneth Marks. I didn't know who would be calling, but I had a pretty good idea what they were calling about.

"Mr. Ruzak?"

"Yes?"

"I am below the building, in the parking garage."

"What building?"

"Your building, Mr. Ruzak. I have a delivery for you."

"I guess it isn't FedEx."

"No, Mr. Ruzak. It is not FedEx."

"Let me throw some clothes on and I'll be right down."

I was fully dressed, didn't understand why I had lied, and was forced by my own lie to cool my heels an extra five minutes before heading down. Lying is the worst kind of buffoonery. The parking garage, like a lot of underground setups, was poorly lighted, having the lowest-wattage fluorescents you could buy, but I saw him right away, standing by a pillar about twenty feet from the elevators: a very big man wearing a jogging outfit and tennis shoes. On the ground beside him were two large paper grocery bags.

"I'm Teddy Ruzak," I told him unnecessarily.

"It would be best if you did not know my name," he said. He had a wide, flat face, a crooked nose, and large cauliflower ears like a boxer's. His huge hands were gloved and I could detect the faintest hint of wood smoke clinging to him.

"Oh, I'm all for what's best," I said. "My struggle is figuring out what exactly that is."

He picked up the paper bags and held them out. I wondered if they contained exactly a million apiece. It would fit with Marks's personality, very symmetrical, very balanced. I hesitated before taking the money. I should have been relieved. After all, ol' Crooked Nose could have put a bullet through my head just as easily as handing over two million dollars. Maybe I hesitated because another splinter had lodged itself into my brain at the phrase "confirmed your information."

I thanked him, took the bags, and we awkwardly disengaged, because this really wasn't the time or place for pleasantries—what do you say to a bagman? I walked quickly to the elevator without looking back and didn't turn until I was inside and the doors were closing. When I turned, he was nowhere in sight. Upstairs, I immediately pushed the two sacks under my bed, but there was no hope of sleep now. Lying over them, I was as restless as the princess over the pea; I was like that narrator in Poe's "The Tell-Tale Heart." So I climbed out of bed and paced the apartment as I waited for dawn. I had that same funny feeling I'd had right before they found Lydia's skull on the mountaintop. I was holding vigil. I kept telling myself I was safe now and Felicia was safe. Everybody was safe; it was over. I had started out a broke, unlicensed detective and now I was a millionaire. But the truth was, a crime had been committed, and I was about to find out I was up to my wide hips in it.

CHAPTER THIRTY-EIGHT

FELICIA CALLED A FEW HOURS LATER. SHE WAS CRYING. I'D NEVER heard Felicia cry, and at first I didn't know who it was. Like a lot of people's, her crying voice was different from her regular voice.

"Have you seen this morning's paper, Ruzak?"

"No. Why?"

"When does it stop? When will it stop, Ruzak?"

I told her I'd call her back, then jogged down to the Walgreens and bought a newspaper. I read the front-page story as I walked back to my apartment. I read it a second time before calling her back.

"Have you had breakfast?" I asked.

An hour later, she pulled into the space next to mine at the Krispy Kreme on Kingston Pike, and her left leg seemed to take forever getting out of the car, it was so long—not the car, her leg. She was wearing white shorts, a striped long-sleeved shirt with the sleeves rolled to her elbows and the collar turned up. She had piled her blond hair on top of her head, which I'd heard women do when they have no time to fuss with their hair. Her makeup was perfect, though, and she didn't look like somebody who had been wailing on the phone just an hour before. I cry for ten minutes, and for days my face looks like somebody's used it for a football.

"This better be good, Ruzak," she said. "You better have a good explanation for this."

"Let's go inside," I said. "Look, the HOT sign is lighted."

"What's in the shopping bags?"

"I'll show you inside."

I ordered two coffees and four regular doughnuts. I followed her with the tray to a table in the far corner, away from the door and the glass facade, to which I positioned my back so I could watch the conveyor belts carrying their precious cargo.

"How's Tommy?" I asked.

"He's fine, and how have you been, Theodore? Cut the crap and tell me what's going on."

"Let me pose it as a hypothetical. . . ."

"Hypothetical? You're going to pose another hypothetical. Well, you want to know something, Ruzak? I have a hypothetical, too. Would you like to hear my hypothetical?"

She sipped her coffee, set down the cup, tore a doughnut in two, and took a bite. One of the delightful things about doughnuts is the way a fresh one will almost dissolve on your tongue. Krispy Kreme recommends microwaving the day-olds on high for eight seconds to simulate the fresh-from-the-hot-oil taste.

"There's this old man, see," Felicia said. "And one fine morning he's taking his morning constitutional and this big black truck roars past him on—"

"It wasn't a—"

"Shut up. Roars past him on the road, killing this gaggle of itty-bitty baby birdies, and he's so shocked and outraged, he hires this overweight, underqualified PI to—"

"Investigative consultant."

"Shut up. Who puts the old geezer under hypnosis so he remembers the tag number of the big black *truck* that flattened his precious ducks—"

"Goslings."

"Shut up. Then this nice lady turns up dead in the mountains, a lady who happened to have disappeared at the same time the baby birdies bought the farm in the same neighborhood they happen to have bought it, and after the old fart remembers the tag number he's fished out of a lake—"

"That's one of the things I need to—"

"Shut up! And that left four people who knew the significance of HRT seven one nine: the shrink who hypnotized him, the overweight, underqualified PI, a deputy sheriff with the Knox County sheriff's office, and . . . who else? Oh yeah, the overweight, underqualified PI's girl Friday! Only now there aren't four; there're just three, right, Ruzak? Am I counting right? Because we lost another one last night, didn't we?"

"You know," I said, "when you put it that way, the bodies do seem to be piling up faster than in a Greek tragedy, where everybody seems to die in the end, except the gods, but of course they're immortal and can't die. Felicia, I think I see where your hypothetical is leading, and—"

"You're about to tell me this is a fantastic coincidence, aren't you? You are actually about to say we can't draw any conclusions from the fact that Gary Paul was burned alive while he slept in his own bed, aren't you?"

"The only thing I can really say about that is I don't think the fire was an accident."

She stared at me for a second. *"Really?"*

"Felicia, I should have told you this a couple of weeks ago, but I know who HRT seven one nine is." I told her the full story, from the setup with Mike Carroll in the Marks rental home—which happened to be the same house Gary Paul had died in the night before—to Gary's visit to my apartment, the trip to the lake, and his threat to kill her if I ratted him out. She ate her second doughnut while she listened but let her coffee go cold.

"He threatened my life and you didn't tell me?"

"I figured I didn't have to. Not once I, um, fired you. And I was sure if I told you, you'd go straight to the cops. See, it put me in a delicate position, Felicia. If I told the cops, he'd kill you, or if I told you, you'd go to the cops and then he'd kill you, thinking I did tell. Then he'd kill me. Or he'd kill me first, then kill you out of spite. Or vice versa. Either way, we'd be dead. I couldn't see any way out of it, so I—"

"Oh my God," she whispered.

"Oh my God what?"

"Ruzak, you didn't."

"I didn't what?"

"Jesus Christ, Teddy, you *didn't*." The color drained from her face and for a second I was afraid she was going to be sick.

"What? Oh. No, of course I didn't. I'm not . . . I could never bring myself to do something like that, Felicia. Even for you."

"Oh." She seemed strangely disappointed. "So who did?"

I watched the rows of doughnuts passing beyond the plate-glass window and their brown skin glistened with wet glaze while these two old ladies in paper hats supervised their progress.

"I think I know," I said. "And I think I know why. But I've got to be careful about jumping to conclusions. I jumped to a very big, very bad conclusion a week ago, and now Gary is dead. His blood is on my hands, Felicia; and I know, I know, he's a cold-blooded killer."

I reached under the table and put the two paper bags on the table. She gave me a quizzical look, then peeked into one of the bags. She stared inside for a long time, then looked in the other one. Then she looked up at me.

"How much?" she whispered.

"Two million. I was going to give you half. You know, for your trouble, for what I've put you through."

She was staring at the paper sacks. I slipped them back under the table, tucking them between my feet. "Ken Marks?" she asked.

I nodded. "The man who I think torched Gary brought this to me at two A.M. this morning. Probably came straight over after taking care of Gary. Now there's really only one reason I have it, just one explanation, and I think I understood even before I read this morning's paper, because he said Marks had 'confirmed my information.' See, if he was just knocking off potential witnesses, he wouldn't be paying me two million dollars for information he already had."

She looked hard at me and said, "Huh?"

"This money has meaning beyond its purchasing power, and giving it to me can mean only one thing: Ken Marks is innocent—and he is also guilty. I thought he was guilty of the one thing, but I *know* he's guilty of this thing. And now I've reached the real nub of it, Felicia, because I can walk. I've got two million dollars—well, one million, I mean—and I can go anywhere I want and do anything I want, but all I seem to want to do is sit down and cry. I thought I'd hit the wall before, but now I've hit reality with a capital *W*. Ever since I became a detective, or a nominative detective, I've been struggling with this issue of my moral character. See, I believe Ken Marks is a man of his word and a deal's a deal. If I decide it ends here, it ends here. I could even go back to being a detective, you could go back to being my secretary, and nobody would ever be the wiser. And you could even argue that justice had its day and everybody got what they deserved. Lydia got justice and so did Gary, though of the primitive variety. But still two wrongs don't make a right—or rather, one wrong doesn't make two wongs white."

" 'Two wongs white'?"

"I'm sorry, I'm very tired and talking too fast and that was like a tongue twister, like 'toy boat.' I meant 'two wrongs right.' "

"Ruzak . . ." She was searching for the right words. "Ruzak, what the hell are you talking about?"

"I'm talking about doing the right thing. What's the right thing to do? How can I be a detective now that I'm a material witness toting two million dollars in blood money in a couple of paper bags? Nothing I could have done would have settled things better than they are right now. Gary can't hurt either of us now and, anyway, nothing can bring Parker and Lydia back. On the other hand, I'm soaked to the skin with blood keeping this money and if I don't figure out what to do about it, I'm gonna end up like Lady Macbeth with the 'Out, damned spot' deal going."

"You're going to have to back up and go slow for me, Ruzak."

I sighed. "I called Susan Marks after I read the story. Her dad's been in Paris this past week, but he's coming home in two days. I've got two days to decide: Do I let it lie, which some people might reasonably argue is the right thing, or do I figure out some way to trap him, which other people might reasonably argue is the right thing? Because here's the other thing that occurred to me: What if a deal isn't a deal and Marks decides he can't trust me? Gary killed Parker to protect himself. What's to stop Kenneth Marks from doing the same thing to me?"

She sipped her cold coffee. Her nose didn't quite crinkle, but it did scooch a little—more of a half crinkle.

"I guess just one thing," she said. "Teddy Ruzak, the master of detection."

CHAPTER THIRTY-NINE

Two days later, I was waiting for him just outside the screening area at the Knoxville airport: After 9/11, unticketed people weren't allowed on the tiny concourse. I was wearing a new trench coat with the collar turned up and a floppy hat, not to disguise myself, but because it was raining and the trench coat had large pockets, in which my new semiautomatic made hardly a bulge—plus, like a lot of big men in trench coats, I looked pretty good. I came the closest I ever had to looking the part of hard-boiled private eye. I wasn't completely comfortable, though I looked good, and looking good takes you a long way toward comfort. I may have looked it, but I was a far cry from hard-boiled, and the gun might as well have been a cap pistol, given my proficiency with firearms.

This wide walkway leading up to the metal detectors and screeners was divided by a fountain constructed of boulders hauled north from the Little Pigeon River in the mountains. It was pretty to look at but very loud, a constant humming roar, so friends and family waiting to greet the arriving flights practically had to shout to be heard. The incessant sound of running water also had an effect on my bladder; I had been to the men's room twice since arriving at the airport. I stood apart from the group, near the big windows that overlooked the gates and the runway. I watched as the plane touched down and slowly taxied to the gate. I looked at my watch. Right on time. That was good, because I had people waiting for us back at the office and I was adverse to keeping people waiting as a general principle.

He was walking by himself, pulling a little rolling carry-on. He didn't see me, or if he did, he didn't recognize me. I fell into step with him and said, "Mr. Marks," raising my voice a little to be heard over the roar of the falls.

He barely slowed down. "Mr. Ruzak." So maybe he had seen me, or was adjusting brilliantly to the surprise. Another thing that separates the very successful from the rest of us is their ability to adapt to rapid change.

"Have a good flight?"

"I had a long flight, Mr. Ruzak."

"You must be tired, and then there's the jet lag. I wouldn't bother you, Mr. Marks, but there's been a development."

He didn't ask me what the development was. He just kept walking toward the escalators that took you down to the baggage-claim area.

"Gary Paul died three nights ago when the house he was renting from you burned to the ground."

He still didn't say anything, just stepped onto the escalator, which was too narrow to stand abreast, so I rode a couple steps back from him, and for the first time, I noticed a bald spot on his crown, which might explain why he wore his hair so long: It wasn't a fashion statement; it was a comb-over. For some reason, I felt an irrational wave of pity for Kenneth Marks wash over me. It wasn't too late to call this off, and besides, who was I to think I could outwit a guy like Kenneth Marks, who made a living going toe-to-toe against the best and brightest business minds in the world? It was like a dog playing chess with Bobby Fischer. We got off the escalator and I followed him to the baggage claim, where he stood stiffly erect, his posture absolutely perfect, and again this struck me as quintessentially German, the quasi-militarist precision of the man. But speaking of precision, the Swiss are known for their watches—and army knives.

"I hardly see what that has to do with me, Mr. Ruzak."

"Really? Well, maybe not, but it's got everything to do with our little deal, and that's what we need to talk about."

"Very well."

"Not here. I don't know what your schedule is like, but if you don't mind, I'd like to take you back to my office."

"Why?"

"There's someone I want you to meet."

"Mr. Ruzak, I believe I told you my flight was quite long. I'm tired. Perhaps in a day or two . . ."

"I'm afraid it can't wait, Mr. Marks. See, a potential witness has come forward, and the three of us need to sit down and hammer this thing out before the whole shebang blows up in our faces."

He raised an eyebrow at me. "A potential witness?"

"I'm afraid so."

"A potential witness to what?"

"I'd really rather not talk about it here, Mr. Marks."

He thought about it, or at least I assumed he was thinking about it. But you shouldn't always assume just because someone falls silent that they're thinking about something.

"Very well," he said.

His luggage was one of those hard-sided numbers about the size of a large cedar chest and must have weighed about a hundred pounds. I know because I pulled it off the conveyor belt for him and walked behind him, pulling his luggage to the sidewalk outside like his coolie. A big black Lincoln was parked there, engine idling, and as we stepped out, the big crooked-nosed man with the cauliflower ears swung his bulk from the driver's seat. He gave me a quick nod, one rich man's henchman to another, and snapped open a large umbrella, holding it over the man as Ken Marks turned to me.

"I'll follow you there," he said.

"I'm parked in the garage. Why don't you have your driver pull up and I'll follow you?"

"Very well." Mr. Crooked Nose held the door for him and he disappeared behind the tinted glass.

Downtown Knoxville was a twenty-five-minute drive from the airport, which was actually not in Knoxville but in Alcoa, named for the aluminum company that was the major employer there. The rain couldn't decide whether it wanted to be fitful or torrential; I kept having to adjust my wiper speed. I'd always liked this drive on Alcoa Highway into Knoxville, with the high ridges on either side of the road, and especially in the fall, when the leaves changed, though spring wasn't bad, with all the dogwoods blooming, the white-and-pink blossoms seeming to float on pillows of bright green. The blossoms had fallen and the rain turned the leaves a deep emerald green and whispered as it fell to the carpet of rotting leaves from the year before, the compost that fed the saplings. Life was like that, indefatigable: After meteors and ice ages and cataclysmic upheavals, wars and famines and droughts and plagues, life just kept coming back for more. It's been fashionable since Hiroshima to be down on the human race and our chances for survival, but I'm an optimist, like I've said. I've never really believed we'll end our days in a single orgasmic instant of fire or go down in a long twilight struggle against forces more in love with death than with life. Even stuff like Ebola and AIDS and global warming don't concern me too much. Even though I lack the spiritual component to combat that kind of despair, I really don't think human beings have an apocalypse in their future, beyond the inevitable blowing up of the sun in about four billion years. It's easy to get down on ourselves, but if the race is really in trouble, what Kenneth Marks and Gary Paul did wouldn't be crimes and, probably most importantly, Parker Hudson wouldn't have given a flip about the deaths of six baby geese.

Crooked Nose double-parked in front of the Ely Building and waited on the sidewalk, holding the umbrella over Marks's balding crown while I searched for a parking place on Church. I saw Marks talking on his cell phone and I wondered, first, whom he was talking to; second, if Crooked Nose was the thug who'd started the fire that killed Gary; and, third, if I would ever find a place to park in this town that never seemed to have enough parking spaces. I finally found a spot on Gay Street and it took me about five minutes to maneuver my little Sentra into the spot. I'd never been good at parallel parking.

I hoofed it the three blocks back to the Ely, my floppy hat pulled low over my forehead, the gun bumping against my thigh. Marks said something sotto voce to Crooked Nose, who got back in the car. I breathed a sigh of relief. The muscle would stay outside, which indicated a measure of trust on Marks's part. He followed me up the creaky stairs, and my labored breathing sounded very loud in the close space. Marks glided silently as a ghost.

We stepped into the little secretary's area and shook the rainwater off our coats. I took off my hat and hung it on the rack by the door, then shrugged off my coat and hung that on the peg below the hat. Marks was staring into my office, at the back of the man's head sitting in one of the visitor's chairs. I nodded toward the secretary's desk as she came around to take his coat.

"Mr. Marks, this is my secretary, Felicia."

"How do you do," she said. "Can I get you anything, Mr. Marks? We have coffee, juice, Evian, soda . . ."

"The office sprang for one of those minifridges," I told him.

"Nothing, thank you." He looked at his watch.

"I guess I'll have some coffee," I told her, and waved him into my office. I made the introductions. "Mr. Marks, this is Mike Carroll."

Marks barely glanced at him. He sat in the other chair with the same Teutonic stoicism as the first time he sat there, which seemed a very long time ago. Mike was nervous, kind of rocking in the chair, ankles crossed. He was wearing one of those woven leather ankle bracelets or anklets and a COME TO JAMAICA, MON T-shirt.

"How long is this gonna take?" Mike asked. He watched her set my coffee by my elbow and added, "Nobody offered me anything."

"We got any half-and-half in there?" I asked her.

"I'll check, Mr. Ruzak. Mr. Carroll, what would you like?"

"You got any diet Coke?"

"Just regular, I think."

"What about Dr Pepper?"

"I don't think so. I'd have to look."

"If you don't have Dr Pepper, I'll take a Mountain Dew."

She bent over the open half fridge and said, "We don't have any Mountain Dew. How about a Pepsi?"

"What about the Dr Pepper?"

"No . . ."

"Mr. Ruzak," Marks said. "Do you think it's possible we could discuss the matter you have insisted we discuss this morning?"

"All right, give me a Coke," Mike Carroll said.

She handed him his Coke and me my half-and-half.

"Will there be anything else right now, Mr. Ruzak?"

"I don't think so, Felicia."

"Do you need me to stay and take notes?"

"No," Marks said, raising his voice a little. "No notes."

"Maybe no notes are necessary, Felicia," I said.

"Okay." She flashed a smile in Marks's direction and went back to the secretary's area. From my desk, I could see her right shoulder and half her head during the rest of the meeting.

"Perhaps now you can tell me why I am here, Mr. Ruzak," Marks said.

"Yeah. I'd like to know the same thing," Mike said.

"There were just a couple of things I wanted to clear up," I said. "A few dangly little threads. See, for the past couple of months, I've been operating on this working theory, and now it's not fitting together so well, and I thought maybe you two could help smooth out the edges a little."

"I don't know what the hell you're talking about, Ruzak," Mike Carroll said. "And I don't give a shit about your theories or rough edges. Like I told you before, I don't know nothing about any murder of anybody."

"I'm glad to hear you say that, Mike. I've been going back and forth on that in the R & D phase of my theory—you know, 'What did Mike know and when did he know it?' I really didn't know how tight you were with Gary, but I figured it couldn't be too tight, since you rolled so easy on him when I waved a little cash under your nose. Spilling the beans on that gosling ruse would have been an incredibly stupid move if you were involved in Lydia's murder."

Mike stared at me and said, "Huh?"

"Mr. Ruzak," Marks said. "Who is this man?"

"This man is Mike Carroll. He's a friend of Gary Paul."

"Not a close friend, like he said," Mike said.

"You said he was a witness. A witness to what?"

"That's a good fucking question, because I haven't witnessed shit."

"Come on, Mike," I said. "There's a lady present."

He glanced over his shoulder toward Felicia's area.

"And as a friend of Gary, I thought he might tie up one of those danglies that's been bugging me." I pulled the MISSING poster from my desk drawer and held it up for Mike. "Do you recognize this woman?"

Mike's eyes cut away. "Yeah."

"Who is it?"

"I don't remember her name. I met her a couple times, maybe, but that was over a year ago."

"Who is it?" I asked again. Marks had turned his full attention on Mike.

"Gary's girlfriend," he said in a soft voice. Marks took a deep breath. I slipped the poster back in the desk, closed the drawer, and took a sip of coffee.

"How do you know she's his girlfriend?"

"A couple of reasons, Ruzak. First, he was draped all over her. And second, that's how he introduced her—'Mike, this is my girlfriend.'"

I turned to Marks. "Lydia managed your properties for you while you were overseas?" He nodded. "That's it, then," I said. "That's the piece I didn't have. I couldn't figure what Gary's connection to Lydia was if it wasn't Mr. Marks here. Thanks, Mike. I think I've got it all now, Mr. Marks, and if you don't mind, I'd like to run my working theory by you and see what you think."

He gave another brief nod. He was the picture of studied calm. It played counterpoint to Mike's obvious discomfort.

"Can I go now?" Mike asked.

"I don't see why not," I said. "Mr. Marks probably wouldn't want you here for the next part."

He set his Coke on my desk—I hadn't seen him take the first sip—fairly sprang from the chair, spun around, and headed for the door. I picked up the can so it wouldn't leave a ring and put it back in the minifridge. I grabbed a bottle of Evian because coffee dehydrates you and my mouth was very dry. I sat behind the desk and called out for Felicia to hold my calls.

I took a sip of water and said to Marks, "Did you know Americans spend more on bottled water than on gasoline?"

"Do they?" He had laced his fingers together, his elbows on the armrests of the visitor's chair, staring at me over his diamond rings the same way as the first time he'd sat in this chair.

"That's what I heard," I said. "But it's one of those statistics you sort of take at face value. We live in an age of specialization, Mr. Marks, and I bet eighty or ninety percent of everything we believe is based on something we haven't experienced firsthand. People say it's also the age of cynicism, but we trust a helluva lot, when you think about it. Like during the Cold War: It was pretty much accepted fact that the Soviets were ahead of us or at least equal to us in nukes, when they never actually were. We were always kicking their butts in the bomb department, but it suited somebody's purpose to convince us we weren't. Or those nutritional labels on foods. How do I really know there're X number of carbs in a Twinkie?"

"What," he asked, "is a Twinkie?"

"A snack cake that's supposedly very bad for you. Twinkies seem smaller now than when I was a kid, but the world seems smaller, too, even mailboxes, so it's hard to tell."

"I have had difficulty, Mr. Ruzak," Kenneth Marks said, "since meeting you, in deciding whether these digressions are designed to make their objects uncomfortable or to put them off their guard, or whether there is any design to them at all—in other words, are they a means of avoiding the matter at hand or merely the meanderings of an undisciplined mind?"

"Probably more the latter," I said. "My brain's like that stereotypical guy in his underwear sprawled all over the sofa on a Sunday afternoon." I reached under the desk and pulled out the paper sacks and set them on the desktop between us.

"What is this?" he asked.

"The money," I said. "All of it. You can count it if you want; I don't mind."

"You are returning it?"

"I'm afraid I don't have a choice, Mr. Marks. No matter how I spin it in my meandering mind, this money really came to me under false pretenses, and to keep it kind of elevates, or de-elevates, me into a league I'd really rather not belong to."

"What league? What are you talking about, Mr. Ruzak?"

"The league of bad moral character, Mr. Marks. See, I lied to you to get this money—well, the money wasn't the point of the lie, really—that's one strike. And keeping the money when I know why you gave it to me is the second strike. Two strikes implies a third, which, I guess, is that keeping the money and keeping my mouth shut will probably land me in prison."

"What do you mean, you lied to me?"

"About the tapes. I don't have any tapes or any other kind of proof linking Gary to Lydia's murder. But I figured I needed you to believe that so you'd get Gary to back off Felicia."

"Who is Felicia?"

"My secretary. You just met her. She's sitting right over there. See, I figured Gary was working for you. That was my big mistake, my big boner."

"Your . . . big boner?"

"You bet. And it just goes to prove what sorts of heartache and mayhem can come from erroneous beliefs. I thought you hired Gary to kill Lydia, so when Gary threatened Felicia, I thought the only way to protect her was to go to you and pretend I didn't know that piece of the puzzle and take you up on your offer. Only that wasn't a piece of the puzzle, because the puzzle was something entirely different; I knew it was Gary but thought it was you, and it wasn't you at all."

He was staring at me dead-on when he said, "I didn't kill my wife, Mr. Ruzak."

"I know that now. And my point is, if I'd known that then, I wouldn't have lied and I wouldn't have taken your money, but I did and now Gary Paul is dead, which could lead somebody to believe I just used you for two reasons: to get rich and to get rid of Gary Paul."

He nodded. "It is a very compelling argument, Mr. Ruzak."

"You bet it is, and that makes me nervous as hell, Mr. Marks. Somebody could look at these facts and come to the conclusion that my goal all along was to put Gary six feet under."

"And was that your goal?"

"I'm not that sneaky or that clever."

He nodded. He didn't elaborate, so I didn't know if he agreed with the first part, the second, or both.

"I didn't kill my wife," he repeated softly. "I loved her." And then Kenneth Marks did an extraordinary thing, the last thing I would have expected him to do: He began to cry. He buried his face inside his bejeweled hands and sobbed like a baby. His big shoulders shook and his knees pressed together as he leaned forward, and there was really nothing to do until he could get a grip on himself. I looked over his shoulder toward the secretary's desk. She had turned around and was staring at his bowed back as he cried. I held up my hand, signaling her to stay put.

"Have you ever loved someone so much that the thought of losing her is simply unbearable, Mr. Ruzak?"

I thought about it. "No."

"After she disappeared, and particularly after they found her, the only thing that gave me any peace was the thought of ripping her killer's head from his shoulders. I would fall to sleep every night with the fantasy of dismembering him slowly, of disemboweling him and scattering his steaming entrails as carrion, of ripping his heart still beating from his chest. . . ."

"Okay," I said. "I get it. Let me ask you something, Mr. Marks, because these danglies have been driving me crazy. . . . You didn't know Gary and Lydia were lovers, did you?"

He shook his head. Reminding him of Mike's revelation helped him get a grip on himself, I think.

"I knew him, of course," he said, removing a white monogrammed handkerchief from his pocket and wiping his face. "Or rather, I knew of him. I rented that house to him."

"And Lydia would manage your rentals when you were out of town."

He nodded.

So did I. "See, that dovetails pretty neatly into my current working theory. I wondered how the two of them hooked up, given the fact that Lydia was so shy and a virtual shut-in. However it happened, Gary and Lydia became lovers, and I bet there was some kind of falling-out. Maybe she tried to break up with him, or maybe he was trying to extort some of your money from her, or maybe there was a big fight and he hit her—maybe didn't even mean to kill her—but anyway, that morning he was on his way to the mountains to dump the body when he hit those geese. That got Parker Hudson involved, which got me involved, which ultimately got both Parker and Gary dead. And that leaves just one question, Mr. Marks, beyond the normal, unanswerable ones about the human heart: If you had known they were lovers, would you still have killed him?"

He hesitated only half a breath. "Of course I still would have killed him."

"But without any proof. You never asked to listen to the tapes. You just took me at my word and killed him."

"No, I did not, Mr. Ruzak. Gary Paul confessed."

"He did?"

"I made sure one was forthcoming before I exacted justice."

"Well, that's very thorough. You're a . . . very thorough man, Mr. Marks."

He stood up. "Are we finished, Mr. Ruzak?"

"I think that's the difference between you and me, Mr. Marks," I said as she got up from her desk and came into the room to stand behind him. "If I had known the truth, I wouldn't have asked for your two million dollars. I wouldn't have pretended to know things I didn't know and to have things I didn't have. That's what really gets you into deep water in the moral character department."

"You are going to the authorities, then?" His arms hung loosely at his sides while he clenched and unclenched his fists.

"Well, that brings me to my last lie," I said. "I mean, in regard to this case. I guess to represent it as my last lie ever would be another lie, since the odds of that are pretty slim and it's one of those promises most people are doomed to break. The money is tempting, Mr. Marks, plus the fact that you've shown you're not the kind of man who lets moral issues stand in the way of your desires. Like one day you might decide it's too dangerous to allow me to walk around knowing what I know and do a Gary Paul on me. So the truth is, I've already gone to the authorities."

He glanced over his shoulder at her, then looked back at me.

"Mr. Marks," I said. "This isn't my secretary. This is Detective Leslie Garrison with the Tennessee Bureau of Investigation." Then I added, I'm not sure why, "I'm sorry."

He remained stock-still as she stepped up behind him and pulled his hands behind his back and told him he was under arrest for the murder of Gary Paul. We stared at each other as she read him his rights, and his expression didn't change. After she asked him if he understood his rights, he said to me, "You are a . . . very complicated man, Mr. Ruzak."

"It'd be easy to think the worst of me at this moment," I admitted. "Like Hamlet—was he insane or just acting insane? I just want to do the right thing, Mr. Marks. Sometimes that brings more grief to people than doing the wrong thing, but it's like that old saying, It's better to be lucky than smart."

CHAPTER FORTY

Two days after the arrest of Kenneth Marks, the police picked up the man he hired to torch Gary Paul, the wood smoke–smelling crooked-nosed man, whose name turned out to be Kaczmarczyk. That had to be Polish, and I felt a little like an honest Italian burdened with the stereotype of the Cosa Nostra.

Two months later, the case was still getting a lot of press. Strangers were recognizing me on the street and some even crossed it to shake my hand. The phone was ringing off the hook, mail was pouring in, and people were showing up at the door. Even a couple of those network news-magazine shows had called me, interested in doing a story. Felicia told me she could put in her full forty hours if she could bring Tommy to work on the days when the babysitter fell through, and I said sure, the more the merrier, and the kid turned out to be a terror, crawling all over the furniture, tearing stuff out of my filing cabinets, and jumping into my chair every time I got up, spinning in it like he was at the teacup ride at Disney. Felicia and I took a meeting about the Tommy issue and she said he'd be much calmer if there was a TV somewhere in the office where he could watch his shows, so the firm sprang for a television and cable service so he could loll in his pajamas in Felicia's area and watch *Blues Clues* and *Little Bear,* and whenever an episode came on with Little Bear's big seafaring father in it, he'd point at the screen and yell, "Roo-ZACK! Roo-ZACK." And Felicia would laugh one of her nose-crinkling laughs.

One morning when Felicia had brought Tommy with her, I went outside just to get a breather from the bedlam, and there was Susan Marks sitting on my stoop, hugging her knees and looking at nothing in particular, just like the day she came to ask for my help. I sat beside her on the steps and looked at nothing with her.

"I can't even begin to imagine what it must be like," I said.

"Matt's the one I'm really worried about," she said. "He's had a total meltdown. He lies in his room all day with the door closed, listening to Led Zeppelin."

"Well, everybody has to find their own way."

"You're so . . . philosophical."

"I don't blame you for being sore," I said. "But you gotta understand I wasn't trying to trick him—well, I did trick him when I brought him here that day. I was talking about the other trick, the one that got Gary killed. But it really wasn't a trick on my part, since I thought your dad was involved in Lydia's death. I've learned a big lesson about going off half-cocked, but like most big lessons, it came with a pretty hefty price tag. Some people might say I'm too trusting. For example, I trusted myself that I knew the truth, and that got Gary Paul killed. You know, that thing about unintended consequences. Are you talking about this with anyone? I know this great lady doctor who might be able to help."

She didn't answer. Instead, she pulled a long white envelope from the pocket of her khaki shorts and held it out without looking at me. Inside was a check for $500,000.

"What is this?" I asked.

"A check for five hundred thousand dollars."

"The reward?"

She nodded.

"But that was for the arrest and conviction. Nobody was arrested or convicted. They were offed in a house fire."

She didn't say anything.

"It's like blood money," I told her. "And rewards are offered for doing something honorable."

"You won't take it?"

"Okay," I said. "I'll take it." I didn't want to add insult to injury by arguing with her about it—plus, it was half a million dollars—so I stuck the envelope in my coat pocket.

"What did you decide?" she asked.

"About what?"

"The dog."

"I haven't yet. I've been, um, kind of wrapped up in my work."

"It should definitely be a Great Pyrenees," she said. "The personalities would mesh perfectly."

"What, they're dim-witted?"

"They're guardians," she said. "They're bred to watch over things, like sheep or goats. Very gentle and loyal and big and . . . and kind." She still hadn't looked at me. A tear rolled down her cheek and she brushed it angrily away with the back of her small hand. I should have taken that hand, seized it, pressed it to my breast, and promised her the hurt would go away and everything would be fine and she would never feel pain again, but I was through with the empty promises.

"You're never going to go out with me, are you?" I asked. "That's why you brought up the dog."

"I can't even tell you what I'll be doing next week," she said. She finally looked at me. The sun peeks through the clouds and says, I'm still here.

"Well," she said, sighing. "I'm late for work."

She stood up and I stood up and there was really nothing to say. I had a couple of suggestions, like usual, but I held my tongue. She started away, her arms folded over her chest. Suddenly, she turned, came back to me, and, rising on her toes, kissed my cheek and called me "Mr. Ruzak."

I went back upstairs. We were hip-deep into summer; it was eighty degrees by ten o'clock, and despite the two fans, one in my office and one in Felicia's area, the dry-cleaning fumes lingered like the smell of a dead animal rotting beneath someone's porch. I figured maybe with this five hundred grand, I could move into better space, but I had already signed the contract to remodel and still had seven months to go on my lease.

Just before lunchtime, Felicia ushered in a little guy with a cheap suit and an even cheaper haircut. She left him in one of the visitor's chairs to run back and answer the phone and to tell Tommy for the six hundredth time to be quiet.

"Mr. Ruzak," he said. "My name is Walter Hinton and I'm with the Tennessee Private Investigation and Polygraph Commission."

"Oh," I said. "You bet. Good to see you. You want anything? Coffee? Coke? Evian? We just sprang for a refrigerator and it's fully stocked. We even have lemonade, if you don't mind the kind in those little pouches with the plastic straw."

"I'm actually more interested in seeing your license."

"My license?"

"Your license to privately investigate criminal and civil matters in the state of Tennessee. You see, Mr. Ruzak, we've reviewed our records and can't locate either your application or a copy of your exam."

"That's probably because I haven't applied or taken the exam. I was meaning to take the exam, but a murder case came up and I missed the test date."

"So you are aware you must be licensed in the state of Tennessee?"

"Oh sure, but see, the thing is, I wasn't what you might call actually practicing anything. I was consulting."

"Consulting?"

"Yeah. The name on the door's a little misleading, mostly because people have trouble adjusting to new ideas. It says 'The Highly Effective Detection & Investigation Company,' but really I'm an investigative consultant."

"I'm sorry, Mr. Ruzak, but I fail to see the difference."

"It's more a distinction than a difference. Are you here to shut me down?"

"I'm here to determine if you're in violation of Tennessee statutes."

"Would it make any difference if I told you I'm already on the list for the next test?"

"Only if you shut your doors until you pass and receive your license from the state."

"Things are really hopping, Mr. Hilton. . . . Hilton. Any relation to the hotel people?"

"No, no relation, because my name isn't Hilton; it's Hinton."

"Oh, sure. I should have written it down. Do you get that a lot?"

"Get what a lot?"

"People who think you're related to the hotel Hiltons."

"No, because my name isn't Hilton; it's Hinton. Mr. Ruzak, are you trying to provoke me?"

"I wouldn't dream of provoking you, Mr. Hinton. I know what that's like, someone getting your name wrong. People get mine wrong all the time. When I first opened up shop, I couldn't even get the right name on the letterhead, but I straightened all that out."

"It just seems to me you're trying to muddy the waters, confuse the issue."

"I've certainly been guilty of that. I was saying that with things so busy around here, the issue with the license puts me in a difficult position."

"In all honesty, Mr. Ruzak, the state could care less about your position. The law—"

"Oh, I'm a firm believer in the law. One of the reasons, maybe even the chief reason, I went into this business in the first place."

"Then you'll understand if the state fines you and secures a court order to shut down your operation here."

"I was thinking about taking a vacation."

He smiled a humorless, bureaucratic smile.

"At the end of which, you can take the test, we can review your application, and, if so warranted, we'll issue you a license."

"I can't think of a more satisfactory resolution," I said. We shook hands and I walked him to the door.

Felicia said, "Busted."

"Maybe I need a vacation," I said. "One of the biggest mistakes people make is rushing through traumatic experiences looking for closure. Nobody takes the time to absorb anything anymore."

Like he always did when he caught me standing still, Tommy came over and sat on my foot and held up his fat little hands.

"Ride! Ride!" he shouted, lifting his wide face up at me.

"So now I cancel all your appointments and take the phone off the hook?" Felicia asked.

I grabbed Tommy's hands and lifted my leg straight out, whooshing him about two feet off the floor. He screeched with delight. "Roo-ZACK! Roo-ZACK!"

"I don't know, what do you think?" I asked.

"By the time he gets that court order, you'll have taken the test."

"You're assuming I'm going to pass."

"You don't have a choice, Ruzak."

"Well, we could probably afford the fine," I said. I lowered Tommy to the floor, pulled the envelope from my pocket, and showed her the check. She grabbed it out of my hand and stuffed it into her Louis Vuitton knockoff purse. At least I *hoped* it was a Louis Vuitton knockoff purse.

"I need a raise, Ruzak," she said.

"Done," I said. Meanwhile, Tommy was back on my shoe, shaking his fists at me. I gave him a couple more rides, then swung him by the wrists onto the love seat, where he curled up and hooted with joy.

I looked at Felicia, and she was actually smiling at me. She pulled the hair back from her face and asked, "Did I ever thank you for saving my life?"

"I'm sure you did," I said.

"Well, in case I didn't, thanks."

"You're welcome."

I sat down at my desk and looked out the window. The sun was directly overhead and bright summer light filled the space between the buildings. Felicia left with Tommy; they were going to the Subway at Market Square and she asked if I wanted anything. I told her I'd brought my lunch. The phone kept ringing, but I let the machine pick up while I stared out the window at the brick wall. I heard the outer door open and close again, and I said, "Hello, Eunice."

"Goodness, how did you know it was me?"

I swung around in my chair to face her. She was wearing a yellow summery-type frock and a bonnet over a poofy blond wig. She looked like what Dolly Parton might look like in another thirty years, depending on the extent of plastic surgery she might get. She was wearing the same orthopedic shoes, though. She sat in a visitor's chair and plopped the ubiquitous purple purse in her wide lap. Purple purse, yellow dress. Mrs. Eunice Shriver clearly did not know how to accessorize.

"I saw your reflection in the window," I explained. I made a show of pulling out my yellow legal pad and clicking out fresh lead in my mechanical pencil.

"I see you're quite the celebrity now, Theodore," she said.

"I'm thinking of writing a book about my exploits," I said. "The working title is *The Gosling Affair.* What do you think?"

"It's not the sort of book I would read," she sniffed.

"What's your taste? I'm thinking *Gone with the Wind* or maybe those Harlequin romances. Or those true-crime paperbacks."

She let the question slide past her. Maybe it was too intimate a detail. "It's a poor title, Theodore. People will think it's about a love triangle among birds."

"You know," I said, "you might have a point there. I can't stand those books with the anthropomorphic animals, like *Watership Down* or that one they made us read as seniors, *Animal Farm.* It's kind of a creepy literary device and it disturbs my sense of the cosmic order. I have a couple other working titles. *Murder Most Fowl. The Wild-Goose Case. Fowl Play.* But there was a movie a few years back with that name; I think it starred Mel Gibson and Goldie Hawn. It was spelled differently, maybe, but I think there was a scene that involved birds—not geese, but chickens. I don't remember much more about it, except that Mel Gibson showed his ass in that movie. I was also leaning toward *Theodore Ruzak: The (Unlicensed) Master of Detection,* which sounds a little self-serving, which is why I put the *unlicensed* part in."

"Theodore," she said. "I really didn't come all the way downtown to discuss literature with you."

"I didn't think so."

"It smells like a child's been in here."

I gave the air a sniff, but all I could smell were dry-cleaning fumes (they were worse the hotter it got) and her perfume or body powder, or whatever it was.

"That would be my secretary's," I said. "She brings her son in occasionally."

"Oh. I thought perhaps you were diversifying into day care."

"I hadn't thought of that. It's generally a good idea not to throw all your eggs in one basket."

"Theodore," she said, "I am a busy woman and a paying client, and I would appreciate it if you would stop changing the subject and going off on wild tangents like talking animals and books and movies in which Mel Gibson exposes himself."

"You're right," I said. My stomach growled. My pimento cheese sandwich was no more than five feet from her in the minifridge by the bathroom door.

"Have you any leads in my case?"

"Not many, but I've ruled out the mayor."

"I'm not sure that's altogether prudent."

"I can't find a motive," I said. "Do you even know the mayor?"

"Goodness, what a question!"

"In fact," I said, "I can't really find a motive for anybody to kill you. Why would anyone want to kill you, Eunice?"

"Do you doubt, Theodore, after all I've done, after the kind of life I've led, that I would come to the twilight of my life with no enemies at all?"

"I don't guess many people do, even the Pope. Maybe certain people do, like hermits or mentally disabled people. I'd guess it'd be hard to hold a grudge against the retarded. Although there's always stuff in the paper about some state wanting to execute a retarded guy, and that's like all of society being your enemy."

She puffed out a hard jet of breath and said, "I have the perfect title: *Theodore Ruzak: The Long-Winded Detective.*"

"I am profligate," I admitted. "Particularly with breath. And thought. I waste a lot of thought. If my life had taken a different path, I'd be sitting in some ivory tower right now, working on a paper about the economy of thought. But that would make me like that televangelist who preached against the evils of prostitution while he cruised truck stops."

"That is a horrible indulgence, Theodore, though quite understandable. A man such as you must get quite lonely at times."

"Oh, no. I said I would be *like* that. I've never done anything like that— never even thought about it."

"Then why did you bring it up?"

"I'm not sure now, but it probably was related to something we were talking about."

"I am an old woman and my memory is certainly not what it used to be, but I'm fairly confident, Theodore, that our conversation had nothing to do with prostitutes."

"Well," I said. "There you have it."

We smiled at each other for a moment. We were on the same wavelength, which was comforting and disturbing at the same time.

"But I was going to say," Eunice Shriver said, "there are certain people whom I have named in the list I gave you who would be more than happy to see me six feet under. Another reason I came today is to give you an additional name."

She reached into her purse and handed over a single sheet of typing paper. I wondered why she'd bothered. She could have just told me the name, but maybe she wanted everything in writing.

I looked at the name and said, "Oh, come on, Eunice."

"Would you not say that revenge is a very strong motive for murder?"

"Eunice, you had nothing to do with the death of Parker Hudson and you know it."

I had raised my voice a little, and it was probably that more than what I said that made her stiffen and pull back in the chair.

"Also," I said, "how would his poor widow know that you did?"

"Because," and now her voice dropped to a whisper, "because Parker and I . . ."

"Eunice."

"We were . . ."

"Just stop, Eunice."

"Lovers!" She pulled the white hankie from her purse and dabbed her eyes. I was about to light into her, but that was something her kids did all the time and it sure hadn't fixed anything.

"This is pretty serious," I said. "And Mrs. Hudson knew about it?"

"Not during the time of our torrid affair, no. Later."

"Eunice, you didn't call Mrs. Hudson, did you?"

She didn't say anything. She wasn't looking at me, but over my shoulder toward the blank brick wall on the other side of the alley.

"Jeez, Eunice, talk about salt in the wound. Why would you do something like that?"

"Because the truth will out, Theodore. The truth will always out. We were taking our usual morning stroll around the lake, Parker and I, when we saw that awful man Gary Paul hit those goslings. Parker saw inside the car and shouted, 'There goes Lydia!' "

" 'There goes Lydia'?"

" 'There goes Lydia!' And I asked him who this Lydia was and he told me."

"He told you? He told you what? Oh. He was seeing her, too?"

All she could do was nod. I said, "So you killed Lydia because you were jealous?"

Another nod.

"And you told all this to Mrs. Hudson?"

"I couldn't keep it in any longer," she whispered.

"Yeah, you seem to have a problem with that. Okay, look, this is what we're going to do." I wrote a name and phone number on the top sheet of my pad, tore it off, and handed it to her. "This lady is tops in her field, Eunice. She specializes in the treatment of serial criminals and adulteresses."

" 'Dr. Stephanie Fredericks,' " she read, frowning.

"Call her and set up an appointment. Today, Eunice. I'm one hundred percent certain she'd love to meet you. You're worth at least one, maybe two articles in *The American Psychiatric Journal.*"

"Do you really think so, Theodore?"

"I'd bet half a million dollars on it."

She went limp with relief. That's all she was really after: a plan of action, a road map to the way out. She even gave me a hug at the door.

Felicia and Tommy came back about fifteen minutes later, while I was eating my pimento cheese sandwich at my desk. Tommy ran straight to me, crawled into my lap, and grabbed the Clausen pickle spear from the paper plate. Pickle juice ran down his forearm and dripped off his elbow onto my $75 pair of dress slacks. Then he wiped his sticky face on my $150 dress shirt, closed his eyes, and fell asleep.

Felicia came over to move him to the love seat, but I told her it was okay because with his head right under my nose, I could smell his lavender-smelling hair instead of the dry-cleaning fumes. She returned to her desk and I sat there with her kid in my lap, and I was thinking this was it. This was what I had been waiting for all those years on the night shift with the aching somewhere in the vicinity of my heart, not Tommy Kincaid snoozing in my lap, per se, though that was part of it, but the whole thing. For the first time in a long time, I didn't feel like Mr. Sad Sack Teddy Ruzak schlepping through the second half of his life like he'd schlepped through the first. For the first time in a long time, I didn't feel so crummy. For the first time in a long time, I actually felt pretty damn good.

THE HIGHLY
EFFECTIVE DETECTIVE
Goes to the Dogs

ALSO BY RICHARD YANCEY

ADULT FICTION
The Highly Effective Detective
A Burning in Homeland

MEMOIR
Confessions of a Tax Collector

CHILDREN'S FICTION
The Extraordinary Adventures of Alfred Kropp
Alfred Kropp: The Seal of Solomon

THE HIGHLY
EFFECTIVE DETECTIVE
Goes to the Dogs

RICHARD YANCEY

Thomas Dunne Books
St. Martin's Minotaur
New York

THOMAS DUNNE BOOKS.
An imprint of St. Martin's Press.

THE HIGHLY EFFECTIVE DETECTIVE GOES TO THE DOGS. Copyright © 2008 by Richard Yancey. All rights reserved. Printed in the United States of America. For information, address St. Martin's Press, 175 Fifth Avenue, New York, N.Y. 10010.

www.thomasdunnebooks.com
www.minotaurbooks.com

Library of Congress Cataloging-in-Publication Data

Yancey, Richard.
   The highly effective detective goes to the dogs / Richard Yancey.—1st ed.
      p.   cm.
   ISBN-13: 978-0-312-34753-6
   ISBN-10: 0-312-34753-7
   1. Private investigators—Fiction.   2. Dogs—Fiction.   I. Title.
   PS3625.A675H55 2008
813'.6—dc22

                                                                              2008018098

First Edition: August 2008

10 9 8 7 6 5 4 3 2 1

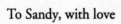

To Sandy, with love

NOVEMBER 7

CHAPTER ONE

I WAS SITTING AT MY DESK, STARING OUT THE WINDOW INTO THE drizzly gray light falling behind the Ely Building, when Felicia's voice came over the intercom.

"Ruzak, what are you doing?"

I jerked in my chair. I startle easily, which might explain why I haven't seen a scary movie since *Aliens,* and I only saw that because of Sigourney Weaver.

"I hate November," I said, raising my voice a little, like a lot of people who use intercoms or talk to foreigners. "I've lived in Knoxville for over half my life and I can't remember one single sunny day in November."

"Maybe you should invest in a light box."

"Light box?"

"This big panel of bright light that depressed people sit in front of."

"Why do they do that?"

"Because they're depressed, Ruzak."

"No, I mean, what does the light do?"

"I'm not sure, but I think it stimulates something in their brain."

"I don't think my brain's problem is lack of stimulation."

"Probably not," she agreed. I wasn't sure why we were chatting over the intercom when she sat about twenty feet away, though we had remodeled recently, adding a wall and a door, turning the one big room into two smaller rooms. Felicia had said a detective needs privacy when consulting with his clients about their case. I suspected it had more to do with a secretary's need for privacy when consulting with her boyfriend about their lunch plans. But that was cynical thinking, and I was at war with cynical thinking, the chief reason for half the world's problems, in my opinion. You have to trust that most people act in good faith. Otherwise, you might as well build your bunker, stock up on the canned goods, and invest in the kind of firepower Sigourney used against the mother alien in the sequel. One of the things I couldn't understand in that movie was all the slobber. Those creatures seemed very insectlike to me, and I didn't think insects salivated. Of course, they weren't real monsters and it was only a movie.

"Now what are you doing?" she asked.

"Wondering if insects salivate."

"You know, that's really weird. I was just wondering the same thing."

"Really?" It would be an extraordinary coincidence if she were. "Well, I know mosquitoes have spit. They inject it into the bite to facilitate blood flow."

"Ruzak, only you could get from light boxes to mosquito spit in ten seconds."

I didn't think she was paying me a compliment. I asked, "What's going on?" which was more polite than saying, "Why are you hassling me over this damned intercom?"

"There's somebody here to see you."

I didn't think I had any appointments, so I asked, "Do they have an appointment?"

"He says he doesn't need one."

My heart rate clicked up a notch. People who don't need appointments are not usually the kind of people you want to meet with.

"Okay, show him in."

The door opened and I recognized him right away, with the square-shaped head, the ill-fitting suit, the slight paunch and rounded shoulders. I could see Felicia over his shoulder making a slicing motion across her throat and I nodded toward her, saying, "Thanks, Felicia, I'll take it from here."

He sat in the chair in front of my desk, I sat in the chair behind my desk, and he was smiling with great satisfaction.

"Mr. Ruzak, do you remember me?" he asked.

"Oh," I said. "You bet I do. I've always been pretty good with faces. Sometimes I have trouble remembering names, but one look at a face and I've got it locked down. I still remember what my ninth-grade art teacher looked like. Can I get you anything? We've got practically everything, even Starbucks coffee."

"No thank you," he said, crossing his legs and setting his briefcase on his lap.

"You sure? Once a week, my secretary picks up a pound. That way I avoid the lady on the cup."

"What lady?"

"You know, the creepy Starbucks lady. Although she is on the bag too, but it's usually my secretary who makes the coffee, so I don't have to look at her."

"You don't have to look at your secretary?"

"Oh, I don't mind that. I was talking about the Starbucks lady."

His smile had fled. "I don't know what you're talking about, Mr. Ruzak."

"She's on all the cups. Check it out next time you're at Starbucks."

"I don't go to Starbucks."

"Well, it is an acquired taste, like beer."

He shook his head quickly, as if he were clearing out the cobwebs, and said, "You must know why I'm here, Mr. Ruzak."

"I've got a pretty strong suspicion, Mr. Hilton."

"Hinton."

"Hinton. Hinton. That's right. Sorry."

He pulled a computer printout from his briefcase. "Mr. Ruzak, I've brought your test results. . . ."

"Okay," I said. "I've already seen them. I know you didn't come looking for excuses, but I was never very good with tests."

"I," he said, "don't care."

"I didn't think so. I don't suppose you looked carefully at my door before you came in. Right below the 'Highly Effective Detection' name thingy? 'Theodore Ruzak, Investigative Consultant.' We added that so potential clients wouldn't confuse me with your traditional detective-type setup."

"Your clients might be confused, Mr. Ruzak. And, based on your test results, you are most definitely confused. But the state of Tennessee is not confused. All applicants must pass this test in order to obtain the license to practice private detection."

"And that's a good thing," I said. "You wouldn't want just any yahoo dicking around with detection, private or otherwise."

"No, we do not."

"Well, I'm already signed up for the next test, and this time I've got high hopes of passing it. My problem was I didn't sleep well the night before, and this time I'm planning to take a pill. Not a prescription, but something over-the-counter."

"That's entirely up to you, Mr. Ruzak."

"Well, that's a relief and one of the reasons this is such a great country, Mr. Hilton. Hillon. Hellion. *Hinton.* Multiple shots at the target."

"Right. And while you're reloading . . ." He pulled a document from his briefcase and slid it across the blotter toward me.

"What's this?" I asked. My name was in all caps in the left-hand corner, like this: THEODORE RUZAK d/b/a THE HIGHLY EFFECTIVE

DETECTION AND INVESTIGATION COMPANY a/k/a "THE DIC".
Above it was this: THE STATE OF TENNESSEE VS.

"A cease-and-desist order, Mr. Ruzak. Effective immediately, you are no longer in business."

"Wow. Just like that?"

He was smiling at me like every villain in every B movie I've ever seen. If he'd had a mustache, he'd have twirled it.

"Just like that," he said.

"You know, I'm not much for irony, but this strikes me as ironic."

"How so?"

"Up till this minute I was making a living off the fact that people do bad things and haven't answered for them, and here you are shutting me down."

"I don't see the irony in that."

"Well, like I said."

"I understand from your application you used to be a night watchman. Perhaps you could apply for that job."

"Does career counseling come with your work?" I asked. "That part of the service?"

"There's no need for bitterness, Mr. Ruzak."

"I guess not in general. But this is a particular case." I was regretting offering him the coffee. "I was thinking about the movies before you came in. If this was a movie and I was your typical hard-case gumshoe, I'd tear up this court order and throw the pieces back into your face."

"I'm a lucky man, then, that you are neither hard-case nor a gumshoe."

He stood up. I stayed down. Felicia appeared in my doorway.

"So that's it?" she asked. She was looking over Hinton's shoulder at me. "That's all you're gonna do?"

"You have to the end of business today, Mr. Ruzak," Hinton said, tipping his hat in my direction before slipping it on his square head. "Or I come back with the Knox County Sheriff's Department."

He left. Felicia sat in the chair he vacated and stared at me.

"I flunked the test," I told her.

"You never told me you flunked the test."

"I meant to. Okay, that's a lie. What I meant to do was take it again and hope for the best."

I braced myself for the explosion. But all she did was drop a piece of paper on top of the court order.

"What's this?"

"What's left in the bank account."

"Really? I thought we had more than that."

"That's what we have." She crossed her arms over her chest and waited.

"Okay," I said. "But let's not jump the gun here. The next test is coming up in a couple of months. There's enough here to cover both our expenses till then. Think of it as a paid vacation."

"You're such a . . ." She searched for the word.

"Dumb-ass?"

"No."

"Mediocrity?"

"Uh-uh."

"Ne'er-do-well?"

"*Optimist.* What's the plan in two months when you flunk it a third time and all the money's gone?"

"It's hard for me to plan for failure."

"That's really strange coming from you, Ruzak. You would think that'd be second nature by now."

She spun out of the chair and was gone, slamming my door behind her. No more than thirty seconds later—time to grab her purse, maybe—I heard the outer door slam.

Alone with my thoughts—and my ferns, which were slightly droopy, making me wonder if I had them too close to the cold windows—I stared out into the alley below, into a world bled colorless by the rain, at the jumble of old filing cabinets and bent metal trash cans and dead stalks of weeds glistening in the rain. They say even the greatest minds suffered from melancholy, though I wasted another minute or two trying to think of a single genius who suffered from the blues. Lincoln, maybe, though he'd had a bit more on his plate than I did.

A voice cried out from the wilderness of the vestibule.

"Hello? Hello, is anybody home?"

I sighed. I knew that voice. I opened my door and Eunice Shriver shuffled in, wearing a wool overcoat speckled with rain and carrying a canvas tote. She plopped her eighty-plus self into one of my chairs and waited for me to sink into my leather executive chair, which had developed a squeak and, as I sank, I wondered if that might affect its resale value.

"Theodore," she said, "you do not look well."

"It's this weather," I said. "You know, rainy days and Mondays."

"Rainy days and Mondays?"

"Always get me down. It's a song."

"I do not listen to the rap music or that abhorrent hip-hop."

"Neither do I. That song's pretty old."

"Meaning I should know it since I am, too?"

"No, meaning it predates rap and hip-hop by at least a generation."

"Theodore Ruzak." She sniffed. "Music critic."

"More an aficionado than a critic, Eunice. I struggle against judgmentalism."

" 'Judgmentalism'? Is that a word?"

"I don't know. I'm no lexicographer." I almost added I was no detective, either, but that bordered on bitterness and self-pity. Our reactions to personal catastrophe are minefields to be gingerly navigated. I wondered if I had read that somewhere, or if it was original. Sometimes I thought things I ascribed to myself only to find out days or weeks later that somebody else said it about a hundred years ago.

"Every time I see you we spin off on tangents, Theodore," she said, waving her mottled, big-knuckled hand in a circular motion, to demonstrate a tangent.

"Well, like the poet said, the truth lies in the parentheses."

"What poet?"

"I don't know."

"Then how do you know he said it?"

"Well, I may not know who said, 'Ask not what your country . . .' But that doesn't mean it wasn't said, Eunice."

"Kennedy said that."

"I know."

"Then why did you say you didn't?"

"I didn't say I didn't. I was making a point."

"Well, perhaps there's a first time for everything." Eunice was eighty-six, and I figured the weather must be wreaking havoc on her joints. Thinking about her aching joints relieved some of the pressure in my chest—or rather moved the pressure a bit to one side, because empathy resides at a different spot than self-pity. I think the ancient Egyptians figured out that one.

"Theodore, I have come today for two reasons."

"I'll guess the first," I said. "You want to know if there's any progress on your case."

"Effective, Mr. Detective," she said. "Highly effective."

"There isn't," I told her. "Eunice, nobody is trying to kill you. People love you. They wish only the best for you."

"You are hopelessly naïve."

"Oh, you bet. But you've put me in the position of trying to prove a negative."

"Have you looked into the bag boy at Fresh Market?"

"The one with the beady eyes?"

"The one with the mole. Beady Eyes was fired months ago."

"He was?"

"I made quite sure of that!"

"Well, in that case he might be holding a grudge, but bag boy is one of those professions where you can generally find work anywhere."

"One should never underestimate the maliciousness of bag boys."

"Eunice, you know what it took me a long time to learn? We're not as important as we think we are."

"And what is that supposed to mean?"

"It means believing somebody's out to get you won't make you important, and neither will confessing to crimes you didn't commit."

"I believe you just called me a liar."

"I don't think you can be a liar, per se, without the intent to deceive. Besides, even if you're right and somebody is trying to kill you, I can't do anything about it."

"And why is that?"

I told her. She accused me of making it up just to get her off my back. I showed her the court order.

"Oh, Theodore, why didn't you study?"

"That's the distressing thing. I did."

"Well, you're still young. You'll land on your feet."

I nodded. "I've got my fingers crossed there's an opening at Fresh Market."

She laughed. I'm convinced old ladies have the best-sounding laughter on earth. She picked up her tote and plopped it into her lap.

"I'm glad you told me," she said. Somehow my losing the business had lifted her spirits. Like mine, her ache must have shifted. "Because I've begun a little project that could be quite demanding on your time. And mine, too, of course."

She fumbled in the tote.

"You're knitting me a sweater," I said.

She hauled out about half a ream of typing paper and slapped it on my blotter. I read the title on the cover page: *Theodore Ruzak, The Highly Effective Detective.* It was an eye-catching title, but I managed to tear my eyes away to look at her, cheeks that rosy red of a lot of old ladies, eyes sparkling in the center of their puffy folds.

"You remember we discussed committing your story to paper some months back," she said. "I've decided to take the liberty."

"Committing my story to paper?"

"Of course, the devil is in the details, as they say, and I've reached a point in the narrative where I simply must have your input."

"You're writing my life story?" I flipped through the pages. I saw a lot of *Ruzak*s and a lot of *Eunice*s, and every now and again somebody ejaculated, as in " 'That killer's as good as caught!' ejaculated Theodore." The thought of crazy old Eunice Shriver writing a book about me was flattering and unnerving at the same time. "Why?"

"To immortalize you!" she fairly shouted. "Holmes had his Watson. Marple had her Christie. Nancy Drew had her Keene. Ruzak shall have his Shriver!"

"Oh, Eunice. Eunice, that's flattering as all get-out; I'm touched, really, but—"

"There are gaps, of course. Some things that I do not know, details and conversations and other matters that only you could know. I have been focusing on our relationship for the most part, but they'll want to know more about the actual case and your secretary, I suppose, and how precisely you managed to bag the killer."

"They? Who's 'they'?"

"Why, your readers, naturally!"

"Eunice, I don't have any readers."

"You will!"

"I don't want any readers."

"Nonsense! What detective in his right mind doesn't want readers?"

"I'm not a detective."

"You were!"

"Then I'm not in my right mind." I scooped up the manuscript and held it out for her. She didn't take it. The loss in her eyes was profound, and I looked away.

"You think I'm ridiculous," she said, voice quivering.

"No."

"A silly old woman with delusions of literary grandeur."

"Of course not."

"I wrote poetry when I was younger."

I wasn't sure what that had to do with anything, but I told her that was terrific. I was impressed. And how in the world could I accuse her, of all people, of being delusional? I kept holding out the manuscript until my forearm began to ache.

"If you really feel it's necessary," I said, "I guess you could just make up the rest."

"What rest?"

"The gaps."

"But this isn't fiction, Theodore."

"It would probably work better that way," I said. "Maybe you could put under the title: 'Based on a True Story.'"

She snorted with disgust. I figured it was disgust, anyway. Is it possible to snort with something else? Is there another emotion that causes you to snort?

She leaned forward and snatched the papers from my cramping fingers.

"I shall finish with or without your help, Theodore. Do you know why?"

"No. Why?"

"Because at the ripe old age of eighty-six, I have finally stumbled upon my life's calling. I shall be known to posterity as the chronicler of the great Teddy Ruzak's exploits."

She stuffed the manuscript back into the tote and pushed herself out of the chair. We argued all the way to the door. Then I gave up. What did I care if she wrote about me? You have to have purpose in your life. The fact that I had just lost mine made this painfully obvious. Loss makes a lot of things painfully obvious.

CHAPTER TWO

I HUNG AROUND FOR ANOTHER COUPLE OF HOURS, MISTING THE
ferns, changing the voice-mail message, composing a letter to my clients about
"pressing circumstances," and writing a note to stick on the front door. "Tem-
porarily Unavailable." Ever the optimist, I had no plans to close up shop for
good. I had more than enough cash in the bank to last until the next go-
around and now more than enough time to bone up for the test. I'm a firm believer in that old saw about try, try again. But I wondered how kindly the state
of Tennessee would treat my application, seeing that it had to get a court order to shut down my illegal operation.

I shut down Felicia's computer and cut the lights. The office fell into a
kind of premature twilight. I bumped down the thermostat to sixty-five and
checked to make sure the fax machine was unplugged. Then I hung in the
doorway, one foot over the transom and one foot in the room, jingling
the keys, knowing I'd be back but not knowing if I would ever *really* be back.

I swung the door closed and locked it. I tapped the etching after my
name, INVESTIGATIVE CONSULTANT, with my index finger, and thumped down
the wooden stairs, the naked bulb dangling above throwing my shadow
against the wall, the silhouette of my trench coat flapping in my descent like
Batman's cape.

I passed the dry cleaner's on the first floor. The walls hummed with the
sound of the machines, and I could see Gustav, the German proprietor, la-
boring over a shirt-pressing machine. A couple months back, Gustav had offered to do all my suits at a 20 percent discount. I had thanked him but
explained I was doing my cleaning with those in-your-dryer bags from Sam's
Club. He reacted as if I had just admitted to shooting house cats for sport.

On the stoop of the Ely, I inhaled deeply and then blew out my breath,

watching the white plume roil in the cold air. Ever since I was a kid, the phenomenon fascinated me. The rain was as fine as the aerosol emitted from my
mister, which sat upstairs on the window ledge beside the row of ferns. What
about the ferns? I should load them into my car and take them home. But I'd
have to climb those stairs and open that door, cross through two rooms, past
my big desk and the squeaky leather chair. Maybe I'd come back tomorrow.

I walked a half block west to the Park Rite lot that backed up to the Ely.
I was parking there because I got tired hoofing it downstairs every hour to
feed the meter—or trying to remember to hoof it downstairs every hour.
Sometimes I got wrapped up in something or my mind strayed, and I'd find a
ticket beneath my wiper. The city was gleeful about writing tickets.

The temperature wouldn't rise much above forty today, and the forecast
called for freezing rain overnight. The sky was an unbroken sheet of gray. The
red reflections of cars' rear lights chased their bumpers on the shimmering
pavement, and their tires hissed as they passed, the water remembering the
tread for a moment before the fresh rain wiped the road clean.

An old man leaned against the lamppost at the corner of Walnut and
Church. Blue jeans, a ratty tan jacket, tangled, gray-streaked hair down to his
shoulders, a full beard, also laced with gray, that grew past his Adam's apple,
holding a scrap of cardboard where he had scrawled, "We all need a little help
now and then. God Bless." He was a regular. I'd seen him almost every day
since September. One block west was the main library, where the vagrants
congregated year-round, sitting in the magazine area, staying warm or cool,
depending on the season. The library wasn't far from the mission on Broadway, which didn't open its doors until late afternoon. If I was a vagrant (something not too far outside the realm of possibilities), I'd hoof it farther south
for the winter. I'd go south until there was no south left.

At the four-way stop where Walnut met Church Avenue, I looked over at
Ratty Jacket and found him looking back at me. In that moment, I made a
life-or-death decision that would change both our lives.

I rolled down the window and he trotted over, chin tucked as he ran, and
I dropped the spare change from my cup holder into his calloused palm. He
commanded God to bless me, and then I reached over, grabbed my floppy hat
from the passenger seat, and passed it out the window to him. It was too big
for his head. The rim bobbed just over his bushy eyebrows, which were shot
through with gray like his hair and beard. His eyes were wide with astonish-
ment at my generosity. He grinned, touching the brim with one gnarled finger
as I pulled away. He looked seventy at least, but probably was in his sixties.

I glanced in the rearview mirror, and he was still standing in the middle
of the street, head turned toward me, a distorted, tan-and-blue figure in the
rain-smeared glass.

CHAPTER THREE

I took Kingston Pike west, through Sequoia Hills with its hundred-year-old mansions behind wrought-iron gates and the big Greek Orthodox church, not far from the synagogue and the fundamentalists' private school, past the Fresh Market where old Eunice Shriver fingered the bag boy out to get her, through the Bearden Hill area, and on the back side of the slope I turned left into the parking lot for the Humane Society. It was the only Spanish-style building I'd ever seen in Knoxville. The Spanish never had a strong presence in eastern Tennessee to my knowledge, and I always suspected the building originally housed a Mexican restaurant.

The place stank of ammonia mixed with the air freshener used to mask the stench of the ammonia. Cages lined the walls in this outer room, and the cages were occupied by cats lolling on carpet-covered ledges a couple feet above the floors of the cages. A big tabby lifted its head and blinked sleepily as I passed. My right eye twitched in response: I'm mildly allergic to cats.

The clerk (or attendant or whatever her title was) stood up and came to the counter. Maybe nineteen or twenty, with short-cropped black hair and a silver ring through her left nostril, her name was Amanda. She was a student at UT, studying philosophy. That probably helped, working at this place, which always struck me as a way station between deliverance and oblivion. She was clad completely in black: black halter that terminated an inch above her pierced navel, tight, black, hip-hugging jeans, and black combat boots. It wasn't hard for me to picture her administering the lethal dose to some unwanted animal. I didn't pretend to know much about philosophy, but what I did know didn't favor an optimistic mindset.

"Hey, Ruzak," she said, placing the paperback she had been reading face-down on the counter, folded open to keep her place. She was reading *The Bell Jar*. "What's up?"

"The state closed me down today," I said.

"Really? How come?"

"I flunked a test."

"We have an opening washing out the runs."

"I'll keep it in mind," I said. "Just wondering if you got in anything new this week."

"Let's check it out."

She grabbed a set of keys from a hook, and I followed her through the big metal door into the back wing of the building where the dogs were caged. We were greeted by a cacophony of barks, howls, whines, yips, and snarls. Some of the dogs I recognized. Butch, the pit bull, who had arrived earlier in the month and was doomed; nobody wanted to adopt a pit bull. Sassy, a Border collie with one bad eye, half shut and weeping with some kind of abscess, yellow gunk congealing in the long hair beneath her eye. Geronimo, a handsome German shepherd mix with a nasty disposition, though that might have sprung from an intense hatred of his confinement. Some dogs poked their snouts against the wire mesh, spittle flying from their mouths, furious; others cowered in the back of their cage, heads lowered, tongues dangling, like winded sprinters. Amanda must have recently washed down the cages: the concrete floor was slick, and the steel drain covers glistened with moisture.

"Okay!" she shouted over the bedlam. We had reached the end of the row. "He's new. That one just came in last night. And that one over there, she's new. It's a she, right? Yeah."

I peered into the cages, one by one. The dogs watched me. Amanda watched them watch me, and then she watched me, thin, pale arms folded over her small chest.

"Can I ask you something, Ruzak?" she asked. "For six weeks you've been coming here, and I take you back here and you stare at these dogs and then you come back and stare some more, and you haven't even asked to take one out. What are you looking for?"

"The right dog."

"Why don't we do this? You tell me what breeds you're interested in and, when one comes in, I'll give you a call."

"Well, it's not the breed exactly. I mean, I'm not partial to any particular breed. I've always believed in the saying that the perfect dog finds you."

"I've never heard that saying."

"It's all a little academic anyway. My lease doesn't allow pets."

"Then why are you looking for one?"

I didn't say anything. She was still watching me. The dogs were still watching me. I stood with my hands stuffed into my overcoat pockets.

"Maybe it isn't the dog you're looking for, per se," Amanda said finally.

"I have a very rich life," I told her. "An abundant existence." I wasn't about to let her existential malaise infect me. I looked into the cage immediately to my right. Some kind of low-slung beagle mix stared back. It wasn't barking, just lifting its narrow head and panting, creating the illusion of a grin. I pointed at it.

"Can I see him?"

"Sure. Go straight through that door into the courtyard and I'll bring him out. His name's Archie."

I sat on a concrete bench under the bare, outstretched arms of a dogwood, the branches black from the rain. The water gathered at the ends and formed droplets that hung, quivering, before gravity took them down. Amanda came out after a few minutes, cradling the beagle, which she lowered to the ground about ten feet from the bench. Archie looked up at her, his thin tail a white-and-tan blur, bouncing off her shins with his front paws. Amanda clapped her hands and pointed toward me, and Archie took off, leaping onto my lap and placing his tongue beneath my chin. I could smell his breath and suddenly I was twelve again, playing with my first and only dog. I'd never fully recovered from that dog's death, but I always told myself that was because you never fully recover from death, even the ones that aren't your own. Nearly a year had passed since my mom died, and I still woke up some mornings with a hard nugget of grief lodged in my gut. It had surprised me in the beginning; I always thought of grief as a hollow kind of feeling, but real grief isn't a void; it's hard and glittering and sharp as a diamond.

Now I had muddy paw prints all over my tan overcoat and this dog was nibbling the soft flesh under my chin.

"Okay, Archie, okay," I told it. I lowered it to the ground and it immediately put its paws on my leg, begging to be back in my lap.

"He likes you," Amanda said.

"He's probably not picky."

"He's small, which is good for an apartment," she said.

"It's a moral dilemma," I said. "I signed an agreement not to bring an animal into the building, but beyond that, if I get caught I'll have to bring him back here."

"So you buy him some time. You could look at it that way."

I looked her way. She might be prettier if she went back to her natural color and ditched the hoop in her nose. She must have been freezing out here in this rain, bare-armed and bare-midriffed.

"How did you decide on philosophy as a major?" I asked her.

She shrugged. "It's interesting."

"What does somebody do with a degree in philosophy?"

"I'm prelaw."

"Oh." I thought about telling her the world probably needed more philosophers and less lawyers, but that might lead to a debate, and I didn't have the stomach or the nerve to get into a philosophical debate with a philosophy major with the personality of a lawyer.

"What's ol' Archie's story anyway?" I asked.

"Brought him in a couple days ago. No collar, no implant. Just a stray, Ruzak."

"Implant?"

"You know, some vets put in those tracking chips. GPS."

"I think I read something about that," I said. "Made me think maybe we should do that with children."

She laughed for some reason.

"He's getting cold," she said. "I better get him inside."

I followed her back into the kennel. Archie smiled at me from behind his bars. His short hair shone with moisture, and I thought of otters.

"How much time does he have?"

"It's hard to say."

"I gotta think about it."

She shrugged. I followed her to the front room. Her shoulder blades poked out her back when she hugged her arms, she was so thin. Back among the cats, I sneezed.

"You got a business card?"

I did, but no business to go with it. I scrawled my home number on the back of the card and told her I wouldn't be in the office for a while.

"But don't hold him on my account," I told her, meaning Archie. "If somebody else wants him."

"Do you? You haven't said."

"I have to think about it. One thing, I'm not sure how wise or ethical it is getting a dependent on the same day I lose my sole source of income."

I sat in my idling car in the parking lot for a few minutes, watching the drops hardly larger than pinheads kiss the glass and looking past the raindrops to the magenta façade of the building. My one-bedroom at the Sterchi would seem empty when I walked in the door. I thought I should spring for some deep-pile carpet. Hardwood floors encourage echoes.

I stopped at the Food City on the corner of Kingston Pike and Northshore, to pick up a flank steak and some black beans, and I stood in one aisle at least three minutes trying to remember if I had any rice in the pantry. If I was wrong and didn't have any rice, I'd be forced to return to the store or opt for the beans without rice, which would make me feel cheated, like I was being denied something I rightfully deserved.

It turned out I did have one bag of Success Rice left in the pantry. I set up a TV tray at the end of my bed and watched a special on global warming on the Discovery Channel while I ate, just another thirty-something bachelor eating alone in his underwear, watching television. The tray was an old one, from a set I inherited from Mom. For as long as I could remember, we ate our family dinners set up in front of the old Magnavox in the family room, so Dad wouldn't miss a minute of Walter Cronkite. Somebody had told him once he resembled Walter Cronkite, and I suspected that's why Dad was so hooked on him. Dad lacked Walter's gravitas, though. His cheeks were ruddier, too, and his nose bigger, his voice higher pitched. His voice really didn't match his size. Maybe that's why Dad wasn't the greatest salesman in the world: you saw this big, barrel-chested Walter Cronkite look-alike coming at you, and when he opened his mouth he sounded like Squeaky the Clown.

Watching the Discovery Channel convinces you of three things: The world is a wonderful, wondrous place; it's going to hell in a handbasket; and you're partially to blame. I discovered that just using my toaster pumped about a hundred tons of carbon into the atmosphere every year.

I turned off the TV after the special—just doing my part—took a shower with colder water than usual, and tried to read an online manual Felicia had printed out, before I flunked the last time, called *Passing the PI Exam, Tennessee Edition*.

I fell asleep with the thing on my chest, clutching a highlighter.

NOVEMBER 8

CHAPTER FOUR

THE PHONE RANG A LITTLE AFTER TEN. IT WAS FELICIA.

"Did I wake you?" she asked.

I admitted she did. She asked if I had had a late night. I said I was up studying.

"See, that's what disturbs me about you, Ruzak. You studied before the last test and still flunked. Maybe you're going about this all wrong. Maybe you need some vices to overcome."

"Well," I said. "I think too much. I'm overburdened with memories. I'm extremely sensitive to loud noises and ethical quagmires, and I've got a soft heart." I told her about giving my hat to the old bum and the dog named Archie.

"I was thinking more along the lines of alcohol or gambling or even cheap, meaningless one-night stands. You know, the stereotypical hardboiled detective thing."

"How would that help?"

"It might give you some depth."

I wasn't sure, but I thought maybe she was implying I was boring.

"I'm not a very accomplished drunk," I told her. "Some drunks are belligerent or funny or loud or sentimental. I just fall asleep."

I asked her if she wanted to have lunch. She asked if I had looked out my window. I looked out my window. The low-slung clouds had departed and the midmorning sunlight was harsh, reflecting off the rows of icicles glittering like silver thorns on the bare branches of the trees and the crystalline stalactites hanging from the power lines.

"Downtown got hit the worst," Felicia told me. "Over an inch."

"I was going to the office to pick up the ferns," I said.

"Probably best to wait till this afternoon."

"How about dinner?" I asked. "I'll take you and Tommy to Steak-N-Shake." Steak-N-Shake was Tommy's favorite.

"We'll have to take a rain check," Felicia said. "Bob's off tonight." Then she changed the subject. "I hope you're not going to spend all your time studying for this test, Ruzak. Maybe you should join a gym."

"Okay. I know I'm out of shape—"

"That's not what I meant. Or maybe one of those continuing education classes they offer at the university. I mean, dear God, you're interested in practically everything."

"I have been thinking about a photography class," I said. "Or videography—if that's a word. You know, I could write off the cost of the class that way."

"You remember Beatrice from the diner? We were talking the other day and—"

"Don't set me up."

"I wasn't—"

"Don't try to set me up, Felicia. I don't need setting up. As a matter of fact, I've got a little more on my plate than I can handle right now."

"You're kidding."

"Why? Why do you think that's something I'd kid about? Hang on. I've got another call."

I pressed the mouthpiece against my stomach and stared out the window at the ice-gripped landscape. I had a terrific view of the railroad yard from my bedroom. On a clear day, you could see the tracks stretching far into the horizon, until they disappeared into the mists of the Smoky Mountains.

I brought the receiver back to my ear.

"You still there?" I asked. "Sorry. That was Amanda."

"Oh. Who's Amanda?"

"This girl philosopher I know."

"I'm sorry. You said . . . girl philosopher?"

"We've begun to mesh. Say, would you say it's unethical of me to adopt a dog, seeing it's forbidden on my lease, and if I get busted I probably won't get kicked out but the dog sure will?"

"You could always say you were pet-sitting."

"Well, the issue was ethics, and I'm pretty sure lying like that would be that. Unethical."

"You never mentioned any Amanda to me."

"We keep our personal lives personal, remember?"

I think I pissed her off with that remark, because she got off the phone pretty quick. I looked out the window one more time and thought Nature, like a woman, was beautiful, but treacherous . . . or maybe they were beautiful by virtue of their treachery.

"It's ironic," I said to the empty room, "that I debate ethics right in the middle of a lie about a girl calling." If I had a dog, I could talk to it and not to an empty room. If you talk to a dog, you're just being a kind owner. But talk to an empty room and you're being a weirdo.

The thought of staying inside until that afternoon was unbearable, so I dressed, pulling on an extra pair of socks ("Layers, layers, layers," my mom always lectured) and my tan overcoat with Archie's muddy prints still embossed on it, and took the elevator down to the parking lot beneath the building.

The sunlight had that late-fall-early-winter fierceness, bright but heatless, hard-edged, bordering on cruel, the way it cut the shadows of the trees and the buildings along Gay Street, and a million little suns sparkled in the ice that hung from the branches and glittered like rows of teeth belonging to some under-the-bed monster along the edges of the awnings. Nearly every building along this stretch of Gay was being renovated, into condos mostly, even the old Tennessee Theater Building, and one-bedroom lofts there were going for four hundred thousand dollars a pop.

At dawn, the salt trucks must have covered downtown, because I encountered no ice on the road on the seven-minute drive to the Ely Building. I turned left into the Park Rite lot and parked beside my building. The attendant, a guy named Lonny, left the sanctuary of his little lean-to and sauntered over as I climbed out of my Sentra.

"You're two weeks late," he informed me.

"I wanted to talk to you about that," I said. I told him I was taking a sabbatical and wouldn't be using the space for the next couple of months.

"We can't hold it," he said, meaning my space. "What's a sabbatical?"

"A working vacation."

"What are you working on?"

"I'm not, really."

"Then why'd you say you were?"

"I was trying to sound important."

He laughed and lit a cigarette. He wore a blue jacket too thin for the weather, jeans, and brown work boots. He accompanied me toward the front of the Ely, and the sand he must have shoveled earlier to clear the ice crunched beneath his boots.

"Actually, I've got to study for my PI exam," I admitted. "I just dropped by to pick up my ferns."

Smoke roiled from his nose. "I didn't know you were a PI."

"I'm not. I've got to pass the test first, hence the sabbatical."

"I'm starting trucking school in January."

"I've always admired truckers," I told him. "All those long, lonely hours behind the wheel."

"You're kidding, right?"

"I have a romantic streak."

He gave me a look, like he suspected I was trying out a pickup line on him.

"Seriously, you can't just hold my space?" I asked.

"Not unless you want to keep paying."

"I'm thinking that might be a foolish use of my funds."

"Because you might fail?"

"I'm trying to get out of that habit," I said. We had reached the front steps. I wondered how I would manage it, sitting in that little shacklike structure for eight hours with nobody to talk to. It probably wouldn't be hard for me at all—before I almost became a detective, I had worked fourteen years on the nightshift as a security guard, sitting in an armless chair, watching video monitors showing empty halls.

"What habit?" he asked. His hands belonged to an older man, the skin bunched tight around the knuckles, fingers stained by tobacco, slightly red from the cold.

"The habit of planning for failure instead of success. I like to think of myself as an optimist, but sometimes the evidence points the other way."

"I could talk to the boss about holding it," he said. Back to the real issue at hand.

"Hey, I'd appreciate that, Lonny."

We stood in silence for a second, then he said, "S'posed to warm up this afternoon. Toppin' forty-five."

"At least the sun finally came out," I said.

"Yeah-a. He lifted his face, turning it slightly to the left to bathe in the light. "Gotta enjoy it while you can."

I thanked him again and went up the narrow stairwell to my office. Yesterday's mail lay on the floor and I scooped it up. Bills. I unlocked Felicia's desk, grabbed the checkbook, and sat behind my desk. I wrote the checks, stuffed the envelopes, and then got up and started a pot of Starbucks coffee, turning the bag around so I wouldn't have to look at the lady. While I waited for the coffee to brew, I hunted for some stamps, but came up dry. I went back to my desk and drank my coffee. When two-thirds of it was inside me, I got up again (I never drain the dregs; I don't know why) and filled my mister from the bathroom tap. The sunlight could not penetrate into the alley; the arc of the sun was too low this time of year.

I was leaning over the wide ledge, misting the final fern, when something caught my eye in the alley below. My finger froze on the trigger. I brought my face closer to the window. My breath fogged the glass and I couldn't see. I wiped the moisture away with my shirtsleeve and peered again into the narrow space. It was a trick of light below, in the jumble of refuse crowded against the wall of the building behind me; it had to be. I threw the latch and, grunting with the effort because the window must have been literally painted shut, heaved the thing open, bending over the fern so the outstretched tips tickled my Adam's apple, and squinted two stories down, into the face of a dead man, wearing ratty old jeans and a brown jacket, with a beard encrusted with ice and eyes staring up into mine, unblinking and wide with horror.

CHAPTER FIVE

I DIALED 911, AND AFTER I DIALED 911 I DIALED FELICIA'S NUMBER.

"There's a dead body in the alley," I told her.

A second of silence, then: "What alley?"

"The alley behind the Ely." I tipped my cup and the lukewarm coffee caressed the tip of my tongue. "I think it's the panhandler."

"What panhandler?"

"The one I gave my hat to yesterday."

"Are you sure?"

"Sure there's a body or sure it's the guy from yesterday? Pretty sure about both."

"Ruzak, are you okay?"

"I'm a little shaky. I shouldn't be drinking coffee on an empty stomach. I wanted some Krispy Kremes but I was afraid of black ice."

"Black ice."

"You know, that ice on the road you can't see and all of sudden you're spinning out of control at forty-five miles per hour. So I drove straight to work and I was misting the ferns before I lugged them downstairs to my car, though I probably shouldn't have done that. They're heavier now with fresh water, but if I hadn't I wouldn't have seen the dead body. Well, I don't know for a hundred percent certain that he's dead, which raises a conundrum. If he's dead, I think there's a good chance that's a crime scene down there and I don't want to muck up any evidence. But if he's alive, I have a moral responsibility to do everything I can to save him."

"Did you call the cops?"

"They're on their way."

"You want me to come down there? You don't sound right."

"I'm okay. He has my hat, though."

"Your hat?"

"Yeah, I gave him my big floppy hat yesterday . . . protection from the elements." I gave a dry, little laugh. "Anyway, I'm gonna have to explain why he has my hat."

"Ruzak, I don't have a sitter for Tommy or I'd—"

"No, I'm okay, really." I wondered what happened to Bob. She had said Bob had the day off. Maybe she didn't like to leave Tommy alone with Bob—but why wouldn't Felicia like that? Maybe Bob got called in on a fire emergency. That sounded redundant to me. Weren't all fires emergencies? My head began to hurt.

"Are you there?" she asked.

I told her I was.

"I'll stay on till the cops get there."

"No, really, that's okay. I just called to let you know. I better get down there."

"Don't touch anything, Ruzak."

"Why would I do that?" I snapped. Then I said, "Sorry. It's the damn coffee. I'll talk to you later."

I hung up, slung my coat over my shoulders, and pounded down the stairs and onto the sidewalk, turning left into the parking lot, and Lonny came out of his little shack, a cigarette dangling from the corner of his mouth.

"Where's the ferns?" he asked.

"Upstairs," I answered. He fell into step beside me as I marched toward the back of the building. The sun actually felt warm against my back. I stopped at the southwest corner of the Ely and turned to Lonny.

"I'm ninety-nine percent certain there's a dead body in that alley," I said. He blinked at me a couple of times.

"You're shittin' me."

"I've already called the cops."

He stood behind me as I pivoted to look into the alley. A wrought-iron gate blocked the entrance, but the gate's latch was broken and it hung open about a foot. Five feet in, the man lay crumpled against an old rusting filing cabinet, legs draped over a black plastic trash bag that had broken open, his face with its glittering ice mask craning upward, as if he were looking at the bright blue ribbon of cloudless sky between the buildings.

"You think he's really dead?" Lonny whispered.

"I don't see him breathing," I said.

"Exposure, poor bastard," he said. "The cold must've killed him."

I had seen dark marks on his forehead from my window, but at street level, with his head thrown back, my angle was bad. They looked like some kind of hieroglyphics from two stories above, but I didn't think so. I didn't think anyone had scribbled hieroglyphics on his forehead. I stepped into the little opening between the gate and the wall of the Ely, raising my hands so I wouldn't touch anything, and rose to my tiptoes. I lost my balance and stumbled forward. Lonny clawed at my overcoat, trying to catch me before I tripped and landed flat on my face, but he missed. I didn't fall, though. I found my balance and now, with only a couple of feet separating me from the body, I could see clearly what someone had written on his forehead.

YHWH.

"What is it, Ruzak?" Lonny, hovering at the gate, hissed at me.

"Letters," I said, lowering my voice and not sure why. *"Y-h-w-h."*

"Y-h-w-h? What's it mean?"

His arms were flung straight out from his sides, and he clutched in his right hand the scrap of cardboard I saw the day before: *We all need a little help now and then. God Bless.* I didn't see my hat.

"Hey, I know that guy!" Lonny said. "I had to run him off the lot a couple times."

Where was my hat? "What's his name?" I asked.

"No clue, man."

I shuffled backward, out of the alley, and Lonny lit a cigarette. He held out the pack and I shook my head.

"Somebody told me I need more vices, but I smoked one time when I was thirteen and it made my brain feel like Swiss cheese."

"Swiss cheese. Right." Lonny's hands were quivering.

"And every time I drink I get very sleepy. Not so much with beer, though."

"Once I drank a fifth of bourbon and put my head through a wall."

"A solid wall?"

"Drywall. So it didn't hurt much."

"People used to use it as an anesthetic."

"People still do."

We waited for the sirens. I turned away from the dead man in the alley. It felt like the watched-pot phenomenon.

"You see any blood?" he asked.

"No."

"Got drunk, passed out, and froze to death."

"Before or after somebody wrote on his forehead?"

"Maybe he wrote on it himself."

"I gave him my hat," I said. "Just yesterday."

I lifted my face toward the cloudless sky. The Discovery Channel had shown examples of my carbon output as big black blocks, each block representing a certain amount of greenhouse gas, pouring into the atmosphere in choking abundance. This November sky made that difficult to believe. But if science has taught us anything since Galileo, it's taught us you can't always trust your senses. Ever since I heard about it, I was troubled by the string theory in physics. I didn't pretend to understand everything about it, or even a hundredth of it, but the thrust of the argument that there might be an infinite number of equally plausible universes, that reality as I knew it wasn't the only reality, had cost me at least six hours of sleep, cumulatively. I was relieved to read that the string theory was falling out of favor with some highly placed eggheads, one of them saying that it didn't even rise to the level of being wrong.

"Why'd you give him your hat?"

"It was raining."

I looked down at Lonny. He was at least a foot shorter. He was looking up at me.

"What's your dog's name?" he asked, nodding toward the stains on my coat.

"I don't have a dog."

"You give him that, too?"

"I went to the pound and met a beagle named Archie."

"I would have taken you for a cat man."

"I'm allergic."

"I'm allergic to shellfish."

"I saw this show on . . . well, I can't remember now, but it was one of the networks, about this woman who was allergic to her own sweat. She basically suffered from an autoimmune response to her own body."

"You gotta wonder why something like that happens," Lonny said. He flicked his cigarette into the lot, where it bounced and rolled until it hit the front wheel of my car.

"Genetics," I said. "DNA."

"I'm talkin' about God."

"Oh. Right."

"You believe in God, Ruzak?"

"I was raised Southern Baptist," I said. "My old man was a lapsed Catholic."

"I'm a Methodist, but I haven't been to church in fifteen years."

"I can't approach the whole thing like a child, you know, like Jesus said to somebody, I think in the Temple. It definitely wasn't the Mount . . . anyway, I think too much, which tends to keep the profound things at arm's length— sort of the opposite of what you'd expect."

We heard the sirens approaching. Lonny lit another cigarette.

"If he was a goddamned banker, he'd be at Fort Sanders by now with a drip going," he said.

The first responder was a truck from the Knoxville Fire Department. Two guys jumped out, neither of whom were named Bob. Lonny and I stood behind the gate and watched them check the old man's vital signs. One EMT felt for a pulse while the other shone a light into his eyes.

"He's gone," the guy with the light announced. He sported a bushy mustache. You don't see many men over thirty with facial hair these days, and those you do see usually practice one of those macho professions or have no profession at all, like the dead man in the alley with YHWH tattooed on his forehead. Maybe it *was* a tattoo and I just didn't notice it the day before.

An ambulance pulled into the lot and, while they were unfolding the gurney, a cop car parked behind my back bumper. The cop's name was Middleton. He took our statements while they carried the body through the gate (the gurney was too wide to fit through the opening). They had to turn the old guy sideways to get him out because he had gone stiff, and his arms remained outstretched as if he had fallen frozen in an attitude of flight.

I told Middleton about my encounter with the deceased the day before and how I discovered him in the alley. Lonny didn't have much to add, except the fact that he had seen him off and on for over three months and once had to chase him out of the parking lot.

No, we didn't know his name. No, we didn't know where he came from or how long he had been working Church Avenue. No, we had never seen him with anyone else. No, there didn't seem to be anything wrong when I gave him my hat.

"Why did you give him your hat?" Middleton asked.

"It was raining."

They had loaded up the body into the ambulance by this point. They slammed the back doors, sauntered to the front, and the ambulance slowly and silently pulled out of the parking lot. It seemed odd and disquieting. No crowd had gathered, either, as you might expect. The sidewalk was deserted and it was nearing lunchtime. Middleton scribbled in his pad. We followed him into the alley. He touched the piece of cardboard with the toe of his shiny black shoe.

"That's his," I said. "He was holding that yesterday."

Middleton threw a leg over the rusting filing cabinet and walked to the opposite corner of the Ely, head turning back and forth as he scanned the ground. I turned the opposite way, to poke about near the gate for my hat. What happened to my hat? Did he give it to somebody? Did he lay it down somewhere and forget about it? Except for the handmade sign, there was nothing else I could see as evidence of the old man dying here—or even having been alive here. No discarded liquor bottles, no cigarette butts, no bag of belongings. Hadn't I seen a backpack resting against the stop sign on Walnut?

Middleton returned, broken glass crunching under his polished shoes. He was just a kid, no more than twenty-one or two, I guessed. At that age, I had already flunked out of the police academy and been denied readmittance.

"Got drunk, passed out, and froze to death," Middleton said, echoing Lonny from a few minutes ago. He flipped his notebook closed. "But we'll see what the coroner says."

"You see the letters?"

"What letters?"

"The letters tattooed or etched on his forehead."

He gave me a look. I had left that out in my statement, so I told him what I saw. He didn't bother to write it down.

"Okay, one more thing. I'm gonna need your names and numbers, in case there's anything hinky in the ME's report."

It turned out Lonny's last name was Bradford, like the fruitless pear trees that grew so abundantly in East Tennessee. Middleton paused after writing down my name.

"Ruzak. The detective, right?"

"Not anymore. Well, actually, not ever."

"He's on sabbatical," Lonny offered.

"I remember seeing your name in the paper," Middleton said.

He drove away and, after he drove away, Lonny lit another cigarette.

"You wanna grab some lunch?" he asked me.

I hadn't even had breakfast, but I told him no. I wanted to get my ferns home. For some reason, I was feeling very protective toward them.

CHAPTER SIX

FELICIA HAD LEFT A MESSAGE ON MY ANSWERING MACHINE, SO AFTER I ate a pimento cheese sandwich, I called her back.

"He's definitely dead," I told her.

"What happened?"

"They think he passed out drunk and froze to death."

"That's sad."

"I didn't see a bottle, though. And my hat's missing."

"Foul play, Ruzak? Somebody killed him for your hat? I've seen that hat. It's not that nice. Why did you give him your hat in the first place?"

"Because it was raining."

"Maybe another bum stumbled over him and took your hat. And his bottle."

"That could be. Are you busy later?"

"I'm going out of town."

"You are? You didn't tell me."

"Sorry, Mom."

"Where are you going?"

"I'm taking Tommy to Kentucky for a couple of weeks to visit with his grandparents."

"What about Bob?"

"What about him? Why are you always so worried about Bob's whereabouts?"

"I'm not."

"Well, you're sure making inquiries all the time. Bob has to work, if you must know."

"That should be a nice trip," I said. "Watch for ice, though. Especially around Jellico Mountain."

"That's on my list, Ruzak."

I told her about the letters on the bum's forehead.

"What do you think that means?" I asked.

"What the letters mean or what it means that they were on his forehead?"

"Either one."

She had no idea. Neither did I. We mulled over in silence for a few seconds our mutual lack of any idea.

"Are you still there?" I asked.

"Yes, but I gotta go. Tommy wants lunch."

"I just had a pimento cheese sandwich."

"O-*kay*. . . . Ruzak, are you trying to keep me on the phone for some reason?"

"I guess I could be a little spooked. I think I would be okay if he had died with his eyes closed. You know, I look down and there he is, staring at me."

"He wasn't really staring, you know."

"Or if somebody else found him," I went on. "I know this sounds egocentric and I have a problem with that, but it feels like, I don't know, that he was meant for me."

"*What?*"

"The day before the state shuts me down, and I didn't tell you about the cop, but he reminded me of me, except he obviously graduated from the Academy, and then I gave him my hat—not the cop, the bum—and it feels like I'm coming to some sort of epiphany or reaching a kind of existential critical mass—one of those moments when you can hear the muffled strike of the hammer."

"Hammer?"

"You know, the hammer of Fate with a capital H."

"I think you're reading too much into the whole thing. Some homeless man freezes to death and you happen to be the one who finds him."

I could hear Tommy shouting in the background, an incoherent, desperate sound. Tommy was Felicia's kid by a guy who ran out on her when she was pregnant, and there were problems with the kid. I could picture him, tugging on her clothes, his wide face twisted into a grimace.

"You have to go," I said.

"I have to go. Don't have a crisis on me, Ruzak. Maybe you should get out of town, too. Go someplace warm for a while."

That's it, I thought after I hung up. That's what was getting to me, besides the letters on his forehead and the way he seemed to be staring at me.

Why didn't he get to some place warm? The mission would have been open, and I knew for a fact that the Catholic church on Northshore kept its doors unlocked 24/7. If he passed out drunk, why didn't we find a bottle in the alley? Of course, he might have died of a heart attack or stroke or any number of other causes. Maybe he had pneumonia or cancer or some other, more exotic disease. There are so many things that can kill you; it's amazing we live past forty.

I tried to tell myself it wasn't because of those letters on his forehead or my own moribund mindset or the nature of my former business that convinced me—absolutely convinced me beyond all doubt—that that old man had been murdered and left in that alley as if he were just another bit of refuse, another bag of garbage.

NOVEMBER 15

CHAPTER SEVEN

I NOTICED A TALL, PALE-SKINNED, DARK-HAIRED WOMAN STANDING ON the steps of the Sterchi Building as I turned into the parking lot. She was wearing a calf-length gray overcoat with matching gray gloves. She reminded me of your classic femme fatale from those old Humphrey Bogart movies. Thin, seductive, soft-spoken . . . and deadly.

I pulled into my space and saw her walking toward me, and even her makeup made me think I'd stumbled into a Philip Marlowe story: her lips were the color of arterial blood.

"Teddy Ruzak?" she asked. Her heels were gray, too, and their clicking echoed in the confines of the underground garage.

I told her I was. She flashed a badge and said, "Detective Meredith Black, Mr. Ruzak. Knoxville Homicide."

"It's the old man in the alley," I said. "Somebody killed him."

"I'm afraid so."

"I knew it."

"Do you have a few minutes? I've been trying to reach you by phone . . ."

"I was meeting with my biographer. Sure. You want me to come downtown?"

"This won't take long. Can we talk upstairs?"

She meant my apartment. Immediately I thought about the dishes piled in the sink and the view through my open bedroom door: the dirty socks, the pile of newspapers, the collection of coffee mugs on my nightstand.

"Sure. That's no problem."

We took the elevator to the third floor, and she stood a couple steps behind me as I fumbled with the keys. I always got nervous around cops. Cops and pretty women. And big dogs. Closed spaces. Dark, unfamiliar locales.

Bikers. Certain members of the clergy. Like a priest is much more intimidating to me than a Protestant minister.

"I've been meaning to tidy up," I said over my shoulder as I stepped inside. The blinds were drawn and the place had all the light and charm of an Egyptian tomb. I flipped on a light and went immediately to the sink, glancing down the little hall to the bedroom. The door was not fully open, so maybe she wouldn't notice.

"Can I get you anything?" I asked. "Water, but it's tap, sorry, or I could make a fresh pot of coffee. . . ."

"No, thanks," Meredith Black said. She was kind of hovering near the door as if she were waiting for something, and I guessed that something was for me to gather my thoughts and start acting like a normal, innocent human being.

"Let me take your coat," I said.

"Thanks." She shrugged the coat into my hands. Underneath she was wearing a gray jacket over a crisp white blouse. A diamond solitaire hung around her neck on a sterling silver chain. Without thinking, I checked out her left hand. No ring. I draped her overcoat carefully over the back of a bar chair and motioned her toward the sofa.

"So you knew it was murder?" Meredith Black said. She left the *how?* unspoken.

"Well, when I said I knew, I didn't mean I knew."

She smiled. She had good teeth. Very white and straight. You could tell a lot about people based on the condition of their teeth. Socioeconomic status. Their sense of self-worth. Their personality type. In life, there are biters and there are chewers. Meredith Black, I was guessing, was a biter.

"It just didn't make much sense to me," I said. "The idea that he just passed out and froze to death. Of course, I'm no doctor and even if I was, I didn't examine him or anything. I didn't even touch him. I figured it could have been a heart attack or a stroke, but I had this gut feeling, based on a couple of factors, that nothing natural killed him."

"What factors?" She was leaning forward, chin thrust forward, elbows on her knees. Her knuckles were red, a little chafed, probably from the cold.

"I didn't think he was new to the, um, lifestyle, which meant he knew where to go to survive the cold. I guess I should tell you right off I had an encounter with him the day before. It was raining and I gave him some change—and my hat. My hat was missing, and people like him don't toss a perfectly good hat. But I may have thought that because the hat had been mine and we tend to inflate the value of our possessions. . . . sorry; I ramble when I'm nervous."

"Why are you nervous?"

"I kind of lost my job a couple weeks ago and, you know, that sort of thing can yank the rug right out from under you, and I don't mean just in the financial sense."

She nodded. "Sure. You were a PI, right?"

"Investigative consultant. Never quite reached the PI level, which is what led me to lose my job. The state didn't grasp the nuance."

She reviewed the statement I gave to Officer Middleton. How I found the body and if I had seen anything or anyone suspicious that morning or the day before when I handed the old guy my hat. How often I had seen him hanging on the corner panhandling. She wanted to know what we said to each other when he came to my car.

"I didn't say anything. He said 'God bless,' or something like that. That's it."

"Where did you go next?"

"Where did I go? I went to the pound."

"The pound?"

"The Humane Society down on Kingston Pike. I'm kind of in the market for a dog. It's still in the planning stages because I've got a lease issue. There's a philosophy student named Amanda who works there." I realized she wanted to know my alibi. "Then I went home. No. First I stopped at Food City and picked up dinner. Flank steak and beans. Black beans. I came home and ate in my bedroom. Not that I normally eat in my bedroom, but the hardwood in here makes the kitchen area kind of echoey. . . . And the next morning, the morning I found him, the only reason I went downtown was to retrieve those ferns over there. I wasn't planning on going into the office for the next couple of months, and I didn't want them to die." I told her about seeing his face, calling 911, and then calling Felicia before going downstairs.

"Felicia?"

"My secretary. She's not here. I don't mean *here* here. We aren't . . . she doesn't . . . we don't . . . She's in Kentucky visiting her parents."

"Okay. So after you tell Felicia, you go downstairs and meet . . ." She consulted her notebook. "Lonny Bradford?"

"Right. Lonny. Only I didn't know his last name till the dead guy turned up. I never asked. That happens a lot in the service sector. You know, everyone's on a first-name basis."

"What else do you know about Lonny?"

"Is he a suspect?"

She didn't answer. She just smiled at me with those bright, even teeth. Biter.

"Well, not much," I said. "He's studying to be a long-haul trucker. Or going to study for it. The only other thing I've got is my impression of him, which is he's a pretty nice guy. Oh, and he's a Methodist."

"A Methodist?" She wrote that down.

"What are you, Mr. Ruzak?"

"What am I?" The question was so open-ended I didn't even know where to start.

"Methodist, Baptist, Episcopal?"

"I guess you could call me a lapsed Baptist. My mother was keen on that, but it never quite took with me. My father was a nonpracticing Catholic. He dropped the whole thing when he married my mom, but it's one of those things you can never really get away from. The minute he realized he was dying, he demanded to see a priest. Even then, though, I suspected he was hedging his bets. The sad fact is it's more the terror of death than the joy of life that drives us to God."

"That's very interesting, Mr. Ruzak."

"Can I ask why all this matters?"

"We think whoever killed him also wrote those letters on his forehead."

"*Y-h-w-h.*"

She nodded. "Yes."

"That was the other factor that made me think this was a crime. What do they mean?"

"YHWH is the tetragrammaton, Mr. Ruzak. The four-letter, unpronounceable name of God."

CHAPTER EIGHT

THE OLD GUY'S NAME WAS JOHN MINOR, CADILLAC JACK, OR SOME-times just Cadillac to those who knew him on the street or at the mission on Broadway, where he ate most of his meals. He had a record. Vagrancy. Trespassing. One count of B&E: he had served two years of a suspended sentence in Bushy State Prison for jimmying the lock of a package store on Middlebrook Pike. No one Meredith Black had talked to could say exactly when John Minor showed up in Knoxville, why he came, or where he had come from. He was a loner and rarely talked about himself or his past. He claimed to have served some time in the military, but so far they hadn't found any record of his service. He said he had no family. He'd been tested at Bushy Mountain, and diagnosed as mildly retarded. That was all anyone seemed to know about Cadillac Jack.

"How did he die?" I asked.

"He was beaten to death, Mr. Ruzak."

"And you think the killer might be some kind of religious fanatic or something?"

"Did you notice the letters when you gave him your hat?"

"No, but it was raining and the whole exchange lasted about thirty seconds. I could have missed it."

"No one who knew him can remember seeing them before," she said. "And nobody remembers him being particularly religious."

"Down on Market Square there's that homeless preacher guy, you know the one? He stands on the corner shouting Bible verses and promising eternal damnation to everybody who ignores him."

She nodded. "I know who you're talking about."

"Maybe you oughta talk to him."

She smiled. Perfect teeth always reminded me of my own drawbacks in the orthodontics department: I have a slight overbite and those stubborn stains on the canines.

"We just might do that," she said. She had put away her notebook. The interview was over. She shot up from the sofa—there's no other way to describe it, she rose so fast—and extended her hand with those pink, raw-looking knuckles.

"Thank you for your time, Mr. Ruzak."

"Oh, you can call me Teddy."

"Thank you, Teddy. And I'm Meredith."

"Meredith, that's terrific," I said.

"If you can think of anything else . . ." She handed me her card.

I dug in my wallet for one of mine.

"I don't need that," she said.

"No? No, I guess you wouldn't." I put it back in my wallet, my face flushed, like a guy rejected in a pickup bar. Her perfume was of the musky variety. She also seemed awfully young to have made detective; she looked like she was still in her twenties.

I gave her coat back and, on the way to the door, she said, "So you live alone, Mr. Ruzak?"

"One of the reasons I was at the pound that day," I said. "Now that my doors are shut I'm spending a lot more time here and there's only so much TV I can take."

"I have two dogs, Wally and Beaver."

"I loved that show when I was a kid," I said. I started to tell her my favorite character wasn't the Beav or Wally but Lumpy, the fat kid next door, but thought she might interpret that as my identifying with Lumpy because of his size. I didn't want to draw attention to mine, and the fact was I had no idea why I liked Lumpy. Too much time had passed. "What breed?"

"Dobermans."

Probably the only Dobermans on earth with the names Wally and Beaver. We shook hands again at the door.

"We'll be in touch," she promised, and was gone before I could ask the question that immediately leapt to mind.

Why?

Amanda called that afternoon. From work, according to my caller ID. I assumed she was calling about Archie. I was wrong.

"The cops just called me," she said.

"Detective Black," I said.

"I don't remember her name. Some transient was murdered in your alley?"

"Well, it's not *my* alley, per se. She's just being thorough, checking out my alibi."

"So you knew this guy?"

"No, not really. I gave him my hat that day. I thought you might be calling about Archie."

"No, I was calling to tell you the cops are checking you out."

"I don't take it personally. How is Archie?"

"He misses you. Every day he asks where you are."

"I'm gonna talk to my landlord."

"Think it'll do any good?"

"No. But you've got to try."

"Offer them money."

"Like a bribe?"

"Oh, Ruzak. You offer to give them a deposit for any damage. That's usually how it's arranged."

"It probably would be better not to come to the table empty-handed. Thanks."

"I'm just looking out for Archie," she said. I could detect a smile in her voice. "She asked if you were wearing a hat."

"A hat?"

"I told her I couldn't remember."

"I've got one of those anonymous personas," I said. "I blend in."

"That must come in handy in your line of work."

"Well, I can't think of a single instance where it has."

She laughed for some reason. Some girls laugh only from the neck up. Amanda's laugh originated deep in her belly.

"Hey, you wanna hang with me sometime, Ruzak?"

"Now when you say hang? . . ."

"Maybe grab a cup of coffee. My treat. I know you're unemployed right now."

"Oh. Well." She wasn't my type, really, with that quasi-Goth look and the thinness. The dyed-black hair and that pin in her belly button.

"That's okay," she said without a hint of disappointment in her voice. "You probably have better things to do—like looking for your lost hat."

"No," I said. "Sounds terrific. I'd love to."

"I like you, Ruzak," she said. She still sounded amused. About my saying yes? About my desire for a dog? About my being nondescript? I wondered, given my intuitive understanding of the ineffableness of human beings, how I ever hoped to make a go at being a detective. It was like trying to use an electron microscope to look at a quark. Or maybe more like using one to measure the circumference of the sun.

NOVEMBER 20

CHAPTER NINE

ON THE CORNER OF THE THEOLOGIAN'S CROWDED CREDENZA, NEXT TO the row of bobbleheads of Jesus, Moses, and Buddha, sat one of those four-cup brewers, and the professor offered me a cup from it after I sat down. The coffee slipped over the lip of the pot with the consistency of crude oil. He handed me the cup printed with a *Far Side* cartoon, the one with a big-headed kid in class raising his hand and saying, "May I be excused? My brain is full."

"I think I saw something in the paper about this case," Professor Heifitz said. He was a small man, pushing seventy, I guessed, with a bald, conical-shaped head, small, quick eyes, large ears, and an equally impressive nose. Our noses and ears never stop growing; I've never looked into what evolutionary purpose that serves, but I guess it has something to do with our fading senses. "But I don't recall any mention of the tetragrammaton."

"It might be one of those elements of the crime they hold back—in the event they identify a suspect."

"Have they?"

I shook my head. "I don't think they'd tell me if they did. I mean, it's not as if we have any kind of working relationship and, more importantly, I think I might be on their list."

"Ah. So that's it. You want to take yourself off their list."

"I'm sure that must be it. Self-preservation. I don't really have an alibi. I was alone that night."

"Rather like the victim himself."

"He wasn't alone. Somebody beat him to death."

"As I said."

"Ah," I said, thinking simultaneously that I was being infected by the academic miasma about me and of Eunice Shriver's book: *Ah! ejaculated Ruzak. I understand now.* "I guess there'd be nothing lonelier than that."

"It's an interesting bit of information," Professor Heifitz said. "The tetragrammaton is not what I would consider common knowledge."

"That's what I'm thinking," I said. "Along with hoping that the 'what' might help with the 'why,' which might lead to the 'who.' "

"Which led you to me."

"I thought about dressing up like a bum—or dressing down like a bum, I guess—and hanging out at the railroad yards, but I've got that common fear of the homeless, plus the fact that I don't speak the lingo. They'd make me in two seconds."

He smiled without showing his teeth. Our teeth don't continue to grow past adolescence, but often that illusion is created as our face shrinks. He scooped a couple of dice from his desktop and commenced to rolling them in his hand. He played with those damn dice for the rest of our meeting.

"So what's the significance of the tetragrammaton?" I asked.

"I've no idea how it relates to this crime," he answered. "Obviously it holds some sort of significance to the killer, but I'm a theologian, not a psychologist, Mr. Ruzak."

"Right," I said. "I'll get with the Freudians later."

Again with the grin. "Perhaps you should start with the Jungians. All right. The tetragrammaton, as you already know, consists of four letters, rendered most commonly as *YHWH* but also as *JHVH, JHWH,* and *YHVH,* representing four consonants of the Hebrew alphabet: *yod, he, vav,* and *he.* Your Detective Black was correct when she told you the word is unpronounceable. The word, when it is rendered orally, is *Yahweh.*"

"The name of God?"

He nodded. "The name God gave himself in the burning bush. The tetragrammaton has been called 'the secret name of God' and appears often in the Dead Sea Scrolls and other ancient Hebrew literature. After the Exile in the sixth century B.C., the name fell out of favor, replaced more generally with the common noun, Elohim. Interestingly, Yahweh is only one of these so-called 'secret names.' There were others. During the eleventh century, mystics known as *ba'al shem* claimed to work wonders and gain hidden knowledge by evoking the tetragrammaton and the other, more esoteric names of the Divine. The practice closely resembles certain shamanistic beliefs . . . that by knowing something's name one can master it or gain power over it."

"Gain power over God?"

"Or channel the power, to borrow a phrase from parapsychology. That would be more precise. By evoking God's hidden name, you gain a portion of his power."

"A power trip."

"Who has not, at some time or other, Mr. Ruzak, hungered for a taste of the Ultimate Ground of Being? To the ancient Hebrews, God is first and foremost the Creator, above and apart from his creation, inexpressible in language, and thus his name is rendered unpronounceable, a reflection of God's unknowable nature."

Not knowing what to say, I bought some time by raising the *Far Side* cup, allowing the lukewarm caffeinated sludge to touch my lips. *My brain is full.*

"Any of these—what'd you call them?—ba'al shems still running around ba'al shemming?"

"Not to my knowledge, no, but echoes of the practice remain in kabbalism and certain fundamentalist sects of the Christian church."

"And is that part of the practice, the writing on the forehead?"

He shook his head. "I've never heard of it."

"Does this seem plausible to you: You've got some disturbed individual with this fixation on at least two things, this tetragrammaton business or God in general and homeless people; and he feels he's been chosen to 'deliver' these lost souls back to God, sort of like a *Catcher in the Rye* syndrome only with old transients and not kids, or those hospice workers you read about who are offing the terminal patients right and left."

"Again, I'm not a forensic psychologist, Mr. Ruzak. But I will say mercy killings usually don't take the form of a savage beating. It is hard to imagine a more brutal way of 'saving' someone."

I thought of the stories of Job and the Crucifixion, but I didn't bring it up. I had no desire to go toe-to-toe with a theologian.

He looked at his watch. It swung loosely on his withered wrist when he lifted his arm. "Is there anything else, Mr. Ruzak? I'm late for class."

"Just one more thing," I said. "I was wondering . . . do you find it tough, your line of work? I mean, in these times is faith more like clinging on the edge of a cliff by your fingernails than taking up arms against a sea of troubles?"

"Clarify your question, Mr. Ruzak. Are you asking if faith is harder now than it was in the past?"

"I'm asking if we've finally gone too far and killed off God."

"Oh, I believe God is more resilient than that, Mr. Ruzak. He is more than happy to suffer us for a few more millennia."

CHAPTER TEN

WALTER NEWBERRY WAS A BIG MAN, A FORMER MARINE, SEMI-PRO boxer and recovering alcoholic who found God literally while lying in a gutter on Magnolia Avenue. He came to at three in the morning, face-down, and when he pushed back from the concrete he saw the warning sign that read NO DUMPING/EMPTIES DIRECTLY INTO RIVER, with its picture of a fish. At that moment he heard Jesus calling him to begin his rescue mission, which he financed entirely through private donations.

"Saw this show on Discovery last Easter," I told him. "About how the early Christians traced a fish in the sand as a secret sign in Imperial Rome."

We were sitting in the mess hall of the mission house on Broadway, about five blocks from the spot where he fell ten years ago, landing on his stomach, which saved him from choking to death on his own vomit. Lunch was finished and the kitchen was already prepping for dinner. The mission was entering the busy season.

His massive head gave a nod. He was wearing a tight white T-shirt, blue jeans, and brown work boots. His right bicep sported a SEMPER FI tattoo.

"And early celebrations of the Last Supper always included fish," he said.

"That's one thing that struck me as a fat kid going to church," I said. "All the eating in the Bible, especially in the New Testament."

"And drinking. Look at all the metaphors Jesus used involving wine and vineyards. And his first miracle took place at a feast. He often referred to the Kingdom as a place of feasting."

"Way to a man's heart?"

"And his soul. What can I do for you, Mr. Ruzak?"

"Tell me about Cadillac Jack."

"Showed up about seven or eight months ago. Never said where he was from, but his accent was pure Yankee. Real quiet. Always came late for the meals, sat in the corner up there, near the door. I try to talk to all the folks who come in, but he was a tough nut to crack."

"So you didn't—crack him?"

He shrugged, staring over my shoulder at the plate-glass window facing Broadway.

"I will say this: Over sixty percent of the people who come through those doors have some kind of mental condition . . . borderline schizos, manic-depressives, you name it. Over ninety percent have a substance-abuse problem."

"Including Jack?"

He nodded. "Including Jack. And he was what I'd call . . . slow. You could tell in five minutes that the elevator didn't go all the way up, you understand what I mean?"

I told him I did. "Anything else? Anyone who had a beef with him?"

"Not that I know of. He always struck me as pretty harmless. Gentle. I remember one time, he came in with this stray cat . . . or kitten, I guess, that he found on the street somewhere. He was crazy about that cat, and I bent the rules a little for him. Let him bring it inside. Don't know whatever happened to that cat. Probably took off on him."

"Anybody around here he was especially close to, besides the cat?"

"Yeah. Guy named Jumper."

"Jumper?"

"Yeah. That's what they call him; never heard his real name. Haven't seen Jumper in a while, though, but that isn't unusual. He probably went south with the hummingbirds."

I asked him to describe Jumper. I scribbled down his description. Newberry watched me scribble.

"I already gave all this to that lady cop," he said.

"Well, it's not a competition."

"You gonna tell me your interest?"

"I was the one who found him."

"So?"

"So, well . . . have you ever been in the position where you've got nothing better to do and not doing something is sort of like embracing death?"

"Brother, now you're tugging at the knot."

"You ever hear of the tetragrammaton?"

"The tetra what?"

"Grammaton. The four-letter secret name of God."

"I always spell his name with three letters."

"Let me ask you this. You get any . . . oh, I don't know how else to put it, fanatics in here? Frothing-at-the-mouth religious types?"

"There's very few atheists in foxholes, Ruzak. It's all in your perspective. A fanatic to you might be a good Christian to me."

"No, I think this would be somebody a little more wild-eyed."

"You're welcome to come back at six. We get more preachers, proselytizers, and table pounders than you can shake a stick at."

I wrote my home number on one of my cards and asked him to call if he thought of anything else or if Jumper reappeared.

"You should come back," he said. "Work the serving line. Thanksgiving's coming up. We could always use an extra hand."

"I'll think about it."

"Do you know him, Ruzak?"

"Know who?"

"Jesus."

"We've never met."

"You're wrong about that, you know."

My face felt hot, the same reaction I had when Amanda asked me out.

"That's my conundrum," I confessed. "The knot I pull at. It's been my experience it just gets tighter."

NOVEMBER 27

CHAPTER ELEVEN

WHAT'S THE MATTER WITH YOU, RUZAK?" FELICIA ASKED AS SHE WIPED Tommy's mouth for the fifth time. "You look like crap."

"Crap!" Tommy barked.

"Don't say that word," Felicia told him. "It's not nice."

"But you said it, Mommy," Tommy said. The table jiggled as he swung his pudgy legs.

"I've been thinking seriously about picking up one of those light boxes," I said. Nature goes niggardly with light in late November. Midmorning could just as well be midafternoon, to judge by the light eking through the cloud cover. I slurped my coffee. This was my first time at the Market Square Diner, which had opened a couple of months after the former occupant, The Soup Kitchen, had cleared out. Felicia and I had lunched at The Soup Kitchen before it closed. I had been sorry to see it go. So sorry I'd refused to try this new place, as if to do so betrayed an old friendship.

"Seriously," she said. "What's up with you, Ruzak?"

"Ruzak!" shouted Tommy.

"Don't do that," Felicia scolded him, as if *Ruzak* was on par with *crap*.

My eyes strayed from her face. Through the window on my right, I could see the southwest corner of the square and the Suntrust Bank building, where in warmer months the crazy preacher man waved his pamphlets and exhorted the lunchtime crowd to dump Mammon for Jesus.

"Do you believe in God, Felicia?"

"This is important?"

I nodded. "Yeah. That's the bigger question. Is it really important anymore?"

"It's about that bum, isn't it?"

"Jack. His name was Jack Minor. They called him Cadillac."

"Why?"

"I haven't found out yet."

"You haven't . . . Ruzak, what have you been up to?"

"Just asking around, really."

"Asking who?"

"This professor of religion at UT. Guy who runs the mission on Broadway. And Thanksgiving I worked the line for a few hours."

"What line?"

"The food line at the mission."

"And you're doing this because? . . ."

I shrugged. Our food arrived. Tommy had the pancakes from the kids' menu. They were in the shape of a mouse's head, vaguely Disneyesque. A huge glob of butter perched precariously on top of the heap. Felicia spread it over the pancakes using her butter knife, eyes darting from my face to Tommy's plate.

"Let the cops handle it, Ruzak."

"I called them," I said. "Or her, actually. Detective Black. You know what she said? She asked if I knew how many homicides occur in the greater Knoxville area in a single month."

"How many?"

"I don't know. But the implication was they weren't going to bust their ass tracking down the killer of some anonymous transient."

"So that means you have to?"

"It's no big deal," I said. "And I'm not violating the court order or anything. I mean, nobody's paying me."

"And nobody's paying you to study for your exam, either. Time, like money, should be invested in something that has some kind of return, Ruzak."

My omelet was a little runny. I wiped up the yellow slop with the edge of my toast. I hated it when she lectured me, as if I were Tommy's big brother.

"And somebody *is* paying, Ruzak," she went on. "You look terrible. And you smell stale."

"Stale?"

"Stale, like you haven't changed your clothes in a week."

"Just my jeans. It doesn't make sense to wash denim after just one—"

"When's the last time you had a haircut?"

"I always let it grow in the winter," I said. "To conserve heat. Eighty percent of our body heat is lost—"

"Don't go over the edge on me, Ruzak."

"No. No, I'm at least fifty feet from the edge. Fifty to forty feet . . ."

"Seriously, why don't you pack up your study guides and hit the beach for a couple of weeks?"

"I was never a big fan of beaches. When you think about it, jumping in the open water is like running through the woods in your underwear. Plus I'm self-conscious about my body."

"Look around this restaurant, Ruzak. How many skinny people do you see?"

"Not as many as I saw on Thanksgiving."

"Oh, Ruzak. I'm gonna call 911: Your heart is bleeding."

"Families, Felicia, whole families . . ."

"Right; that's right, Teddy, and if you don't pass that exam, maybe next Thanksgiving you can join them on the other side of the steam table—you, me, and Tommy."

He looked at her at the sound of his name. Syrup hung from his bottom lip and dotted his chin. I pulled the napkin from my lap and ran it over the lower half of his wide face. He grinned at me. "Ruzak!" he shouted, and Felicia shushed him.

"I burned my thumb," I said, showing her the reddened pad. Half my print was gone. "On the steam. Made me think a determined killer could erase his prints that way."

"He'd be determined but not too bright."

"You read about them cutting off the fingers of their victims to hamper identification. They could just burn the prints off."

"I think they usually torch the whole body. Why are we talking about this over breakfast?" She glanced at Tommy, who was tracing designs in the puddle of syrup on his plate.

"So you do believe in God?" I asked again.

"I was raised to."

"But you don't now?"

"Frankly, Ruzak, I don't give it much thought."

"Whoever killed Cadillac did. I think he thought about it a lot." I told her about the tetragrammaton. "I thought it was just drawn on his forehead, Felicia, maybe with a piece of charcoal or even a Sharpie. But Detective Black told me it was *carved*. Somebody took some kind of sharp implement and cut it into his forehead. It looked dark to me that morning because of the frozen blood."

She glanced at Tommy, then leaned over the table and hissed sharply, "Ruzak, I'm not going to warn you again."

"Sorry. My point is, whoever did this thought it was very important to leave the secret name of God on his victim's forehead."

"Maybe Cadillac was a human sacrifice."

"And the killer puts God's name on him like a claim ticket?"

"Or like a parent writes their kid's name in their jacket."

"Right: 'Here, Yahweh, you left this down here; better pick it up.'"

"And that's where Teddy Ruzak, pseudo PI, comes in. Keeper of God's lost-and-found."

"You're saying I should drop this."

"Oh, yeah. Now you understand."

I picked up the check, since Felicia and Tommy came on my invitation. Felicia insisted on leaving the tip (as a former waitress, she never thought I tipped enough), and popped Tommy's hand when he tried to snatch the bills from the table.

On the sidewalk, she zipped his coat. The wind had picked up, and the clouds now looked like a sheet of corrugated steel above us. We walked south, away from the main square where the city sponsored free concerts in the summers. After we had walked about a block, Felicia leaned toward me, lowering her head slightly, and I could smell peaches.

"Don't turn around, but there's some old woman following us."

"Okay."

"She was in the restaurant, too."

"It's Eunice."

"Eunice who?"

"Shriver. No relation to the Yankee Shrivers. You remember her, the chronic confessor."

"Oh. Right. Why's she following you, Ruzak?"

"She's taken up a different kind of confessing."

Felicia gave me a look. I said, "She's writing a book about me."

"You're kidding."

"I can't figure out why, but she's been following me for a couple of weeks now. I've decided not to confront her. She's really old and working through some issues. They're issues I'd rather she work through alone."

Tommy ripped free from Felicia's grip and bulled his way between us, slipping his gloved paw into my right hand, taking Felicia's left with the other. A stranger might mistake us for a family.

"I wonder why you feel more kinship with the corpse in the alley than a living person who might need your help," Felicia said.

"What's wrong with Eunice Shriver I don't think I'm qualified to help."

"So what do you thinks qualifies you to help Cadillac Jack?"

"Sorry, I forgot. Teddy Ruzak, pseudo PI."

"You're sore."

"I haven't been getting much sleep," I admitted. "I can't get it out of my head, Felicia. I looked out that window and he's staring up at me, and from that height you can't tell . . . you can't tell if he's looking back or looking at nothing, and that's what's getting to me—the possibility that that's exactly what he's looking at: nothing; nothing at all."

CHAPTER TWELVE

I was taken aback at her car when, after she strapped Tommy into his car seat, Felicia turned and asked me if I wanted to come over for dinner.

"Now whose heart is bleeding?" I asked her. The wind drew a thick strand of her blond hair across the bridge of her small nose, and she pulled it away, tucking it behind her right ear. Suddenly I felt like bursting into tears.

"No way," she answered. "This is purely selfish. I've got to keep you healthy or it's back to the unemployment line."

"Actually, I guess you could say I sort of have this kind of date tonight."

"Really?" She reacted as if I had told her I had just crapped my pants, her nose crinkling the same way it did when she laughed. But she wasn't laughing.

"I'm having coffee with my pet consultant."

"You don't have a pet."

"That's what I'm consulting about."

"Seriously, who are you dating, Ruzak?"

"Nobody you'd know. She works at the pound."

"Oh. The philosopher."

She ducked her head a little, fumbling with the door handle of her Corolla. I was no mechanic, but the front tires looked a little bald to me, and I wondered how Bob, being a fireman and supposedly very up on safety issues, could let her drive around like that.

"She's prelaw," I said. "Which makes me suspect the philosophy thing is just a cover."

"A cover for what?"

"Rapacious greed."

She laughed. "Doesn't sound like your type, Ruzak."

I held the door for her as she slid in behind the wheel. She pulled down the visor and flipped open the mirror to check something in her reflection. I didn't know what she was checking. Tommy was yelling my name and Felicia told him to be quiet. I opened his door to say good-bye. He tugged on my wrist and ordered me to get in. Felicia told him to let go of Ruzak. As the car pulled away from the curb, the kid flattened his nose against the window. I raised my hand, then dropped it into my overcoat pocket before turning away.

I stopped at a vending machine to buy a paper. I doubted there'd be anything about Cadillac, but I had been checking every day, and why break the habit now? I tucked the newspaper under my arm, crossed the street into the little park, and sat on a bench beside Eunice Shriver. She was hiding behind her own copy of the *Sentinel*.

"So how's it going?" I asked.

She lowered the newspaper and said, "I have reached a crossroads."

"Best to take the one less traveled."

"That could be my life's epithet," she said.

"Epitaph," I corrected her. "Big difference."

"I have not wished to bother you, Theodore," she said. "Some battles we are doomed to fight alone."

"Right," I said. "Eunice, I saw you outside the mission. You shouldn't be hanging around down there. It's a terrific place to get mugged."

"You were there," she pointed out.

"But I've got about fifty pounds on you and I can affect a menacing air."

"Menacing, Theodore? You?"

"I've got facets you've never seen, Eunice."

"Yes! Facets! That's exactly what I'm after."

"What you're after," I echoed. "Eunice, I've been thinking about this little project, and the more I think about it, the more I'm convinced you've chosen the wrong subject. You're like a blind person trying to describe the color blue. Why don't you write *your* story? I'm sure it's much more interesting than mine."

"But Theodore, I can't drop it now; I'm nearly halfway done!"

"You're kidding."

"Look at my hands."

I looked at her hands. She said, "I've been having to wrap them at night in warm towels. The pain from typing all day becomes quite intense by eleven or twelve."

"Maybe you should dictate it."

"I thought of that, but I loathe the sound of my own voice."

"Most people do," I said. "Because the bones in our head distort the sound."

"Oh, my," she said. "My." She dug into her canvas tote and retrieved a pad and a pen. " 'The bones in our head,' " she mumbled as she scribbled.

"So what's this crossroads you're talking about?" I asked.

"Theodore, I'm going to need much more involvement from your end."

"Eunice, from the beginning I think I've made it pretty clear I don't want any involvement, from any end."

"I need to get inside your head."

"That would make it about one person too crowded for me."

I had hurt her feelings. She lowered her head and studied her scuffed orthopedic shoes.

"Vernon tells me I'm foolish, too," she said softly. Vernon was her oldest child. I'd never met Vernon or any of her children, but I had the impression he was the one she was closest to. Maybe I should talk to Vernon, I decided, if you can make a decision that begins with the word *maybe*.

"Well," I sighed. "I guess if they had tied Michelangelo's hands behind his back, he would have painted the Sistine Chapel with his right foot. Tell me what you need, Eunice."

CHAPTER THIRTEEN

AMANDA AND I WERE SITTING ON THE SECOND FLOOR OF A COFFEE house in the southernmost building of the complex that fronted Kingston Pike, called Hamburg Place. The buildings next to the Pike had that sort of German, sort of Swedish look, with the fancy gables and dark trim, very Alpine-ish, though I wasn't sure if the Alps were even in Germany. Our table overlooked the parking lot. Railroad tracks lay on the other side of the lot, and on the opposite side of the tracks was the golf course. In warmer months, you parked by the tracks at your own risk.

She had clipped back her short, black hair using these wide, silver pins, the same kind my mother used to wear. Black parachute pants, a tight black T-shirt that revealed her pale torso and the silver pin in her belly button. She ordered a double espresso. I got something called the Turtle, a coffee concoction made with steamed milk and hot chocolate.

"So did you talk to your landlord?" she asked.

"How much time do I have?"

"Depends on how many we get in."

"I was wondering," I said. "About his name."

"I named him Archie."

"After the comic?"

"What comic?"

Despite being about ten miles from campus, the shop was crowded with students. Textbooks, laptops, highlighters, overflowing ashtrays, chess sets. Floor-to-ceiling bookcases marched along the walls, with stacks of beat-up boxes of board games—Monopoly and Sorry and Risk—jammed between them.

"Maybe an old boyfriend?"

"He just looked like an Archie to me."

"That's good," I said. "I prefer human names for animals. Not like Fido or Stinky."

"Stinky?"

"My first—and only—dog was named Lady."

"Let me guess. Bulldog."

"Collie."

"At least you didn't name it Lassie."

"Lassie was a male."

"Not on the show."

"My dad named her. She died one summer when we were on vacation. I had a total meltdown. He told me I couldn't have another dog until I could demonstrate some self-control."

"And you couldn't?"

"Not to his satisfaction."

"You didn't get along?"

"I never saw him much. He was a salesman."

"The traveling kind?"

"The mediocre kind. He had to work very hard for the very little we had." "I haven't spoken to my father in six years."

"Divorce?"

She nodded. She finished her espresso like a Russian sailor knocking back a shot of vodka.

"Parents," she said, and shuddered.

The guy sitting alone at the table behind her was typing on his computer, the white wires from his iPod dangling from his ears. He was smirking, maybe at something he was listening to or reading, an e-mail or MySpace comment, and I said, "Did you hear about that study that found Americans have only about two close friends?"

"No."

"It struck me how disconnected everything is, though we're more connected now than in any time in human history."

"Do you really think about things like that?"

"Three hundred million of us and growing, yet we're lonelier than ever."

"Maybe you're projecting."

"That's the thing. I don't want to get a dog simply because I'm lonely."

"Isn't that the best reason to get one?"

"I think it has more to do with my savior complex."

"Oh, God. Not one of those."

"I was a kid," I said. "I thought that damn dog died because I wasn't there to save her. I thought if only I had been there . . ." Something caught in my throat. You never really stop grieving. It just goes into hiding, like a filovirus into the dark recesses of the rain forest.

She reached across the table and placed her hand over mine. Her fingers were ice-cold.

"I like you, Ruzak," she said. "You got heart."

"A hemophilic one."

"There are worse kinds."

I walked with her across the parking lot. I watched our breath congeal into mist and mingle.

"Sit in the car with me a minute," she said.

Her car was a late-model Monte Carlo. She cranked the engine to get the heat going, then threw herself over the seat at me, wrapping those pale, thin arms around my neck and smashing her lips into mine. Her tongue was insistent against my front teeth. I could taste the acidity of her espresso. Her cold fingers dug into the hair on the back of my head.

When she came up for air, she said, "You know what I think your problem is, Ruzak? You're a little in love with death."

She grabbed my right wrist and lifted my arm, pushing my hand under her black T-shirt. I was struck by the contrast between the warmth of her chest and the coldness of her fingers.

"Don't tell me you're gay," she whispered.

"I'm not," I said.

"Kiss me again, Ruzak. Hard."

I kissed her again, my arm twisted awkwardly between us. I worried about my two-day-old beard, if it was irritating her soft skin. It seemed strange to me, her accusing me of being in love with death when she was the one in black; I'd never seen her wear a different color.

She broke the kiss and I removed my hand from beneath her shirt. She glanced in the rearview mirror and then unsnapped her pants and commenced to wiggle out of them.

"What's going on?" I asked.

"Tell me you're a virgin. Please." Her cheeks were flushed. The foggy window behind her shone with the ambient light of the single streetlamp about two cars away.

She pushed me back against the seat and straddled me. Her panties were white. I was surprised.

"Come on, Ruzak," she whispered into my ear. "I haven't been laid in months."

It had been much longer than that for me, but I didn't tell her that. Her hips rotated slowly as her weight pressed down on my lap, with both hands on my shoulders, pushing.

"Don't you like me?" she asked. "I can tell you like me. . . ."

"I do like you," I said. "I do."

"But? There's a 'but' there."

I bit back an inappropriate laugh. "This is just a little . . . sudden."

"Spontaneous." Again she smashed her lips against mine. There was nothing tender about it. Insistent and fierce, bordering on angry.

When I could talk again, I said, "I can't shake the feeling I'm taking advantage of you."

She pushed herself off me and sat behind the steering wheel again, taking it in both hands, like a little girl pretending to drive her daddy's car.

"Sorry," I said. "I've been edgy ever since I found him."

"Who?"

"The old guy in the alley."

"See? You are in love with death."

"I really don't see it that way, Amanda."

"Then why won't you fuck me?"

I didn't say anything. She swung her face in my direction.

"I turn you on," she said. "I felt it."

"Do you believe in God?"

"Huh?"

I repeated the question. She said, "Oh great, one of those. This is just my shitty luck." She hit the steering wheel with the heel of her hand.

"So that means you don't?"

"No, I don't, if you must know."

"The evidence could be interpreted either way."

"Who cares, Ruzak? Who really cares anymore?"

She grabbed her pants from the floorboard and yanked them over her slender hips. "I like you, Ruzak, I really do, but guess what? You haven't been commissioned to save anybody. You may think you're preserving my honor or whatever, but really, all you're doing is leaving me frustrated and fucking angry and thinking I'm unattractive as hell. . . ."

I reached over to wipe off the tear rolling down her cheek. She slapped my hand away.

"Don't fucking touch me."

"Sorry. You're not. It's me. You know it's me."

"I don't want to get engaged or have a boyfriend and, even if I did, it wouldn't be with someone like you," she said. "I don't need a man to complete me. And guess what, I don't need God or Jesus or any of that other bullshit. It's all bullshit, Ruzak. Even love is bullshit. You know what love is? Love is just a complex hormonal response to stimuli. It's genetic memory mixed with the procreative drive. It's the lie we tell our children because the truth is too horrible to say aloud. You're thinking love saves but love does the opposite. Why are you looking at me like that? Who are you, Mahatma Fucking Gandhi?"

"I was just thinking this has got to be the oddest first date I've ever had."

"Fuck you."

"Amanda . . ."

"Get out of my car and fuck you."

"Okay."

I stepped out but left the door open. I leaned in.

"I'll call you," I said.

"Don't you fucking dare."

She started the car and slammed it into reverse before I could close the door. I stepped back in the nick of time. She floored the gas. She stopped long enough to reach over and shut the door, and then she was gone, screeching out of the parking lot. I suspected she was hyped on caffeine, which can be as dangerous as driving drunk.

I sat in my car for a minute or two, and then dug my cell phone from my pocket. Felicia answered on the fifth ring.

"Hey," I said.

"Ruzak?"

"Hope it's not a bad time," I said, checking my watch. I figured Tommy would be in bed.

"What's the matter?" Felicia asked. "I thought you were on a date."

"It's over."

"Something bad happened, didn't it?"

"I've got to get out of this funk," I said. "I was thinking finding who killed that old guy might get me out of it, but now I'm wondering if that's just making it worse."

"Of course it's making it worse."

"I took his mug shot to the soup kitchen," I told her. "The one taken when he was busted for B and E. I showed it to everyone who came by my station. Nobody remembered him. Nobody knew he had even been there. They didn't know the face. They didn't recognize the name. He passed through life as anonymously as a boat in the fog. Do you think I have a complex?"

"Oh, Ruzak, don't get me started. You made some ham-handed pass at her, didn't you, and got your face slapped."

"No, just my hand."

She didn't say anything.

"Are you still there?" I asked.

"Yes."

"Okay. I thought the network had dropped my call."

"You want me to come over?" she asked.

"I'm in my car."

"Well, I could wait till you get home, dummy."

"No," I said. "No. You have Tommy."

"Bob can watch him."

"Bob won't mind if you come over?"

"We're all grownups, Ruzak."

"That's okay. I think I'd rather be alone. Sorry to call."

"Ruzak, drop this."

"I will. I mean, I should."

"And it's a good idea for you to talk to somebody. You know, a professional. Something's going on with you and I'm not qualified to deal with it."

NOVEMBER 30

CHAPTER FOURTEEN

I BROUGHT SOME LILIES FOR MY MOTHER'S GRAVE AND A BOTTLE OF
Old Grouse for Dad's. Mom had buried him among the Baptists, though Dad
had never set foot in a Baptist church, or any church for that matter, since his
twenties. He had asked to be cremated and his ashes scattered over the Smoky
Mountains. Mom claimed to have looked into it before telling him federal law
prohibited dumping a person's remains in a national park.

"Well, Mom," I told her. "I got to get to the printer's, but I wanted to let
you know I'm not a detective anymore. Actually, I guess I never was, but anyway, despite that or maybe because of that, now I'm looking into this case of
a guy I found dead in the alley behind my office. Nobody asked me to and Felicia tells me not to; she says it's dangerous to my mental health, but I can't get
it out of my head, him lying down there in the garbage, like he was looking up
right at me, and I can't get it out of my head that the last thing he saw was the
person who killed him, and I'm wondering if he was still alive when they
carved those letters into his forehead, though the coroner doesn't think so because there wasn't much blood and there'd be more if his heart was still beating. He had seventy-three broken bones, Mom. He was a mess. Face, ribs,
arms, fingers, both cheeks. They beat the living shit out of him. Sorry.

"Damn, it's cold. I prefer February cold to November cold. November
cold seeps right in and you can't shake it, even in a warm room.

"So anyway, I'm supposed to be studying for the PI exam so I can do this
the right way instead of the Ruzak way, but you know, part of this I'm convinced must be genetic; Dad was a corner-cutter, let's be honest. Remember
how he lost that job in Saint Louis, skimming commissions from his crew at
the car dealership? Or how he used to park in the handicapped spaces at the
grocery? Dad thought the fix was in on everything, even elections and pro

football games, so he never saw anything wrong in putting the fix in himself. I'm not being judgmental, Mom. It's not judgmental to face the facts.

"I know what you'd tell me. You'd tell me to pray about all this, and I've tried but I can't get past 'Dear God.' I start and then my mind gets overwhelmed and my thoughts scatter and I feel this weight come down on my shoulders like it's too much, and I feel like a kid poking a big anthill with a stick. That's weird. Then I think most people in my position would choose to escape or anesthetize themselves, which is just another form of escape, I guess. Like the vast majority of homeless people are alcoholics and a big chunk are also mentally handicapped, and this Cadillac Jack was both, but I've checked with every mental institution, hospital, and drug rehab clinic in eastern Tennessee, and nobody has a record of ever treating a Jack Minor.

"The ways to catch a killer are finite, Mom. Forensics, witnesses, victimology, profiling . . . maybe one or two more, but that's about it. I guess I keep looking at Jack because he was looking at me. Maybe to catch his killer I need to look away. Like with God, you're not going to find him by looking for him.

"So that's why I got to stop by the printer's on my way home."

I unscrewed the cap of the Grouse and slowly poured the whiskey over Dad's grave, near the base of the stone, aiming for the spot directly over his mouth. Then I dropped the bottle back into the bag and slipped it into the outer pocket of my overcoat.

"It's the last day of November," I said. "Thank God."

A man was standing on the handicap ramp leading to the side door of the church, watching me as I walked back to my car. He raised his hand and I waved back. I stood by the car for a second, and then decided, What the hell? I crossed the lot and stood on the pavement beneath him while he leaned his forearms on the rail, smiling benevolently down at me with large, perfectly even teeth.

"How are you, Eddy?" he asked.

"It's Teddy, and I'm a little cold," I told Pastor Morris. He was wearing a gray suit and a bright yellow tie with a silver cross tiepin. His goldish-blond hair was swept straight back from his finely sculpted forehead. Pastor Morris was at least six years younger than I was, a fact that made me vaguely uneasy for some reason.

"Want to come inside for a minute?"

"I'm late for an appointment," I lied.

"How's business?" he asked.

"Not bad," I lied again.

"Working through your weekends?"

"As a matter of fact . . ." I said, but stopped there. Let the preacher fill in the blanks; that was sort of his job.

"We surely miss your mother," he said, nodding toward the cemetery. "She was a wonderful woman."

"You think it borders on the profane, my talking to her grave like that?" I had to assume he had seen me out there.

"In what way?"

"Well, you know, talking to the dead, like some sort of ancestor worship."

"Talking isn't the same as praying, Eddy."

"Teddy."

"Just closing your eyes and feeling God's presence—that can be praying, too."

"I caught this documentary on TV not long ago," I said. "About that tsunami in Indonesia. This one Indian guy was with his family on a train, heading for a holiday on the coast, when it rolled in and he never found his son, this twelve-year-old kid. He was just wiped off the face of the earth."

"So what's your point?"

"Well, he never talked about his religion, but I'm betting he said a prayer."

"The Almighty has his own purposes."

"That's the rub, Pastor. Why did he give us a brain if he didn't want us to figure out what those are?"

"Are you asking me why we suffer?"

"No. Because I know what your answer's going to be. Original sin or free will or echoing Christ's suffering or something along those lines. I just can't shake this feeling that God was born on the day the first person died."

I sat for a few minutes in the car. The forecast was calling for the first snow of the season. The preacher disappeared into the church. He was barely three months on the job when he buried my mother, and he kept getting her name wrong at the service. Maybe it didn't make much difference in the eternal scheme of things, but I was pretty upset at the time. The ancient Hebrews invested a lot of time and energy ferreting out the hidden name of God, and not just because God was important to them; *names* were important. I wouldn't be the same person if my name had been Ralph or Anthony or Christopher—or even Eddy, which this preacher obviously thought it should be.

By forgetting her name, he was forgetting her, and the point of the whole exercise was to remember.

CHAPTER FIFTEEN

AMANDA LAID DOWN HER PAPERBACK COPY OF NIETZSCHE'S *MAN AND Superman* when I walked through the glass doors.

"This better be about Archie," she said.

"That's half of it," I said. "Well, a third."

"You don't owe me an apology, Ruzak. What do you have behind your back? Those better not be flowers."

"If it is, am I in trouble?"

"Oh, Christ. They'll just die. I'm here till four and I don't have anything to put them in. What are they?"

I showed her.

"Daisies?"

"It was more of an impulse buy," I said. "I was at the florist's picking up some lilies for my mom's grave."

She grabbed the flowers and laid them behind the counter.

"The second thing," I said, to move off the subject of flowers. "I was wondering if you'd mind putting this on the door."

I showed her one of the flyers I'd been putting up all over town.

"Who's Jack Minor?" she asked.

"The old guy who died behind my building."

"Twenty-five-thousand-dollar reward? Who's putting that up?" She looked at me.

"I collected a pretty big payoff on my first case," I explained.

She stared at me for a few seconds more, then shrugged and dropped the flyer beside the daisies.

"I'll ask the boss."

"The third thing," I said. I took a deep breath. "I've decided to adopt Archie."

"You can't."

"Because I'm underqualified?"

"Because he's dead."

"Oh, no."

"They put him down this morning, Ruzak."

"Why didn't you call me?"

"I did call you. I left a long message on your voice mail."

"I wasn't home. I was visiting my mom."

"I thought your mom was dead."

"I was visiting my dead mom."

"Well, Archie joined the club at ten-forty-five this morning."

"Well, of course he did."

"What's that supposed to mean?"

"I have to go," I said.

"Don't do that. Three more came in last night. Let's check them out."

"No," I said. "No. I still have to cover Cumberland Avenue."

"Carpe diem, Ruzak!" she called after me as I walked to the door. "Carpe diem!"

I sat in my Sentra and put my hands on the wheel. I wondered if she could see me. Bits of snow began to peck at the windshield, no bigger than pencil leads, not soft, fluffy-looking flakes, but flinty pellets, a vindictive snow. The prospect daunted me, trudging up that long slope on Cumberland Avenue in this weather, stapling my "Wanted" posters on the light poles along the section known as The Strip, the main drag through campus. In a day or two, Jack's face would be buried under other announcements and advertisements more interesting to college students, local band dates and roommate-wanted flyers with the little removable strips with the contact information at the bottom.

Covered over. Busted up. Jack was pulp inside, his gut filled with blood, both lungs crushed. The only significant exterior bleeding had been from his forehead, and that was after his heart had stopped. Jack Minor bled into himself; they turned him into a sack of blood and shattered bone, then cut the name of God in a spot no more than an inch from the only part of his brain that had the capacity to conceive of a God.

The cops had found a broken piece of two-by-four near the mouth of the alley, which Meredith Black thought was a good candidate for the murder weapon. The crime techs had found several human hairs that resembled Jack's stuck in one splintered end, but they had no plans to run a comparison. What would be the point of that? Detective Black had six other homicide cases on her desk demanding her attention, cases with leads and tips and real evidence to work from. No witnesses had come forward, and nobody had walked through the front doors of the station to confess. She had a better case with the gang-banger from the East Side who took a bullet in the forehead. He didn't have much of a future, either, but there were people who noticed his passing, for whom each day was different because he died.

Behind a closed door, one person holds down the animal while another injects it with a lethal dose of pentobarbital. The animal is dead in thirty seconds. Then they place it in an oven and burn it. Three to four million times every year. And it's okay; it's the humane thing. Nobody wants this dog. The man holding the needle is performing a necessary service to society. We can't allow these creatures to run wild on the streets. They're a nuisance and a burden.

CHAPTER SIXTEEN

I ARRIVED AT MY APARTMENT A LITTLE AFTER FIVE, IN A DARKNESS THAT struck me as preternatural. There was no message from Amanda. Felicia had left a message to call her.

"I haven't heard from you in a couple days," she said.

"Well," I said. "No news is good news."

"Ruzak, you're not having a nervous breakdown, are you?"

"You know what I think it is? That Hinton guy from the state left the cosmic door open that day he shut us down and some seriously bad karma blew into the room. They killed Archie today."

"Who's Archie?"

"The dog I was going to adopt."

"Oh. Who killed him?"

"The people my tax money pays to kill them."

"Ruzak, I know you've got your heart set on it, but maybe a dog isn't the right kind of pet for you. Maybe you should go with something that doesn't require quite that level of commitment."

"What, like a turtle?"

"Or a hamster, if it's got to be a mammal. What about a parrot?"

"Parrots aren't mammals, and I read somewhere they can live to be a hundred. I'm not comfortable with having a pet that will outlive me."

She changed the subject. "You'll never guess who called me today. Eunice Shriver."

"Why'd she do that?"

"To talk about you. She's a funky old broad. She kept me on the phone for two hours."

"I'll talk to her. People with obsessive personalities should have the decency to keep it to themselves. What did she want to know?"

"It was weird. She kept talking about you as if you were hypothetical."

"What's that mean?"

"Oh, she'd say things like, 'If this guy you barely knew walked into the diner where you were working and offered to give you a job, bing, just like that, what would you say?' "

"Well, that's pretty much what happened."

"Or, 'Say you had this thirty-something bachelor with limited social skills, let's call him Teddy, how do you think he'd approach you, as a woman? . . . ' "

"She wonders if I'd approach you if I was a woman?"

"*Me* as a woman, Ruzak. *Me.*"

"Oh. What did you say?"

"I said I would let him know I was involved in a relationship."

"I've been meaning to call Vernon."

"Who the hell is Vernon?"

"Her son. I'm thinking an intervention might be necessary."

"I think she's harmless. Aren't you flattered?"

"More like unnerved. Her grip on reality is one-handed."

"Right now I'm more concerned with *your* grip," Felicia said. "Have you been studying for your exam?"

"I've been kind of busy."

"Doing what?"

"Looking for my hat."

"Oh, Ruzak."

"Look, I should tell you in case you see them around somewhere: I've made up these posters offering a reward for Jack's killer. Well, not a reward for his killer, but one for information leading to the arrest and conviction of his killer."

There was a second or two of silence, and then she said, "What kind of reward?"

"The monetary kind."

"Christ, Ruzak . . ."

"Only twenty-five thousand."

"Oh, is that all? Ruzak, you're talking to someone who happens to know the balance in your account."

"It's okay," I said. "It's okay. I'm not dipping deep, not up to my neck, just sticking a toe in."

"More like going up to your waist."

"Well, we could quibble."

"You'll have fakes and con men coming out of the woodwork, Ruzak. Anybody with any legitimate knowledge is going to take it to the cops."

"I don't have to pay out unless there's an arrest and conviction. By that time I'll have passed the test and be back in business. And that's all I'm gonna do, Felicia; I promise. No more sleuthing until I have my license. I think he'll be happy with that."

"You think who will be happy?"

"Jack."

"Ruzak, Jack is dead."

"I know. That's how this whole thing started."

"You remember Dr. Fredericks?" she asked.

The shrink. Something knotted up in my chest. I said, lips tight, "Sure I remember her."

"Maybe you oughta give her a call."

"You bet."

I was chilled to the bone, so I took a hot shower, wrapped myself in a towel, and fried some bacon for a BLT in the cast-iron skillet I'd inherited from Mom. Halfway through the frying, the towel slipped from my middle and puddled around my ankles. It's not a good idea in general to fry anything in the nude, but some masochistic switch had been flipped in my psyche, and the hot grease popping on my pale flesh brought me a kind of perverse satisfaction. I thought of those pilgrims who flagellate themselves on their way to shrines, though the odds weren't in my favor that I was on some march to enlightenment. The odds were more likely I was slipping down a slope toward a messy landing. The evidence was there, like Eunice Shriver asking Felicia questions that implied my existence was merely hypothetical. The evidence was there that both Eunice and I had climbed into the same metaphysical boat, and that boat was being carried by a swift current toward the falls.

DECEMBER 4

CHAPTER SEVENTEEN

I SIGNED IN AT THE FRONT DESK, AND THE COP BEHIND THE COUNTER gave me a visitor's pass to clip on my shirt pocket. Then I followed a short young woman, whose uniform struck me as at least two sizes too small for her, through a set of double doors, and down a series of labyrinthine hallways until we reached a door outfitted with one of those keypad-locking systems. The door was labeled HOMICIDE. She blocked my view of the keypad with her body as she punched in the code.

"Last office on the right," she instructed me.

Detective Meredith Black smiled at the sight of me filling her doorway.

"How've you been, Mr. Ruzak?" she asked. She reached across the desk, gave my hand two quick pumps, and waved me to a chair. On the credenza behind her were several photos of her with two kids, a boy and a girl, neither more than ten, I'd guess. No man in any of them. Divorced, probably, or maybe he took all the photos. Or they could be a relative's kids.

I could have filled her in on the details of my escalating existential crisis, but I had been pegged for a kook by law enforcement during my first case, and I was determined this time to present a sturdier façade.

"Thanks for seeing me," I told Detective Black. "I know you must have your fair share of wannabes and hangers-on and rubberneckers."

She smiled enigmatically. I wondered why I had made a list like that. Just doing it up thrust me into the milieu.

"Well, I really don't have that much to share with you, Mr. Ruzak. As I told you on the phone, the case has stalled."

"Don't know if you've seen or heard about this," I said, sliding the poster across her desk. "And I owe you an apology, I guess, for slapping them up all over town without giving you a heads-up. I have this tendency to go off half-cocked."

"Seems counterproductive in your line of work, Mr. Ruzak."

"Oh, practically every personality trait I have is," I said. She was studying the poster. "So I tell myself it's like my old shop class: Sometimes you have to saw against the grain to get the perfect cut."

"It's an admirable gesture," she said, dropping the poster on her blotter.

"Meaning futile?"

She shrugged. "I haven't gotten any calls. You?"

"A couple. Nothing promising."

"Well, then."

She leaned back in her chair and folded her hands in her lap. She wore a gray cashmere or cashmere-looking turtleneck sweater and gray slacks. I noted the prominence of her chin. The chin and those large incisors, that's what Meredith Black led with.

"I've got a couple a working theories I'd like to run by you, if that's okay," I said. She didn't say it was, but on the other hand she didn't say it wasn't, so I went on. "Nothing past the hypothetical stage. There are things I know but more things I don't know, and some of the things I don't know you may know. That's what I need to know, so I know which to keep and which to toss."

"Which what to keep or toss?"

"Theories. For example, what do you know about Jumper?"

"Jumper?"

"According to Walter Newberry, Jumper was Cadillac's only friend in Knoxville. He disappeared near the time Jack was murdered."

"I interviewed Mr. Newberry. I don't remember him mentioning any Jumper."

"Well, he mentioned him to me. So I'm thinking we're dealing with either a suspect or a witness."

"There's a third possibility. It's a coincidence. Jumper's disappearance has nothing to do with the crime."

"Right. So you don't have anything on Jumper?"

She shook her head. "As I said, Mr. Ruzak, this is the first I've heard of him."

"Okay. Well, he isn't really necessary for my working theories to work. He's the best candidate I have for Theory A, but it could be someone else, a Mr. X. By the way, I'm calling the perpetrator in Theory A 'Mr. X,' and in Theory B he's 'Mr. Y.'"

"A, B, X, Y, got it," she said.

"Okay, so . . . Theory A: Jack Minor was murdered by somebody he knew. First, he was beaten to death, an intimate way to kill, right up there with stabbing. Mr. X knew Jack and had some motivation to kill him. Mr. X could be Jumper or another person Jack knew in town. Maybe Jack stole something from him, or Mr. X demanded money from him, or Jack welshed on a bet . . . it could be any number of things."

She was nodding. "Agreed."

"Whether premeditated or spur-of-the-moment, the beating probably occurred where I found him. There's a possibility he died someplace else and the body dumped in the alley, but that would entail some risk for Mr. X. If Jack was indebted in some way to him, I figure Mr. X lured Jack to the crime scene on a pretext, then jumped him."

"I'm beginning to see how someone named Jumper could fit into this scenario."

I took a deep breath. "It's also possible within the paradigm of Theory A that Jack was the instigator—in other words, Jack set up somebody to rob them and lost the fight."

"In that case, Mr. X doesn't have to be someone he knew. I'm assuming Theory B has to do with a stranger killing."

"Right. Mr. Y is a complete stranger, a psychopath with a God complex who knocks off Jack for his own disturbed reasons—that's what behind YHWH. He may have been stalking Jack or other transients, or maybe Jack was a victim of opportunity. . . . Mr. Y sees him that night and lures or follows him into the alley."

"Or perhaps Mr. Y is someone Jack knows."

"That would make him Mr. X."

"My point is, that segment of society is full of people with psychological and emotional problems. It isn't farfetched that Jack knew someone obsessed with religion, and this person decided to make an offering out of him."

"Which is why it seems imperative to me we try to find this Jumper. He might be the key. The one thing Mr. X and Mr. Y have in common is YHWH. Plus the fact that Jumper is the only real lead we have."

"Mr. Ruzak," she said, and her tone was not unkind, "As I've said, the department takes every homicide very seriously, and simply because this homicide involved an indigent doesn't mean we take it any less seriously than someone murdered in, say, West Knoxville. But I hope you can understand we simply don't have the manpower to track down every possible lead in every single case. This case has no witnesses, no promising forensics, and no viable suspects, X, Y, or Z."

"My theories didn't have a Z. You think there could be a Z? A Z would imply a C when I thought A and B covered every possible scenario using X and Y."

She showed me her incisors, chin thrust slightly forward. "Here's one possible C. Jack was murdered by a secret society or cult that worshiped the ancient Hebrew god Yahweh. Either as a ritual sacrifice or because he saw something he shouldn't have seen or stole something he shouldn't have stolen. Like a sacred amulet or code belonging to the cult. Maybe you should look into all the functioning secret death cults in the county. Then, after you nab them, sell the film rights to Hollywood. You could call it *The Yahweh Code.*"

I thought about what she just said. "You think this is funny."

"I think it's pitiful. Not you—Jack. Well, maybe you a little, too." She tapped her well-manicured index finger on the poster. "Don't get me wrong, Mr. Ruzak. Offering a reward is really altruistic and noble, and I promise if any calls come in on it, you'll be notified. As I hope you'll notify us should you develop any leads."

"I have developed a lead and I did bring it to you," I said. "Which you poo-pooed."

"You said it yourself: that's not a lead; that's a theory."

"It's both."

She shrugged. "I can make a few calls about this Jumper person, but I'm assuming you've already done the legwork and come up empty, otherwise you wouldn't be here asking about him."

"I don't believe you," I said. "I don't believe you'll make a single call and I don't believe you take this case as seriously as you would a rich person buying it in West Knoxville. I don't think you care jack squat about Jack Minor. He was a nobody—not anything to anyone except God, if you believe in a God, and maybe that's why whoever did this carved those letters into his forehead, like a return address. And just like Jesus being taken up in a cloud, Jack is gone from our sight, but the ironic thing, he was gone before he left."

I stood up. "And I'm going to find whoever did this, Detective Black. I'm going to find him and deliver him to your doorstep, because you've made it clear I'm all Jack has now. Me, of all people! The most hapless PI to come down the pike since Inspector Clouseau, that's who Jack Minor has on his side."

"The Pink Panther wasn't a PI, Mr. Ruzak," she pointed out, smiling.

"Well, the plain fact is I couldn't think of any famous PIs who are also hapless. Hapless PIs are invisible, too."

CHAPTER EIGHTEEN

LATER THAT AFTERNOON, I WAS ON MY DAILY PHONE CALL WITH Eunice Shriver when another call beeped through. I told Eunice I would call her back because I never could get the hang of clicking the button to put people on hold; I always disconnected them. So I held down the button and picked up on the first ring.

"Good, you're home."

"Amanda?"

"What's your number?"

"You just called it."

"Your apartment number, Ruzak. I'm outside your building."

"I'll come down."

Amanda was sitting on the front stoop, cradling something squirming in a fleece blanket. Being an ace detective, I immediately deduced what it was.

"That's a dog," I said.

"Ruzak, it's Archie."

She pulled back the edge of the blanket and I saw dark brown eyes and a wriggling black nose.

"You told me they put Archie down."

"I know. I lied. Can we go inside? He's freezing."

"Let me make sure the coast is clear."

We took the stairs to the third floor; the elevator was too risky. I threw the deadbolt and Archie leaped out of Amanda's arms as if that was the signal he'd been waiting for. He scampered through every room, skittering on the hardwood, and once he had run the circuit, sniffing along the baseboards and in the corners, he came to a stop in front of me and sat, his tail scraping back and forth as he grinned up at me.

"I think he approves," Amanda said.

"My landlord won't."

"What your landlord doesn't know won't hurt him."

"I'll have to take him for walks," I said. "Sooner or later they'll catch me. That's the thing most transgressors never figure out, Amanda: Eventually, everything in shadow comes into the light."

"That sounds like something from the Bible."

Well, you can bet it didn't come from your pal Nietzsche, I thought. "Why did you lie to me?"

"I was angry. You hurt me and I wanted to hurt you."

"I was that cruel?" It seemed to me the punishment didn't fit the crime.

"Ruzak, you and me disagree on most of the fundamentals, but I think we both can agree that I'm human. Can you think of anything crueler than rejection?"

"Yes. Indifference."

"You're going to reject Archie now, aren't you? Just to get back at me."

I looked down at the dog. His eyes were the color of chocolate and fixed on mine. I'd learned from Animal Planet that you never look away from a dog's gaze; it was a sign of submissiveness. Dogs view humans as two-legged members of the pack, and you had to establish you were top dog. After a few seconds, Archie gave up trying to stare me down and fell to his side, raising his foreleg and offering his belly for a rub. I looked at Amanda.

"He's housebroken, right?"

"He never messed in his pen," she said.

"Guess I gotta get to the pet store," I said.

"I'll come with you."

"Will he bark while we're gone?"

"We'll take him with us. How about it, Arch? Wanna go shopping?"

So that's what we did: piled into my little Sentra and drove to Pet Market on Kingston Pike. Archie rode in Amanda's lap, and she insisted we keep the window down so he could stick his busy nose into the frigid air.

"Dogs have a sense of smell a thousand times more sensitive than ours," she pointed out.

I wondered if that applied to your flat-faced breeds, like bulldogs and pugs.

"What do you want from me, Ruzak? I'm just a volunteer, not a vet."

She was being awfully snippy for someone trying to right a wrong.

"What made you change your mind?" I asked.

"Today was Archie's day. They were coming at five to put him down. So I signed all the papers and paid the fees. You owe me a hundred and thirty dollars, Ruzak."

Pet Market promised the lowest prices in town, but after bowls, food, treats, a crate and bed, collar and leash, an ID tag with Archie's name and my phone number, a chewy toy, a package of dried pigs' ears, doggie shampoo, a comb, and a toothbrush, the total bill came to $312.87. I had no idea they made toothbrushes for dogs.

"What do you think?" I asked Amanda on the drive back. "Is getting a dog like purchasing friendship?"

"What, like buying something that can't be bought?"

"I've always looked at therapy that way. What does a shrink do that your favorite bartender can't?"

"Dispense drugs."

"Alcohol is a drug. And unless you've got a real problem, you can get out of a 'session' for a lot less than a hundred fifty an hour."

She helped me carry Archie's supplies up to my apartment. I set up his crate by the sofa and asked Amanda why I needed to cage this dog.

"A dog crate isn't cruel, Ruzak," she answered. "It gives them a sense of security at night and when you're gone. Dogs can develop separation anxiety. Crates help with that."

I offered her something to drink. I didn't think she deserved a reward for lying to me, but probably deserved one for rescuing Archie and forcing me into the decision I'd been avoiding for reasons I couldn't put my finger on. She accepted a beer and we sat on the sofa while Archie worked on his new squeaky toy, a lamb whose cries I guess excited the part of Archie's brain that still held the ancient memory of the hunt, the death squeals of the kill.

"Everybody has a type," she said. "People they're more attracted to than others. Is that it? I'm not your type?"

"I never really thought about it."

"What is that? Is that a yes or a no?"

"It's neither."

"Look, Ruzak, I'm young but I'm not stupid. You're not gay so I know you must look at women. What kind of women do you like to look at? You a leg man? Breasts? Ass? What?"

"Eyes."

"Eyes?"

I nodded and took a long pull of my Bud Light.

"What color are my eyes, Ruzak?"

"Brown."

"You guessed that because most people have brown eyes. They're green."

"I could have sworn they were brown."

"I don't have large tits. But my legs are okay."

"I've never seen them."

"It's winter, Ruzak. But I hardly ever wear skirts. Is that it, I'm not feminine enough?"

"Oh no. You're feminine."

"No I'm not. Not like my sister. I was always a tomboy; she's the girly-girl. Maybe you'd like my sister better."

"You want to set me up with your sister?"

"I'm just trying to figure you out. I'm attracted to you. I've never been attracted to a big guy before. You're really not my type. I like athletic guys; you know, guys with a nice build. But the biggest thing for me is intelligence."

I wasn't sure, but I thought she had just called me fat and stupid.

"That's a puzzle, then," I said. "Why you would find me attractive."

"I've had dreams about you."

"You're kidding."

"It's the size thing. You're so big and I'm skinny and in my dreams you're holding me down. . . . It's almost like a rape."

"Boy."

"And I'll wake up and, God, I'll be so excited."

She set her empty bottle on my coffee table and scooted closer to me.

"So what do you think?"

"My dreams are usually more mundane," I said. "Me in the kitchen trying to open a can of tuna fish. Things like that."

She put her pale hand on my knee and said, "It's just sex, Ruzak. I don't even expect it to be good sex, if you've got any issues with performance anxiety. We don't have to go steady or get engaged or anything like that. I'm on the pill."

My immediate instinct was to tell her I had AIDS. Then I thought that might be a little over the top and herpes would be better. I could tell her I was in the middle of an outbreak. Her eyes *were* green, but a very dark, loamy green.

"There's somebody else," I blurted out.

She stared at me for a second. "Where?" she asked, and then looked around the room as if the other woman might leap out from a hiding place.

"We've been dating for almost a year," I said.

She pulled away from me and said, "You might have told me before I admitted to having sex dreams about you. What's your goal, Ruzak? Why is it, every time I see you, you humiliate me?"

She grabbed her coat from the back of the sofa and stood up. Archie rose when she did and followed her to the door. It had been a big day for Archie, and Amanda was the one constant.

"I don't believe you, by the way," she said at the door. "You don't have a girlfriend. What's the big deal, Ruzak? Why can't you just tell me you find me gross?"

"I don't find you gross."

"Then what is it? You a monk or something? Are you on a mission from God, Ruzak?"

"This old guy has raised some questions in my mind. I guess they've been simmering on the back burner for some time now," I said, "And there's this principle I try to live by: When you're tumbling down a slippery slope, you don't grab onto anyone. You'll just yank them down with you."

"But what if grabbing onto someone is your only hope?"

I didn't have an answer for that. I thanked her again for saving Archie and she left. Archie pressed his nose against the jamb and whined, his tail waving slowly.

"She's gone," I told him. "And I doubt she'll be back."

A couple hours later, I realized I'd forgotten to give her a check for the adoption fee.

CHAPTER NINETEEN

THAT NIGHT THE DISCOVERY CHANNEL RAN A SPECIAL ABOUT THE ascent of man and the mysterious disappearance of the Neanderthal. Did disease or competition with us wipe them out, or did we murder them into extinction? In the nineteenth century, the Romantics viewed Nature as benign, a glowing reflection of God's grace. Now we know better. Nature is brutal and, if it is feminine, she's not the kind of woman you can trust. Human beings may be her finest achievement yet, but when you get right down to brass tacks, we're meat. AIDS and organisms like streptococcus don't give a crap that we subdued the earth or produced a Shakespeare or put a man on the moon or were the first species to conceive of God. We might not have been the first, though. Maybe Neanderthals got to God first. If true, that raises all sorts of theological issues I didn't feel qualified to deal with.

Two things disturbed my viewing pleasure. One was the dog. While I sprawled on the sofa, he lay on the floor by the television, head between his forepaws, staring at me. It started to get to me after a while. I asked him what he wanted. I offered him a Milk Bone, then a pig's ear. During a commercial, I rushed him outside for a quick walk, during which there was much sniffing but little urinating and no defecation. I worried he might be saving up for a deposit on my hardwood, and I remembered I'd forgotten to pick up some poopie-cleaning product at the pet store.

Back upstairs, he resumed his position by the TV, so it was impossible for me to ignore his stare while I tried to watch Cro-Magnon make his great migration. Maybe this was part of the separation anxiety Amanda had talked about.

"I'm not going anywhere," I told him. He answered with not so much as a twitch of his tail.

A little after ten the phone rang. Archie got up before I did. He followed me into the kitchen and stood there, staring up at me, still as a setter on point. "Hello?" I said into the receiver. Silence. I glanced at the caller-ID display. It said, UNKNOWN CALLER.

"I'm on the do-not-call list," I said, thinking I was queued up in a phone bank. Silence. "Hello?" I said again. The line went dead.

Ruzak back to the sofa. Archie back to the TV. A commercial was on, the one with the two cavemen pissed off at the big insurance company. The phone rang again. Again Archie followed me into the kitchen. I glanced at the caller ID. UNKNOWN CALLER.

"Hello?"

More silence, but this time I thought I could hear someone breathing.

"This is Teddy Ruzak," I said. "Who's this?"

No answer.

"Amanda?" I asked. "Eunice?"

The line clicked, and then I heard the dial tone. I went to the bedroom; Archie's nails clicked on the hardwood as he followed me. I grabbed the cordless phone from its cradle and was halfway back to the sofa when the phone rang again.

I hit the talk button and said, "Look, I don't know who you are or why you're calling, but I'm in the middle of something important right now and the FCC considers what you're doing a serious crime. It's called harassment, and blocking your number won't stop them from finding out who you are."

Silence. I stood by the sofa. Archie sat at my feet.

"I can hear you breathing," I said. My mind raced down the list of the people who might call me. The list was short, and everyone on it wouldn't hold on the line without saying anything. I figured, if this wasn't some random weirdo, that I actually had a lead on the line. "Are you calling about the reward?"

They hung up. I waited for the phone to ring again. I was sure they would call back.

They didn't. Not that night, at least.

DECEMBER 5

CHAPTER TWENTY

I woke fully clothed on the sofa to the ringing of the telephone. I rolled over and the cordless fell off my stomach onto the floor.
Archie was sitting by the coffee table about three feet away, watching me.

"Hello?" I gasped.

"Theodore, you never called me back."

"Eunice? What time is it?"

"Four-thirty."

"In the morning?"

"Old people never sleep; didn't you know that?"

"What's the matter?" I asked, because something had to be for her to call
me at four-thirty in the morning.

"We haven't finished, and I do my best work in the morning."

"Really, Eunice, I'm not in good shape right now."

"Why, Theodore?"

"It's four-thirty in the morning!"

"I am beginning to sense a certain reluctance on your part to help me
with the last worthwhile endeavor of my life."

"Well, I hope it isn't the last thing you do. That would be a helluva coda,
Eunice. Did you call me last night, around ten-forty-five?"

"Now Theodore, wouldn't we both know if I had?"

"Somebody called three or four times and just held the line."

I heard a strange clicking through the earpiece.

"Did you hear that?" I asked. "Something just clicked on the line."

"That may have been my teeth."

"Your teeth?"

"My uppers slipped."

"Eunice, you're not taping me, are you?"

"Theodore, what a question!"

It could be a tap. But who would tap my phone? Archie had not budged since I woke up. Mouth slightly open, bright brown eyes locked on my face, he looked like he was grinning.

"I'm going to hang up now, Eunice," I said. "My dog needs to go outside."

"Dog? Theodore, you don't own a dog."

"I do now."

"Hmm. I'll have to think about the wisdom of using that device."

"Device?"

"The device of using a dog to create sympathy for the character."

"He's not a device, Eunice; he's a dog. And I'm not a character; I'm a human being."

She didn't say anything. I heard another click. I knew from my PI test material that taping someone without their knowledge was legal in Tennessee, but phone taps required a court order. Knowing that didn't kill the little germ of paranoia beginning to replicate itself in my sleep-deprived brain. I told Eunice again that my dog had to go wee-wee and hung up. I didn't get up from the sofa, though. Just sat there and looked at Archie looking at me and waited for her to call back.

"Do you need to go?" I asked him. He didn't move a muscle. Not even a twitch of his tail. Why was this creature staring at me? I've heard dogs are especially sensitive to stimuli that flies under our human radar, things like earthquakes and low pressure systems. Maybe Archie was picking up on something wrong with me, an imminent heart attack or aneurysm.

I scooped him off the floor and put him into the crate behind the sofa. He stared at me through the bars.

"Don't look at me like that," I said. "This is supposed to comfort you."

I threw myself on the sofa and tried to go back to sleep. I couldn't shake the feeling that I was losing my grip on something very important, not my sanity, per se, but my grip upon the familiar, the comfortable world I held so casually until the day Mr. Hinton walked into my office and yanked it out of my hands. Or was it that morning when I looked out my window and saw the dead man looking back at me, God's name emblazoned above his empty stare? I felt as if I had crossed a border into a new country, an immigrant who couldn't speak the language, my vocabulary useless in the Land of the Enigmatic Stare, where Jack Minor and Archie were natives. The string theory had unnerved me, but now I could see the seductiveness of it. In another reality, Teddy Ruzak had his detective license, Archie a house in the suburbs with a big yard and kids to play with, and even Jack Minor a place of his own where the sun shone more than ten days in the winter.

I gave up on sleep. On my way to the kitchen, I glanced toward the cage, and that dog was still sitting there, watching me. I let him out.

"What's the matter with us, Arch?" I asked. I made a mental note to call the vet as soon as the sun came up. There was something wrong with this dog. He couldn't tell me, but maybe a vet could.

"Come on, I'll fry us some bacon."

CHAPTER TWENTY-ONE

WHEN THE PHONE RANG A LITTLE AFTER TEN, I CHECKED THE CALLER ID before answering. It said CITY OF KNOXVILLE.

"Mr. Ruzak," Detective Black said. "How are you?"

"Look," I said. "About yesterday. I guess I overreacted a little."

"Perfectly understandable. I hope I haven't caught you at an inconvenient time."

"Oh, no. All my time is convenient now."

She gave a little laugh, and I thought of those large incisors.

"I made some inquiries after you left, and I think I have a name for you."

Nincompoop would be a good one, I thought, but I said, "A name?"

"Jumper's real name is Reginald Matthews. He's been arrested three or four times on nuisance and reckless endangerment charges. They call him Jumper because he has a penchant for threatening to jump off various rooftops around town. He climbs up and waits for us to get there and talk him down."

"He's suicidal?"

"He may be, but usually when people really want to kill themselves they do."

She told me they had an address for him in Johnson City. I wrote it down.

"He listed his next of kin as Robert Matthews, his son, same address."

"Phone number?"

"Nope, and there's no listing for either of them. I checked."

"I guess you're not taking a drive up to Johnson City."

"Maybe I'm trying to save you twenty-five thousand dollars."

"Hey," I said. "I really appreciate this."

"Just doing my part to aid and abet an unlicensed PI."

I called the Humane Society and learned Amanda wouldn't be in till three. She probably had morning classes. I dialed Felicia's number. She answered on the sixth ring with a voice thick with sleep.

"I woke you," I said. "Sorry."

"I was up late with Tommy," she said. "He had a rough night."

"He's not the only one."

"What's the crisis du jour, Ruzak?"

"I've got to drive up to Johnson City and I wanted to know—"

"I can't go with you."

"I was actually needing a pet-sitter. Thought maybe Tommy would like to meet Archie."

"You finally got a dog."

"Or he got me; it's complicated."

"Why are you going to Johnson City?"

"I've got a lead."

"You've got a—is this about the dead bum?"

"Jack. Jack Minor. Yeah. There may be a potential witness or possible suspect up there."

"Tell the cops."

"Actually, the cops told me."

"Why would the cops tell you?"

"I guess I kind of shamed them into it. I wouldn't bother you, but I hate the thought of locking him up all day, plus I don't know how long this might take. I might have to stay overnight, depending on what I find. Do you mind watching Archie for me?"

"Is this animal housebroken?"

"Well, he hasn't relieved himself in my apartment yet."

"I'm worried about you, Ruzak. I can't figure if this whole thing is you working *on* something or working *through* something."

"Maybe a little of both."

Ten minutes later, I stepped out of the shower to find Archie sitting in the bathroom doorway, watching. I quickly wrapped a towel around my middle; I wasn't accustomed to another set of eyes seeing me naked. Archie had abandonment issues, I decided. That's why he stared, because if he looked away I might be gone.

"I'm not going anywhere," I told his reflection in the mirror while I shaved. "Well, actually, I am going somewhere, but I won't be long and you'll be staying with a very nice lady who has a kid that'll just eat you up."

He didn't react to the sound of my voice. I tried to remember if he'd wagged his tail since Amanda left.

"You ignored your breakfast," I went on. "I gave you a forty-five-minute walk. You don't want your squeaky lamb or a bone. What do you want, Archie? You keep watching me like you want something—what is it? What do you want?"

I turned away from the sink and squatted on the linoleum. I snapped my fingers. Archie stayed in the doorway, ducking his head a little, nose twitching, the tip of his pink tongue protruding between his brown lips.

"Come here, boy. Come on, Archie." I whistled softly. Archie didn't move. "Maybe you've been beaten," I said. "Maybe I even look a little like the guy who beat you and you're wondering why Amanda delivered you back into the hands of the enemy. I'll ask her if there was any evidence of abuse when they brought you in. It's okay, Arch, swear to God, you can trust me."

I stood up and took a step toward him. He got up and took a step back.

"I won't hurt you," I said. He turned and trotted down the hall, nails clicking on the hardwood, turning the corner and disappearing into the family room. Only no family lived here. What did you call the family room of a single person? I hung in the bathroom doorway, chewing on my lower lip. Something was going on with this dog. Maybe that's why his owner abandoned him. Who'd want a dog that stared at you all the time?

Felicia lived in a neighborhood just off Chapman Highway, on the southern edge of Knoxville, a few miles from the town of Seymour. It was only a twenty-minute drive from my apartment, but it seemed much longer with Archie sitting in the bucket seat beside me, staring at my profile. I was so distracted I almost rear-ended a Buick at the stoplight for the entrance to Baptist Hospital. My mom had died in Baptist Hospital, which sat on a bluff overlooking the Tennessee River. During the deathwatch, I would sit in the chair beside the window and stare outside at the opaque water sliding under the Henley Street Bridge.

At the door, Tommy pushed against his mother's legs, trying to get to Archie, hollering, "Puppy, puppy, puppy, I wanna see the puppy!" I set him down just inside the door and those two were all over each other, swapping slobber, Archie's tail a blur of white and brown, until the kid fell laughing onto his back and the dog jumped on his chest, swabbing the decks with his tongue. Felicia gave me a look.

"What?" I asked.

"Now, what do you think is going to happen when Buster has to leave?"

"His name is Archie."

"He looks more like a Buster."

"I didn't name him."

"Curse of the foster parent."

"He doesn't wag his tail for me," I said.

"He's going to eat the legs off my coffee table, isn't he?"

"I don't know what he'll do, to tell the truth," I said, watching Tommy and Archie frolic at our feet. "All he's done with me is stare. Here's his stuff."

"Just set it there by the door."

"Bob around?"

"No. Why?"

"Just wondering. You think I'll ever meet Bob?"

"Anything's possible."

"You'd think I would have by now."

"Do you want to meet him?"

"It's like we're Superman and Clark Kent: never in the same room together."

"Which one would you say is Superman?"

"That's funny, Lois."

"You sure about this trip, Ruzak?" she asked.

I nodded. "There's a reason Jumper took off right around the time Jack got killed. I find Jumper, I find the reason. I find the reason, I maybe find the killer."

"You sound like Charlie Chan."

"I'm a human being, Felicia."

"Wasn't Charlie?"

"I mean, I'm not a fictional character."

"Who said you were a fictional character?"

"Nobody, but somebody implied it pretty strongly around four-thirty this morning."

"Oh, Ruzak, a guest at forty-thirty? Who was it, that Amanda person?"

"Eunice Shriver."

She cocked her head to one side and her nose crinkled.

"It was on the phone, Felicia," I said. "Okay, I better hit the road. Archie, come here, boy."

Archie ignored me. He had a grip on Tommy's wrist and was play-growling deep in his throat. Tommy was laughing so hard that tears streamed down his face.

"Archie," I said. "Come say good-bye to Daddy."

"Daddy?" Felicia asked.

"All right," I said. "That's okay. He's made a friend."

I turned on the stoop to say good-bye, but the door was already closing. I saw Tommy on the floor, Archie squirming in his pudgy arms and Felicia fussing at both of them. Then she threw the deadbolt.

CHAPTER TWENTY-TWO

Johnson City, named for the seventeenth president, was situated in the far northeast corner of Tennessee, about one hundred miles north and a thousand feet higher than Knoxville, in an area alternately called the Tri-Cities (the other two being Bristol and Kingsport) and the "state of Franklin." During the Civil War, this portion of the state seceded from the Confederacy and petitioned the Union to be admitted as a state, following the model of West Virginia. Johnson City, like Knoxville, was a college town, home to East Tennessee State University.

It had snowed over the weekend, the snow followed by a cold front that plunged the temperature into the teens. The hills encircling the city glistened pure white, but the snow piled beside the road and in the parking lots was that dirty-orange color that reminded me of deli mustard.

Holiday banners festooned the lampposts along State of Franklin Road, and the cars of Christmas shoppers packed the mall parking lot. This would be my first Christmas without family. Dad had a couple of brothers living in upstate New York, but I wasn't close to my uncles. Dad had trouble getting along with family, though he never met a stranger he didn't like.

I was thinking about that as I pulled into a space near the food court entrance to the mall: The focus of the season is family, but the thrust of Christmas, the point of the whole damn thing, is the stranger and the outcast, the anonymous losers living among us. Mary and Joseph bunked with animals in a barn and Jesus, who was God on earth after all, spent his first night in a food trough. When I was a teenager and the absurdity of this first hit me, I made the mistake of telling my mother, who was offended down to her Baptist shoestrings. I was convinced that we were worshipping a deity crazy as a bedbug and, if he was, what did that make us? She rewarded me with a slap across my mouth. Atheists and their fellow travelers point to Islamic terrorism as a wake-up call that we'd better abandon God or the biblical disasters attributed to him will pale in comparison to what we'll end up doing to ourselves. In other words, God may not be dead, but keeping him alive endangers the human race.

I wondered if Jack's killer was getting at something along those lines with the tetragrammaton. Maybe he wasn't a religious fanatic at all. Maybe he was a psychotic atheist, though more people have justified their crimes by citing their love of God. In our time, the devil is out as the scapegoat. They say the 9/11 hijackers screamed "God is great!" right before they murdered three thousand people.

According to the Knoxville PD, Robert Matthews lived only a few blocks from the mall, but I had decided on the drive up not to attempt contact till later in the day. Odds were he'd be at work and I might get only one shot at this, since he might be harboring a fugitive. Plus, it was now after one o'clock and I was starving.

I ate at the Ruby Tuesday in the mall, then returned to my car and located the apartment complex where Robert lived or might live. I parked a couple of buildings away from his unit and commenced my surveillance. Gas was pushing three dollars per gallon, so I cut the engine and buttoned my coat up to my neck. Within an hour, I fell asleep.

CHAPTER TWENTY-THREE

Dusk was creeping in from the east when I woke up a couple hours later. It was so cold my nose had gone completely numb. I stepped out of the car and stamped my feet on the frozen pavement, and the sound of it was very loud in the frigid air. I was feeling a little spongy; there was no other word for it.

Robert Matthews lived in apartment 213 in Building C, and I trudged up the stairs to the second floor, unbuttoning my coat as I ascended: I didn't want to be mistaken for a pervert, which I associated with men in buttoned-up overcoats.

I rapped on the door. I blew hard into my cupped hands. My knuckles had turned bright red. What if I had died of hypothermia in the Sentra? How long before somebody found me? It was a persistent worry since I moved from my parents' house, that I would die alone in my apartment, and days would pass before somebody noticed I was missing. Now I had a dog, and what would that animal do if his owner fell over from a massive coronary or aneurysm and couldn't put out the Alpo for a week? The thought was too terrible to contemplate.

The door opened and a woman in her late thirties, maybe, eyed me standing on the welcome mat.

"I'm looking for Robert Matthews," I said.

"He's not here."

"But this is his address?"

"Who wants to know?"

"Teddy Ruzak."

"Who's Teddy Ruzak?"

"Me. I'm Teddy Ruzak. I'm a PI out of Knoxville and I'm trying to find his father."

"His father doesn't live here."

Behind her, I could see a toddler with half his fist in his mouth, naked but for a diaper, his knees the color of charcoal.

"When will Robert be home?" I asked.

"Who is it, Liz?" a man called from inside.

Liz rolled her eyes and called over shoulder, "Somebody looking for Reggie!" She gave me the once-over and said, "He just got home."

"Who?" He appeared behind her, wearing a grease-stained pair of overalls with his name stitched on the right breast: ROBERT.

"Teddy Ruzak," I said. "How's it going?"

He ignored the question. "Are you a cop?"

"He's a PI," Liz said.

"Technically, I'm an investigative consultant."

"What the hell does that mean?" Robert asked. He had a small, pinched face, reminding me of those mammals that emerged from their primordial holes after the dinosaurs bit the dust.

"Basically it's a reflection of the age we live in," I said. "I'm a specialist."

"What do you want with Reggie?"

"I think he might be involved in a murder."

"Murder! You got some kind of ID or something?"

I handed my business card to him through the half-open door.

"'Highly Effective,'" he read. "That what you are, highly effective?"

"Well, there's good days and there's bad days."

He stared at me for a long moment. His wife was staring at him, and the toddler was staring at her. I stared at nothing and tried to look trustworthy.

"All right," he finally said.

"Robert," Liz said.

"It's okay," he assured her, and I followed them into the small family room with a sofa that had seen better days, worn carpeting, and cheap plastic vertical blinds over the sliding glass doors leading to the patio, where Fisher Price and Mattel were staging a major invasion. The kid, whose name I never caught, stared at me, gnawing on his knuckles, a dab of something the color of peanut butter on his knobby elbow. Robert offered for Liz to fetch me a beer. I thanked him, but I was still feeling a little spongy and asked instead for a cup of coffee. Liz left to brew some.

"Now, what's this about Reggie?" he asked.

I gave him one of my flyers.

"Twenty-five thousand dollars," Robert murmured. He studied the picture. "This isn't Reggie," he said.

"No. It's a man named Jack Minor. He was found murdered in an alley last month. Actually, *I* found him murdered in an alley last month."

"There ain't no way Reggie murdered anybody," Robert said.

"Reggie ever mentioned Jack Minor to you? He may have used the name Cadillac."

"I haven't spoken to my father in eight years."

"Is there a reason for that?"

"Oh, no. No reason. Just been real busy. Jesus Christ! What do you know about Reggie Matthews, Ruzak?"

"I know he's been in and out of treatment centers, been arrested more than a couple of times, and likes the view from tall buildings. Down in Knoxville he's called Jumper, though that's a misnomer since I don't think he's actually ever jumped. And the most significant thing I know is your dad vanished around the same time his friend Jack Minor was murdered."

Liz came in the room with a cup of coffee for me and a Miller Lite for Robert. She planted herself on the settee by the television. The kid picked up a stuffed bear and waddled over to me, holding it out.

"He wants you to hold it," Liz said. I thanked him and pulled the bear into my lap. It was missing an arm, and the white stuffing bulged from the tear. There was something disturbing about that.

"Reggie ran out on me and my mom when I was twelve. Very seldom I'd get a postcard or a phone call, then about eight years ago he completely disappeared. I just thought he drank himself to death."

"You didn't know he was in Knoxville?"

"I didn't know where the hell he was and I didn't care. He was nothing to me."

The little boy, emboldened by the big man with the red nose accepting his gift, commenced to bringing me other toys he scooped up from the floor, until I had a lapful.

"Okay, buddy, enough of that," Liz told him, but he ignored her.

"What about other relatives? Brothers, sisters, cousins?"

"Nobody," Robert said. "Nobody at all."

"Why did he leave Johnson City?"

"He was never in Johnson City, far as I know. Me and Liz moved up here last year."

"That's odd," I said. "Last time they arrested your dad, he listed this apartment as his address."

His eyes narrowed over the neck of his bottle, and Robert said, "So?"

"So if you haven't seen or heard from him in eight years . . ."

The kid, having relocated all the toys in the room to my lap, hoofed it down the hallway and disappeared into another room. Liz didn't notice; she was watching Robert.

"He probably just gave them my name as the next of kin and they looked it up," he said with a shrug.

Their boy returned with a toy rifle longer than he was and, face split wide with giggles, offered it to me. Liz fussed at him but I said it was okay, and leaned the rifle against the arm of the sofa. The kid barked a laugh and raced back down the hall.

"Was your dad very religious?" I asked.

"Was he what?"

"There's a theological component to the crime," I said. "Whoever killed Jack had some kind of obsession with God."

"The only thing that obsessed Reggie was Jack Daniels."

"How about you?"

"You think I didn't learn my lesson? I never touch hard liquor." He tucked his empty bottle between his thighs. His knuckles were encrusted with grease. If I were Liz, I wouldn't let him near the furniture until he had showered and changed out of the grungy overalls.

"No, I meant how do you feel about God?"

"What is this? Are you a PI or a Jehovah's Witness, Ruzak?"

"Neither."

"Then why the hell are you here?"

"Well, that's a good question and something I've been wrestling with. I'm a big guy, but no matter how big you are, there are some questions that'll always be bigger. My gut tells me Reggie didn't kill Jack Minor, but he may know who did and that's why he took off. He's afraid he's next. So my theory is—to answer your question—my theory is, given your classic fight-or-flight response, Reggie has 'gone to ground,' to a place where he feels safe."

"He wouldn't be safe here," Robert said. "I hate that sonofabitch's guts."

At that moment, his son reappeared, head, eyes, nose and cheeks hidden under my next present, fat little arms outstretched, stumbling along a little bowlegged toward me, until he bumped into the sofa and fell back on his diapered butt. Liz rose from the settee and moved toward him as he yanked the floppy brown hat from his round head and waved it toward me.

"Sorry," Liz said to me.

"It's okay," I said, taking my hat from the child squirming in her arms.

"Nice hat," I said.

CHAPTER TWENTY-FOUR

I DROVE TO THE LOT ON BEHIND ROBERT MATTHEWS'S APARTMENT and parked on the backside of Building C. There was a six-foot space with a walkway between the buildings, so I could see the base of the stairs leading down from Unit 213. Night had fallen, and the temperature could not have been much over twenty degrees. A hard freeze was coming.

I called Felicia's number and got her voice mail. I hung up without leaving a message. Ten minutes later, my phone rang.

"Where are you?" she asked.

"Sitting in my car. Hey, listen. I'm gonna be a little later getting back than I expected."

"How much later?"

"An hour. Or a day. It depends."

"On what?"

I told her. She asked, "Are you sure it's your hat?"

"There's a stain on the brim," I said. "Mustard from a hotdog I had at Sonic. It's my hat."

"Do they know they're busted?"

"I didn't confront them about it, though maybe my reaction to the mustard stain gave me away. I don't know; I'm not much of an actor."

"He did it. Jumper. There's no other reason to hide him."

"Unless they're protecting him from the killer."

"Nope."

"Why nope?"

"Twenty-five thousand reasons why nope, Ruzak."

"For all they know I'm the killer—that was my line of thinking."

"And the reward is the bait to lure the witness from his hole?"

"Right."

"Hmmm. Robby doesn't sound that sophisticated."

"He's a mechanic."

"So?"

"So mechanics intuitively understand the principle of interlocking, moving parts. Anyway, I figured they needed time alone to debate the pros and cons of coming clean with me."

"So what's your plan?"

"Wait awhile for the call. I figure it'll be sooner rather than later. How's Archie?"

"He's watching TV with Tommy. They've exhausted each other."

"Any unnatural staring?"

"No, just the natural kind. Why?"

"I'm starting to think it's something about me and not the dog."

"The odds are better. Oh, and Eunice Shriver called again."

"Why?"

"Because you won't give her your cell phone number and I really wish you would. I would have, but she hung up before I had a chance."

"She hung up on you?"

"She was pretty pissed she couldn't get hold of you. This is none of my business, Ruzak, but I don't think that old woman is quite right in the head. She threatened to cut me out."

"Cut you out?"

"Of the story. Well, her exact words were, 'I'll be forced to red-pencil you.' "

"Have you ever heard of the string theory?"

"No, but I get the feeling you have, and now you don't have anything better to do than to tell me."

"Boiled down to its nub, basically there are an infinite number of possible existences, and everything that could possibly happen *does* happen in one of these, um, alternate realities."

"Wow. What's that have to do with string?"

"Maybe reality is like a rope, which is made up of thousands of tiny individual strands of fiber or strings, each one having its own integrity but part of the larger intertwining."

"Intertwining?"

"Right. So maybe in this rope there's a string where I *am* a fictional character."

"And another string where you're not?"

"The question is, Which string am I in?"

"It seems pretty far out there, Ruzak. The possibility that you're the product of an eighty-six-year-old woman's imagination."

"It's lost some of its luster in the scientific community," I admitted. "And even if it were true, what can I do about it?"

"Beg her to let you win the lottery."

"A lot of money would be nice, but I'd rather have the answer."

"The answer to what?"

"Oh, you know, what's it for. If there's a purpose. If the unconnectedness is an illusion and God really does have a plan."

Above me, in the moonless sky, the stars shone winter-bright in the dark matter—the stuff that made up 98 percent of the universe, the stuff that scientists had so much trouble understanding, which meant we couldn't grasp 98 percent of the reality surrounding us.

"Ruzak, are you there?"

"I guess I am. I hope so," I said. "Felicia, do you think I should have slept with Amanda?"

She didn't say anything at first. "Does it matter what I think?"

"I mean, I'm not talking about the carnal act per se, though it's been some time since I—"

"Ruzak, I'm really not comfortable talking about this."

"I don't mean her personally, that's the thing. And not the sex part, but the idea that we're only afforded a finite number of opportunities to . . . to . . . to . . ."

"Connect with someone?"

"Or forget that we can't. That ultimately, because of the dark matter that separates us, we can't."

"You've lost me, Ruzak. Look, you need to walk away from this. You need to drive back to Knoxville right now, and in the morning you can give the police what you know and let them handle it. It's their job, Ruzak. Your job is to study for the PI test, because it's next month, and if you flunk that test I'll never forgive you. Do you hear me? I will never forgive you, Ruzak."

"I gotta go," I said.

"Teddy—"

"Somebody's calling through," I said. "I'll call you right back."

"Mr. Ruzak," Liz Matthews said after I picked up. "I hope you're not too far down the road."

"Not too far," I said.

"I have a confession to make."

"So do I. I'm not down the road. I'll be up in two minutes."

CHAPTER TWENTY-FIVE

ROBERT HAD SHOWERED AND CHANGED INTO A PAIR OF JEANS AND AN ETSU sweatshirt. He occupied the lounger in one corner, the flyer crumpled in his hand. With the fingers of the other, he nervously combed his damp hair. Maybe they put the kid to bed or locked him in his room, I didn't know, but he wasn't around to bring me any more presents. Liz was sitting on the sofa next to her father-in-law, Reginald "Jumper" Matthews, thin-faced like his son, white-haired, splotchy-skinned and shrunken-looking in a denim shirt two sizes too big for him. I guess the shirt belonged to Robert. And the baggy jeans. And the athletic socks on his jittery feet.

"Is this for real?" Robert asked, waving the flyer in my direction.

"It's for real," I said. "And if Reggie helps us nab this guy, he gets every penny."

"You hear that, Dad?" Liz asked. Reggie nodded. She turned to me. "You understand, Mr. Ruzak, we wanted to clear all this with Reggie first."

"You bet," I said. "What did you see, Reggie?"

"Hold on," Robert said. "Maybe we need to talk about it first. How do we know you won't take this information and keep the money? Maybe we should talk about some kind of up-front money."

"That's not the offer," I said. "The reward hinges on the arrest and conviction of the killer."

"Look, Ruzak, a couple weeks ago my old man shows up at my door scared shitless. Look at him—he's still scared shitless. Me, I'm thinking he's gone out of his head again with the booze or God knows what else, saying they're comin' for him next, and today you show at my door looking for him, and what am I supposed to think but maybe he's right, maybe somebody is after his ass. So I gotta think after his safety, you know what I mean? I gotta look out for Reggie. If this is on the up-and-up, I don't see how a little earnest money's gonna hurt. Maybe ten percent down, fully refundable if the information doesn't pan out."

"I'd be okay with that," I said. "If we put the money in some kind of escrow account."

Robert's eyes narrowed. "What, you don't trust me?"

"Looks like there's a lack of that on both sides."

"Not me," Reggie spoke up for the first time. "I trust you." He looked at Robert. "He's got a good face."

"Christ, Pop," Robert said.

"I don't understand why you're offering it in the first place," Liz said to me. "Who put up this reward money?"

"If you're asking who hired me to find Jack's killer, nobody did. The money is mine."

"So why, Ruzak?" Robert asked. "Who's Jack to you?"

"Nobody—except I'm the one who found him, and that's the issue."

"You're like the Good Samaritan, huh?"

"Well, as I remember the story, the guy he helped actually lived to tell the tale."

I looked at Reggie. "We don't need to complicate this. Reggie gets the cash when I get the killer."

"And when you screw up and the crazy mothers come after my dad, then what? You cover the funeral expense?"

"Well," I said, trying to puzzle it out—I had no idea how I'd stumbled into such a complicated negotiation. "Maybe we can set up some kind of protection program along the lines of the FBI—"

"And who foots the bill for that? We got him back into treatment, but my insurance don't pay for that or his Prozac, and who's gonna pay for his upkeep until these bastards go to trial?"

"Robert," Liz said. "We had this problem before Mr. Ruzak showed up."

"It's Reggie's information," I said, hunting for the shears to cut the Gordian knot. "Maybe it should be Reggie's decision."

Everyone looked at Reggie. He didn't say anything. Robert finally said, softly, "Reggie ain't been capable of making a decision for twenty years."

"You're my boy, and listen at the way you talk to me," Reggie said. "Maybe I just won't tell nothin' to nobody."

He crossed his arms over his thin chest and stuck out his grizzled chin defiantly toward Robert.

"Here's what I'm willing to do," I said. "Half the reward deposited in an interest-bearing account in Reggie's name, plus half his living expenses until we get this guy behind bars."

"You don't need to worry about that," Reggie said, "because I ain't no charity case. I'm leavin' tonight."

"Right, Pops," Robert said. "That's what I'm workin' on here." He turned to me. "Deal, but you're protecting him henceforth and henceforward, Ruzak. Understand? I got a wife and little kid to think about."

We shook hands on it, and Liz asked if I wanted another cup of coffee. I accepted, hoping the caffeine would suppress the gnawing hunger in my belly: I hadn't eaten anything since lunch at the mall. She went into the kitchen. Reggie called after her, asking her to fetch him a glass of ice water.

"One thing first," Reggie said to me. "I ain't goin' back to Knoxville."

"I don't see how we can avoid that," I said.

"They said they would kill me if they ever saw me again."

"Who?"

He looked away. His hands worried with each other in his lap. The knuckles were oversized, or maybe he just had thin fingers. Liz returned with my coffee and his ice water. She told Robert she was going to check on the kid and she disappeared down the hallway.

"Who killed Jack Minor?" I asked.

Reggie muttered, " 'Bout two in the mornin', me and Jack was on Church, walkin' toward Gay Street. They come walkin' up the other way. Three of 'em. One of 'em's singin'."

"Singing?"

"The big one. One big, one medium-sized, one little—scrawny kid."

"A kid?"

"They all kids. No more'n nineteen or twenty, I'd say. Drunk. They come up on me and Jack, and the big one say, 'Give me your hat, old man.' "

I swallowed. "He wanted the hat?"

Reggie nodded. "Jack told me somebody gave it to him, didn't even have to ask, just gave it. So Jack tells the kid, 'No; it's my hat.' Big kid, he starts shovin' Jack around, tryin' to grab it off his head. I say, 'Caddy, ain't worth it; give it up.' But Caddy don't listen. So 'nother one, the medium-sized one, he sneaks around Jack's backside while he slappin' with the big kid and grabs it off his head. So Jack goes after him, and the big one jumps him from behind." He set his glass on the floor between his feet and hid his face behind those large knuckles. "They took turns on him, 'cept the skinny one. He was like me, both of us yellin' for 'em to stop. Didn't do no good. Big one drug him into the parking lot, and the other one finds this two-by-four lyin' in the alley there . . . they take turns on him with that two-by-four, and the big one, he's wearing the hat. He's wearin' Jack's goddamned hat while he beats him to death!"

Reggie broke down then, putting his head between his knees, his narrow shoulders shaking. I looked over at Robert, who was looking back at me.

"What were you doing during all this?" I asked.

Reggie lifted his head and the look in his eyes forced me to look away.

"Nothin', Mr. Ruzak," he said. "Nothin' at all."

CHAPTER TWENTY-SIX

THE SKINNY KID NOTICED REGGIE TAKE OFF DOWN CHURCH, AND shouted something to his buddies. One of them chased him down—Reggie wasn't sure which one—screaming, "You're next! You're next, mother-fucker!" But the kid was drunk and gave up the chase after a few blocks. Reggie hid in the Hilton parking lot, debating whether to find a cop or re-turn to the alley to check on his friend. After a couple of hours, he risked it, finding Jack and my hat in the alley behind the Ely. He left Jack there, but took the hat.

"Why didn't you go to the cops?" I asked.

"Ain't you been listenin'? They said they was goin' to kill me! I hitched a ride out of town at first light."

"That's not the only reason," Liz said gently.

"You were afraid they'd suspect you?" I asked Reggie.

"I been to prison six times," Reggie said. "Last time Bushy State. I ain't goin' back to prison."

"Can you describe them?"

"Big one, the hitter, he was blond, bright blond, like it was dyed, you know? Had a crew cut and a goatee. Medium one real small eyes, pig eyes, and the little guy, long hair down to his shoulders, baby-faced, hardly no chin. Don't remember much else. Big one wearing a UT sweatshirt but, you know," he shrugged. "It's football season."

"How about names? You catch any names?"

Reggie shook his head. "Called each other 'bro.'"

"'Bro' like *brother*?"

"Yeah, like *brother*."

I walked him through the story again, to see if he'd remember more detail and also to see if he remained consistent. He lost it again at the part where "the big one" found the two-by-four.

"Who is Yahweh?" I asked suddenly.

"Don't know any Yahweh."

"So you don't know what the letters Y-H-W-H mean?" I pressed.

He slowly shook his head. Robert said, "Okay, I'll bite. What do they mean?"

"Somebody took a sharp object and carved those letters into Jack's forehead," I said, looking at Reggie.

"Then they must've done it after I took off," Reggie said.

"Any idea why somebody would do that, Reggie?"

Again, he shook his head. He muttered something like "God, I need a drink," and lowered his head, hands kneading his bony knees.

Liz left the room. I sipped my cold coffee. Robert stared at me, and Reggie stared at his own lap.

"You have to go to the cops," I told him.

"No, Mr. Ruzak. No cops."

"You have to tell them what you saw."

"They'll kill me."

"I won't let that happen."

"They'll arrest me. They'll think I did it."

"They will question you," I said. "And maybe get your DNA and probably polygraph you. I can help you find a lawyer, if you want."

"I ain't nothing but a broken-down drunk, Mr. Ruzak, and the doctors got me on pills to control my moods now, but I ain't crazy."

"I know the detective in charge of the case. She's very sharp, and I also think she's very fair. I promise you she'll take you seriously."

"You can't promise that."

"What about Jack?" I asked. "Don't you want to do right by him?"

"Right by him?"

"You want them to get away with it, Reggie? Is that what you want? Because I guarantee you they will if you don't come forward. He's not high on their list, Reggie; the police aren't going to pursue this unless we make them, you and me. And you and me, we're all Jack has now. Are you going to turn your back on him?"

"There ain't nothin' I can do for him now."

I ignored him. Things that had been simmering were beginning to boil over the lip of the pot. "Maybe not, but if three kids on a lark can get away with beating a homeless man to death, we've reached the bottom of it. As low as we can get, and if you turn away now you're not just turning away from

Jack, you're turning away from the next guy these kids decide to kill simply because they can.

"I don't know if you're a religious man. I'm not or never thought I was, but I've lost a lot of sleep since I saw the name of God on your friend's forehead, and I think it says somewhere in the Bible that what you do to the least of these you do to him, and you could look at it that way, if you're a religious man, that God was murdered that night. If he's in us and we're in him, God is murdered every night. And what's been getting to me is the fact that we've used up the not-knowing-what-we-do excuse. By God, if we don't know by now what we're doing, we're in big trouble and not just in the theological sense.

"We can't be as good as God and, if he's really there, I don't think he expects us to. I just think he expects us to be human—not as in a species, but as in his . . . crop. You know, the dinosaurs had their time—their season—now it's our season. It's our turn until he decides to let something else have a chance to get it right."

Liz returned during my rant, standing at the juncture between the hall and the family room, staring at me, a beat-up brown knapsack in one hand.

"What the hell was that?" Robert asked. "What the hell *was* that?"

"Sorry," I said.

CHAPTER TWENTY-SEVEN

Take care of my old man, Ruzak," Robert told me at the door. "Or I'll slap a wrongful death suit on your ass and you'll be out a helluva lot more than twenty-five grand."

"I gotta kiss him good-bye," Reggie announced and shuffled down the hall before anyone could stop him.

Liz put her hand on my arm. "Thank you, Mr. Ruzak," she said. She was holding my hat. I took it from her but hesitated before setting it on my head. It didn't feel right, wearing evidence to a capital crime.

"His pills are in the bag," Liz said. "Make sure he takes them. And you better get rid of any alcohol in your house."

"He isn't allergic to dogs, is he?" I asked. "I have a short-hair, but there may be dander issues."

She shook her head. "I don't know."

Reggie rested his gnarled hand on my forearm to steady himself on the way down the stairs. I could feel his son's eyes on the back of my head as we descended. First I adopted a dog, now a homeless man. I was going to need a bigger apartment if I kept this up.

At the intersection of State of Franklin Road, as we waited for the light to change, Reggie said, "You know Steve Spurrier, the football coach? He went to high school here. You like football, Mr. Ruzak?"

"I used to play it," I said.

"Yeah? What position?"

"Left guard."

"I could see that."

"I like to watch it—it's great to fall asleep to on a Sunday afternoon."

"Don't watch TV like I used to," Reggie said.

"Golf is good, too, for a nap," I said. "And tennis."

I pulled off the interstate to hit the Wendy's late-night drive-thru. I asked Reggie if he wanted anything. He leaned forward, squinting at the menu, rubbing his thighs.

"Oh, boy," he breathed. "Ain't been to Wendy's in years. They still have the Frosties?"

I ordered a medium Frostie for him and an Italian Frescata sandwich for me. I would have preferred a burger, but his bringing up football had made me uncomfortably cognizant of my size.

Back on the interstate, heading south, I gripped the wheel with one hand and my Frescata sandwich with the other. Reggie dug out dripping mounds of the nondairy frozen treat with his plastic spoon and sucked through pursed lips.

"Tell me about Jack," I said.

"I told you twice already."

"No, I mean the living Jack. What was he like?"

"Real good guy. Always shared what he had, no matter what it was. If he had a couple bucks and you were busted, he gave you one."

"He ever talk about his past?"

Reggie shook his head and his tongue darted between his lips. "Said he was in Nam. Lost everything when his old lady kicked him out for drinkin'."

"But where was he from? How'd he end up on the streets? What happened to him?"

Again, he shook his head. "Like I said, he didn't talk much."

I couldn't remember Reggie saying Jack didn't talk much, but this wasn't an interrogation and my job wasn't to lean on Reggie Matthews. He had that delicate air of someone breaking the grip of dependency. It hung around him, like a pall. You sense it in recovering addicts and jilted lovers, or anyone who's had their crutch abruptly yanked away.

"Was he religious?"

"Why's that matter?"

"His little sign mentioned God."

"That wasn't his. I made that sign."

"You let him use it?"

He nodded. "We worked that corner in shifts."

"So was he? Religious?"

"I never seen him pray or go to any church, if that's what you're askin'. He was retarded, you know. Not bad, but there was a lot he didn't get."

"I'm just having trouble understanding why one of those kids carved those letters into his face."

"Sick joke, you ask me."

He dropped his plastic fork into the empty cup and jammed it into the holder between the bucket seats.

"Now I'm cold," he complained, scrunching down and folding his arms over his chest. I cranked up the heat.

"Pretty esoteric joke," I said. "I don't know many people besides priests or rabbis or religion professors who'd get it."

The hairs on the back of my neck stood up. What a dufus you are, Ruzak, I told myself. I looked over at Reggie, hunkered down in the bucket seat, knees pressed together, squinting through the windshield as if we were on the road on a bright spring day.

In the art of detection, it's not just asking the right questions. You have to ask the right people the right questions.

"How far is the campus from the Ely Building?" I asked.

"How the hell would I know?"

"No more than a mile," I guessed. "Walking distance."

"All right," he drawled. He was waiting for the punch line. I didn't have it, but I suspected I knew who might.

CHAPTER TWENTY-EIGHT

I fetched a couple of old blankets I inherited from my dead mother to fix up the sofa for Reggie. He gave the middle cushion a tentative push. Then he announced he was still a little hungry, so I found a couple of Roma tomatoes in the crisper drawer, dropped a couple of pieces of bacon in the pan to fry, popped a couple slices of bread into the toaster, and tore the wilted edges from a couple of leaves of lettuce for a BLT. Reggie sat on the edge of the sofa and worried his hands in his lap.

"Where's your dog?" he asked.

"He's being sat by my secretary."

"Sat?"

"Well, it's a pretty long drive and he's a new dog. I didn't know how he'd handle it."

"Is he vicious?"

"Oh, no, but I wouldn't say he's issue-free. I adopted him—or somebody adopted him for me. That's more accurate."

I hadn't had a sleepover in years. Amanda had sort of offered. I wondered what it meant, if it meant anything, that I ran a girl out my door but welcomed with open arms a homeless man who might be a sadistic killer. Human beings have a tendency to read meaning into everything, like that woman a few years back in the Bible Belt who saw an image of the Virgin in the dried grease of her frying pan. Back in the fall, I read this story about a kid who threw his mom's cell phone in the microwave—I don't remember the reason, but the kid was a teenager—and Mary appeared in the ruined LCD. It would be odd for the Mother of God to choose to reveal herself in a cell phone, but once the story got around, pilgrims began to appear at their trailer.

Reggie ate his BLT at the kitchen counter, taking it with a tall glass of milk. I dug into his backpack and found the pill bottle.

"Here," I said, dropping a tablet by his elbow. "Says you're supposed to take it with food."

He grunted and tapped the pill with the nail of his index finger.

"Jumper's antijumping pill," he muttered.

"Why did you want to jump all those times?" I asked.

"Wouldn't you?"

I decided to change the subject. "Why did they call Jack Cadillac?"

He shrugged. "Maybe 'cause it rhymed."

"You really don't know that much about Jack, do you?"

"I know he had a taste for beef jerky. He liked baseball. He had arthritis and a bad leg. Said it was from shrapnel—friendly fire in Nam."

"The police checked into that," I said. "They didn't find any record of him in the service."

"Said he was a Marine."

"Maybe he just thought he was. Although I'm not sure retardation leads to delusions. Maybe he just lied."

Reggie sighed. "Does it matter?"

"I guess not."

"I still ain't really sure why I'm here."

"In the morning we're going down to KPD headquarters."

He shook his head. "No, I am not."

"I'll protect you," I said. "I have a gun."

"You gonna shoot our way out of the police station?"

"I meant I can protect you from Jack's killers."

He laughed a bitter bark of a laugh. "Where the hell did you come from, Ruzak?"

"Well, I was born in New York, but Dad moved us around a lot, always in the southerly direction. I guess if he'd lived longer I'd be in Key West."

I wondered if I was reading this old guy wrong. Maybe he killed Jack after an argument and that's why he was reluctant to talk to the police. He knew their skills in interrogation exceeded mine. Maybe the whole story of the marauding college kids was a lie. But why, then, come back to Knoxville with me? To dispatch the meddlesome gumshoe? Would someone—Felicia maybe—find me in a couple days, black and bloated in my bedsheets, God's name carved on my forehead?

I had forgotten to check messages, so while Reggie washed up for bed I listened to about thirty seconds of silence while whoever called hung on the line. The caller ID had registered the same thing as before: UNKNOWN CALLER. Someone was reaching out.

DECEMBER 6

CHAPTER TWENTY-NINE

I WAS ON THE PHONE WITH FELICIA FIRST THING IN THE MORNING. Actually, it was the second thing, after a cup of black coffee and a slice of toast with apple butter. For some reason, every time I had it, I thought of the first day of school.

"Why are you talking so softly? I can barely hear you," she said.

"I don't want to wake up Reggie."

"Who?"

"Jumper. I brought him home last night."

"And the reason you brought him home? . . ."

I told her. I also told her I was relieved I didn't wake up bludgeoned to death.

"Ruzak, if you were bludgeoned . . . never mind. When are you picking up this dog?"

"I'm swinging by right after I take care of Reggie."

"Good. I'm letting you deal with Tommy."

"Why am I dealing with Tommy?"

"You know why. You do it just to buy time, Ruzak, but what good is that?"

"Maybe it's the one thing you can buy but can't keep."

"Do you make this stuff up, or are you just regurgitating something you read in *Reader's Digest*?"

"That happens," I admitted. "I'll think of something and I'll get all excited and my ego tells me it's original. It's like a default setting if I can't remember if I read it somewhere. My dad subscribed to *Reader's Digest* for his bathroom reading, and those are chock-full of the pithy quotes. Dad always used to tell me not to eat anything bigger than my own head, and I always wondered if that came from *Reader's Digest*."

"I wish I could have met your father," Felicia said. "One thing I would ask him is, 'Why, Mr. Ruzak. *Why?*'"

"What if I brought him a stuffed dog?"

She stayed right with me. It was one of the things that I liked about her.

"I think he would throw that stuffed dog back in your face."

"This could be a sign," I said. "Maybe Archie wasn't meant for me."

"I'm not keeping this dog, Ruzak."

"I was just putting a feeler out."

Next, I called Detective Black.

"You found Jumper," she said.

"Reggie, right," I said. "He wants to talk."

"Does this mean I get the twenty-five grand?"

"He didn't do it. I'd tell you the whole story, but I don't want to compromise the case."

"How would that compromise the case, Mr. Ruzak?" I could detect a smile in the question, and I thought of those large canines.

"I don't want to create any unnecessary inconsistencies."

"Your statement implies there are *necessary* inconsistencies."

"See what I mean? How's ten for you?"

I woke up Reggie and told him he needed a shower before we left. He protested.

"I washed up last night," he said.

"And a shave," I said. "My stuff's in the cabinet beneath the sink."

"What is this?" he asked petulantly. "We goin' to a funeral?"

I fried him a couple eggs while he got ready. He was sitting at my counter, sopping up the runny yolk with a slice of toast, when my phone rang.

"Theodore," Eunice Shriver said. "I am coming over."

"Eunice," I said. "You can't come over."

"I am tired of chasing after you like Alice's rabbit."

"I won't be here," I said.

"You will be there if I say you'll be there!"

She slammed the phone down. Reggie was staring at me, a dab of egg quivering on his freshly shaved chin. He looked younger without the stubble; most older guys do.

"Who was that?" he asked.

"A god from an alternative string," I said as I flipped to the *S*'s in the phone book. I looked at my watch; I didn't have time to get into anything protracted, but an intervention seemed to be imperative.

"A what from a what?"

"Or maybe she would be a goddess, but the thing about the pantheists is their deities never made anything from scratch; it was always earthier than that, like Zeus frolicking with all those mortal women."

He picked up on the sixth ring. He didn't sound happy to be picking up.

"What?" he barked.

"Is this Vernon Shriver?" I asked.

"Who wants to know?" He possessed the native accent, slightly nasal, sharp in the middle, rough on the edges, like a hunk of half-grated cheese.

"Teddy Ruzak. I'm a . . ." What was I? ". . . a friend of your mom's."

"Did you say Ruzak?"

"Teddy Ruzak, that's right."

"Listen, buddy, I don't know who you are, but this isn't funny."

"It isn't?"

"You're from her workshop at the university, aren't you? Some wise-ass college kid."

"I'm a bit long in the tooth for that. The reason I was calling—"

"Mister, I don't have time for your jokes. Teddy Ruzak is the name of a character from Mom's book, so tell me what you want and stop yanking my chain. I'm late for work."

"I'm in the book," I offered.

"I know you're in the friggin' book; I just said that!"

"I meant the phone book," I said. "You can look me up."

"So Mom pulled the name out of the phone book. What's that prove?"

"Well, I guess that's my dilemma at the moment," I answered. "Trying to prove I exist. *Cogito, ergo sum.*"

"Huh?"

"Let's hang up, you call the number for Teddy Ruzak, I'll answer, and there you'll have it."

"I'm not calling anyone. I'm late."

"Then I'll be quick. Your mother just got off the phone with me and I'm a little worried about her."

"Ain't we all, pal."

"No, I mean seriously worried. I know I just said 'a little,' but really I mean seriously. I think there's been a break from reality."

"Ruzak—or whatever your name is—my mother's grip on reality's been loose for the past twenty-five years."

The line went dead. "You know," I said to Reggie. "Ultimately, there's only so much one person can do."

"And it ain't never nearly enough," he said, and I thought maybe I had found a kindred spirit, a fellow amateur philosopher, here in this very oddest of circumstances. But then, I thought, that's where you usually find the most kindred of spirits.

"But you have to try," I said. "Otherwise, you might as well be a fictional character. Though they tend to try harder than us."

"I couldn't save him," he said, his lower lip coming forward slightly, quivering in agitation. "I had to run. They would've killed me if I didn't."

"Look, Reggie, the police want these monsters off the street as badly as you do."

"This ain't gonna get them off the street," he said. "It was dark, I was drunk, and I got no names. What's the police gonna do? Round up every kid at UT? All this is gonna do is let 'em know I talked and then I don't care how many locks you got on this door or how many guns you got stashed under your pillow."

"Maybe you could ask them for some protection."

"Right, like they're gonna protect somebody like me."

"Maybe you should knock over a liquor store. That way they'd have to arrest you, kind of a de facto custody arrangement."

He got a funny look when I said that. I interpreted it as fear.

"Everything's going to be okay," I said.

"That's not a bad idea," he replied.

CHAPTER THIRTY

A UNIFORMED FEMALE OFFICER LED REGGIE AND ME THROUGH THE doors marked AUTHORIZED PERSONNEL ONLY, down a long corridor, then into a conference room with armless, thin-cushioned folding chairs around a church social–type folding table. She took our drink orders, and after a couple of minutes returned with stale, weak coffee in white Styrofoam cups. She promised it would be just a couple more minutes and closed the door behind her.

"Relax," I told Reggie, whose bottom lip was edging out again.

The door opened and Detective Black came in with two men in tow, one in his shirtsleeves, a badge hanging just below his prodigious gut. The other was wearing a suit. Tailored. With gleaming Florsheims below his cuffs.

She made the introductions with an arctic smile that reminded me it had been over two years since I'd been to the dentist. What was wrong with me? Humans don't usually crash spectacularly, which was why, when they do, it's such startling news. We tend to crumple more than fall, a slow descent into chaos that actually accelerates after our end. The absolute stillness of Jack Minor lying in that alley was deceptive. A human cadaver is a busy thing as the organs and tissues break down.

The suit's name was Beecham, and he was with the district attorney's office. The guy with the belly was Detective Louis Kennard.

As Detective Black checked the batteries on her tape recorder, Kennard turned to Reggie and said, "Hey, Jumper. Remember me?"

Reggie shook his head, lower lip now in full protuberance mode. His eyes were on the tabletop.

"I pulled you off the roof of the Marriot in '98."

Reggie didn't move a muscle. I said, "He's a little shaken up by all this. But he's going to cooperate. Right, Reggie?"

"I'm sorry," Beecham said. "Are you his attorney, Mr. Ruzak?"

"Not exactly."

"Not exactly," he echoed. "Then what exactly are you?"

"Well, I was an investigative consultant. For about nine months. Then the state closed me down over a technicality and now, you know, I like to keep my hand in."

"Mr. Ruzak is offering a reward for Jack's killer," Detective Black said. "I suppose he's here to protect his investment."

Beecham leaned over and whispered something to Meredith Black. She whispered something back. Kennard was smiling smugly, massive forearms folded across his chest. His cologne was very strong.

Finally, Beecham broke off the discussion with Meredith and said to me, "We'd like to talk to Mr. Matthews alone."

"Oh, no way," Reggie said. "Ruzak stays or I go."

"Try and I'll arrest you," Kennard said pleasantly.

"Here is the situation, Mr. Ruzak," Beecham said reasonably. "Mr. Matthews is here to give a statement. He's not under arrest, but it's totally outside the department's protocol to question a witness in the presence of a third party."

Reggie gave me a desperate look, as if to say, *Don't go!* I reached across the table and patted his hand before standing up.

"I'll be right outside," I said, more to him than to them. Detective Black opened the door for me and then closed it behind me. I lowered myself into the chair in the hallway beside the door, the little foam cup in my big hand, and steeled myself for the wait. I had read somewhere that the average person spends three years waiting—in lines, at traffic lights, on the phone, in the doctor's office—a fact that was both distressing and useless. I had been running into a lot of those kinds of facts lately. I wondered if Eunice was camping out on my doorstep, red pencil hovering over my ejaculations, poised for the coup d'état—or would that be more of a coup de grâce?

Thinking of Eunice brought on this panicky feeling in my gut, as if my own thoughts didn't belong to me, and I tried to comfort myself with that old saw about fearing for your sanity confirms that you're just fine, that crazy people never think they're crazy. Going crazy wasn't like coming down with a cold—but that was hardly comforting. I told myself I should be more myopic when it came to my understanding of reality. Most people are—painfully so. I suspected I was trying to keep too many balls in the metaphysical air. I couldn't seem to discard even the most worthless bit of information, like the fact that Einstein's brain weighed less than the average human's. Or that the higher your IQ, the more zinc and copper are contained in your hair. Or that every day we fart out a pint of gas. There's only so many neurons in the human brain (about a hundred billion), and I was loading them up with crap. What did it matter that blondes had more hair than brunettes or redheads? How was that going to help?

I had been sitting in that hallway for nearly an hour when the door opened and Meredith Black stepped out. I stood up.

"It's okay," she said. "He's agreed to take a polygraph."

"Why are you giving him a polygraph?"

"It's SOP."

"What about a sketch artist?"

"What *about* a sketch artist?"

"To get some composites of the guys who did this."

She gave my forearm a reassuring pat. "One thing at a time, Mr. Ruzak. Look, this is going to take a while. Why don't you let us give you a call when we're done?"

I looked at my watch. "There is one thing I need to do," I said. Something felt squirrelly about this, something about the set of this detective's jaw, but I couldn't put my finger on it. Besides, if things got really hinky I was sure Reggie would demand to see a lawyer.

"Call me on my cell," I told her.

"Of course," she said. She flicked a smile at me as casually as a lifelong smoker flicks his Bic.

"Okay," I said, not moving. "Okay, okay. I'll be back in a couple of hours."

"It would be better," she said, "if you waited for my call."

CHAPTER THIRTY-ONE

THE TETRAGRAMMATON," I SAID TO DR. HEIFITZ, "IS HARDLY COMMON knowledge. You remember saying that?"

The harsh late-morning light of early December shone through the smudged window behind me, and the shadows of the bobbleheaded icons were long on the credenza.

He gave a quick, impatient nod of his weathered pate.

"And what is your point, Mr. Ruzak?" he asked, shaking his dice; I could hear them clicking together inside his fist.

"I have a witness who says the killers were college-aged kids."

"Killers? There was more than one?"

"Three young males."

"And you suspect something along the lines of a Yahweh death cult?"

"Well, I wouldn't rule out that possibility, though my witness says they behaved more like drunken rowdies than religious fanatics."

"As I think I told you, Mr. Ruzak, I know of no sect or cult that specifically emphasizes ritual sacrifice in the name of Yahweh."

"Right, and that's not why I'm here. I'm here because there's also a possibility that at least one of these young men, given the location of the crime and the ages of the perpetrators, was a college student."

"Ah." He leaned back in his chair, lacing his pale, thin fingers together in front of his chin. "Ah."

"And not just your run-of-the-mill undergrad frat boy. Someone either with a background steeped in some pretty obscure religious esoterica or maybe—and that's why I'm here—maybe someone who's taken a few religion classes. . . ."

"You're asking me if I think one of my students could be involved."

"You ever cover the tetragrammaton in class?"

He nodded slowly. "I have. It's part of a graduate lecture series on Judaism offered every spring."

He closed his eyes while I described the three guys Reggie saw, as if to better picture them in his mind. Then his eyes opened and he slowly shook his head.

"I'm sorry, Mr. Ruzak. After thirty-five years of teaching, the faces begin to blend into a single amalgamation: Adam the undergrad, if you will."

"So you don't recollect any odd kind of kid maybe a little fixated on God?"

"Being fixated on God is not odd, Mr. Ruzak. Or if it is, most of us are odd, then. Ninety-six percent of Americans profess a faith in the deity."

"I'll have to take your word on that," I said. "Though that's one of those statistics that gives you hope and bums you out at the same time. If everybody is buying into the system, why is the system so troubled?"

"I," he said, "am not troubled."

"What do you think . . . how difficult would it be for me to get my hands on the class roster for last spring?"

"All our rosters contain personal information zealously guarded by the university, Mr. Ruzak."

"You could black out the personal stuff," I said. "I just need the names. Phone numbers would help, too."

"I'll have to get it from the registrar's office. It might take a day or two."

He showed me to the door. I turned at the threshold to confide, "I think I'm in that tiny percentage who can't decide the question one way or the other."

"I like to comfort myself in such times with the fact that it hardly matters."

"How so?"

"If God exists, our belief or disbelief has no consequence."

"I always heard it did, in terms of where we spend eternity. But that gives me some hope, Professor. You know, there's this old lady who thinks I don't exist, at least on the physical plane, that I'm a figment of her imagination."

He showed me his large yellow teeth. "Perhaps I should pinch you."

"I suffer, therefore I am? But it could be the pain is part of her creation, too."

"It certainly is part of God's," he replied.

"I thought all that was Adam's fault."

"Yet the creation is still God's. If it isn't, we're in one helluva pickle, aren't we, Mr. Ruzak?"

CHAPTER THIRTY-TWO

WHAT DO YOU THINK?" I ASKED FELICIA. "WHEN YOU'RE EIGHTY, WILL you be more or less anxious about eternity?"

"I think I'll be damned tired. Where are you, Ruzak?"

"Stuck in traffic on the Pike." Over two hours had passed since I left the police station and Detective Black still hadn't called. Thinking maybe she had tried my home number, I retrieved my messages, but all I had was two hang-ups, which I was sure came from Unknown Caller, and a long sales pitch from a company in New Jersey, offering me a once-in-a-lifetime deal in stock futures. If I ever had real money, the first thing I'd do is dump it in the lap of a fancy-pants investment counselor with a single order to sink it so far out of my reach it would take a bulldozer to dig it out.

"Any idea when you might be by to get this animal? I don't need a specific time, just an ETA before midnight."

"Right after I pick up Reggie. They were setting up a polygraph when I left. It's making me a little nervous."

"How come?"

"They didn't polygraph me."

She laughed for some reason. I told her about my meeting with Dr. Heifitz. Then I told her about the hang-ups at home and Unknown Caller.

"You're about to share a hypothetical," she said.

"Here it is: three college kids on a drunk stumble across Jack and Reggie on Church Avenue. At least one of them attended the professor's seminar on ancient Jewish apocrypha, and in a burst of regret or maybe just to toss in a red herring, cuts the tetragrammaton into the old guy's forehead. But one of them, maybe the same one who cut God's name, is having trouble dealing with what they've done, and one day sees my poster on campus. He calls my number, but then he can't make himself say anything."

"Hmmm," she said, though "*hmmm*" isn't technically a word. "Here's an alternative hypo: Reggie got in a fight with Jack over your hat, killed him, and made up the whole story about the kids to cover his murderous ass."

"I would hate to think my hat was the spark."

"It's in your hypo, too."

"That part wasn't hypothetical. Reggie said those guys wanted my hat."

"It all boils down to your misplaced philanthropy."

"But if you went through life avoiding unintended consequences, you'd never get a damn thing accomplished." I lifted my foot off the brake pedal and inched forward about half a car length. Why did I come this way? If I had her number, I'd call Eunice Shriver and tell her to write me onto I-40. I wondered how people would behave if our theology contained a promise from God that he would answer just one prayer in their lifetime.

"Do you ever pray?" I asked Felicia.

"Every Saturday, right before they draw the lottery numbers."

"I guess I do, just not formally. Sometimes, stuck in traffic like now, I go, 'Please, oh please,' and I guess that's a kind of prayer."

"Weird. I was having one of those this very moment. Please. Oh, please."

"Okay," I said. I promised I'd call as soon as I got Reggie back from the clutches of the curiously thorough Knoxville PD.

Forty-five minutes later, I was standing at the front desk signing in, when the double doors leading to the back swung open and the big-bellied Detective Kennard stuck his conical-shaped head through the opening.

"Ruzak!" he barked. He crooked his finger at me, but he didn't step aside to let me pass.

"You may want to hang out here for a while," he said. I smelled garlic on his breath. "He's downstairs getting booked."

Stupidly, I said, "Who's getting booked?"

"Jumper. He says he wants to talk to you, but we gotta get him processed first."

"Why did you arrest him?"

"He confessed."

"That's impossible."

"Think so?"

"I want to talk to him."

"You're not listening, Ruzak. I just said after we process him."

"I want to talk to Detective Black."

"She's at lunch."

"It's two-thirty in the afternoon."

"Late lunch."

He waited for me to say something else. I didn't have something else to say. He left and I sat in the small waiting area and flipped through an old *People* magazine while I waited. Ten pages were devoted to Oscar Night's fashion flubs.

What now? Dear God, what now? Had I read it all wrong? He did run when Jack died, but why would he come back if he was guilty? Did he figure if some thickheaded out-of-work PI could track him down, the Knoxville PD certainly could? Maybe they showed him the crime scene photos and he collapsed in a paroxysm of remorse. His relationship with his son wasn't peachy, to say the least. He must have known if he showed up on his stoop fessing up to murder, Robert would probably turn him in, so he invented the drunk-frat-boys story as cover.

A uniformed officer escorted me to the visitors' room. Reggie was waiting on the other side of the glass, dressed in an orange jumpsuit, the receiver already pressed to his ear.

I picked up the receiver on my side and said, "What happened?"

"They arrested me, Ruzak, what do you think happened?"

"Did you kill him, Reggie?"

He stared at me for ten agonized seconds, and then began to cry and laugh, both at once, and I noticed for the first time that Reggie Matthews was missing most of his teeth.

"Just don't tell Bobby," he cried. "Don't tell my boy. It'll break his heart, Ruzak. It'll break his heart."

And that's all I got from Reggie Matthews, besides the mixture of laughter and tears, and I thought of those mammoth, gravity-defying roller coasters, the ones where your feet dangle in empty space as your body is whipped and spun around, and you worry about your wallet falling out of your back pocket, and the way we scream through that controlled fall, the one we normally endure, when you think about it, with someone we love by our side.

CHAPTER THIRTY-THREE

DETECTIVE BLACK CLOSED THE DOOR TO HER OFFICE AND, AS SHE passed me on the way to her chair, I caught a whiff of her perfume, causing a swelling in my nasal cavities.

"What happened?" I asked.

"He confessed."

"And you believe him?"

"Of course not, but I decided to arrest him anyway."

"Detective Black—"

"Please, call me Meredith."

"Okay, Meredith . . . nobody could ever accuse me of being the most logical person who ever came down the pike, but the 'why's' don't make any sense to me."

"What do you mean?"

"Either his confession is true or it isn't. If it is true, why did he come down here today? If it isn't true, why would he lie?"

She stared at me for a second before answering. "The only thing I know, Mr. Ruzak, is Reggie Matthews admitted to taking a piece of two-by-four to Jack Minor's head."

"He didn't have to come," I said. "I didn't tie him up and drive him over here in my trunk. Why would he make a big show of cooperating and then confess to murder? But if he is innocent, what happened in that room after I left which would make him confess to a capital crime?"

"Boy," she said. "You got me. We did show him the crime scene photos. After that, he broke down and told us the truth."

"The truth."

"The truth," she repeated, nodding.

"He beat his best friend to death."

"That's right."

"Over my hat," I said.

"He didn't say what started the argument."

"Then Reggie took a broken piece of glass and carved God's initials into Jack's forehead."

She shrugged. "We didn't discuss that."

"Why?"

"Does it matter?"

"I think it does."

"Well, you're not the lead detective on the case, are you?"

"Something's wrong here," I said.

"No, something has finally gone right here. Solving a crime is what we detectives call a good thing."

"Unless the solution is based on a coerced confession."

"I take great offense at that, Mr. Ruzak."

"Well, I take great offense at this whole setup. I could see two buddies having a falling out. I could even see Reggie beating him—though it goes against my gut; Reggie doesn't strike me as the violent type—but I can't see him mutilating the body like that. For one thing, I don't think Reggie Matthews knows Yahweh from a hole in the ground."

She didn't say anything. The teeth were out, though.

I went on. "I haven't been a detective very long, not even a year. Well, I was never really a detective beyond the most generic definition of the word, but don't the elements of a crime have to fit into its solution?"

"Mr. Ruzak, there are some elements to every crime that remain mysteries."

"You people pushed him. You wore him down. That's why you got me out of that room."

"Who are you?" she asked. "Are you Mr. Matthew's attorney? Are you related to the suspect in any way? You're not a detective, you just told me that, so who are you, and what is your business in this case?"

"I just want Jack's killer," I said. "That's all I want."

"Me, too. And I think I got him. You may think otherwise, and on that we'll just have to agree to disagree, Mr. Ruzak, and let a court of law decide who's right. In the meantime, maybe you can use that twenty-five thousand dollars you saved today to hire an attorney for Mr. Matthews. Since you're so convinced of his innocence."

"I'm not convinced of anything," I said, rising from my chair. "Except this: If Reggie Matthews is innocent and you guys are innocent, there's only one reason he'd confess to a crime he didn't commit."

I made for the door, walking on the balls of my feet, like a sprinter cooling down from a dash, strangely lightheaded, with a tingling in my fingertips.

"What's the reason?" she called after me.

"Fear," I said.

CHAPTER THIRTY-FOUR

I CALLED FELICIA FROM THE CAR. I GOT HER VOICE MAIL. I LEFT A message.

"Hey. It's me. Ruzak. Teddy. You know . . . hey, Reggie confessed. I'm not sure what that's about, but I'm pretty sure he pulled this for a little protective custody. Maybe he's thinking he can recant at any point and they'll have to let him go. Or maybe he is guilty and I'm just plucking at straws because *I* can't let this go. Anyway, I thought if you were around I could pick up the dog. Thanks. Okay. I'll be at my place. 'Bye."

The cold front had followed me down from Johnson City; the temperature hovered around twenty and the radio warned of a hard freeze coming. Everything, from the traffic lights to the naked branches of the dogwoods, had that terrible stillness, that sharply etched quality of a photograph that made you feel like a voyeuristic interloper in a landscape at once familiar and alien, like a lonely man looking at a picture of a beautiful woman.

A small figure in a worn gray coat was huddled on the stoop of the Sterchi Building as I pulled into the lot. I wondered why she didn't wait in her car; she could at least keep warm that way.

"Eunice," I said, my six-foot-five frame towering over her small, gray, bent-backed lump. "Eunice, what are you doing?"

I noticed her white wig was slightly askew. She raised her head so I could see her face, the nose a startlingly bright red, the rheumy eyes squinting, although most of the light had already bled from the day.

"*You*," she muttered, as if I was the last person she expected to see on the front stoop of his own apartment building.

"Come on," I said. "I'll brew you a nice hot cup of tea."

I slid my hand beneath her elbow and pulled her up. She was heavier than

I expected; maybe it was all the layers of clothing, the gray coat, the matching gray muffler, the man's red flannel shirt, the athletic sweats with the elastic bands at the ankles. She grabbed the ubiquitous tote and slung it over her shoulder as we eased our way across the frozen concrete to the front doors.

Upstairs, she collapsed on the sofa, cradling the canvas tote in her lap, the tan blotches on her hands sharply contrasted against the paleness of her skin. I set a pot of water on the stove to boil and positioned only half my butt on the bar stool at the counter: You never know when you might have to make a break for it.

"I talked to Vernon this morning," I told her.

"I don't know anything about that conversation," she said.

"He doesn't believe I'm real."

She waved her left hand in a gesture of dismissal. The right maintained its death grip on the tote.

"Why should he, after all?" She wasn't looking at me. She had that "third space" stare of a prophet—or a mystic, I guess, since we don't live in an age of prophets.

"I guess there's nothing that says he has to," I said. "Though it would be nice."

"I am very angry with you, Theodore," she said.

"Well," I said.

"And disappointed. You have deeply disappointed me."

"Eunice, I never asked you to write a book about me."

"About you," she snapped. "About *you*. Oh, I am sick to death of you, Theodore Ruzak!"

She hurled the tote at my head. I ducked. It skittered across the bar and landed on the kitchen floor, disgorging a stack of paper that spread out, fan-like, across the linoleum.

I picked up the top sheet and read the first sentence: "I'd had this dopey idea to be a detective ever since my mother gave me an illustrated Sherlock Holmes book for my tenth birthday." It wasn't the sort of sentence that compelled me to read on, but I'm no literary critic.

Behind me, Eunice Shriver continued to rant.

"It's ridiculous. Absolutely ridiculous! No detective in history has been so woefully underqualified, distracted, lazy, and incompetent. What person in their right mind is going to believe you set up shop as a private eye without even realizing you needed a license?"

"Fools rush in?"

"I can always change your looks. Make you thinner, chiseled, steely-eyed. I toyed with making your eyes steel-gray, as a matter of fact. But I cannot change these basic character flaws that *in themselves* make you completely unbelievable as a character!"

"Look at it this way," I offered, shoving the stack of paper back into the tote. "You're plowing new ground."

"Here is the thing," she barked, still not looking in my direction. "Your story . . . if you want to call it that, has less substance than a takeout menu."

"Then let it go."

She swung her gaze in my direction, but still wouldn't look directly at my face. Her eyes were focused on some point just over my head.

"Eunice," I said. I went to the sofa and lowered myself into the cushions beside her. I pulled her cold, withered hand into mine. "Eunice. I'm going to pose a simple hypothetical."

"Fat chance!"

"What if you just went to bed and when you got up it was gone? Would you be sad or relieved?"

"Both. I cannot abandon you in midstream, Theodore. It would be like God stopping with the fishes."

"I'm sensing a disconnect here. Between you and God and me and the . . . the fishes. Do you feel my hand, Eunice?"

She didn't say anything.

I rubbed her hand hard between both of mine, feeling her arthritic knuckles slide beneath my palms.

"I'm real, Eunice. I have an existence outside your imagination."

"That is a terrifying thought," she said.

I was about to ask her why when my buzzer sounded. It broke the existential spell. I swung through the kitchen on the way to the intercom to turn off the burner; the water was boiling over the lip of the pot.

"Ruzak?"

"Amanda?"

"Amanda?" Eunice called from the sofa. "I know of no Amanda!"

"Can I come up?" Amanda asked.

"Right now?"

"No, not now. I thought I'd just ask now and come back in a couple of hours."

"Come on up," I said, and hit the green button. I returned to the kitchen to drop the teabag in Eunice's cup.

When the knock came on the door, Eunice said, a bit panicky, "Who could that be?"

Amanda stood in the hallway holding a white plastic bag with THANK YOU! written in red on the outside.

"I'm hoping you haven't eaten," she said.

"I haven't," I said, and stepped to one side so she could pass. I caught a whiff of fried rice. Amanda stopped when she saw Eunice on my sofa.

"Oh," she said.

"Amanda, this is Eunice Shriver, no relation to the famous Shrivers."

"That Maria is an anorexic so help me God!" Eunice cried.

"Maybe this isn't a good time," Amanda said.

"I can't think of a more perfect one," I said, taking the bag from her and setting it on the coffee table, about a foot from Eunice's broad knees. "You like hot tea? I'm guessing this is Chinese."

Amanda nodded. She eased herself onto the edge of a bar stool, staring at Eunice. I refilled the pot and turned on the burner. I kept meaning to invest in a teakettle.

"I detest Chinese food," Eunice told Amanda.

"I didn't know," Amanda said.

"Gives me the runs."

"Maybe you got hold of some bad noodles," I said. "I have some Campbell's in the pantry."

"Chicken noodle?"

"I think it's cream of potato."

"Dear God!" She made a sour face. Amanda gave me a look.

"It's a very long story," I told her. "Eunice, how about a grilled cheese sandwich?"

So that's how we supped: Amanda and I on noodles and rice, sitting crossed-legged at the coffee table, Eunice on grilled cheese and baby dills, the dish in her lap.

"Where's Archie?" Amanda asked.

"Sleepover," I said.

"Who is Archie?" Eunice demanded. "Who are all these people I don't know, Theodore?"

"Is this your grandmother or something?" Amanda asked.

"I am his creator!" Eunice said, not without a touch of pride.

"Eunice is writing a book about me," I said.

"She is? Why?"

"I'm still not sure. This is really good," I said, meaning the food. "You didn't have to."

"I took a chance you'd be here. I wanted to apologize for last time."

"What happened last time?" Eunice asked.

"You should know," I said. "That's what I've been trying to tell you, Eunice. If this was all in your head, how could there be things that you don't know?"

"I'll tell you, if you'll give me a complete inventory of the contents of your hall closet."

"I'm not following this," Amanda said.

"It's a philosophical dilemma," I said. "Right up your alley."

"It seems more psychological."

"But physiology is muscling that out," I said. "Everything's getting traced back to whacked-out brain chemistry."

"I don't want you to hate me, Ruzak," Amanda said.

"I don't."

"I want to be your friend."

"You are."

Eunice was watching us, pivoting her head, a tennis match.

"We could slow it down a little. I can move fast sometimes, I know that," Amanda said.

"Right."

"It's just you're not like other guys I've dated. I've been conditioned, you know? A burger, a movie, and right to the mattress."

I cleared my throat. I would have been uncomfortable with this without Eunice Shriver sitting two feet away.

"I just don't want to give you the wrong impression," I said. "It's like I said before: It goes against my general principles to get wrapped up while I'm untangling some issues."

"Sometimes it helps, though, having someone there to help you untangle them."

"I can't deny that."

"Teddy Ruzak does not have a love life!" Eunice interjected.

"That's what we're working on," Amanda said with a smile. Smiling wasn't something she did often but, when she did, it was a good smile.

"He is as celibate as a monk!"

"Tell me about it," Amanda said.

"Theodore Ruzak has not had sexual relations since 1998!"

"Whoa," Amanda said. "Really?"

I didn't say anything. Any answer would be humiliating.

"Did Miss Marple have a lover? Hercule Poirot? Did the greatest detective of all time, Sherlock Holmes, have a sweetie?" Eunice's chin rose indignantly.

"Well, I always wondered about him and Watson," Amanda said.

"Watson got married," I pointed out.

"And your point?" Amanda asked.

Eunice said, "Theodore, I have not formed a good impression of this girl."

"Oh, no," Amanda said.

"She should be discarded."

"But you don't even know me," Amanda said, reasonably.

"Oh, I know you," Eunice said. "I know you."

"I get it," Amanda whispered to me. "It has its own interior logic. Since you're her creation, anything connected to you is part of it, too."

I shrugged. It had come to that. Shrugging.

"Well," I said. "You're the philosophy major. I've been hugging Descartes like a long-lost brother lately. How do I know she isn't right? How do I ultimately confirm my own existence?"

Amanda stared at me for a second, a smile playing at the corner of her lips. Then she leaned toward me, grabbed my face in both her hands, and pressed her lips against mine. I tasted pork-fried rice. From the sofa, I heard Eunice gasp. Amanda pulled away, no more than a couple of inches, so her loamy eyes filled my vision.

"Now what, Ruzak?" she murmured.

It struck me how uninhibited she was, even at the feet of crazy ol' Eunice Shriver, who, for all Amanda knew, was perfectly capable of grabbing a carving knife from my kitchen and plunging it into her recalcitrant back.

"That is better," I said.

At that moment, my cell phone rang. I fumbled for it. Amanda leaned back and sipped the dregs of her tea. Eunice watched me, open-mouthed.

"Ruzak, where are you?" Felicia asked.

"Home," I said.

"Why didn't you call me?"

"I did. I left you a voice mail."

"Well, I haven't been home; what did you expect?"

"I wasn't expecting much of anything, really."

"Look, Tommy and I and this damn dog are four blocks away."

"Four blocks away from what?"

"From you, dummy. I'm picking up Bob from work." Bob worked at the fire station downtown, about six blocks from the Sterchi.

"Who is that?" Eunice asked from the sofa.

"Who is that?" Felicia asked on the phone.

"Felicia," I said to Eunice.

"What?" Felicia asked.

"Felicia?" Eunice asked.

"Who's Felicia?" Amanda asked.

"Who's that?" Felicia asked.

"Eunice," I said to Felicia.

"Ruzak, that didn't sound like an eighty-six-year-old woman to me," Felicia said.

"Oh. Amanda," I said.

"What?" Amanda asked.

"I'm telling Felicia your name," I said.

"The dog philosopher?" Felicia asked. "And Eunice? How many strays are you going to take in, Ruzak?"

"Hmmm," I said. All eyes were upon me. "Nothing's been planned, really."

"Is that the girlfriend?" Amanda asked.

"There is no girlfriend, per se," I managed to get out.

"Damn right!" Eunice ejaculated.

"Ruzak, did you tell her I was your girlfriend?" Felicia asked.

"Of course not," I said. "Maybe you should swing by tomorrow."

"This isn't good for Tommy," she said, meaning the situation with Archie. "The sooner he's back with you, the better."

She hung up. I set the phone on the kitchen counter.

"Felicia, my secretary," I said. "She's bringing Archie back."

"Who is Archie?" Eunice asked.

"Ruzak's dog," Amanda said.

"Theodore doesn't own a dog," Eunice said. "It would be completely contradictory to his character."

That did it. I picked up the phone and dialed Vernon's number.

"Vernon," I said after he had barked that East Tennessean version of a greeting: *Hell-uh!* "This is Teddy Ruzak and I have your mother."

I heard him take a deep breath. "You are one sick—"

I cut him off. "Here, she wants to talk to you."

I held the phone toward her and she commenced to frantically waving her hands, like a football referee signaling the end of a play. She mouthed the word *no.*

"Well," I said into the phone. "I guess she doesn't. But you need to come over. You got something to write with? I'll give you my address."

"I'm callin' the FBI," he promised.

"I'm thinking the psychiatric ward at Saint Mary's might be more appropriate."

"You think this is funny, don't you?"

"I don't think it's funny at all, Vernon. It's downright disturbing . . . on so many levels."

I gave him my address.

"If this ain't on the up-and-up, I'm prosecuting you, mister," he promised before hanging up.

"I won't go," Eunice told me.

"You have to," I said. "He's your flesh and blood, Eunice. I'm neither, in either possible universe. He can get you some help."

My buzzer sounded. Felicia and the dog. I buzzed her up. Amanda pulled me aside and said, "Tell me the truth. She's the one you told me about, isn't she?"

"She's my secretary," I said. "She has a boyfriend."

"You have a thing for her. You can hear it in your voice."

"Really? No, I just like her, that's all. She has pleasant knees."

"Pleasant knees?"

"You know, well formed."

"Oh, Christ."

"You should understand the year 1998 was just a supposition."

The door burst open and Tommy barreled into the room shouting my name, "Roo-zack! Roo-zack!" and, behind him, Archie the beagle mix, trying hard to keep up, putting its front feet on Tommy's rear while the kid pawed at me. Felicia hovered in the doorway, taking in the scene.

"Hi," Amanda said to Felicia. "You must be Ruzak's crush."

Felicia gave me a look. Amanda smiled and said, "Your pleasant knees gave you away."

Eunice glared at Felicia. "Hello, and how are you, little Miss Felicia?"

"Well, Ruzak," Felicia said. "I guess one of those cosmic strings is unraveling, isn't it?"

CHAPTER THIRTY-FIVE

IT WAS AN AWKWARD SITUATION, MORE OF A TANGLING OF THE VARIOUS strands than an unraveling. Amanda's was the first to peel away: she crooked her finger at me and I followed her into the hallway.

"Be honest with me, Ruzak," she said. "Is there anything here worth pursuing?"

"What do you think?"

"Don't answer my question with a question."

"Socratic method," I said, hoping to make a philosophical connection. That's life's rub, connection. Between the dog and Eunice and even Jack with the staring eyes beneath God's name was Teddy Ruzak clutching the tugging butt-ends of the balloon strings as they urged him upward toward . . . what? You wondered sometimes if life was just a slow rush toward gibberish.

"What? Ruzak, do you ever get at what you really mean?"

"It's been a lifelong struggle," I admitted.

I offered to escort her to her car; downtown Knoxville can be scary at night, but she acted offended at my offer. As she walked to the stairs, I watched, admittedly, her rear end.

Back in my apartment, I discovered Archie in Eunice's lap, Tommy squatting at her feet, and Felicia sitting on one of the bar stools, her expression bemused.

"Vernon's on his way to pick her up," I told Felicia, with a nod toward the old lady.

"You told that girl you had a crush on me?" she asked.

"She's extrapolating."

"From what?"

"From a lie."

"What lie?"

"I told her I had a girlfriend."

"Don't get a crush on me, Ruzak. Where's the street person you took in?"

"They arrested him."

"Why?" Felicia asked.

"He confessed."

"Good," Felicia said. "Case closed."

"I think he's lying," I said.

"Why would someone lie about that?"

"I'm working on the answer, but I think it has something to do with fear."

Vernon Shriver arrived thirty-five minutes later. He was pushing forty, with a wide, flat face and smallish eyes, short like his mother, but I didn't see much of a resemblance, so maybe his looks came from the Shriver side.

"You Ruzak?" he asked at the door, as if he still wasn't quite buying this whole setup. I told him I was, in the flesh, and the tripartite talks began in earnest. Vernon seemed more interested in getting her to accept my autonomy than getting her out the door, which was my ultimate goal. He kept slapping me on the forearm, saying things like, "I feel him, Momma; he's right here; how could I feel him if he wasn't here?" But it was like four-foot swells crashing against a seawall. Eunice refused to budge, from either her convictions or my sofa.

"What about going to Vernon's place?" I asked. "You could stay with him for a few days." I took him aside and said, "She can't stay here and can't be alone. What choice do you have?"

"This is messed up," he said. "You messed her up, Ruzak. I'm gonna look into this." I wasn't sure what he meant by that.

Felicia sat beside Eunice and spoke to her quietly while Vernon and I argued. Tommy enticed Archie from Eunice's lap and commenced to playing a game of tug-o'-war on the floor in front of the TV, using an athletic sock that he had found somewhere, probably under my sofa. Archie growled, shoulders hunched around his apple-shaped head, and Tommy mimicked him, showing his baby teeth as he grred.

Eunice began to nod, clearly connecting to whatever Felicia was saying. Vernon asked if I had anything to drink. I offered to make some coffee. He asked if I had anything stronger, so I handed him my last Budweiser.

"Part of it's my fault," he said, more mellow after a few swallows. "I took away her TV."

"Why?"

"All those damn infomercials. And that goddamned QVC channel, forget about it! I walk in one morning and there's five Cuisinarts on the kitchen counter and an Ionic Breeze in every room, including the plug-in models for the john."

"Maybe she needs a more supervised environment," I said.

"You offering?"

"I didn't encourage this," I said, a bit defensively. "I tried to put the kibosh on it, but the more I tried, the more stubborn she became."

"I go by every day," he said. "Or every other day, to make sure she's taking her meds and there's food in the house."

"What about her car keys?"

"Took them once and she went on a hunger strike."

"I guess I'm lucky that way," I said. "To be spared that. My mom died last year."

"You're lucky that your mom died."

"I meant the role reversal. I don't know how good a parent I would have been to her."

"Well, my own kids won't talk to me, so if I live to be her age, I'm screwed."

He was finished with his beer, Felicia was finished with her speech, and Eunice, I guessed, was finished with her recalcitrance. She allowed Felicia to help her rise from the sofa. I fetched the tote.

Vernon said, "Hide that damned thing."

"I will follow you home," Eunice said to Vernon.

"No, Momma, I'll drive. We'll pick up your car later."

"I am a burden to you," she said.

"No, Momma."

"It is a terrible thing," Eunice announced from the doorway. "All this . . ." waving her hand in my general direction, but I got the idea she was getting at something much bigger.

And then they were gone, and I stood in the middle of the room, clutching the tote.

"If you threw that into a fire," Felicia said, "would you burn up, too?"

She turned toward Tommy and Archie, still frolicking on the floor.

"Come on, kiddo," she called. "We're late for dinner."

"Hey," I said. "Thanks. For everything."

"Do you really think I have pleasant knees?"

"You bet." I was blushing.

"That's sweet . . . and weird—what's her name?"

"Amanda."

"Not your type, Ruzak."

"She *is* a little moribund."

"Pushy. I see you with some sweet, naïve thing, a type-B personality."

She took a deep breath, steeling herself, and called again to Tommy. He ignored her. She looked at me. I walked over and scooped up the dog. Tommy's pudgy arms shot up and he hopped up and down, trying to wrest the animal from my grip. Felicia grabbed his wrist.

"Say good-bye to Archie," she said. "If you're good, Ruzak might bring him over for another visit."

"You bet," I said. "That's a promise."

Tommy burst into tears. I was sure Felicia had set him up for this good-bye, had told him Archie was Ruzak's dog, not his, and every hello implied a good-bye. But the kid looked shocked, as if leaving Archie behind was the last thing he expected. I communicated my question to Felicia with my eyes— *Why not?*—and she shook her head angrily. She pulled Tommy toward the door, as he reached for the animal in my arms with his free hand, his face scarlet and glistening.

"Hate Roo-zack!" he hollered. "I *hate Roo-Zack!*"

There was no comforting him, so I tried to comfort Archie as he whined and scratched at my forearms to join Tommy.

"I'll call you later," Felicia shouted over the ruckus. "And congratulations!"

"For what?"

"For nabbing the killer!"

The door slammed and, after that, the silence. I was alone again, except for Archie, who leapt from my arms and scratched frantically at the door, going up on his hind legs and pawing at the wood just below the doorknob.

Later that long night, as Archie, exhausted, lay curled in front of the door, waiting for his boy to return, I pulled a random page from Eunice's manuscript and read this:

> *You would think living alone would free me from all the normal burdens of responsibility that people complain or worry about, but all living alone does is increase your psychological weight, as if your soul were living on Jupiter. It tends to make you more important to yourself and exaggerate your problems to the point that they're insurmountable afflictions.*

The passage got my heart rate up. Not only did it strike me as eerily prescient, it even sounded like something I would say. Either Eunice Shriver had found her way into my head or I had indeed found my way into hers.

DECEMBER 7

CHAPTER THIRTY-SIX

I HAD TROUBLE FALLING ASLEEP—GO FIGURE—SO THE PHONE RINGING at two A.M. broke only the lightest of dozes. I noted two things before answering: Archie's staring from the bedroom doorway and the display on my cordless, UNKNOWN CALLER.

"Hello?" Silence answered, but for a slight background hissing. It might have been someone breathing; it might not. "You keep calling, but you won't say anything," I said. "Like God." Maybe that's it. Maybe that was as far as he would reach. I chased that thought away. Time to get focused. "I'm going out on a limb here, but I'm guessing you're connected in some way to the murder of Jack Minor. That's his name—he had a name, you know; he wasn't just some faceless vagrant, some useless parasite. He was a man, a human being like you and me.

"Maybe you know what happened, maybe you were involved or know who was involved, but you should know a man is sitting in jail for the murder, and you and I both know he isn't guilty. He's there because he thinks it's the safest place to be right now, and he's left it up to me to save him. That's ironic, since he wouldn't be sitting there right now if he hadn't put his trust in me.

I heard a sound like a sigh, pitched in an upper register, like a child's . . . or a woman's.

"I'll double the reward," I offered. "Fifty thousand dollars."

No answer. I looked at Archie, his big brown eyes shining in the ambient light coming from the bathroom. For almost thirty-four years, I had slept with a light on. I had read somewhere that God is to us as we are to dogs, that the gulf separating our intellects must be, if God is God, wider than the universe. Archie sensed I cared for him. He sensed his entire existence relied upon my tender feelings. But my thoughts were unfathomable, unknowable, and so he stared, unable to reach me except through signals as easily interpretable to me as mine were ineffable to him.

"You know," I said into the phone. "This is a little like praying. I talk and hope you are listening, and I don't expect a reply. At least, not a direct one. Look, I can't help you and you can't help me—or yourself—unless you tell me what you want. What do you want?"

Silence.

"One way or the other, I'll find you," I said, but the promise sounded hollow in my own ears. "I won't stop till I do, so why don't you make it easy for both of us? It's the *why* more than anything. I got the *what* and the *when* and the *where*. I even have the *who,* sort of. The *why* is what I'm getting at. You don't have to tell me who. Tell me why. Why is Jack dead? Why was God's hidden name carved on his forehead?"

A tiny voice whispered, a girl's voice, "He'll kill me."

I started to ask Who? but that would break my promise not five seconds after I made it. There should be more lag time between a promise and its breaking.

"There's gotta be a way we can do this," I said. I worked furiously at it, while Archie rested his chin between his forelegs, watching me.

"You don't have to actually tell me," I said. "I'll just ask a question and all you have to say is 'yes' or 'no.' How's that?"

That offer met with a long sigh. I couldn't tell if it was an acquiescent sigh or not.

"Do you know who killed Jack Minor?" I asked.

"Yes," came the answer, escaping from the receiver like air leaking from a tire.

"It wasn't another homeless man who killed him, was it?"

"No."

"There were three of them," I said.

"Yes."

"Students at UT?"

"Yes."

"Okay," I said. "Okay." I swung my legs out of the bed and ran a hand through my hair. Archie moved when I moved, sitting up, eyes locking onto me, lowering his nose toward the carpet.

"Were you there?" I asked.

"No."

"But you heard about it?"

"Yes."

I stood up. Archie rose with me. I shivered in my boxers. I felt larger somehow, or maybe the room just felt smaller.

"You weren't there, but somebody told you about it."

"Yes."

"And they made you promise not to tell anyone."

"Yes."

"Or they would hurt you?"

"No. Yes." I heard something on the other end that might have been a sob.

"It's going to be okay. You're doing the right thing. Don't be afraid."

"Yes."

"Doing the right thing is hardly ever easy. Otherwise, there'd be more right things being done. One thing you gotta keep to the forefront is the fact that keeping vital information from the police about a crime is also a crime."

"Yes."

"I can help you," I said. I wasn't sure I could, really, but these crumbs she was dropping marked the only path toward justice. "Tomorrow I'm getting a list of names of students. If I showed you that list, could you highlight a name or two for me?"

I waited for her answer. Archie padded to the edge of the bed and sat down about a foot from my cold feet. He looked up at me.

She didn't answer. I went on. "Tomorrow night, eight o'clock at World's Fair Park, at the base of the Sunsphere. Look for the guy in the floppy brown hat. Can you do that? Can you do that for me? Can you do that for Jack?"

Archie and I waited for the answer.

CHAPTER THIRTY-SEVEN

THE PHONE RANG AGAIN AT EIGHT-THIRTY, SNAPPING ME OUT OF A restless sleep.

"Yep," I said instead of "hello."

"Ruzak?"

"Oh, yeah."

It was Felicia, raising her voice to be heard over Tommy's wails in the background.

"Tommy wants to talk to the dog."

"Right now?"

"And then I want to talk to you."

Archie still manned his station by the bedroom door. I whistled, snapped my fingers and called his name, but he remained in his sphinxlike pose.

"I'm thinking I might remind him of his former owner," I said. "And it wasn't a happy relationship."

I held the receiver by the dog's ear while Tommy brayed on the line. The tip of Archie's tail twitched, and the end of his tongue swiped over his nose.

Felicia came back on the line.

"I'm meeting you for breakfast," she said.

"You are?"

"You have other plans?"

I admitted that, as usual, I was planless. An hour later, we were sitting in a booth at Pete's Diner. Felicia was wearing a chartreuse turtleneck, a long black skirt, and matching black boots. The day was overcast, with snow likely in the afternoon.

"Reggie Matthews is innocent," I said after the waitress left to turn in our order. Western omelet for me, a bagel and fruit cup for her. I told her about my conversation with Unknown Caller.

"Could be a prank," she said. "Some college kid sees your flyer and decides to have a laugh at your expense."

"It'd be hard to think of a sicker joke," I said.

"They didn't actually offer you any information, Ruzak."

"No, but she did offer *con*firmation."

"You're about to lay a hypo on me, aren't you?"

"One of the guys who did this told his girlfriend, swore her to secrecy and, I think, threatened her to keep her mouth shut. But it's been weighing on her conscience, and one day she sees my number on the flyer—"

"Or she sees the dollar sign on the flyer."

"Could be a little of both, but you shouldn't always assign the worst motives to people."

"What if the boyfriend's setting you up? He knows you're poking around and this was his way of finding out what you know. Then you, being the crackerjack detective that you are, set up a clandestine meeting in a dark, deserted place—"

"I'll bring my gun."

She pushed her plate a few inches toward me and folded her arms on the tabletop, leaning forward slightly, so I got a whiff of White Diamonds by Liz Taylor.

"Now about this dog, Ruzak. Some things in life are impossible. Sometimes those things are the things you want the most. And the sooner you develop your own personal solution to that dilemma, between the wanting and the can't-having, the better off you'll be."

"You're teaching Tommy a lesson? Why can't he have the dog?"

"Bob's allergic."

"Oh."

"Don't do that. Don't say 'oh' like that."

"It's just an 'oh.'"

"Nothing is just what it is with you."

"I guess you're saying I never learned the lesson you're trying to teach Tommy."

"I guess I'm saying exactly what I'm saying. It's incredibly hard for me to imagine a scenario in which your mentioning my knees has any meaningful context."

"It might have been a non sequitur. You know I have that problem."

"What problem?"

"With linear thought."

"Ruzak, what goes on in your head never bothered me much. It's part of what makes Ruzak, Ruzak. It's what's going on in your heart that's bothering me."

It hit me, finally, what she was getting at.

"I don't have a crush," I protested. "I really don't. I was dealing with a high-pressure situation. She's not subtle, this girl, and it was a desperate moment."

"You could have brought up your old girlfriend from high school," Felicia pointed out. She reached up with her left hand and tucked a strand of her hair behind her ear.

"She's married. To a guy named Bill Hill."

"So would Amanda know that?"

"It's been more than a couple years since high school. What kind of guy carries a torch for sixteen years?"

"Oh, Ruzak, and I always took you for a romantic."

"Again, my only defense is you're the one woman I know who's around my age and around *me*—"

"A random choice?" She was smiling.

"Sure. No. I mean, I don't really know why I brought up your knees. I'll never do it again. It's not as if I said you had ugly knees. Pleasant and well formed, I think I said, and that part wasn't a lie. I've admired your knees for some time now, though I'm no voyeur or pervert; I mean, I don't have a knee fetish or anything like that, though I'm sure there's men—and women—who do; you can have a fetish on practically anything. Well, not practically. *Literally.* Anyway, it's been my experience—or observation, I guess I should say—that a lot of women don't have any kind of knee structure to brag about, not even those fashion models, whose knees tend toward knobbiness, very unattractive," I said rapidly, and sipped my cold coffee.

"Bring the cops along," Felicia said.

"What?"

"To your rendezvous tomorrow night. That way, they can bust whoever shows up: the girl as a material witness or the perp as the . . . well, the perp."

"I'll call Detective Black."

"You could have used her as your excuse."

"She has a mean smile."

Felicia laughed. "What about her knees?"

"I never looked, to be honest."

"What do you suppose that means? That you took the time to notice mine but not hers?"

I looked right into her eyes and said, "I don't ascribe any meaning to it at all."

CHAPTER THIRTY-EIGHT

OF COURSE, SHE COULD HAVE POINTED OUT, CORRECTLY, THAT THAT was my biggest problem: I ascribed meaning to everything, even to things that had no meaning or no potential meaning, like the letters on Jack Minor's forehead, or that my concern for life (the ferns) that brought me to the office the morning after Jack's murder had anything to do with my finding him. Life is pretty damned random, and maybe it was the randomness that terrified me.

I called Detective Black the minute I got back to the apartment, the omelet resting uneasily in my gut. I distrusted my digestive powers. Growing up, I was always the nauseated kid, puking in the school bathroom before the big test.

"What if I told you I've turned up a corroborating witness?" I asked her.

"A corroborating witness to what?"

"Reggie's story."

"Which one, the one he told you or the one he told us?"

"The first one."

"The one about the three college kids who committed murder just for the heck of it?"

"Right. That one." I filled her in on Unknown Caller. "I'm meeting her tomorrow night at World's Fair Park."

"Well, let me know how that goes."

"You don't want in on it?"

"I would definitely want in on it if there was anything to be in on."

"Don't you think that might make the being in on it difficult if you're not there?"

"I appreciate the offer, Mr. Ruzak, but at this point we're satisfied we're in on the only story that matters."

"How come?"

"Because nobody in Reggie's position would confess to something he didn't do, Mr. Ruzak." It was taking some effort, I could tell, for her to remain civil.

"That's exactly why he confessed," I said.

"Why is exactly why?"

"His position. He doesn't trust his son to keep him safe—it wasn't hard for even someone like me to find him. And he didn't trust me to keep him safe. So he confesses to you, knowing you'll lock him up, which gives me time to find the real killers."

"Wow. That's a heck of a theory. A man risks life in prison because he's afraid he might lose his life out of prison."

She was right: It *was* a heck of a theory, but no theory is perfect. Look at all the holes in Darwin's.

"He's hunkered," I said. "He figures he might as well hunker in jail where he'll be safe while he waits for this to play out. He can recant at any time, and then what do you have? There's nothing else tying him to the crime."

"You think he's that smart?"

"Just because you're a semisuicidal homeless alcoholic doesn't mean you're not smart." I didn't tell her I had sort of planted the seed of this idea. She might perceive it as bragging.

DECEMBER 8

CHAPTER THIRTY-NINE

WORLD'S FAIR PARK, SITUATED BETWEEN THE UNIVERSITY OF TENnessee campus and downtown Knoxville, was built in 1982. There's a pavilion and an amphitheater set amid acres of rolling green park. The nearly three-hundred-foot-tall Sunsphere near the center of the original park dominates the landscape downtown, with its shiny gold dome sitting atop its Eiffel-Tower-like scaffolding. For years there was a restaurant at the top, but they closed it down; I'm not sure why.

At seven-forty, I was standing at the base of the sphere, wearing my mustard-stained floppy hat and my trench coat, both hands stuffed into the pockets. In the left was Professor Heifitz's class roster. In the right, the .45-caliber gun I bought from Wal-Mart, back when I naïvely thought I had a fighting chance to become a real detective, before I flunked the PI exam, before the state shut me down for flunking, before I found Jack Minor's mutilated corpse in the alley when all I wanted to accomplish that day was rescue some ferns.

I could hear the traffic along Cumberland Avenue, the main drag through campus, and see the flickering headlamps of the cars on the interstate. To the west, I guessed from the apartments across the street from the museum, a dog barked, a clipped, hard-edged sound in the frigid air.

At a quarter after eight, she still hadn't shown. I decided to give her another ten minutes. It couldn't have been more than a couple minutes later when the first blow landed between my shoulder blades. I stayed on my feet, stumbling forward a couple of steps. Behind me, I heard the scraping of shoes against concrete. The second blow landed in the lower back, a kidney punch that dropped me to my knees. My hands came out when I went down, to brace my fall. Kneeling, I fumbled in my pocket for the gun, and took the next blow at the base of the skull. I pitched forward, meeting the concrete with my nose. I heard a *crunch* and tasted blood rising from the back of my throat. Much warmer than the surrounding air, the blood steamed as it hit the pavement, pouring from my broken nose.

A hand grabbed my right wrist and yanked it up to the base of my neck. I howled. A knee pressed into the small of my back and I felt the warmth of someone's breath in my ear.

"You want to be next?" a male voice hissed. "That what you want, motherfucker?"

The fingers of his free hand dug into my hair and yanked my head back. I swallowed a wad of blood and snot.

"Don't fuck with us, Ruzak. We know where you live."

He shoved my face straight down. I managed to twist my head just in time, so my left cheekbone hit first and not my smashed nose. All I accomplished with that maneuver, though, was a smashed cheekbone.

He released me. I pushed myself up. Then he kicked me in the ribs, and the toe of his shoe wasn't soft, like a sneaker, but hard, like a reinforced work boot or steel-plated cowboy boot.

I flopped back down, gun completely forgotten, clutching my side. I suspected he'd broken a rib.

"Stay down, Ruzak," he said softly.

I took a few deep breaths and pushed myself back up. He kicked me again, twice, taking care to hit me in the same spot, where he could cause the most pain.

"What the hell is the matter with you? Stay *down*."

I started to get back up. He snorted with frustration, a kind of hiccuping laugh, and let me have it again, until I heard another crunching sound and felt a stabbing pain deep inside my chest. I wondered if a rib had punctured my lung. My vision was clouding, but I tried to get up.

"Moron," he said, and commenced to kick again. My legs moved against the ground, propelling me forward, like a Marine in an obstacle course. He must have kept pace beside me, because he managed to land his kicks in the same spot each time.

"Give up, why doncha? Why doncha just give up?"

One last time I tried to rise. He wasn't expecting it and missed the spot in my side, hitting instead my solar plexus. I collapsed, writhing and gasping for air, but hung onto consciousness long enough to hear his last words before darkness overwhelmed me.

"Nice hat," he said.

CHAPTER FORTY

I HAD A VERY ODD DREAM IN WHICH I WAS A DOG. I'M ASSUMING I WAS Archie, because I was sitting on my kitchen floor watching my human self peel a carrot. As I stared, the carrot began to squirm and wriggle, growing fatter and longer until it morphed into a rattlesnake as thick as my arm. I kept working as the snake whipped about, peeling off the skin, long glistening strands of it falling into the sink as its blood ran down my forearms. The snake's mouth came open, revealing three-inch fangs. The human-me just kept peeling. The dog-me barked.

I woke up in a hospital bed, an IV line snaking from my arm. Someone stirred in the chair beside me, rose, and came to stand beside the bed. I smelled White Diamonds.

"Hi, Ruzak," Felicia said. "How do you feel?"

"Floaty."

"You have Demerol in your drip."

"Oh. It's pretty good stuff. . . . How bad is it?"

"Not too bad. A fractured rib, a broken nose, a few lacerations here and there. You'll live."

I eased my hand to my face and touched the bandages over my nose.

"I was bushwhacked," I said.

Her eyes seemed very large in the subdued lighting of the hospital room. She had pulled her hair back, but I couldn't tell if it was in a bun or a ponytail. As the year had grown old, Felicia's hair had grown darker. She had begun the year a Dolly Parton blonde. Now the color was nearing a Penelope Cruz brown.

"You were lucky," she said. "Lucky he didn't kill you and lucky we got to you as soon as we did. You might have gone into hypothermia."

"Got to me?"

"I figured you'd call me. So when I didn't hear from you, I called you. When I couldn't reach you, I called Bob—he's on duty tonight and the station's only about a half mile from the park."

"Bob found me?"

She nodded, smiling, and her nose crinkled in the middle.

"You said you wanted to meet him, remember?"

"He didn't have to do anything like mouth-to-mouth, did he?"

She laughed and shook her head. "If he did, he didn't tell me about it."

"Would he?"

She laughed again. "Anyway, I didn't want you to wake up by your lonesome."

She laid her hand on my forearm, just below the IV. Her hand was cold.

"Did you get a good look at him?" she asked.

"No. He jumped me from behind."

"Well, it's a helluva price to pay, Ruzak, but at least now we know you were right about Reggie."

At that moment, the door swung open and Detective Black strode into the room. Felicia removed her hand from my arm.

"Well, Mr. Ruzak," Detective Black said. Her nose was bright red and the color was high in her cheeks.

"I was right about Reggie," I told her.

She showed me her teeth in what I took for Meredith Black's version of a noncommittal smile.

"Hello," she said, turning to Felicia. "I'm Detective Meredith Black with the Knoxville PD."

"This is Felicia, my secretary. Well, technically, my former secretary."

"Girl Friday and dog-sitter," Felicia corrected me.

"Oh," Meredith said. "Nice." She turned back to me. "Feel up to giving me a statement?"

"I better go," Felicia said.

"Okay." Meredith smiled in her general direction.

"Why don't you stay?" I asked. I looked at Meredith. "I got an armful of Demerol and I have trouble organizing my thoughts in the best of circumstances."

"I don't understand," Meredith said.

"I think Teddy wants me to stick around, as a kind of interpreter," Felicia said.

"He seems lucid to me."

"Appearances can be deceiving," Felicia said. "I used to think he was pretty smart."

"It really doesn't matter to me," Meredith said. She slipped into the chair

Felicia had vacated and dug a tape recorder from her purse. It was a very large, tote-sized purse.

"Here's the deal," I began, and brought the Knoxville PD up to snuff. Felicia hung by the door, arms folded over her chest. If Bob was working, I wondered, where was Tommy? And what about my dog?

"So I guess this girl was a no-show," Meredith said.

"I don't know. I didn't see her, but that doesn't necessarily mean she wasn't there."

"And she didn't give you a name over the phone?"

"If she had given me a name over the phone, I wouldn't have set up the meeting in the park."

"Seems an awfully convoluted way to go about it," Meredith observed. "And risky. Luring you to a public place like that. Why not jump you in the parking lot under the Sterchi?"

"Well, I really can't answer that," I answered. "I'm not in his head."

"My point is, why would they arrange something so elaborate and risky just to send you a message to back off? All these calls basically an act to lure you over there tonight? It doesn't make sense."

"Not much has since I found him," I said, meaning Jack.

"I'm just wondering if there's an element to this you've left out."

"I don't think so. . . ."

"You're asking me to believe that the three people involved in this crime, if there were three people, involved a fourth person in their conspiracy to commit an act that blows any chance they have of getting off scot-free."

I thought about what she said. Then I asked, "Huh?"

"Reggie's confession was reported in the newspaper. Odds are they know somebody's taking the fall for them. Why would they do something which sends the message we got the wrong guy?"

"I don't know. All I know is my nose is broken."

"Maybe this has nothing to do with the death of Jack Minor," Meredith Black said.

"How couldn't it?"

"I think only you could answer that question, Mr. Ruzak."

From across the room, Felicia exploded.

"Oh, Jesus Christ, I'm not believing this! He's had the living shit beat out of him; he might have frozen to death out there tonight; and you're sitting there accusing him of lying about the whole thing! Where do you people get off? Ruzak's got a lot of problems, God knows, but one of them isn't dishonesty. He's the most honest person I've ever known."

"It isn't a matter of Mr. Ruzak's honesty," Meredith snapped back. "It's a matter of consistency and logic."

"Well," I said. "Those two things do happen to be problems."

"Shut up, Ruzak," Felicia said. "Why are you giving in to this . . ." She started to call her a name, then backed off. ". . . person?" She turned back to Meredith. "It is consistent and it is logical. I don't think it was a setup. Or it didn't become a setup until after the last phone call. I think she's a girlfriend of one of these guys. He told her about Jack, then one day she sees Ruzak's poster on campus. She starts calling him, but she can't bring herself to say anything until yesterday."

"Why?" Meredith asked. Her tone was sharp, but she was smiling, ever the biter.

"Why the hell does *why* matter? Maybe she really loves the guy and doesn't want to see him go to jail for the rest of his life. Maybe she's scared—she told Ruzak he would kill her—maybe she's both, in love and scared, and then she finds out an innocent man is going to pay for something her boyfriend did and that finally makes her talk.

"Look, this isn't brain surgery. All you have to do now is take that list and go through the names. Because his name is on that list. His or one of the other's or maybe all three. There's no other reason he'd do this. You wanted to know why he risked it—that's why."

"It isn't a long list," I said. "Twenty-seven names, twenty of which are male."

"Don't make us do it," Felicia said to Meredith.

"Excuse me?"

"Don't make me and Ruzak go down that list. Can you imagine what the *Sentinel* would do with that story, how the Knoxville PD sat on its ass while some boneheaded loser PI who isn't even a PI caught the real killers?"

Meredith looked down at my broken face. I said, "She never wanted me involved in this." The remark about the boneheaded loser PI stung, but I knew Felicia was just driving home a point.

DECEMBER 9

CHAPTER FORTY-ONE

My breakfast the next morning was surprisingly good for a hospital. Eggs, toast, two pancakes, and a glass of orange juice. I asked the lady who brought the food when I could go home, and she said as soon as the doctor cleared me. So I ate my breakfast and waited for the doctor. I studied the IV in my arm and worried about a staph infection; a hospital really is the worst place to be sick: The longer you stay, the higher your odds of getting seriously ill from something that had nothing to do with your being there.

Felicia called to check on me.

"I don't know when I can leave," I said to her, half complaining, half explaining.

"Can you get a ride home?" she asked, which I took to mean she couldn't be that ride. Probably something to do with Tommy, or Bob, or both—or neither. There were whole areas of Felicia's life that I knew nothing about.

"I'll figure something out," I said. "You probably saved my life last night, and I don't think I thanked you."

"Was that a thanks?"

"More of a lead-in. Thank you. And make sure you thank Bob for me."

"It couldn't have worked out better," Felicia said. She sounded tired, and I wondered how much sleep she had gotten the night before. "Now that our pal Meredith has the list."

"What if the list proves to be a dead end?"

"Ruzak, at some point you have to say enough."

"Maybe I shouldn't, though, as long as Reggie's behind bars."

"You have more important things to do, like studying for your PI exam."

"Right. Um."

" 'Right um'?"

"Well, sometimes circumstances force you to look at things with a fresh eye."

"Meaning?"

"Meaning maybe detective work and I aren't a good fit."

"If you really mean that, why are you thinking about doing more with this case?"

"I'm not sure how much that has to do with me being a detective."

"Oh, Christ. You're so . . .'"

"Boneheaded?"

"You're sore about that."

"A little."

"I was trying to make a point, that's all."

"That's what I figured."

"It has its advantages, you know. Being a bonehead."

"Name one."

The silence that ensued weighed on us both. Finally, I said, "I'm worried about Archie."

"Archie's fine. I swung by your apartment on the way home and picked him up."

"How'd you get in?"

"I took your keys."

"So how will I get in?"

"Turn the knob. I didn't lock it. Your keys are on the kitchen counter."

"So Archie's with you?"

"Until you come by and get him. And the sooner, the better, Ruzak."

There weren't too many names on my list of people I could count on to give me a ride. I called the Humane Society.

"I'm in the hospital," I told Amanda.

"What happened?"

"A bad guy jumped me."

"Oh, my God! Are you okay?"

"Well, the doctor just came through and said I could go home."

"Did they catch the guy?"

"Not yet, but they have his name."

"What is it?"

"I don't know."

"You just said they had his name."

"They have his name on a list."

"Dear Jesus, how many people attacked you?"

"It's kind of a long story. The reason I'm calling is I need a lift back to my apartment."

"My shift doesn't end till three."

"Oh. Well, maybe I'll call a cab, then. I think they need the room."

"No, no, don't do that. I'll make a couple of calls. Give me an hour, okay? I'll be there."

"Okay."

I decided to get dressed and hit the john before she arrived. The last thing I wanted—well, not the last in the absolute sense—was her to see me in a hospital gown. I had trouble buttoning my shirt over the bandages protecting my ribs, and pulling up my pants proved a challenge of physical engineering. I hurt like hell after it was over, and double-checked my wallet for the subscription for painkillers the attending physician had written. I was surprised to find my gun in the pocket of my overcoat. You would think a hospital would have tighter security procedures.

I avoided my reflection in the bathroom mirror, but the little glances I shot that way were not encouraging. Both eyes had shiners, giving me a raccoonlike appearance. I wondered if my nose would come out crooked after the bandages came off, and what that would do to my overall appearance. Might it give my otherwise bland features some character? Well, I thought, at least my basic optimism is still intact.

I sat in the chair by the bed and tried to gather my thoughts, though the effects of the Demerol still lingered. A thought would dash across my mind and I would chase after it, like Alice after the rabbit, until it hopped down my cerebral hole and was gone.

There could be only one reason I was jumped the night before. Like Meredith said, it was a huge risk, and the only thing that made the risk worth taking was a name on the list I promised Unknown Caller I had. At some point, from the time I set up the rendezvous and last night, this guy found out about me and the list and decided he didn't have a choice but to try to warn me off the case.

I had accomplished that, at least: narrowing his options. That spawned another half-formed thought, or more of an emotion struggling to become a thought, and that emotion felt a lot like fear.

I was still chasing rabbits when Amanda walked into the room, took one look at my smashed-up face, and brought a hand to her mouth.

"It looks worse than it feels," I told her.

"Lean on me," she said.

"The doctor says I might need to use a cane for a few weeks."

"This has something to do with the dead guy in the alley, doesn't it?"

I nodded. "He's running out of options," I said. During the elevator ride and the long, slow walk to the parking lot, with my big self draped over her skinny frame, I told her about the list and Unknown Caller.

"And now I've got a bad feeling," I said, as she helped me lower myself into the passenger seat of the Monte Carlo.

"I bet you do," she said.

I shifted in my seat as she drove, trying to find a comfortable position. That had been a problem of mine for some time. I said, "I mean, about her. He can't trust her now."

"You think he'll hurt her?"

"I'm just wondering if the reason I didn't see her last night was because she wouldn't come, or if it was because she *couldn't* come."

"Oh, God."

"But it's one of those things where there's nothing you can do. I've been faced with that a lot lately. From Jack in that alley to Eunice Shriver, even to Archie, with all that angst-ridden staring."

"I don't think dogs suffer from angst, Ruzak."

"Well. The point is, fear is a very useful emotion. We're capable of it for a reason. It's supposed to spur us to action, the flight-or-flight thing, but I've got nothing to fight and nothing to fly from, really. There's no way to find her. All I can do is pray she's safe."

"Maybe she'll call again."

"I doubt it. She's afraid, too. She was afraid before, obviously, but now she's very afraid. Now she's terrified."

I asked her to swing through the Buddy's Barbeque drive-thru on Kingston Pike; I was starving. I had a pulled-pork sandwich and side of coleslaw. Amanda ordered a hot-fudge cake.

"I live on these things," she confided.

"Don't you worry about things like proper nutrition, saturated fat content, and stuff like that?"

"No more than you," she said, eying my sandwich.

In the lobby of the Sterchi, we passed a man whose name I knew only as Whittaker. Whittaker was the assistant apartment manager.

"Ruzak?" he asked.

"I had a little accident," I said.

"Looks slightly larger than little. I need to talk to you. I got a report that you've violated your lease."

"How so?"

"You're aware we're a pet-free facility?"

"I think I remember something about that."

"We've had reports, Mr. Ruzak."

"Look, he's been seriously injured," Amanda said. "He needs to get off his feet."

Whittaker ignored her. "Are you denying you've taken a dog into this building?"

"I was affirming that I knew I couldn't keep a pet."

"Are you?"

"I just did."

"No, are you denying you have a dog?" he asked, his voice rising.

"I do not currently have a dog, no," I said carefully.

Amanda edged us toward the elevator. Whittaker trailed behind, hot on the scent.

"You do know, as the assistant manager of this facility, that I have the right to enter your apartment at any time to conduct an inspection of compliance with your lease agreement?"

"I wasn't specifically aware of that, but I'll take your word for it."

"I'll be happy to supply you with a copy," Whittaker said. "We take enforcement very seriously here at the Sterchi, Mr. Ruzak."

"Oh, I'm a firm believer in enforcement," I replied. "But as of this moment, I don't have a dog."

The elevator doors slid closed, and we left Mr. Something Whittaker or Mr. Whittaker Something behind.

"You got rid of Arch?" Amanda asked.

"Felicia took him. But I have to get him back."

"Felicia of the pleasant knees."

She walked me to the sofa.

"Comfy?" she asked.

"Not really."

"Maybe you should lie down in the bed."

"I'll get used to it."

"We should have got you a cane. Or a walker, like old ladies use."

I asked her to fetch me the cordless. There were no new calls and no messages.

"Seriously, Ruzak, tell me what else you need."

"I did forget this," I said, showing her the prescription.

"I'll go get it filled," she said, snatching it from my hand.

"You don't need to do that."

"It's no big deal," she said, and headed for the door. "There's a Walgreens right on Gay Street."

Then she was gone. I sat on my sofa and thought I'd never seen her so animated. Sometimes all we need to feel alive is to feel useful.

After fifteen minutes of me staring at the TV remote lying on the coffee table, trying to work up the energy to get up and grab it, the phone rang. The number that popped up looked familiar, but I couldn't place it.

"Ruzak!" Vernon Shriver barked at me. "Where is my mother?"

"I haven't seen her," I said. "I just got home from the hospital."

"Why were you in the hospital?"

"Somebody beat me up."

"That don't surprise me. Well, she isn't home and she isn't here and she isn't at the church. What do you think?"

I told him I had no idea what I thought, but promised to call if I heard from her. He called me a name and hung up.

Another forty-five minutes went by, and still no sign of Amanda. I wondered if Walgreens was giving her a hard time about the prescription because, obviously, she didn't look like somebody whose name could be Theodore Ruzak.

Felicia called to ask if I got home okay.

"Did you take a cab?" she asked.

"No," I said. "I took Amanda. I mean, Amanda gave me a ride. I mean, she drove me home."

"Amanda," she said. "Well, you know what this means."

"What?"

"She's got a real thing for you, Ruzak. I just don't understand your reluctance."

"I'm not the any-port-in-a-storm kind of guy."

"It's her knees, isn't it?"

"They do have a certain knobby quality."

Another half hour went by before Amanda finally returned, the white paper Walgreens' drug sack in one hand and a small duffel in the other.

"What now?" I asked.

"I decided to run by my place and grab a few things. You're gonna need some help until you get back on your feet."

"You're moving in?"

"Just for a few days. Is that a problem?"

I sat very still, trying to think of one way in which it might be. She laughed.

"Don't worry, Ruzak. You're in no condition to hanky-panky, even if you wanted to. I'll bunk out here on the sofa."

She dropped her duffel to the floor and commenced to rummaging through my pantry. She was wearing stretchy black pants that accentuated her glutes as she bent over.

"You must eat out a lot," she called over her shoulder. She leaned on the kitchen counter, unwrapping a Twinkie. I wasn't sure, but it may have been my last Twinkie.

"There's no tree," she said, looking around. "Don't you celebrate Christmas?"

"I used to put up a tree for Mom," I said. "This is my first Christmas without her."

"Maybe that's the problem," Amanda said. "A Freudian element."

"I'd hate to think so."

"All I'm saying is, maybe older women turn you on."

"Well," I said. "I watch a lot of old movies, and I always had a thing for Sophia Loren."

"Oh God, Ruzak, she's nearly as old as Eunice Shriver."

"I think that's why I've been so indulgent," I said. "Not because of Sophia Loren, but because Eunice showed up right after my mom died."

"Do you do that a lot?" she asked, finishing off the Twinkie and licking the white cream from her fingertips. What the hell was in that cream, anyway? "All the navel gazing?"

"More than I should," I admitted. "Probably I'm trying to keep the cosmic scales balanced against the people who should, but don't."

DECEMBER 20

CHAPTER FORTY-TWO

My first impression of Reggie Matthews through the bullet-proof pane was how much better his looks had improved since his incarceration: neatly shaved, his hair shorter and thicker looking, calm and well rested. More than poor diet or lack of exercise, it's fear and anxiety that tear our appearances apart. Reggie didn't have to worry anymore where his next meal was coming from, or if he'd find a warm place to sleep for the night. Or if he was doomed to suffer a useless, unjust death at the hands of a punk.

"Reggie," I said into the telephone receiver. "You look terrific."

"You don't. He really did a number on you, Ruzak."

"It's reached that point where it looks worse than it feels."

"That's the point to get to, all right."

"Reggie," I said. "They're finished with the list."

He wet his lips. "They caught 'em all?"

"They caught nobody. Reggie, the list didn't pan out. Every guy on it had an alibi or didn't fit the descriptions you gave."

"So?"

"So I told Detective Black it didn't change the fact that I was attacked by somebody who warned me off this case. That this girl calling me and that guy jumping me could only point to your innocence."

He nodded. "And what'd she say?"

"She said I'd make a terrific witness for the defense."

"Well, sure."

"Reggie, here's the bottom line: You're going to trial next month for a murder we both know you didn't commit. Now, the Knoxville PD is playing this close to the vest—Meredith won't say what she'll do—but my guess is they'll fold their hands if you recant now. They don't have anything of any substance except your confession."

"I ain't recanting, Ruzak."

"How about Johnson City?" I asked. "You must have felt reasonably safe there."

"Are you kidding me?" he said with a laugh. "You hear from my boy?"

I nodded. "I told him you were doing just fine, but he asked to talk to you and I had to lie."

"What'd you say?"

"I told him you were walking my dog. What're you going to do when he decides to drive down for a little visit? Or he picks up the paper and reads about your trial?"

"Did you give him that money?"

"I did."

"Then he don't have any reason to come down. He never wanted much to do with me, Ruzak, even when he was little. You wanna know somethin'? I'm feelin' the best I have in years. Even gone off my medicine. I got a whole month to let this thing work itself out."

"These kind of things don't just work themselves out, Reggie. Maybe you should factor this into your decision: she hasn't called me since the attack, and the list is a dead end."

His eyes narrowed at me. "So?"

"So there's nothing the police can do and, more important, there's nothing more I can do. The only option left is for you to recant."

"Not yet."

"I don't get it," I said. "What are you waiting for, Reggie? The police think they have Jack's killer, so they're not looking. I've got no leads, so I'm not looking. And I sincerely doubt these guys are going to waltz into the station and confess. You're betting the police will have to let you go if you recant at the eleventh hour, but you don't know that for sure. They still may take you to trial, and men have been sent to the death chamber on less in this state."

"Ah, come on, Ruzak, what's the matter with you? It's almost Christmas. Don't you believe in miracles?"

I gave up after that. He seemed awfully cocksure for somebody whose fate hung by a thread. I left the prison, hobbling across the parking lot, leaning on the cane Amanda had bought me, carved from hickory with a gold handle in the shape of a duck's head. Bunting hung from the lampposts, bronze horns on a green background with HAPPY HOLIDAYS written in red beneath them. Somebody had thrown a few strands of Christmas lights around the evergreens by the entrance, the kind with the fat, multicolored bulbs, which was the only kind of lights I could remember from childhood; I think my childhood predated the minilights.

The overcast sky was spitting a fitful snow, and I walked slowly to my car, planting my feet carefully on the slick pavement. To the west, on the other side of the river, seven-foot-tall Christmas trees, red, green and white, glimmered on the roof of the First Tennessee Bank building, the tallest structure downtown.

I leaned the cane against the passenger seat and started the car. I felt heavy, weighed down. Foolish, too, to put so much stock into the list from Professor Heifitz. I wasn't attacked because a name was on a list; I was attacked because he must have found out she had talked to me and I deserved a stern warning.

It took over forty minutes on the Pike to get to West Town Mall and another ten to find a parking place, and that one tucked in the farthest corner. Driving was not a painless exercise, and Amanda had offered to chauffer me, but I told her my independence was about all I had left. She seemed to understand. I had hoped that that would lead to a discussion about her moving out. It didn't.

I had lived alone for so long, her being in my apartment was both comforting and disconcerting. She was gone most of the day; the semester was over, but she had picked up more hours at the Humane Society. I discovered Amanda was a night owl. I'd wake up in the middle of the night to the sound of her raucous laughter on the phone, and she spent a lot of time on her laptop, crafting her MySpace. Archie enjoyed having her around, though. She was an old friend from his pound days, and it took his mind off whatever it was about me that troubled him.

Two days after I left the hospital, Vernon Shriver called me.

"We found her," he said without even saying hello.

"Where was she?"

"Hiding out at her preacher's house. I got her safe now. Put her in that home on Middlebrook Pike, you know the one?"

"I think I've heard of it. Wasn't that the one where the old guy killed himself a couple years back?"

"That's the one. Killed his wife, too. Think she had terminal cancer."

So Eunice Shriver was safely tucked away in a rest home, only they don't call them rest homes anymore for politically correct reasons that were hard for me to discern. Still, if anybody needed a rest, it was Eunice. I'd read somewhere that dementia wasn't a matter of *if* but *when*. You live long enough, you get it. Those ninety-year-olds with the minds sharp as tacks, they're doomed, too, if they beat the odds and make it another ten years. All the advances in medical science can't change the fact that the human body is designed to last for only so long. And still, in the twenty-first century, nobody can say for sure why we die, what makes our cells eventually stop doing what they're designed to do. Maybe this is the root cause of our sense of outrage and betrayal when the inevitable comes.

Felicia was waiting for me in the food court, wearing a red scarf and dangly ruby earrings, her hair pulled back into a cascade of blondness that fell to the middle of her back. She had colored her hair again. She smelled like cinnamon, though I might have been picking up the rolls from the Cinnabon place four tables away.

"Sorry," I said. "I couldn't find a spot."

"You should have used a handicapped one."

"I don't have a sticker."

"Ruzak, half the people parked in them don't, either, and half of those who do, shouldn't."

"Integrity begins as a personal issue," I said.

"You know, sometimes you say things that sound very smart but, if you really think about them, they kind of crumble apart like old cake."

She had taken the liberty of buying my lunch, a steaming steak-and-cheese from Charlie's Steakery. They served the fries, the greasiest I'd ever had, in a paper cup. Felicia had salad from McDonalds.

"Reggie won't recant," I told her.

"He's getting three squares a day and twenty-four-hour, taxpayer-provided protection. He figures he can wait till the last second and they'll have to let him go. Would you recant?"

"I wouldn't have confessed in the first place."

"Well," she said. "At least it's over and you can concentrate on more important things. Like passing your PI exam. Three weeks, Ruzak. You better be ready."

"I could let it go," I said. "If it weren't for her."

"Who her?"

"Unknown Caller. What if something happened to her? Why hasn't she called me?"

"Because it worked. He beat you up to send her a message, too."

"She said he would kill her."

"Has there been anything in the papers? Any story on TV? And even if he did do something to her, what're you going to do about it? She had the opportunity to be straight with you and she chose not to."

"One thing that puzzles me," I said. "Why did she call me and not the cops? That way she gets him locked up and unlocks up an innocent man."

"Maybe it's more than fear," Felicia said.

"She loves him?"

She shrugged. "It happens."

A frazzled-looking woman hurried by our table, arms loaded down with bags, two kids in tow as she talked on her cell phone.

"I haven't bought the first present," I told Felicia, watching the woman. "What does Tommy want?"

She gave me a look. "What do you think?"

"They do have hypoallergenic breeds."

"You know something? Whenever you say a word over four syllables there's this caressing thing that goes on with your mouth."

"Floccinaucinihilipilification."

"Flocci what?"

"It's the longest word in the *Oxford English Dictionary*."

"What does it mean?"

"The estimation that something is worthless."

"Like knowing the longest word in the *Oxford English Dictionary*. What was it again?"

"Floccinaucinihilipilification."

"Wow. That was practically orgasmic."

"Amanda asked me why I kept a dictionary in the bathroom."

"Do you think that's significant? That I say the word orgasmic and you think of Amanda?"

"Oh, nothing like that's going on. She sleeps on the sofa."

"Let me ask you something, Ruzak. Are you human?"

"She did ask me if I was gay. I told her I wasn't, but what if I am?"

"You're not gay, Ruzak."

"I've never been attracted to a man, but maybe that's only because I haven't been around the right man."

"I don't think the fact that you're not attracted to this girl means you're not attracted to girls. Does she still throw herself at you?"

"Once, the night she moved in, but that was more of a gentle toss."

"So when does she plan to move out? You're ambulatory now."

"I don't know how to broach the topic."

"How about, 'Hey, thanks for the help, but I'm okay now?' "

"I'm figuring it won't be long. She'll want to spend Christmas with her mom."

"So am I," Felicia said, pulling a compact out of her purse to check her face. Her red lips puckered at the mirror. "Not her mom, mine up in Kentucky."

"This'll be my first Christmas since Mom died," I said. "I'm thinking of spending it at the mission. The food wasn't all that bad at Thanksgiving, and it'll give me something to do."

"You need that," she said. "Something to do."

"The other thing I thought of was working the list myself. You know, maybe the cops missed something. I doubt they checked out all those guys' alibis. I've got a copy of it." I tapped my pocket. The idea had been to show the list to Reggie, but in the middle of our conversation it struck me how useless that would have been.

"You know what the secret to happiness is, Ruzak? Knowing when to give up."

I nodded. "That's it. You've hit it right on the money. Knowing which battles to fight and knowing the time to walk from the fray. But it's like great sex. Afterward, when the moment's done, there's the 'what next.' I don't have any what-next."

"You don't have the sex, either."

She dropped the compact into her purse and pulled out a small notebook. The tip of her tongue came out as she studied whatever was written in it.

"What is that?" I asked.

"Shopping list, Ruzak."

"I haven't bought the first present," I said.

"I know, you already told me."

"Do you ever worry about dementia?"

"Only when I'm with you."

"Eunice's son committed her to a rest home."

"They don't call them rest homes anymore, Ruzak."

"I know. Why is that?"

"Does it matter?"

"That's my other problem," I said. "One of my other problems. Figuring out what matters."

"Here's what matters," she said. "Knowing for certain I've taken care of everyone on the list."

She noticed me staring at her.

"What?"

" 'Everyone on the list,' " I said.

"Even the mailman. He loves M&Ms, so I have to hit the Candy Factory before I leave."

"There were twenty-seven names on that seminar's class roster," I said. "Twenty of which are male. Felicia, Detective Black told me they interviewed every guy on that list. Every *guy* on that list."

I pulled the list from my pocket and showed her.

"They never talked to the girls," I said.

She let the notebook fall closed and said, "I'll drive."

CHAPTER FORTY-THREE

I MADE THE CALLS FROM THE PASSENGER SEAT OF FELICIA'S COROLLA. The first and third were picked up by an automated voicemail system, and I hung up without leaving a message. We could always swing by the addresses later. The second, fourth, and fifth also went to voicemails, these with personalized greetings, but I didn't leave a message on those, either. I didn't want to spoil the element of surprise.

"School's out for the semester break," I said. "We might not get anybody."

The sixth call was answered on the tenth ring, right as I was about to hang up.

"Hello?"

I glanced at the list. Angela Cummings. "Angela," I said. "This is Teddy Ruzak."

A good ten seconds of silence, and then the line went dead.

I looked over at Felicia. "I think my network dropped the call."

Felicia started the car. "Bullshit," she said, and whipped out of the parking space. Then it took ten minutes just to get out of the lot and onto Kingston Pike, where the brake lights twinkled very Christmaslike. Felicia banged her palm of the steering wheel.

"Damn, damn, *damn*," she said.

"You should cut over on Papermill to the interstate," I said.

"Really, you think? Thank you *so* much, Ruzak, for stating the obvious! Why do you men do that?"

"Here's my theory—"

"Screw your theories! You have more theories than China has people!" She laid on the horn and yelled, "Come *on!*"

It took twenty-five minutes to get eastbound on I-40. Felicia asked for the address again, and I gave it to her, on Seventeenth Street, about four blocks north of the Strip on campus.

"Okay, okay," she said, alternating between slamming on the gas and pumping the brake. "I think I know where that it is."

It turned out to be in a row of brownstones converted into student apartments. The entire block had a deserted feel to it, an atmosphere of abandonment, with the leafless oaks and maples and Bradford pears, and the small yards of winter-killed grass.

Felicia parked on the street about half a block to the north. She cut off the engine and we sat in silence for a few minutes, looking at the house. Someone had wrapped silver tinsel around the porch railing.

"She's had plenty of time to scoot," Felicia said.

"And probably won't come to the door when she sees it's us," I added.

"You're the detective, Ruzak. Now what?"

"Maybe she called him," I said. "Maybe he'll show up."

"Maybe they live together and he has a knife to her throat."

"Maybe we should call the cops."

"Maybe that's the dumbest idea I've ever heard after the way they've screwed this up," she said.

"Well," I said. "If she isn't inside, she's somewhere else. . . ."

"Oh, you're so good."

"And she'll either come back or she won't."

"Right."

"Or she's still inside trying to figure out what to do."

"Calling first was a stupid idea," she said. "I say we stake it out. If she's in, at some point she has to come out. If she's out, odds are at some point she has to go back in."

"Okay," I said.

And so we waited. After about fifteen minutes, Felicia checked in with the sitter, telling her she got tied up at the mall and she might have to stay through dinner. She hung up and looked at me.

"Aren't you going to call Amanda? She might be worried."

"She's at work," I said, avoiding her eyes.

"Maybe you're just in denial, Ruzak. You really are attracted to her, but you're afraid of getting your heart broken."

"Or the opposite," I said. "The last girl broke it and maybe I'm afraid it'll be mended."

The hours drew out, and the snow began to grow fatter, taking longer to melt on the windshield and actually surviving on the exposed tree branches. Every few minutes Felicia started the car to keep us warm. It was nearly three o'clock when she said, "I can see why you're so enamored by this detective deal. Such heart-pounding excitement."

She scrunched down in her seat, pulling the red scarf tighter around her neck. I didn't smell cinnamon now, but peaches with a hint of coconut.

"I'm hungry," she said suddenly.

"There's a Walgreens on the corner," I said. "I'll get us something."

"No. I'll go. You're the big strong man. Did you bring your gun?"

"Why would I bring my gun?"

I watched her walk down the sidewalk toward Cumberland. When I couldn't see her anymore, I watched the house. I looked for any sign of life, any movement in the windows. Nothing.

Felicia came back with some candy bars, a couple of Mountain Dews, and a bag of Bugles.

"Bugles!" I said. "I haven't had those since I was a kid." I tore open the bag and popped a handful into my mouth. Felicia watched me, amused.

"It takes so little, doesn't it, Ruzak?"

The light began to fail. Despite the massive dose of caffeine from my soda, I started to get a little heavy-lidded. I think I dozed off. The next thing I knew, Felicia's head was on my shoulder, her left arm across my body, her hand curled into a fist in my lap, and my world was the smell of coconuts. It was cold inside the car and it was hard to see through the snow-dusted windows, but I didn't wake her. I put my hand over hers, to see if it was cold. I told myself, if her hand was cold I would wake her so she could get the heater going. Her hand didn't seem that cold to me, so I didn't wake her.

Then she stirred—maybe because I touched her—and her arm moved around my waist and she pressed herself closer, moving her head to my chest, and she made some low sound in the back of her throat, a contented purr. I wondered if I was Bob—or a memory of Bob, a kind of Boblike echo—and I had found myself in a situation rooted in a false pretext, the equivalent of a stolen kiss.

Back when I was a security guard and Felicia was a waitress at the Old City Diner, I would make small talk to keep her by my table, because, frankly, there was something about the way her nose crinkled when she laughed. At seven o'clock, my shift had ended; hers had just begun. It was the only hour of the day when our orbits overlapped, and I flattered myself that something might be born in the area formed by the intersection of our spheres.

She wore a white uniform and those thick-soled white shoes over white stockings, her hair always swept back into a tight bun, only a few wisps of blond would hang down in the back, and at the time I wondered how her hair would feel between my fingers. Now that same thick hair was inches beneath my nose, and the smell of coconut made me think of piña coladas, which led to tropical breezes and the rustle of palm trees and the feel of sand beneath your toes, the foam of crashing waves, and the water fading into the sky, even that old Rupert Holmes song, "If you like piña coladas and getting caught in the rain . . ."

I sat very still, skirting along the edge of the moment, maybe the only opportunity I would ever have to touch Felicia's hair. Fifty years from now, would I chase sleep on my deathbed, haunted by my cowardice, my failure of will at the critical hour on that snowy night when she lay curled in my arms? Sometimes we're afforded some space before we must screw our courage to the sticking place, and that's all we need, a little time to steel ourselves. Then there are moments like this one, where the courage must be drawn from some inner reserve before that singular moment is gone forever. With no warning, the test comes, and whatever is beneath the mask you present to the world, the elemental *you*, stripped of pretense, is exposed. Reggie Matthews had one of the moments and, when that moment came, Reggie Matthews ran. In a way, he was still running.

And speaking of runners: Consider Ruzak inside this snow-encrusted car, in the gloaming of an early winter day, as he begins to shiver and not because it's cold. What should I make of him, when even the simplest act forces him to freeze like a tightrope walker teetering on the rope, absurdly paralyzed in midstride, in that instant before the fall?

Really, Ruzak, how much courage does it take to touch a pretty girl's hair? I raised my hand to touch Felicia's hair.

CHAPTER FORTY-FOUR

AND WHEN I DID, SHE SAID, "RUZAK, WHAT THE HELL ARE YOU DOING?"

"Nothing," I said, dropping my hand. She pulled away, touching her hair where I had almost touched it.

"Did I fall asleep?"

"I think we both did."

She pulled down the visor and checked out her face in the mirror.

"Oh God," she said. "I think I drooled."

I looked down at my shirt, but didn't see any evidence of dribble.

"Great," she said. "We probably missed her."

I looked down the street. "Maybe, but here comes somebody."

He was wearing a Tennessee orange hoodie and blue jeans, walking toward us from Cumberland Avenue. A short guy, painfully thin, with long dark hair that pooled in the folds of the hood, hands jammed into the hoodie's pocket. He approached us with his head down, so I didn't get a good look at his face. He turned up the walk of the house. The door swung open as he mounted the porch; she must have been watching for him. He disappeared inside.

"Okay," Felicia breathed. "Now what?"

"I don't know," I said. "I thought he'd be bigger."

"You said you didn't get a look at him."

"No. But I had the impression he displaced a lot more air."

"What the hell does *that* mean?"

"You know, like he was more lumbering than lithe. I say we chance it. We might not get another shot at this."

I started to open the door. Felicia grabbed my forearm.

"First tell me what we're chancing, Ruzak."

"We're going to knock on the door."

"We could have done that hours ago."

"We didn't know she was there."

"We still don't know she's there. This guy might not be connected at all. Or maybe her roommate let him in."

"Only one way to find out."

I heaved myself out of the seat. My battered torso sang a little protest song. I leaned against the car, holding my cane, as Felicia got out and met me on the curb. A snowflake clung to her eyelash.

"I'll get to one side," I said. "Between the window and the door. You do the knocking."

"They can see us coming," Felicia murmured as we approached the brownstone.

"He's here now," I said. "I doubt they're hovering by the door, watching."

I leaned on the wall, trying to catch my breath in the thin winter atmosphere. I made a mental note to always carry my gun with me. Then I mentally tore up the note—I'd forgotten I was getting out of the detective business.

I didn't know what I was going to do with my life. Maybe I'd try to get into college and study something that might one day benefit mankind, like medicine. *Dr. Ruzak to the OR, stat!* I watched a lot of the Discovery Health Channel, and the operating room scenes never grossed me out. I wasn't sure how far that went to qualify me to practice medicine, but I wasn't so old yet I had to close that door.

Felicia knocked. We waited. She knocked again.

" 'Who's that?' " Felicia whispered. " 'Oh, just that beefy detective and his trusty sidekick. Let's let them in!' "

"You could kick down the door using your ninja powers," I suggested.

"And they prosecute us for breaking and entering," she said, which sort of acknowledged that she did have ninja powers.

"They're college students," I said. "I say we go Pavlovian. Yell 'Pizza!' "

"My hands are so cold it hurts to knock."

"What do they want?" I asked rhetorically. "They want us to leave. So we don't. We stay until they realize we won't."

"They've probably already run out the back door."

"You know," I said. "I didn't even consider that."

"You're born for this work, Ruzak, you know that?"

She knocked again, this time an urgent *rap-rap-rap*.

"Somebody's coming," she whispered. "I hear them."

I pressed my back against the wall, in case they were checking her out through the window. I heard the latch turn and the door came open a few inches. I held my breath so the person on the other side wouldn't see it fog.

"Yes?"

"Angela Cummings?" Felicia said.

"Yes?"

"Angela," Felicia said, her tone both kind and urgent. "We know he's here and we want to help. We want to help him and we want to help you help him."

"I don't know what you're talking about," I heard Angela say. "I really don't." But the door stayed open a crack. Felicia should stick her foot between the door and the frame. That was PI 101, but I couldn't expect Felicia to know that.

"We know he's the one," Felicia said. "The police don't, not yet, but close this door and in five minutes they'll have the SWAT team in position."

"He's not. He didn't. They caught the guy who did. He confessed."

"Caught the guy who did what?" Felicia asked. "I thought you didn't know what I was talking about. Look, we're not here to arrest anyone. We just want to talk."

"We?"

I pushed away from the wall and stood behind Felicia. Through the crack, I could see one large, teary eyeball over a slice of nose.

"Hey," the girl said, her voice rising. "I don't know who you people are or who sent you—"

"I'm Teddy Ruzak," I said. "And Jack Minor sent me."

CHAPTER FORTY-FIVE

Behind the girl, a shadow moved, then spoke. "Angela, you better let them in."

The door abruptly swung closed. Felicia looked over her shoulder at me, the red scarf cupping her delicate chin.

"I think she disagrees," she said.

The door opened again, and Angela stepped back to let us pass. Several feet into the gloomy entryway stood the kid in the hoodie. Angela closed the door and threw the deadbolt, and then the four us stood there, and nobody seemed to have anything to say.

"I didn't kill him," the kid said.

"But you were there," I said. "With the guy who did."

He didn't say anything. I went on, "Three of you, and then you mutilated his corpse."

"I didn't," the kid whispered. "I never touched the guy. Eric cut the letters."

"But it was your idea. Angela had told you about the tetragrammaton. Was that some kind of joke?"

"No." He shook his head. In the weak light spilling from the kitchen behind him, he had all the physical presence of a drug addict. I still couldn't make out his face. "We panicked, man. That other guy, his buddy, he saw us. He saw everything. So Brice took after him, chased him down the street, left us there with the body and we didn't know what to do. So I said, 'Let's make it look like some crazed serial killer did it.' But I didn't do it; I didn't cut him up; it wasn't me. I was saying let's leave a note or something and Eric said we can't leave a note—there'd be fingerprints—and anyway, we didn't have anything to write with, so he found a broken bottle in the alley . . ."

He choked up. Angela brushed past me and stood by his side, pulling his hand into both of hers.

"I said we gotta do this. We gotta do this and in a couple days we'll write a letter to the cops calling ourselves the Yahweh Killers or something like that so they'll think it's some kind of weird cult or something."

"Brilliant plan," Felicia said.

"We were drunk! I mean, shit, I've never been in trouble. I've never even had a fucking traffic ticket! Brice went crazy on the old guy over that hat. That fucking hat!"

"He *is* crazy," Angela said softly. "I told you not to hang out with him."

"Brice was the one who beat me up," I said.

Angela nodded. "I told Liam I was meeting you at the park, and he told Brice."

"You gotta understand," Liam said. "I can't go to prison. Jesus Christ, I'm supposed to graduate this spring!"

"And get married," Angela said softly. "Please, Mr. Ruzak, I've been telling him to go to the cops. They'll go easy on him if he cooperates, right? Won't they cut him a deal if he agrees to testify?"

"I never touched him," Liam cried. "I never touched the old fuck!"

"Stop that," I said. "Don't call him that."

"You shouldn't call him that, Liam," Angela said.

"Where are they? Where are Brice and Eric?" I asked.

"Man, you don't know. Eric isn't so bad, but Brice will fucking *kill* you, man."

I said to Angela, "So after I called you, you called Liam. What about Brice and Eric?"

She shook her head. "I called Liam. Just Liam."

"Did you call them?" I asked Liam. "Do they know that I know?"

"Are you serious? I waited until my shift was up and then I came over here to figure out what to do. I don't know what to do!"

"That's okay," Felicia said. "We do."

CHAPTER FORTY-SIX

THEY SAT IN THE BACKSEAT ON THE SHORT DRIVE FROM CAMPUS TO downtown, holding hands. Angela urged him into saying the Lord's Prayer with her. I finally got a look at his features: sallow, pinched, pocked by acne scars, and for some reason I thought of Ichabod Crane.

"I'm sorry you got hurt, Mr. Ruzak," Angela offered as we waited for the light to change on the corner of Cumberland and Main. "It's my fault. I saw the flyer on campus and I don't know why I couldn't say anything on the phone. It wasn't about the money. I'm a good person. Liam's a good person. And Eric, he just does whatever Brice tells him to do."

"Eric's a moron," Liam said. "They're both fucking morons."

"I told him not to hang with Brice," Angela said.

"He won't let 'em take him alive," Liam said. "He told me that, if it ever went down."

"What a shame," Felicia said. "I'll miss him."

Liam started to cry. Angela slipped her arm around his shoulder and he collapsed into her chest. She stroked his black, greasy hair and whispered, "It's okay, baby. It's okay. It's going to be okay. Put yourself into the Lord's hands now. Ask Jesus into your heart. Tell him you're sorry and he'll forgive you." I had the feeling I was hearing a reprise of a speech she had given many times. "He loves you, Liam, he loves you so much and you know what? So do I. I don't care what you did. That's what it's about, baby. Love. Love, love, love, baby." She kissed the top of his head. "All things for a reason, baby. All things for a reason."

"Tell that to Jack Minor," Felicia muttered.

"Here's what I don't get," Liam said, his voice coming up muffled between his girlfriend's breasts. "You, Ruzak. I don't get you. Who the hell was that old guy to you? Why the hell do you care?"

"Ruzak is on a mission of God," Felicia said. "His humble instrument."

"Oh, Christ," Liam moaned.

"He's a roundabout operator," I said. "Inscrutable."

The dome of the Sunsphere shone in the night sky behind us; a golden halo shimmered in the falling snow, a circle of beatific light. Why the hell did I care? I didn't answer, because I had come to the point where I understood the question was irrelevant. Only one question really mattered, and it wasn't that one. Maybe Jack Minor lying dead in my alleyway was the answer, or maybe it was just another way of putting the same question that we've been asking since we dropped from the trees and rose on two legs to survey the landscape: Hello, are you there? Can you hear me? Who are you and what do you want?

The answer eludes us.

DECEMBER 24

CHAPTER FORTY-SEVEN

By midmorning Amanda had packed up, her old duffle by the door with Archie beside it, his dog senses tingling at the impending disintegration of our little pack. I was up by eight, showered and dressed, and made a quick run to the Krispy Kreme while Amanda snored on the sofa. I took Archie with me for a little private time.

"Look," I said, as he stared at me from the passenger seat. "You and I have to come to some sort of understanding here. For better or worse, fate's dumped you into my lap, and we both had better get used to it. I think what gets to me most is this feeling of expectation or dread, the way you just stare at me, like you're afraid I'm going to wig out on you. I'm really a fairly balanced person. I tend to think too much and get too wrapped up in trivialities, sort of a borderline autistic—don't think I haven't thought of that—but that doesn't mean I'm a bad person or, more to the point, a poor owner. I promise to give you a warm place to sleep and tasty kibble and take you on walks and play with you. Well, as long as my super doesn't kick you out—I'm going to have to work on that problem. The point is, I appreciate the fact that you're an excellent listener; it's really impressive the way you seem to cling to my every word, but there's a reason we tell little kids not to stare, you know?"

Amanda was up by the time we returned with the doughnuts. I also picked up a couple of their medium-brew coffees. Like soft-drink products, coffee always tasted better from a restaurant.

"Maybe I should stay," she said. Without her makeup, she looked about twelve years old. "You're going to be alone for Christmas."

"I'm working down at the mission tomorrow," I said. "And you should be home with your family."

"Do you like me, Ruzak?" she asked.

"Sure I like you. I can't thank you enough for helping me through all this."

"You know what I mean."

"I have this difficulty," I said. "This fear of foisting my foibles on others."

"That's stupid," she said. "If everybody waited until they were perfect—"

"Oh, I know I'll never get to that point. I'd just like to be a little more sure of what I want."

"The plain truth is you don't find me attractive. Why can't you say that? And if you're afraid you'll hurt my feelings, tell me what's worse: finding me unattractive and lying about it or thinking I'm gross and telling me the truth?"

"That's sort of a false choice."

"So you do find me attractive, and this is all about you not knowing what you want?"

"Well."

"Ruzak, how can you decide what you want unless you try it? It's like deciding you don't like sushi without ever tasting it."

She licked the glaze from her fingertips. Before I allowed myself to think, I leaned forward and kissed her sugary lips. Our eyes met for an instant, and then she slapped me very hard across the left cheek.

"Bastard," she said.

I offered to walk her to her car. She told me she was perfectly capable of walking by herself.

"I'll call you," I said.

"Don't."

She wasn't gone five minutes when the phone rang. I was so sure it was her, I didn't bother to look at the caller ID.

"Hello, Mr. Ruzak," Detective Black said. "Just wanted to let you know we got Brice Carlson last night."

"Alive?"

"Surrendered without incident. He was holed up at his parents' house down in Polk County. Denies everything, but Eric Reston broke yesterday and confessed."

"It's done," I said.

"All but the shouting."

"Well," I said. "Thanks for letting me know."

"We'd like to go after him for the assault on you," she said. "We've got Angela's and Liam's testimony and we can get Brice's cell phone records—Liam stated he called him that afternoon."

"I don't think so," I said.

"Excuse me?"

"I don't think so. You've got him on Jack. That's enough."

"You're sure?"

I told her I was, down to my shoestrings.

"Okay. I had one more thing."

"What's that?"

"An apology. You were right and I was wrong. You know," she said. "In six years as a homicide detective, I've never encountered a case quite like this one. I've never had an eyewitness confess to something he didn't do. I just wanted you to understand there was no bad faith involved. We honestly thought we had the right guy."

It was more of an acknowledgment than an apology, but I didn't press it.

"And if you hadn't stuck to your guns, an innocent man might have paid a very dear price."

"Right," I said. "One's enough."

"One's enough?"

"I mean Jack. Don't get me wrong, detective, I'm glad we got these boys, but it's one of those things that bring closure but no satisfaction."

"I don't understand what you mean, Mr. Ruzak."

"Three college kids on a drunk kill a harmless homeless person over a hat. My understanding is this Brice character was nothing but a punk and a thug, but these other two weren't bad kids, just weak, and now they have no future, and Jack is dead, though I guess you could say he didn't have a future, either. It just seems so . . . useless."

"Sounds to me like somebody's got the Christmas blues."

"Oh, I'm an optimist at heart," I said. "But if you're gonna get in the water, you gotta risk a riptide or two."

A day after his father's release from prison, Robert Matthews showed up at my door with his dad in hand and a chip on his shoulder.

"I oughta punch you in the face for what you did to my old man," Robert said.

"Ruzak didn't do anything to me," Reggie said.

"Did I ask for your input?" Robert asked him. "Look, Ruzak, we had a deal and I'm not leavin' town without the balance of what you owe me."

"What I owe Reggie, you mean."

"Whatever!"

"The reward was, I think, um, rewardable upon arrest and *conviction* . . ."

"That's not what you told me in Johnson City."

"But if you read the flyer—"

"You told me one half right now and the next half when somebody went to jail. Well, I read the papers. Somebody's in jail—where's my twelve-fifty?"

"*My* twelve-fifty," Reggie said.

"Whatever! Plus the fact I should sue you for breach of contract, Ruzak, kidnapping under false pretenses; I don't know, I'm not a fucking lawyer, but they threw my dad in prison after beating a false confession out of him, and you didn't even bother to tell me!"

"They didn't beat me," Reggie said. "I confessed falsely of my own free will."

"In fact," Robert said, jabbing his finger at my nose, "you lied about it! You told me he was living here!"

"He asked me not to tell you."

"Why?"

"Maybe that's a question you should ask him."

"Look, I didn't come all this way to bandy words with you, dickhead."

"Bandy?"

"I just want what's mine."

"Mine," Reggie said.

"Whatever!"

"Let me get my checkbook," I said.

So I wrote out a check to Reggie Matthews for $12,500. Then I handed the check to Reggie. I wished them both a Merry Christmas and a Happy New Year. I closed the door and heard Robert saying loudly in the hall, "Dad, if I let you keep it, it'll be gone in a month!"

I felt bad for Reggie, but told myself that whole setup was an accident of nature, which really had nothing to do with me.

After getting off the phone with Detective Black, I took Archie for a walk, wrapping him in my overcoat for the trip outside lest Whittaker or one of his spies was on the prowl. Then I went back upstairs, where I put on a pot of coffee because I still had half a dozen Krispy Kremes left and nobody to share them with. Archie sat at my feet and stared while I chewed.

"Not good for you," I said. "And besides, nobody likes a beggar."

And of course I thought of Jack when I said it, and not how I usually thought of him, tossed on a pile of garbage, dead eyes wide open, but the day before, standing by my car in the middle of the street, the questioning look when I passed my hat through the open window. *God bless*, he murmured. The way he appeared in my rearview mirror as I drove away, clutching that hat, astounded by his good fortune, a solitary figure standing on a street corner in the rain, as ubiquitous and forgettable as any street person.

Beggars can't be choosers. If wishes were horses, a beggar could ride. My mother had a boatload of sayings, a seemingly endless supply of bromides for every possible occasion, I guess because clichés are the convenient hooks we use for hanging our hats of uncertainty.

I washed up in the kitchen sink, scrubbing my hands until the knuckles turned raw. Something felt like it was slipping inside, so acting on instinct—

maybe the same instinct that drove me to give Jack my floppy hat—I put Archie in his cage and headed downstairs for my car.

I stopped at Walgreens first and purchased a stocking with an embroidered puppy on the front, filled with bones and chewies and a little packet of breath fresheners, sort of like Tic Tacs for canines.

A year ago on this night, I was at Mom's house leafing through old photos of Christmases past. There's Dad pulling another shirt from a box. There's Teddy with his first bike. There's your cousin Ernie from New Jersey, don't you remember him? I wondered what happened to those albums—did I stick them in my closet? Our old house in Fountain City had a big fireplace where Mom hung our stockings, three in a row, until Dad died, and then there were two. Where did those end up? I tried to remember if I had a box in the closet labeled "Christmas." If I found mine and put it out tonight, how much faith did I have it would be filled to overflowing on Christmas morning?

I pulled into the Park Rite lot beside the Ely Building and Lonny came out of his little booth, a cigarette dangling from his mouth.

"Saw they caught the bastards," he said.

I nodded. "They did."

He trailed behind me as I trudged up the walk toward the entrance.

"You oughta take a look at the alley."

"Why?"

"They cleaned it up. Put up some little tables. Looks like the outside of a little French bistro back there now."

"That'll be nice when the weather warms up."

He hovered beside me at the door. I wasn't sure what he wanted.

"You don't have to work on Christmas, do you?" I asked.

He shook his head. "Naw. Gotta scramble tonight, though—still don't have all my shopping done."

"Me either."

I went upstairs, past the dry cleaners, three flights up to my door, where someone had posted a sticky note on the frosted glass: *Mr. Ruzak please call me. I need your help.* I didn't recognize the name. There was a small pile of mail on the floor below the slot. I scooped it up and dropped it on Felicia's desk. It was cold inside; my breath fogged around my head as I went into my office. A fine patina of dust covered the desk, the globe in the corner, the bookcase with the full leather-bound set of the *Tennessee Rules of Evidence* that Felicia had mail-ordered to give my shelves some gravitas.

The blinds were drawn. Funny, I couldn't remember doing that. I pulled the thin cord to open them and stared out the window to the alley three stories below. The glass fogged with the impression of my breath, evidence of my autonomy: take that, Eunice Shriver!

In an instant, scientists tell us (in theory born in the mind of a priest), the universe spontaneously burst into existence, spewing out the matter that would form you and me a few billion years later, after violent cataclysms, stars and proto-planets smashing into each other, after mass extinctions and millions of years of evolution, the arrival of Teddy Ruzak in this moment, slouching in his rumpled overcoat, scrubbing his three-day-old beard with the back of his hand, standing before a foggy window slightly pigeon-toed, with a crooked nose and a bent walk, a triumph of Nature's inscrutable design, the current occupant in this empty space, at once obscure and of paramount import.

It was like I told Angela: I knew the *who,* the *what,* and the *where.* It was the *why,* the motive. Someone once said we were here because the universe needed a way to look at itself. We were Creation's eyes.

I closed the blinds and turned from the window. I knew these rooms like the back of my hand, but that didn't change the fact that I was still in the dark.

I had solved the case but not the mystery.

CHAPTER FORTY-EIGHT

I STOPPED AT THE BARNES & NOBLE, THEN DOUBLED BACK TO Middlebrook Pike. The home was maybe five miles from the bookstore, and it took me forty-five minutes to get there, the traffic was so bad.

The receptionist at the desk took my name and told me to have a seat, and another ten minutes crawled by. Here's Ruzak again, putting in his time, filling his quota. Finally, an attendant wearing hospital-type gear, including the soft-soled shoes and scrublike top, escorted me to a room they called the Solarium. The lighting was weak and washed out, a feeble, whispery-thin light; maybe the room was more solariumish in the summers.

Eunice Shriver was sitting in a rocking chair by a door marked FOR HOS-PICE PERSONNEL ONLY. All the window seats were taken. I didn't recognize her at first. She'd always been meticulous about her makeup, and now I saw her for the first time without it. They had taken her wig away, too, and her natural hair was thin and wispy. I could see her irregularly shaped, bone-white scalp. She was wearing a purple terrycloth robe and matching slippers.

"Well," she said as I pulled up a chair. "Look what the cat drug in."

"Merry Christmas, Eunice," I said. I pulled the Barnes & Noble bag out of my coat pocket.

"What's that?"

"It's for you. Sorry, I didn't have it wrapped."

She peeked into the bag, pursing her lips.

"It's a journal," I said. "And also a pen. See, the cap has an *S* on it."

"Why an *S*?"

"*S* for your name."

"My name is Eunice."

"I know. The *S* is for *Shriver*. They didn't have an *E* pen. I looked."

"Well. Thank you, Theodore." She laid the bag on her lap.

"I didn't know if they allowed you to have your computer or typewriter or whatever it is you use to write, so I thought you could use this journal."

"Yes, so you did."

"What, you don't want to write anymore?"

"Oh, I finished the book."

"You did?"

"And I have several publishers interested in it."

"You're kidding."

"I most certainly am not kidding. I shall use a pen name, of course."

"Why?"

"Did Poe use his real name? Did Conan Doyle?"

"Actually, I think they did."

"I picked the name of a local author, though this person's quite obscure, something just shy of a hack, so I'm certain they won't mind."

"What's her name? So I know where to look in the bookstore."

She told me. I said, "Eunice, that's a man's name."

"Ever hear of George Eliot?"

"No."

"Well, there you have it."

"Did you change my name too?"

"Dear heavens, why would I do that?"

"So I wouldn't sue you for libel."

She laughed. Even her eyes seemed washed out in this room of dying light. Ah, Christ, Eunice! Ah, Christ, light! I was gripping the arms of my chair, hard. Something was definitely stuck in my craw. But every time I tried to trap it or tamp it down, it skittered away.

Across the room, beside the upright piano against the wall, a five-foot Christmas tree stood, wrapped in gold tinsel and festooned with red and silver balls. An angel sat on the top, listing to one side so she appeared to be cocking her head toward the ground while she strummed her harp, trying to keep time with an earthly rhythm section. It occurred to me that any attempt to straddle the divide was doomed to failure. The distance between faith and reason was widening, and the time had come to pick sides.

"Eunice," I said. "Do you ever get scared?"

"Why should I be scared?"

"I mean, you must think about it. You know it can't be much longer. Do you think once it's done, it's done and there's nothing afterward? Like those crash tests when the car hits the wall. I guess that's it. Is it a wall or is it an open door, or like a—like some kind of—I don't know, like a porous membrane, opaque but—but through it we shall pass? Because here's the problem as I see it: If it is a wall, then you'll never know you were wrong."

"I would prefer not to," she said.

"But what I'm asking . . . what I'm trying to get at . . . Eunice, are you ever afraid? It won't be long before you'll either meet oblivion or its utter opposite. I'm sure you've thought about it."

"I do not worry about what's next, Theodore. I worry about what's left."

"So 'What's next?' is a pointless question because it can't be answered?"

"Well, that hasn't stopped people from trying to answer it, has it?"

"That's the rub, I guess. In my line of work, you gotta go where the evidence leads you. Take something along the lines of three drunk college kids murdering a mentally incompetent homeless man. What's that evidence of? We all have a destiny, and Jack's is to be beaten to death and dumped on a pile of garbage? Or Jack is being punished for some grand transgression, either in this life or another? Or God gave these boys free will so they could murder a harmless old man just for the hell of it, just because they could? Don't all these possibilities point away from an all-knowing, all-loving, all-powerful Presence and toward that wall, and we're the dummies behind the wheel?"

She stared at me for a long moment.

"Oh, Theodore," she said. "You're so marvelously inept, so hopelessly lost. How I love you."

She placed a withered hand over mine and gave it a squeeze.

"Here's what it is," she said, squeezing. "Here's what it is," squeezing, "and I am so happy, so very grateful that you are mine." Squeezing.